Ready for takeoff

Brye Hamley leaned toward his sister. "Lark," he said. "Won't be easy. But—" He paused, as if to gather enough words to express himself. "Mum worked herself to death on Deeping. You look so like her."

Larkyn bit her lip.

"Be a good thing," Brye finished, sitting back with an air of finality, "not to see you grow old before your time."

Fresh tears reddened Larkyn's eyes, and a jolt of emotion tightened Mistress Philippa's throat as she watched brother and sister. She recognized the emotion exactly for what it was. It was envy. She gritted her teeth against it.

"You want me to do this, then?" Larkyn asked.

"You have to," Prefect Micklewhite burst out. "It's not as if you—"

Philippa hissed. "For the last time, hush, you old fool!" The Hamleys stared at her, and Lark's cheeks flushed.

"Larkyn Hamley," Philippa said curtly, "do you want to go to the Academy of the Air?"

Ace Books by Toby Bishop

AIRS BENEATH THE MOON
AIRS AND GRACES

Airs
Beneath
the Moon

TOBY BISHOP

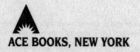

ACE BOOKS, NEW YORK

THE BERKLEY PUBLISHING GROUP
Published by the Penguin Group
Penguin Group (USA) Inc.
375 Hudson Street, New York, New York 10014, USA

Penguin Group (Canada), 90 Eglinton Avenue East, Suite 700, Toronto, Ontario M4P 2Y3, Canada
(a division of Pearson Penguin Canada Inc.)
Penguin Books Ltd., 80 Strand, London WC2R 0RL, England
Penguin Group Ireland, 25 St. Stephen's Green, Dublin 2, Ireland (a division of Penguin Books Ltd.)
Penguin Group (Australia), 250 Camberwell Road, Camberwell, Victoria 3124, Australia
(a division of Pearson Australia Group Pty. Ltd.)
Penguin Books India Pvt. Ltd., 11 Community Centre, Panchsheel Park, New Delhi—110 017, India
Penguin Group (NZ), Cnr. Airborne and Rosedale Roads, Albany, Auckland 1310, New Zealand
(a division of Pearson New Zealand Ltd.)
Penguin Books (South Africa) (Pty.) Ltd., 24 Sturdee Avenue, Rosebank, Johannesburg 2196,
South Africa

Penguin Books Ltd., Registered Offices: 80 Strand, London WC2R 0RL, England

This is a work of fiction. Names, characters, places, and incidents either are the product of the author's imagination or are used fictitiously, and any resemblance to actual persons, living or dead, business establishments, events, or locales is entirely coincidental. The publisher does not have any control over and does not assume any responsibility for author or third-party websites or their content

AIRS BENEATH THE MOON

An Ace Book / published by arrangement with the author

PRINTING HISTORY
Ace mass-market edition / January 2007

Copyright © 2007 by Louise Marley.
Cover art by Allen Douglas.
Cover design by Judith Lagerman.
Interior text design by Kristin del Rosario.

ISBN: 978-0-441-01462-0

ACE
Ace Books are published by The Berkley Publishing Group,
a division of Penguin Group (USA) Inc.,
375 Hudson Street, New York, New York 10014.
ACE and the "A" design are trademarks belonging to Penguin Group (USA) Inc.

PRINTED IN THE UNITED STATES OF AMERICA

10   9   8   7   6   5   4   3   2

For Susan Allison,
who sowed the seed

I am much indebted to the following people for their judgment, talent, knowledge, and generosity: Nancy Crosgrove, R.N., N.D., and Equine Therapist, and all the denizens of Second Wind Ranch in Newport, Washington; the young equestrienne Margaret Schroeder; my agent Peter Rubie, faithful through thick and thin; my editor Susan Allison, for her vision, patience, and graciousness; Zack Marley, for reading with a critical eye, and Stephanie Phillips, the same; Catherine Whitehead, trusted first reader; the members of Redmond Riters, who are Richard Paul Russo, Kij Johnson, Melissa Lee Shaw, and Mark Bourne; and of Tahuya Writers Catherine Whitehead, Dave Newton, Niven Marquis, Brian Bek, and Jeralee Chapman. It is an honor to have worked with all of you.

PROLOGUE

BEYOND the barn's single, unglazed window, the stars began to dissolve, one by one, drowning in the chill gray light of dawn. The cows huddled together, head to tail, for comfort and for warmth. The goats stood silent and uneasy in their night pen, listening to the little dun mare laboring in the box stall. It had gone on all night, Char and her mistress grunting and groaning together. Now, as the sky began to brighten, Char's time had come at last.

Char pushed. Larkyn Hamley, boots braced in the wet straw, pulled. Birth fluids soaked her tabard and her tangled skirts, and filled the stall with an odor both acrid and sweet. Lark knew the smell to be the essence of coming life, of the force that made the crops grow and the moon wax and wane. It was also the scent of death, of the melting of one time into another. Larkyn Hamley was a girl of the soil and the seasons, and her blood surged with the power of the moment, the alchemy of life striving to be.

"Once again, Char," she panted. Salty sweat dripped in her eyes, but she had no hand free to wipe it away. She tried to lift her shoulder to get the worst of it, but a fresh spasm wracked Char's body, and Lark set herself again to pull on the foal's slick fetlocks. "Lovely girl," Lark said. "That's my brave girl. Once again!"

The mare's sides rippled with effort. Lark's hands cramped, and she begged Kalla for strength, even though she, an Uplands farm girl, had no right to pray to the horse goddess. It was for Char, poor little Char, her foundling.

Lark knew nothing of horses except what the dun mare had taught her. Horses were rare in the Uplands, and there had never been one on Deeping Farm, nor in the village of Willakeep. Lark had stumbled upon Char standing ankle-deep in the icy waters of the Black River, her ribs standing out like the curved pickets of the haymow, and her hide, the color of smoke from the autumn chimneys, torn by brambles. Neither Lark nor her brothers knew then that Char was with foal, but now, just as sharp-toothed winter began to loosen its bite on the Uplands, she had come to term.

The foal lay widdershins, hind feet first. Lark had tried everything she knew to turn it, without success. Once it was on its way, there was nothing left but to see it through. She gasped for air, in rhythm with Char. She tugged, and Char groaned. The mare gave one last heave. There was a deep, rushing sound, and the foal's body slid, limp and awkward, legs asprawl, to the matted straw.

A gray shroud, streaked with red, masked its nose and mouth. Lark ripped at the gelatinous stuff with her fingers, clearing the tiny muzzle. She bent, and blew fiercely into the foal's nostrils. A shuddering breath rewarded her, and a little mewling cry. She cried out herself, exclaiming in wonder as she cradled the wet creature in her arms. His coat felt gluey and rough beneath her hands.

When she was certain his breathing was steady, she lifted her eyes. "Char, look!" she said softly. "Look at your little one!"

The mare always responded to Lark's voice, had done so even on that very first day, when she was so weak she could barely walk. Lark had coaxed her, stumbling step by stumbling step, through the fields to the barn. But now, Char lay exhausted. Her ribs barely moved, and her black forelock tangled in her long eyelashes. Even as Lark watched, the little mare's breathing slowed, and her dark eyes fixed on some point only she could see.

"Oh, no," Lark whispered.

Lark was a country girl. She knew the look of death, from slaughtering days, from accidents, from her own mother's illness. She understood the dimming of the light in the mare's eyes, the rattle of her last breath, her sigh of release, the stare into nothingness.

Lark, little more than a child herself, hugged the motherless foal to her breast, and cried. She gave in to her grief and exhaustion and shock, and sobbed.

The foal began to mewl and wriggle in her arms, reminding her of the dawn chill. Her wet clothes were icy, and the foal, too, was wet and cold to the touch. She had to get him dry.

She had brought a pile of old towels to the barn with her when she saw that Char's time had drawn near. Now she plucked one from the stack and gently rubbed the foal's head and neck. He struggled to his feet, leaning against her, long-legged, big-eyed, quaking with weakness. She steadied him with one hand, and reached along his withers and spine with the other to scour away the remnants of the birth sac.

The slow morning sun slanted through the window. Lark felt it on her cheeks. It would be gilding the frosty grasses in the north pasture, glittering on the fallow fields to the south, shining on the slate roof of the farmhouse, silvering the scraps of late snow. It brightened the stall so she could see that the colt was as black as the blackstone of the Uplands that gave the river its name.

She slid the towel down the foal's ribs, and stopped. Something stayed her hand, some solid, living structure beneath the towel.

The foal made the little choked sound again, a sob of his own. With care, Lark pushed him away from her to see what it was that grew below his withers, behind his shoulders.

What she saw filled her with awe and dread.

Everyone knew that an animal such as this belonged to the Duke, and the Duke alone. Oc was a tiny and beleaguered duchy, with scarce resources. Its desolate coastline lay open to the sea lanes, coveted by other duchies, by bigger principalities. Creatures such as this, Char's foal, were Kalla's special gifts. They were Oc's most precious resource, the envy of every duke, prince, and king. To tamper with their bloodlines was to commit high treason. Had any of the Hamleys realized . . .

But of course they hadn't. How could they? They could never have guessed that little Char carried such a marvel. That such a being would appear here, on Deeping Farm, was an event of such magnitude Lark could hardly comprehend it.

With trembling fingers, she caressed the colt's slender head, and then held him close, her arms gentle around his fragile neck.

"By Zito's ears, little one!" she breathed. "You have wings!"

ONE

THE hand of spring was rarely gentle in the Duchy of Oc. By day it crooked a teasing finger, coaxing every branch and blade to open, spilling new light over meadows and groves, grassy ditch-mounds, fallow fields awaiting the plow. By night it was a fist, hard and cold, the stars like shards of ice, the northwestern peaks of the Ocmarins ghostly white in the black sky. The last winds of winter glazed the puddles in the paddocks of the Academy of the Air, and rimed the windows of the Domicile. The glass still gleamed with the night's frost as Philippa Winter stepped out of the Hall.

The headmistress followed her to the doorstep, hugging her thin body against the cold. Her hair shone silver in the early sun. Wrinkles fanned from her eyes as she squinted into the light. "Use your judgment, Philippa. You may be in time, after all."

Philippa pulled on her peaked cap, and buttoned her riding coat to the neck. "I'll do my best, Margareth. Either way, I'll be back before dark."

Margareth nodded, and stood watching as Philippa crossed the courtyard to the flight paddock. Philippa wore a woolen vest beneath her riding tabard, and thick stockings inside her boots, but the cold stung her cheeks. She shivered at the prospect of the frigid air aloft.

At her approach, Sunny stamped her feet and nickered a greeting. She tossed her head, tugging at the lead in the stable-girl's hand. Philippa pulled on her gloves before she unclipped the lead to let the stable-girl coil it over her arm. "Thanks, Rosellen." She unhooked the reins from the pommel. "Sunny's as cold as we are, I think."

"Aye, Mistress. She'll be warm soon enough, I expect. Bit of exercise, isn't it, all that way to the Uplands?"

"Indeed," Philippa said. "Sunny will be warm, but I'll be a block of ice."

Rosellen showed her freckled, gap-toothed grin. "Want one of them holding straps, like the first-level girls?"

Philippa snorted. "I'll take my chances." Her mare danced sideways, swishing her tail.

Rosellen stood back, rubbing her reddened hands together. "Must be something important in the Uplands," she said, with a hopeful tilt to her head. "To take you so far, and away from your flight."

"There may be." Philippa braced herself, flexing her knees, and then leaped into the saddle, a perfect standing mount. Other flyers her age depended upon the mounting block, but she disdained it, a matter of pride. "I hope to know by nightfall." She lifted the rein, and Sunny whirled with a rustle of silken membranes. Frost rose in crystal sprays where her pinions touched the grass.

"Well." Rosellen gave a good-natured shrug at her curiosity left unsatisfied. "Good morning to you then, Horsemistress. Safe flying."

Philippa touched her quirt to the brim of her cap, and gave Sunny her head.

LARK had not slept in her own bed since the foal's birth. Her brothers objected, Edmar scowling, Brye saying the colt should get used to being alone, Nick offering to stay in the barn through the night. Lark refused every suggestion. Somehow, she couldn't bear to leave the tiny creature, nor could she bear the thought of someone else being with him. Her brothers gave in. Edmar still scowled, but Nick brought her quilts and pillows, and Brye found an old blanket to tie around the colt to ward off the night cold. Lark left the stall only for meals and the milking, and to churn the butter for Nick's rounds. She abandoned all her other chores. Already it seemed she could hardly remember her life before the foaling.

Brye roused her from a sticky sleep at midmorning, calling to her from the barn door. He didn't come near the stall. All the brothers had quickly learned that the colt could not abide them nearby. He mewled and struggled to get as far away from them as possible, causing Lark to beg them to keep a fair distance. They gave up, one by one, leaving the care of the foal entirely to their sister, taking her chores for her when they could, leaving them undone when they couldn't.

The foal lay sprawled in heavy sleep beside her. She uncurled herself from her bed of straw and blankets, and went to open the top half of the stall door. "I'm here," she answered. The colt lifted his head, and stood, his blanket slipping awry as he shook himself.

"Prefect's come!" Brye's announcement was as brief as possible, but Lark understood the weight of information in his announcement. The arrival of Master Micklewhite, prefect of Willakeep, meant that the horsemistress from Osham must also be near.

Lark unlatched the gate to let herself out. The foal, balancing on his impossibly slender legs, his ears flicking nervously, tried to follow.

"No, no, little one," Lark murmured. She stroked his neck, and breathed reassuringly into his nostrils. "You stay here. I won't be long." She slipped through the gate and latched it. The colt whimpered, and she reached back to rub his stubby mane with her fingers. "Don't cry," she said. "I won't let them take you."

And she wouldn't, she promised herself, as she tried to straighten her skirt and brush the straw and dirt from her tabard. The foal was hers, Duke or no Duke.

"Larkyn?" The querulous voice belonged to Master Micklewhite. "Larkyn Hamley!" Lark grimaced as she turned toward the barn door. She would rather have faced the horsemistress outright than deal with this pudding-waisted, foolish old man. But this was no time to offend Willakeep's prefect. The Hamleys found themselves in a precarious situation, and they needed the support of every authority.

"Coming," she called. She took a step away, and then turned back for one more caress, one touch of the colt's rough fur, one more sniff of his sweet, spicy scent. It was hard to separate from him, even for a short time. It was as if they were connected by some invisible thread, a spider's web of destiny. It stretched only just enough to allow her to do what she must do, then tightened, pulled her back, again and again. She had to force her feet to carry her away, down the aisle to the barn door.

As she walked, she put her hands to her head, and found her hair sticky with straw. She undid her thick braid, and struggled to comb it out with her fingers. Her hair was always a problem, its curls tangling and twisting, defying brush or clasp.

She gave up on it, simply pushing the mass of it back over her shoulders as she came out into the cool sunshine. A freshening breeze blew from the slopes of the Ocmarins. Beguiled by the promise of spring, she lifted her face to the sky.

Her eyes went wide, and her mouth fell open. Her fingers dropped from the tangle of her hair, and she clasped them before her chest. She forgot about Micklewhite, and Brye, and the threat of the Duke's ire. For a long, wondrous moment, she even forgot to breathe.

The great, slowly beating wings were red and translucent, the sun shining through their membranes like lamplight through a parchment shade. The legs were curled close to the body, hooves shining like polished glass. The mane and tail streamed like banners of red silk as the winged horse circled Deeping Farm.

It should not have been possible for such a creature to fly. It was the great mystery of Oc that the horse goddess should endow them with such ability. Surely the cows and goats, twisting their necks up to watch this miracle, must envy the horse its freedom, its power, its impossible grace. Such a sight must make them lament their own earthbound state.

And the rider!

The winged horse dropped lower with each circuit, until Lark could clearly see the tall, slender figure astride it, dressed in the black and silver colors of the Duke, a long divided skirt, a belted tabard with full, fluttering sleeves buttoned tightly at the wrists. A peaked cap was pulled low over her forehead, and her hair was knotted neatly on the back of her neck.

Larkyn gulped, and drew her delayed breath. Nothing had prepared her for the heartbreaking beauty of the woman and the horse descending from the sky. Her eyes stung with it, and her heart sped.

Everyone in the barnyard froze, Brye with his hat in his hands, Micklewhite gaping, Nick in the lane with the oxcart. The winged horse made a last, slow circle above the farm buildings, and then spread its wings wide and still. It glided down over the blackstone fence that lined the north pasture, dropping over the heads of the watchers to come to ground with running steps, cantering across the barnyard, then trotting, whirling with a creak of saddle leather, and coming to a halt. For a long, stunned moment, no one moved. Then Micklewhite, with a little, urgent moan, hurried toward the flyers.

The horsemistress gave him a cool nod, and dismounted, right leg up and over the pommel of the saddle. She touched her horse's shoulder with a slender quirt and spoke some command. The sorrel shook its wings, once, and then began to fold them, rib to rib, the membrane darkening as it contracted, until the length of its magnificent wings tucked in neat layers over the saddle stirrups.

The horsemistress, unsmiling, surveyed the group in the barnyard. "Where's the foal?"

The Hamleys stared at her, immobilized by wonder. It was the prefect who answered, bowing, bobbing his head like a duck in a pond. He removed his narrow-brimmed hat and then stuck it on again, babbling, "Well, yes, of course, Horsemistress, right down to business, naturally . . ."

Brye pointed to the barn, and said, "There."

The horsemistress nodded again, tucked her quirt under one arm, and strode across the barnyard without hesitation. She was tall, with dark red hair and a long, plain face. She wore a slender jeweled insignia, in the shape of wings, pinned to her collar. As she walked, she stripped black leather gloves from her hands and tucked them into her belt.

Lark braced herself in the doorway.

The woman stopped a few steps away, and tipped her head back to look down her nose. "You're the girl? You were present at the foaling?" Her accent was different from that of the Uplands, slightly nasal, with clipped vowels. Her upper lip flexed as she spoke.

Lark's voice scraped in her throat. "Yes. I'm Larkyn Hamley."

The woman eyed her. "Indeed. Larkyn. Unusual name, isn't it?"

Micklewhite, at her elbow, burbled, "Oh, no, not really, Horsemistress. The Uplands, you know, the dialect . . . the country names . . . there's a tradition . . ."

She withered him with a sidelong glance, and he fell silent. "I'm Philippa Winter," she said, and then moved forward with such a sure step that Lark, though she meant not to, fell back. The horsemistress swept into the barn, her heels kicking up little puffs of sawdust. Lark stumbled after her. Brye and Micklewhite followed, Brye's boots making a solid thumping, Micklewhite scuffling along behind him.

The newcomer's spotless riding habit, her clean hands and neatly knotted hair, made Lark uneasily aware that the barn floor needed fresh sawdust, that one of the cow stanchions had a broken crossbar, that the straw in the goats' night pen should be changed. But there was nothing to be done about any of it now, and the horsemistress was on her way to the box stall.

Lark dashed ahead. The colt, as the men drew near, backed away until his rump struck the far wall. Everyone stopped, Micklewhite muttering under his breath, the horsemistress staring at Lark with her eyebrows raised.

"Step aside, please." Philippa Winter took the quirt from under her arm, and Lark thought, for a wild moment, she was going to use it to make her move.

"If you'll just give him a minute, Mistress . . ."

"I've come a long way," the woman said. "And there's no time to waste."

"My—that is, he's nervous around strangers," Lark said hastily. "Men especially."

"I think, my girl," the woman drawled, "that I know how to deal with a winged foal."

"Oh. Oh, well, of course you do, but I—"

"Please." The word was a command.

Still Lark didn't move, though her throat was dry and her heart hammered in her chest. "I've been feeding him by hand," she blurted. "First I took what I could from Char, and now I'm using goat's milk, like we do with the bummer calves. And I've been keeping him warm at night. I've hardly been out of the stall since—"

"You mean to say you've been sleeping here?" Philippa Winter threw a look of fury at the prefect.

The prefect tutted at Lark. "I told you, Larkyn Hamley, always in trouble . . . should have reported the horse . . ."

Old resentments boiled in Lark, and she pointed her chin at him. "What would you have me do, Master Micklewhite? Leave a newborn foal alone all night in a freezing barn?"

The prefect subsided, but gave the horsemistress what was meant to be a speaking glance. She pressed her lips together.

Lark said hastily, "We did try to find Char's owners. No one spoke up, and she was starving and lost . . . I think Kalla brought her to me, especially. To take care of her."

"Hmm." The horsemistress eyed her, one brow arching high. "Why do you think Kalla would choose a backwater like this for one of her creatures?" She gestured with a long, slim hand at the plain surroundings. "I feel sure you have your own little small-god, some spirit of the dirt or grass or something."

Lark closed her eyelids hard for a moment, trying not to be afraid of this woman and the power she represented. It was true, the Uplands had their own deity, a little hunched creature with enormous eyes and ears and a great, embarrassing phallus. The farmers called upon Zito to make their fields fertile, their seeds productive. Kalla, the horse goddess, was represented by a tall, fierce statue of a woman with a horse's head, and a sweeping mane and tail. Lark had always much preferred her, though she had never seen one of the beasts under her protection until the arrival of the foal.

Lark opened her eyes. "Kalla is a goddess of the air. She can be anywhere she chooses. And Char would have died if I hadn't—"

"Ah," the horsemistress snapped. "But she *did* die, didn't she?"

At this barb, Lark's bravado faded. She hung her head to hide her reddening eyes. "I did all I could," she choked. "The foal came widdershins. I had to pull him by his legs, and Char pushing all the while. It was too much for her. She had grown so thin, you see, and though I fed her and warmed her . . ." Her voice broke with fresh grief.

The horsemistress gave an exasperated sigh. "Yes. I suppose so. Sometimes foalings don't go well." She paused a moment, as Lark snuffled into her sleeve. "Well, don't cry, child. It probably wasn't your fault."

Behind her, the colt gave his little whimper. The horsemistress put her quirt under her arm again, and pushed Lark to one side, gently but firmly. She stepped forward, and peered into the stall.

"Hmm," she said.

The black foal, eyes wide and head high, took two mincing steps toward the horsemistress.

A wave of possessiveness swept over Lark. She opened the gate and slipped through. The foal came to her, and she put her arm around his neck, stroked his ears with her fingertips, rubbed his withers with her palm. One day, she supposed, his mane would flow long and fine, like that of the beautiful horse waiting in the barnyard, but it was only a stubby brush now, matched by a wispy tail. The top of his head came just to her breast. His wings folded tight to his ribs, reminding Lark of batwings, satiny smooth beneath her fingertips. He butted at her pockets, looking for the bottle of goat's milk, and whimpered again. "Shush, Tup," she murmured. "You have to wait a bit." She kept a hand on his neck as she looked back at Philippa Winter. "You can see, can't you, Horsemistress? He's mine."

Something powerful flashed from the redheaded woman's eyes. "Really. Are you going to tell that to Duke Frederick yourself?"

Lark's voice grew small, but she would not—she could not—give in. "I will. If I have to."

Micklewhite snapped, "Larkyn! Never a day's peace . . . how dare you defy—"

Lark swung toward him again, anxiety flaring into anger. "What do you think, Master Micklewhite? That I stuck wings on the colt with my own two hands?"

"Mind your snappy tongue, young lady," the prefect began, but the horsemistress put up a hand to silence him.

She nodded to the foal. "What did you call him?"

Lark hugged the colt's neck tighter, taking strength from his warmth. "Tup," she said.

Mistress Winter's mouth turned down as if she had tasted something nasty. "More Uplands dialect, I suppose."

Lark looked down at her soiled boots. At least here, in Tup's stall, the straw on the floor was fresh. She said hesitantly, "It's a two-penny coin we have here. Nick said he wouldn't bet two pennies on the foal's chances. But he made it, so I called him that, a tup."

"Hmm. Well, the name won't do. Naming is the duty of the Master Breeder."

Lark lifted her eyes. Her belly roiled with nerves, but she said as firmly as she could, "But the colt already knows it. And he knows me."

Philippa Winter made an exasperated noise in her throat, and turned away. "You have no idea, my girl," she said, "what it is you've done."

TWO

PHILIPPA pulled off her cap as she entered the Hamley kitchen, and stood folding it between her fingers as she looked around. An ancient pendulum clock ticked in one corner. Two scarred counters flanked an enormous stone sink, and a bare wooden table filled the center of the room. Pots and pans, battered and dented, swung above the sink.

The girl, Larkyn, lifted the lid of the close stove and added twigs to its embers. As these flamed, she pumped water into a kettle, and set it to boil. The older brother—Brye, another name unfamiliar to Philippa—stoked the open fireplace, and then pulled out a chair for her. "Sit you down, Mistress."

"Thank you, Master Hamley." He merely nodded. The grimness of his expression told her he at least understood the gravity of the situation the Hamleys found themselves in.

Micklewhite sat at the opposite end of the table, in a chair that didn't match Philippa's. In fact, none of the chairs matched, though they were in good repair. She found hers surprisingly comfortable, as if generations of Hamley backsides had worn the wood into the perfect shape. Aromas of past meals clung to the shabby curtains and ghosted in the bare-beam rafters. Sealed jars and bags and baskets of ingredients crowded the open shelves. Philippa had no idea what they might be for, but then, she rarely visited kitchens.

Larkyn, at one of the counters, measured tea leaves into a pot. Philippa waited for the brothers to sit, Brye and the younger one, Nick. A third was apparently away, working in a quarry or some such place. Philippa laid her cap on the table, and addressed Brye, who seemed to be the head of the family. "There are all kinds of difficulties we must address, Master Hamley. Larkyn is too young, for one thing."

The girl whirled, her cheeks flushing pink. "I'm fourteen!" she protested.

She was a pretty thing, really, though her black hair was matted, bristling with bits of straw, and though she smelled more like the foal than the foal himself. Her eyes were the delphinium blue of the garden borders at the Academy, and her skin clear and pale. This one, no doubt, could have married whom she liked.

Philippa pursed her lips. "Fourteen. No doubt in the Uplands that seems an age for finding a husband, spawning a flock of children. But at the Academy—"

Brye Hamley laid an oversize fist on the table with a muted thump. "Academy?" he said, his tone low and dark. His sister stood frozen, the color draining abruptly from her cheeks.

Micklewhite squeaked, "Academy!"

Philippa set her jaw. These Uplanders clearly had no comprehension of the gravity of what had happened. She chose the prefect as the repository of her irritation, fixing him with her hardest gaze. "I'm far too late, Micklewhite. The foal has imprinted."

Brye Hamley was as tall as Philippa herself, and powerfully built. He had removed his broad-brimmed hat when they came into the house, revealing a thick shock of graying black hair, bluntly cut at the neck. His eyes were dark, and Philippa thought there must be many a farmhand who would quail before the look he turned on her now. "Explain yourself," he growled.

His tone might have given offense, but Philippa took none. This farmer was sure of himself, and of his place in the world. And they were talking, after all, about his sister. Would that one's own brother had cared half as much!

The kettle began to whistle, and the girl hurried to lift it. She poured the boiling water, and then lifted a little fetish from a hook above the sink and waved it over the teapot. Her small hands moved economically, as if she had had much practice. Philippa watched her, and wondered where her parents were.

"Lark," Brye commanded. The girl turned with the teapot in her hands. Her brother pulled a chair out with his foot, and the child obediently put the teapot in the center of the table, and sat down. Brye returned his black gaze to Philippa and leaned forward into the heavy silence, waiting. The girl, too, waited, her pink lips parted.

Philippa sighed, and crossed her booted feet at the ankle.

"You've allowed one of the Duke's winged horses to bond with you," she began.

No remorse clouded the deep blue of Larkyn Hamley's eyes. "Animals take to me, Mistress," she said. "Goats and cows. Chickens. Even yon great ox in the lane turns his head for a blink at me. I'm a farm girl, after all, born and bred."

"I can see that you are," Philippa said dryly. "Unfortunately, such credentials may not impress the Duke. Or his Master Breeder." She accepted a thick pottery cup from Nick, who was dark like his brother, but smaller and quicker of movement. The hearth fire crackled, and a welcome warmth swept across the stone-tiled floor.

"I suppose you understand the rarity of the winged horses," Philippa said. Micklewhite nodded, and slurped his tea. The Hamleys only gazed at her, each very still. These Uplanders, it seemed, felt no need to fill every silence with chatter. Philippa found this oddly restful, and she wished the situation weren't urgent.

But it was. She turned the cup in her fingers. "Every winged foal is precious, to the Duke, to the Council of Lords, to all of Oc," she said. "The girls who bond with them are chosen with care. Such events are never accidental."

"No, no, of course not, Horsemistress," the prefect began.

Philippa barely resisted smacking the table to get the damned man to hold his peace. She glared at him, and he shrank back in his chair. She said to the Hamleys, "All these girls come from good families."

"I dare say," said Nick with a jaunty air. "But where in the Duchy will you find a better family than the Hamleys? We work hard, we have no debt, we have a good reputation. We own our land and this house. Where would the likes of you and His Grace be without us? Even girls of 'good families' need meat and milk and eggs!"

Micklewhite sucked in his breath, but Philippa inclined her head to Nick. "Of course, Master Hamley. Allow me to apologize for putting that badly." She hesitated, searching for how to go on. "I feel certain I can assure my Headmistress that none of you intended this."

The younger Hamley laughed. "Intended!" he chortled. "We couldn't have imagined it!"

"Have a care, Nick," Brye said. Nick grinned at his older brother.

"You've buried the mare, I suppose."

The girl's eyes flooded with sudden tears, and she dropped her head. Brye Hamley said, "North pasture. Had to."

"Yes, I do understand. But the Master Breeder wants a description. We have no record of a horse of the bloodlines gone missing."

"Half dead when Lark found her," Brye said.

Nick put in, "Lark's a wonder with animals. A soft heart for every beast."

Larkyn said in a choked tone, "She was a little thing, dun in color, with a black mane and tail. We named her for the autumn chimney smoke, that we call char." She sniffed, and wiped her nose on her sleeve. "She was lovely sweet in her ways, Mistress. She let me ride her everywhere, when she was stronger, though I had no saddle nor bridle."

Philippa looked away, digesting this. Abruptly, without apology, she rose from the table and went to the kitchen window. The branches of a rue-tree, laden with spring buds, slanted above the window-frame. Philippa looked past them into the barnyard.

Sunny stood where she had left her, drowsing in the pale sunshine, her pinions drooping. Empty fields stretched to the south. To the north, a lane curved through pastures just starting to show green between patches of graying snow. "Where's the Black River from here?"

Larkyn jumped to her feet and came to stand beside her. She pointed north. "The river forms the border of our farm."

"And that's where you found her?"

"Yes. I was grazing the goats."

"When?"

The girl tilted her head to one side, considering. "In the late summer," she said. "The bloodbeets were in, I remember, and the broomstraw just coming on. Seven months, perhaps."

Philippa pursed her lips, thinking of what had happened at the end of the last summer, presaging the long, dark winter, and the breaking of Duke Frederick's heart. She put her hands on the edge of the stone sink. It felt old under her fingers, old in the way the Academy itself was old, every stone and brick and tile cleaned and repaired many times, cared for by generations past remembering.

She glanced up into the darkness of the rafters, and wondered how long the Hamleys had been on Deeping Farm.

She returned to the table, and the girl followed. Someone had produced a plate of bread and cheese, a saucer of jam, a little dish of some elongated biscuit. The men were helping themselves, but the girl seemed to have no appetite.

Philippa picked up her cup. "Larkyn," she said. "Can you read?"

"Read?" The girl's eyes sparked with indignation. "Of course I can read!"

Philippa suppressed a smile. But the prefect, naturally, could not let it pass. "Larkyn Hamley, mind your tongue!" he said. And to Philippa, "I taught her myself, of course, Horsemistress. In the school in the village."

"We are not an illiterate mountain village." This was Brye. He leaned back in his chair, but his eyes never left Philippa's.

"You can understand the question," Philippa said. "Many are." She thought she had better tread carefully with this man, or have to use the Duke's authority to bend him. She wouldn't want to do that, not with Brye Hamley.

Larkyn said, "I read, and write, and do my numbers. Though most of it I learned at home!" This was directed at Micklewhite, and Philippa enjoyed the reddening of his plump cheeks.

"Well," Philippa said, setting her cup down with a decisive click. "That's settled, then."

"What is?" Nick Hamley asked.

Philippa set her jaw, almost overcome with impatience. She would have to find a way to explain all this to the Duke, to the Headmistress, and to the Master Breeder. Hardest of all was trying to explain it to the Hamleys. "When a young woman bonds with one of the winged horses, it is permanent," she said, her eyes on Larkyn's pale face. "It is irreversible. And it means you must come to the Academy of the Air to train."

The hope that dawned in the girl's eyes caused Philippa a twinge of pain in her breast. Larkyn half rose, her mouth a little open, her eyes violet with emotion. She breathed, "Academy?" She turned to Brye as if in a dream, and then, slowly, she sank down again. The light in her dimmed as surely as if someone had blown out a wick. "Oh," she said softly, and then again, "Oh. No, no, I can't." She turned back to Philippa. "My brothers need me here."

Philippa snorted. These people really understood nothing, and it was setting her nerves ablaze. She turned to Brye, spreading her hands. "I do see the problem, Master Hamley, but the Duke will not, and he answers to the Council. Every horse and rider of the bloodlines trains at the Academy. We can't have a winged horse raised on an Uplands farm. The waste—to say nothing of the precedent—would be disastrous."

Nick said, "Send the colt to the Academy, then. Leave Lark here, where she belongs."

The fiery look Lark cast at her brother was not wasted on Philippa. She raised an eyebrow, and said, "You know nothing of the winged horses, evidently."

Brye said gruffly, "No need. None such in the Uplands."

"Indeed." She nodded. "I am trying to explain. Winged horses are very different creatures from wingless ones, even when they are born of the same sire and dam. They mature at a faster rate, and they are more intelligent, more sensitive, than their wingless brethren. And without exception, a winged horse bonds for life." She let her eyes drift to Larkyn. "The foal can't stay here, and he can't leave the girl. He would die. Such things have happened."

A long silence greeted her flat statement. Nick dusted crumbs from his fingers, and Brye fingered his chin. Lark stared at her untouched teacup, her lower lip caught between her teeth.

More quietly, Philippa went on, "And though it is unpleasant to say so, I must remind you of the penalty for interfering with the bloodlines."

"Confiscate our farm," Brye said.

"At the very least."

Nick added, "Banishment."

"Quite possibly."

Philippa sat back, allowing the Hamleys a moment to consider. Micklewhite opened his mouth as if to speak, but she lifted a forefinger to stop him. It was not that the family had a choice in the matter. They had none. But she hoped to allow them to come to their decision without saying so.

Brye growled, "Will she be safe?"

"There are risks, Master Hamley, commensurate with the privileges. The Horsemistresses of Oc rank only below the Duke and the Lords of the Council. And of course, there are . . ." She let her eyes drift to the window again, to the silvery pregnant branches of the rue-tree. "There are sacrifices."

When she looked back, the light had begun to glow in the girl's eyes again. Larkyn looked down the table at her brothers. "Brye," she said. "Nick. What will you do if I go? Who will cook for you, milk the goat and the cows, tend the hens?"

Micklewhite drew breath once again, and Philippa quelled him with narrowed eyes. Truly, if he didn't keep quiet, she would give herself the satisfaction of striking him with her quirt!

Brye Hamley leaned toward his sister. "Lark," he said. "Won't be easy. But—" He paused, as if to gather enough words to express himself. "Mum worked herself to death on Deeping. You look so like her."

The child bit her lip again.

"Be a good thing," Brye finished, sitting back with an air of finality, "not to see you grow old before your time."

Fresh tears reddened Larkyn's eyes, and a jolt of emotion tightened Philippa's throat as she watched brother and sister. She recognized the emotion for exactly what it was. It was envy. She gritted her teeth against it.

"You want me to do this, then?" Larkyn asked.

"You have to," Micklewhite burst out. "It's not as if you—"

Philippa hissed. "For the last time, hush, Micklewhite, you old fool!" The Hamleys stared at her, and Lark's cheeks flushed. "Larkyn," Philippa said curtly, "do you want to go to the Academy of the Air?"

The girl hesitated only a moment. "I do. And I want to stay with Tup."

Philippa grimaced at the unseemly name, but she nodded. "We'll have to talk about what's involved. First of all, you must stop sleeping in the colt's stall."

"I can't leave him alone! He'd cry all night."

Philippa rose from the table, pulling her gloves from her belt and starting to draw them on. "At the Academy, the girls sleep in the dormitory, in proper beds, and the horses are in the stables, where they belong. The oc-hounds keep them company, until they outgrow the need. Do you have a dog?"

"No." Lark considered. "We have goats, though."

Philippa picked up her cap and unfolded it, deliberately hiding her expression. The situation might have been laughable, if it were not so full of doubt and danger. "Well," she said, turning to the door, pulling on her cap. "A goat may do. And you need some riding lessons."

"I can ride already. I rode Char."

Philippa spun about in the doorway, out of patience. "My girl," she drawled. "Clomping about the country bareback is not riding. You need to learn to use the proper tack, understand the discipline . . . You are signally unprepared for the Academy, yet you must not fail."

Lark stood very straight. "Why is that, Mistress Winter?"

Philippa hesitated. This was the worst part. It was usually made clear to the girls long before they came under her tutelage. She spat it out, not allowing the bitter words to rest in her mouth. "Flyers don't bond a second time. If a winged horse loses its rider, it dies. If you fail, your colt will be put down. There's nothing else to be done."

THREE

"YOU'VE forgotten what it feels like, Philippa." Margareth Morgan, formerly Margareth Highflyer, smiled wearily across her desk. A small fire burned in her fireplace, and oil lamps flickered on the polished wood and brass fittings of her office. An account book crowded with figures lay open before her, her pen laid neatly across it. At one elbow a stack of slender, marbled volumes awaited her attention. Philippa had just such a volume on her own desk in the Domicile, a half-finished term report requiring her assessment and expectations for the riders and horses of her flight.

At Margareth's other elbow lay a huge tome, bound in black leather and stamped in gold. She often, in an unconscious gesture, laid her palm upon it. It was a genealogy, a chronicle of the winged horses of one of the three bloodlines. No one but the Master Breeder and the Headmistress of the Academy of the Air could write in that book.

Philippa rubbed her eyes with her fingers. Her hands were still cold from the long flight. She held them out to the warmth of the fire. "I suppose you're right, Margareth. I have forgotten what that first feeling is—that—obsession, I suppose."

"Like falling in love," Margareth said.

Philippa's hands began to sting as they warmed, and she rubbed them together. "God forbid! I recall it being much easier than that. Can *you* remember?"

"It's been a long time, Philippa, but I can remember something as intense as my bonding. And you should, too."

Philippa sighed. "I know I seem harsh. But she's completely unsuitable, Margareth. She's too young, to start with, and she has an accent like a stable-girl. And the roughest manners I've ever seen in a girl! She was filthy, to boot. She'd been sleeping in the barn."

"How did this happen? Why did no one get word to us?"

"The prefect of the village is a doddering fool. Kalla's teeth, why do we employ such people? Are they fit for nothing else?" She beat an irritated rhythm on the floor with her heel, and looked up to see Margareth hiding a smile behind her hand. "Yes, you may laugh, Margareth. You weren't there. I gather the Hamleys—that's the family—contacted this Master Micklewhite immediately, but instead of fetching the horsemistress from Dickering Park, this incompetent sent a letter by mail coach. The mail coach stops at every hamlet between Osham and Willakeep, and the letter took four days to reach us! So here we are, and the foal's imprinted, and there's no going back."

"Tell me about the foal." The tips of Margareth's fingers played across the stamped surface of the genealogy.

"Even worse."

Margareth tilted her head to one side, waiting. She still wore her hair knotted in rider's fashion, though it had been years since she and Duke's Highflyer had patrolled the coast. Her wrinkled face was brown from years of flying.

Philippa sighed. "The foal's pretty enough, but he's not bred true. You'll know it as soon as you see him. He's black, which could mean a Noble, but he's too small. His legs are like toothpicks. You might think he's an Ocmarin, with his short back, but his croup is too flat."

"You can't judge by that, Philippa. My own Highflyer had a croup like a tabletop. And this foal is what—a week old? His wings haven't even opened."

Philippa shrugged. "True, of course. Eduard will have to rule on it."

"We can speak to him tomorrow."

Philippa frowned. "Margareth—perhaps we should wait. Something's happening here, and it makes me uneasy. How would such a foal be bred? And why would his dam be wandering loose and abandoned in the Uplands?"

"Winged foals have appeared spontaneously," Margareth said. "But it's been a very long time."

"It's been more than a century."

The headmistress nodded. "Two, at least. And I'm trying to come up with an explanation that doesn't mean trouble all around."

"I don't know if the Duke will rouse even for a breeding violation," Philippa said tiredly. "But I must try. And immediately."

"You had better go tomorrow, then."

A spasm of pain shot up Philippa's neck. She winced, and put her hand up to rub it. "Do you think Irina could cover my flight again?"

"I'll speak to her." Margareth stood up, bracing herself on her desk, and bent to blow out her lamp. Her eyes were shadowed, the lids drooping as if they were too heavy to lift.

Philippa leaned toward her. "Are you all right, Margareth?"

The headmistress nodded. "I'm just tired. Very tired." She put a fist in the small of her back and stretched. "Old," she added wryly.

"Nonsense. You're not old," Philippa protested.

Margareth gave her a look as she moved to the door. "Every horsemistress feels old the day she loses her mount, Philippa. And none of us escapes it."

Philippa hurried to open the door for her, trying to ignore the anxiety that rippled up from her belly. Margareth was the closest thing she had to a friend at the Academy. In truth, she could only count two true friends in her life. "You go to bed, Margareth," she said quietly. "Please. I'll find Irina myself."

Margareth nodded. "Thank you. I believe I will." She started toward the stairs, but on the first step she paused. She looked down, the light making hollows in her thin cheeks, shadowing her wrinkled throat. "Philippa . . . be sure to speak with Frederick alone."

"I'll do my best."

Margareth shook her head sharply, and spoke with a little of her old fire. "Not good enough, Philippa. No one else must hear you speak of this foal. Especially not at the palace."

"I know."

Margareth nodded again. Philippa watched her progress up the stairs, chilled by the slowness of her steps. Margareth had flown her Foundation stallion, Duke's Highflyer, for almost thirty years, and wore the scars that proved it. She had been Headmistress of the Academy of the Air for two decades. She had earned her retirement, a house in the White City, time to take her ease on her family's estate. But Philippa dreaded the loss of her friend.

Her own steps, as she walked to the Domicile, were hardly less heavy than Margareth's.

The small, white winter moon was just rising. She paused in the cobbled courtyard to look across at the whitewashed walls of the stables, the neat hedgerows that lined the flight and landing paddocks. How different it all was from the homely Uplands farm! She thought of the ferocity in Brye Hamley's eye when they were speaking of his sister's future, and a wave of emotion, even less honorable than the earlier one, twisted her heart.

"Idiot," she cursed herself. She wheeled to her right, and stalked across the courtyard to the Domicile. She dashed up the stairs and threw open the double doors.

Matron had obviously been waiting for her in the hallway. She dipped a brief curtsy, and reached for Philippa's things. "My, Mistress Winter, so late tonight! I was a bit worried."

"Nonsense, Matron," Philippa said distractedly. "Nothing to worry about. Do you know where Irina is?"

Matron pointed to the reading room, where a fire blazed in the hearth and all the lamps glowed yellow. Comfortable chairs were arranged so that the horsemistresses could read or converse alone or in company. Several were seated now before the fire, talking in low voices or doing paperwork. Irina Strong, a tall, broad-shouldered woman who flew a classic Foundation mare, had stretched her legs across the window seat, with ample cushions behind her, and a book open on her lap. Philippa started toward her. Matron said, "Food, Mistress Winter? Something to drink?"

Belatedly, Philippa recognized the hollowness of her belly. "Please. Anything you have," she said. She walked into the reading room, nodding to one or two of the other women.

Irina looked up from the window seat. "Philippa, at last," she said. "Where have you been so late? Off at the palace again?"

"No." Philippa pulled a chair close to Irina. She felt the curious glances on her back as she sat down.

Irina frowned. "No? But Margareth said—well, I understood you were on the Duke's business."

"Irina, we're all on the Duke's business. Every day of our lives."

Irina's broad face flushed. "You know what I meant," she said. "Extraordinary business."

"Yes." Philippa leaned back in her chair. "Well, it was."

Matron returned with a tray, and pushed a tea table close to Philippa's knee. She set the tray down, whisking the caddy off the teapot with a flourish. "There, now. A sandwich and a cup of tea. Don't let it get cold."

Philippa picked up the sandwich, paper-thin slices of bread layered with wafers of cheese and limp tomato slices. She demolished it in four bites, sure she could have eaten three more. She poured tea into the bone china cup, and cradled it in her fingers, gazing into the delicate tan liquid, remembering the thick pottery mug she had been given at Deeping Farm, and the biting black tea she had drunk from it. She looked around her again at the comforts of the reading room, the polished floor, the richly upholstered chairs, the perfectly groomed women in their crisp riding habits and clean boots. Despite the distinct smell of horse that permeated everything at the Academy, it was an elegant scene. How would the farm girl from Willakeep ever fit in?

"Are you going to tell me?" Irina persisted.

Philippa took another sip, and set down her cup. "I can't, Irina." Irina's lips tightened, and Philippa felt a wave of impatience. "You'll know soon enough, as everyone will, but until I've seen the Duke, I can't discuss it. Margareth and I have agreed it's the best way."

Irina shrugged. "Have it your way, Philippa. Your flight did very well today, by the way. You want to watch Geraldine Prince, though. Her gray was a little skittish."

Philippa said sharply, "Prince? Ridiculous. He's never skittish. What were you doing?"

Irina straightened, and swung her legs out of the window seat. "What do you mean, Philippa? We were practicing Airs, of course. Points and Reverses. Nothing your girls haven't done a hundred times. Surely it's what you meant for me to do!"

Philippa held up an apologetic hand. "Irina, I didn't mean—I wasn't criticizing."

"You should hear yourself," Irina said sourly.

Philippa wanted to snap the same words back at her colleague, but a sudden, dragging weariness overtook her. "No doubt," she said heavily. She pushed the table aside and stood up. "And now that I've made you angry, Irina, I have to ask you to take my flight again tomorrow."

Irina folded her arms, looking up into Philippa's face. "Really."

She drew out the word, exaggerating the nasal accent of her Eastreach upbringing. "And are you going to tell me why you're going to miss another drill?"

Philippa touched a hand to the back of her neck. Her headache had grown unbearable. "No, Irina, I'm not. I should have let Margareth come and ask you herself, but she was exhausted, and now I am, too. Will you do this for me, or must I find someone else?" Her voice had grown sharp, but she was too tired and worried to discipline it.

"Oh, I'll do it," Irina said. "You have seniority, and it's not as if I have a flight of my own. And of course, if you're on the Duke's business . . . *Extraordinary* business . . ." She let the words trail off.

Philippa became aware, as she lifted her head, that all the women in the room were listening to their exchange. She looked down at Irina. "How kind of you," she said. She knew that acid dripped from her words, but she was simply beyond caring. She whirled, and met the curious gazes. It was too much, after such a long and troublesome day. She snapped, "And now, I bid all of you a good night's sleep. I'm in desperate need, myself." With her back straight and her head high, she marched out of the reading room and up to her own apartment. Her bootheels clicked angrily on the polished hardwood of the floor as she mounted the stairs.

TIRED though she was, once she had taken off her riding habit, slipped into a thick flannel nightgown, and braided her hair for the night, Philippa found she couldn't sleep. She pinched the wick of her lamp, and wrapped herself in a quilt to curl up in the wing chair beside her window.

As the most senior of the Academy's instructors, her rooms were spacious and well appointed. Her window looked directly out over the courtyard, with the Hall to her left, the Dormitory to her right. The stables and the paddocks lay open to her view, and if she leaned from her window, she could catch a glimpse of the yearlings in their pasture.

Now she lay back in the chair, gazing across at the gambrel profile of the stables, limned in moonlight. Herbert, the stable-man, came out of the Hall and crossed the courtyard. An oc-hound rose from the shadows and trotted to meet him. Herbert, with a hand on the dog's narrow head, went into the stables, and a moment later the window brightened in his upper apartment. All was in order at the Academy of the Air.

Philippa drew the quilt to her chin, and thought about her exchange with Irina. She knew she wasn't popular with her colleagues. It didn't seem to matter that her flight was the most disciplined, the most accomplished. Only Margareth, and of course Duke Frederick himself, appeared to care that she and Winter Sunset had brought honor and respect to Oc through their service in the White City and at the Prince's court in Isamar. She supposed that, as in her girlhood, her ambition and her discipline attracted envy. Her younger sisters, with their fine marriages and beautiful homes, still regarded her with uneasy resentment, despite the sacrifices she had been required to make. And her brother—

Again the image of Brye Hamley intruded upon her thoughts. She didn't truly know him, of course. But she did not believe for a moment that Master Hamley of Deeping Farm would have arranged his sister's future to suit his own purposes.

Her eyes stung, and she shook herself, furious at her weakness. Tired, she thought. That's all it is. I'm tired.

She forced herself out of the chair, and spread her quilt on the bed again. Matron had ordered her fire set, and a warming stone slipped beneath the sheets. Philippa climbed into bed, and laid her head on the pillow. Her headache began to recede, but images and memories danced through her brain as if she were fevered. Her sisters at Islington House, their silken skirts floating as they descended the curved staircase to meet their beaus. Her mother frowning over her older daughter, trying this hairstyle and that fabric, struggling to make her look more appealing. Her brother Meredith, upon her father's death, with that cold light in his eye as he took her measure. And William's handsome face, laughing at her . . .

"Zito's ears!" she swore aloud, and turned herself about in the bed, away from the view of the moonlit stables. What was it about the events of this day that had brought up old, buried slights? She thought she had purged them long ago, as the discarded bits of experience they were. She couldn't imagine why meeting one un-refined country girl and her rough-edged brother should so upset her own composure.

She thrust the thought away. None of it mattered. She would sleep, and in the morning she would see things in their proper perspective once again. It was simply a matter, as it always was, of discipline.

FOUR

"You'll need a bath if you're to sleep in the house again," Nick said.

He and Brye and Edmar stood in the kitchen, gazing at their sister. The prefect had departed at last, mumbling to himself about laws and the slowness of the mail coach cobs, the insolence of farm girls. Silent Edmar, returned from the quarry, frowned as his siblings recounted the events of the day.

"But I can't leave Tup alone," Lark began.

Brye put up a hand. "Good idea, Mistress Winter had. One of the goats. The milker."

"I don't know if he'll like her," Lark said doubtfully, but Brye, pulling on his jacket, was already on his way out the kitchen door. She seized the long, padded coat she wore for night chores, and dashed after him.

The cows lowed from the far side of the barn, having come down from the north pasture, their udders heavy with milk. Molly, the she-goat, bleated from the night pen, and Tup whimpered in his stall, his little hooves shifting in the straw. Lark glanced up at the cold white moon, already high above the eastern horizon. She was late with her chores, and had given no thought to supper. She hurried to catch up with Brye.

"Let me do it," she said to his broad back.

He unlatched the gate to the night pen and stood back for her to sidle past him. The five goats crowded around her, two she-goats and three billies. She stroked their bony heads and tickled their wispy beards. Uplands goats were famed for the softness of the wool beneath their long, coarse outer coats. In the spring, they were sheared close, and the wool carded for the woollery in Willakeep, where it would be made into capes and cloaks for the highborn ladies of Osham. Molly, the little brown milker, turned sideways to present her full teats to Lark, bleating a plea for surcease.

"I know, Molly," Lark said, rubbing the goat's back. "I'm late. Sorry."

Brye handed her a rope, and she looped it around Molly's neck and coaxed her through the gate into the aisle. The other goats scuffled for position as they peered after Molly.

Molly balked at the stall door, setting her feet and dropping her head. Tup threw up his head, his nostrils widening, his ears laid back. Lark stood with one foot in the stall, one in the aisle. She cast her brother a helpless glance.

"Brye," she said. "It'll never work with you here."

Brye frowned, but he took a step back, and then another. "Wouldn't hurt yon colt to spend a night alone," he grumbled, but he turned his back and moved toward the door.

Lark shot him a look, but she held her tongue. The strange day had worn all their tempers thin. There was a great pile of things to think about, but the heap would look smaller, she knew, when they all were rested. She heard the outer door of the barn open and close, and her brother's heavy footsteps cross the yard. Tup dropped his head, and flicked his ears forward. He gave a curious whicker. Molly shook her wispy beard at the colt.

Lark bent to murmur into the she-goat's floppy ear. "Silly! It's just a different stall. And look, you can't be afraid of Tup! Why, he's hardly bigger than you are! Come along, now. I'll milk you right here." She picked up the waiting bucket, and rattled it. Molly bleated again, and followed the bucket.

Step by slow step, Lark coaxed the goat into Tup's stall, and latched the gate. She put the bucket beneath the goat's swollen teats, and then squatted, leaning her head into the goat's soft flank. Molly groaned with relief as the milk began to ring against the tin.

A moment later Lark felt a push at her hands from Molly's other side. She lifted her head to look across the she-goat's back.

She could see only the arch of Tup's slender neck, bending neatly as the foal tucked his nose beneath the goat's udder. She took her hands away, and let him find the teat. He was nursing! Somehow, suddenly, it seemed the most natural thing in the world.

"Aren't I the fool!" Lark exclaimed softly. "Should have thought of this myself."

She stayed where she was, her hand on the goat's shoulder. Molly rolled an eye at her, and then twisted her head to look at the colt. Tup butted at her gently, and Molly lifted her ribs a little to give him better access. The comforting sound of the foal's suckling filled the stall.

Lark stood up slowly, and leaned against the wall. The foal's legs had steadied, and his eyes, widely spaced in his finely cut head, glowed with intelligence and spirit. His wings clung to his ribs, even when she tried to push a gentle finger beneath them. His coat was rough and soft at the same time, baby fur. His ears were small and pointed. His hooves, so neat and tiny, gleamed like black glass. He was the most beautiful creature Lark had ever seen.

"Lark!" It was Brye, standing in the yard outside the barn. "Leave them to it, Lark. Come to the house."

Reluctantly, obediently, Lark let herself out of the stall. Tup lifted his head to watch her go, but he didn't whimper. She felt both relieved and a little disappointed as she followed her brother across the barnyard. As she passed into the warmth of the house, she noticed that the buds on the rue-tree beside the kitchen door were about to burst into leaf. When had that happened? Spring was rising around her, and she was too distracted to see it.

She came into the kitchen just as Nick passed the Tarn over a bubbling pot, twirling its ragged skirts through the steam. The bathscreen, the painted scenes on its three panels almost worn away by generations of Hamley hands, had been set up in one corner. Nick looked up at her, and indicated the screen with a bob of his head. "Tub's steaming," he said. "Best fetch some clean clothes and pop yourself in." He crossed to the counter to restore the Tarn to its hook. "And wash your hair, Lark. You look like one of your own goats."

She hurried up the narrow stair to the darkness of her room. Without bothering to light the lamp, she pulled a tabard and skirt out of the chest, hoping they were clean. She found smallclothes and stockings in the darkness, and her brush and comb, and carried the lot back down to the kitchen.

Her brothers had gathered around the table. Nick grinned at her. Edmar nodded his wordless greeting. Brye was thumping bowls and spoons on the table, slicing ragged hunks of cheddar from the wheel.

"I'll be quick," Lark said.

"Thorough," Brye commanded, without looking up.

Lark caught sight of her wavering reflection in the side of the soup pot, and then looked swiftly away, chagrined. "Zito's ears," she said. "I've never been in such need of a wash."

"That's my thinking," Nick said, laughing.

Lark ducked behind the screen. "Half an hour, and I'll be a new girl, I promise."

Edmar and Brye were busily chewing their bread and cheese. Nick said cheerily, "No need to go that far," he said. "We all quite like the old one."

Lark tossed her filthy clothes in the corner, and lowered herself into the tub. She smiled as she reached for the fresh cake of mercantile soap Nick had laid out for her. Tup and Molly were managing together. A new and glorious future lay ahead of her. At this moment, it seemed there was no difficulty she could not master. She stretched, and then sank to her nose in the hot water, giving herself up to the pleasure of her much-delayed bath.

THE next morning, Lark woke with a start to sunshine pouring in her window. She was surprised to realize that she had slept the night through without waking. When she had first tucked herself under her thick, age-softened quilt, she felt a qualm at being separated from the foal, and strained her ears for his cry. But she had heard nothing, and it had been too long since she slept in her own bed. She bolted upright, and leaped up to pull on her clothes and hurry to the barn.

She found Tup and Molly curled snugly together in one corner of the box stall. Tup came to his feet when he saw her, and Molly followed him, treading in his footsteps in the straw like a brown shadow. The foal nosed Lark's hands, and his little cry was easier this morning, more of a whicker than a sob. She laughed, and rubbed his cheek, breathing in the sweet musk of his skin. "There now, my Tup," she said. "Full at last, aren't you?" He tossed his head up and down, up and down, as if in agreement. Molly crowded close to be petted. Lark laughed, and opened the half-door. "Come on out, now, you two. The sun's on the yard, and it's lovely warm."

She went about her chores, chuckling over her shoulder as the foal and the goat ambled behind her, making an odd little procession from barn to kitchen to coldcellar. She negotiated the three steps down to the coldcellar with Tup on her heels, and Molly bleating above. Nick was waiting for her, holding the slanted door open. "Now stand back, rascal," he told the foal. "My customers won't want horsehair in their milk!"

There was barely room for Lark and Nick together in the cold-cellar. Tup stood with his forefeet on the floor, his slender hindquarters angled up to the top step, watching as Lark poured the milk through cheesecloth filters into big bottles. He backed away when Nick came out with the full bottles, and Lark came after with the yellow slab of butter she had churned and formed the day before. It glistened in its copper tray, ready to be portioned out to the housewives who would hail Nick's oxcart as it passed their doors.

The ox stood patiently waiting, his stubby horns gleaming in the cool sunshine. Nick pulled the canvas sheet over his cargo and tied it with thongs to the cart's rail. "Best come with me, lass," he teased. "Make sure I do this right."

"I don't like to leave the foal," she said.

He flashed the white smile the housewives of Willakeep loved. "Thought you'd say so. Did you write down that awful woman's receipt, then, for the mash? I'll swap the miller some fresh butter for the grain."

"I did," she said, pulling the scrap of paper from her pocket. She handed it to him, and he climbed up on the wooden seat and picked up the ox's leather reins. "But, Nick," she added, one hand on the side of the cart. "Did you think Mistress Winter was awful?"

"That I did!" he exclaimed, laughing. "Bony and hard, and so snooty you'd think she was a duchess."

"She could be," Lark said as she stepped back. "She might be Lady Something-or-other if she weren't a horsemistress."

"Lady Leanshanks," Nick said with a wink. He pulled his nose down with his fingers. "Lady Longnose. Lady Lackbosom!" He pressed his hands against his chest, pushing up his shirt to make meager mock breasts.

"Oh, Nick!" she said, waving him away. "Be off with you before my butter melts!"

He clucked to the ox, and it stirred to life, its head swinging from side to side as it took its first plodding steps. The well-oiled wheels creaked only once, and then rolled almost silently over the packed dirt of the lane. Nick waved, and settled a wide-brimmed hat on his head. Tup nosed Lark's shoulder, and she circled his neck with her arm as she watched Nick and the oxcart trundle off between the hedgerows.

"Tonight, little Tup," she promised. "Tonight you'll have mash."

She turned toward the house. There were beds to be made, dishes to be washed, soup to be started. Still, she stood for a moment, admiring the neat yard and buildings of Deeping Farm. The midmorning sun warmed her neck, a sure sign that spring was at hand. The rain of the preceding day had washed the landscape clean. Doves cooed in the eaves of the barn, and blackbirds chittered in the hedgerow and the rue-tree beside the kitchen door. It seemed life was about to burst from every tree, every shrub, every dormant bulb and seed. Lark's heart lifted as if it were filled with air, and a strange sensation stirred in her belly. She felt for all the world as if she, too, were about to blossom.

PHILIPPA rose early, and begged a cup of tea and a slice of buttered bread from the kitchens, to avoid the delay of breakfast hour in the Hall. The morning sky was spring-bright, with the gentlest wind from the south. A perfect day for a flight.

She pulled on her gloves as she strolled to the stables. The long-legged yearlings in their pasture raced across the rain-washed grass to nod their heads at her above the fence poles, and then dash away again, tails flying, wings flexing against their wingclips as they galloped and bucked. Philippa slowed her steps to watch them.

There was no lovelier sight in all the Duchy of Oc than these exuberant creatures. They were white, black, dapple gray, red, gold, and brown. Their bodies were more slender, their bones finer than their wingless brethren. Philippa scorned all superstition, and yet, watching these young ones twinkle across the grass, she could almost believe the stories of their descent from the glittering Old Ones. It was nonsense, of course, and no one knew that better than she did. Every winged horse was the result of generations of selective breeding, of the careful, even obsessive monitoring of each of the three bloodlines, of the cautious husbanding of Oc's most precious commodity.

Her own Winter Sunset was of the Noble bloodline, a strain aptly named. Nobles were swift, graceful horses, prized by royals as couriers and escorts. A flight of seven Nobles signified a progress by the Prince himself, and preceded him on foreign state visits. Foundation horses were big and strong, trained for battle, for patrolling borders and defending vulnerable outposts. From the Ocmarin line came slender, agile animals, famed for endurance and intelligence. Ocmarins carried messages to the farthest corners of the principality, and even to other kingdoms.

Thinking of the bloodlines reminded Philippa of her mission, and she hurried on toward the stables. There was nothing easy about the task that faced her this morning. There had been a time when Duke Frederick guarded the bloodlines with a ferocity that commanded respect from the Council of Lords and no small degree of fear from those who worked with winged horses. But it was not easy talking to the Duke these days, nor had it been for the past eight months. The loss of his daughter, his favorite child, had broken him.

Herbert emerged from the stables as Philippa approached, and Bramble, the oc-hound, trotted eagerly forward to greet her. She stroked the dog's narrow, satiny head. Bramble sat, watching her hopefully. "Sorry, Bramble," Philippa murmured. "No time to play today."

"Need your mare then, Mistress?" Herbert asked.

"Yes, please." She adjusted her cap on her head, and smoothed her rider's knot. She was pulling on her gloves when Rosellen appeared with Sunny, flying saddle in place. The sight of her, even now, made Philippa's heart beat faster.

Margareth had been right. The loss of her mount must seem, to a horsemistress, to presage her own death. There was still work to be done, of course, foalings and breedings and girls to be guided and taught. But there could be no substitute for being airborne, for looking down on the green and brown and white landscape, for flying above expanses of blue water, for being above—far above—the mundane details of life on the ground.

Philippa turned toward the flight paddock, Sunny's nose at her shoulder, eager to lift into the chilly golden morning.

The doors of the Dormitory opened, and the twitter of girls' voices reached her across the expanse of courtyard. Time to be away. With luck, she would catch Frederick at his own breakfast. With even more luck, she might find him alone.

FIVE

THE quickest route to the Ducal Palace led directly over Osham. Philippa thrust aside her worries for the brief flight, and gave herself up to the pleasure of feeling Sunny's powerful wings lifting them into the wind, of the rush of the wind in her ears. They followed the twisting ribbon of the Grand River as it cut between the turrets and spires of the White City. Philippa glanced over her shoulder at the copper dome of the Tower of the Seasons, gleaming against the distant green tapestry of the sea. Beyond it the white marble rotunda of the Council of Lords sat like a fat iced wedding cake, aflap with pennants bearing the insignias of each noble family.

In her girlhood, Philippa had spent a good part of each year in the White City, accompanying her mother and her sisters to social occasions, attending concerts, promenading their ponies through the parks. It was far better to fly above it all, as she did now, looking down on the immense houses of the Council Lords, the great brick plaza around the Tower, on the broad avenues where the gentry strolled and shopped, on the cramped neighborhoods of the working people. Sunny's wings beat steadily, tilting as she banked to the north. Philippa shifted her weight to match the mare's angle without thinking about it. They had flown together nearly twenty years, and Sunny knew the way to the Palace as well as she did. They had served there, on the special request of the Duke. The Palace had felt almost as much like home to Philippa as the Academy. Those days, she knew, were now gone, her friend and mentor failing, his heir poised to seize his power.

They approached the Palace from the south and circled to approach from the north. With the wind at her back, Sunny settled toward the park. Philippa sat deep in her saddle, giving the mare her head as her wingbeats slowed and then stopped. As Sunny began her glide, Philippa looked ahead to the Palace grounds. Gardeners were taking advantage of the early spring weather to dig beds and prune dead canes from the hedges. The stables were lively with movement, several of the Duke's flyers visible in the paddock. Philippa wished she would find Frederick about to set out on some affair of state, escorted by a flight of Nobles, as he had done so often during her years here. She knew he had not left the Palace since Pamella's disappearance, and now it seemed likely he never would again.

Sunny descended, her neck stretching, her haunches gathered beneath her. Philippa collected herself as well, elbows in, heels down, helping Sunny to balance, leaning back ever so slightly as the mare's forelegs reached for the ground. The return paddock of the Ducal Palace was long and narrow, and Sunny, exuberant from the short flight, covered the length of it at a hand gallop, shaking her bridle, flaring her tail. Her pinions trailed the spring grass, and it almost seemed she would launch herself once again into the sky.

Philippa lifted the reins. Sunny whuffed and pranced, but she slowed to a canter, and then a trot. Soon she stood, blowing and stamping, as a stable-girl came out to meet them.

"Mistress Winter," the stable-girl said. "Good morning." She was, of course, not a girl at all, but a woman of advanced years, dry and leathery as an old fence, who had been in service to the Duke since his investiture, and to his father before that. In Philippa's time at the Palace, she had come to know her well.

"Jolinda. It's good to see you." The passing years had whitened the old retainer's hair, dried her skin on her bones. Only her eyes were as bright and lively as Philippa remembered them. "Rosellen sends her greetings."

The older woman grinned. "Rosellen! Good girl, that."

Philippa smiled. "I know."

Jolinda took Sunny's reins. "Best get indoors now. Your cheeks are as red as His Grace's roses."

Philippa turned toward the Palace. Its marble and stone facade sparkled in the sun, its windows gleaming. Automatically, she glanced at the southern wing, where she had lived with the other horsemistresses. With the great exception of the raid on the South Tower of Isamar, it had been the happiest time of her life. "How is Duke Frederick, Jolinda? Does he ride?"

Jolinda paused, and Sunny almost bumped into her. "No, Mistress," the stable-girl said. "He doesn't ride, nor hardly go out of his chambers, to hear Andrews tell it. Palace been a bleak place since they lost Pamella."

"She was a beautiful girl."

Jolinda spat into the grass between her feet. "Beautiful, heh. That's as may be. Lady Pamella was a spoiled brat, pure and simple. Drove them tutors wild with whims and tantrums. My own mum would have put paid to such behaviors. But His Grace adored her." Jolinda shrugged, and led Sunny toward the stables.

Philippa strode away in the opposite direction, stripping off her gloves as she went. An oc-hound came to pace beside her, drawn as they always were to flyers. She stroked its head, and its plume of a tail waved. When she had crossed the courtyard, she patted it again. "Wish me luck, my friend," she whispered, and waved it back to the stables. It trotted away, but stopped at the far side of the courtyard, head lifted, eyes fixed on her. The oc-hounds were as sensitive as the winged horses. A pity she had not had one when she was a lonely girl!

Philippa climbed the broad steps, tucking her gloves into the pocket of her riding jacket. As she reached the top, one of the heavy doors swung open, and a tall, thin man in the Duke's livery bowed to her.

"Horsemistress Winter," he said gravely. "What a pleasant surprise."

"Good morning, Andrews." She gave him her cap and her quirt.

"Shall I take your coat, Mistress?"

She shook her head. "No, thank you. I'm a bit chilled."

"Of course. A cold morning for flying." He bowed again. "Have you breakfasted? I could certainly bring you something in the small dining room, and there's a nice fire going."

"Thank you, Andrews, but no." She glanced around at the elaborately appointed entryway. Crystal and silver and brass shone everywhere. A maid in a long apron was polishing the tall mullioned windows, and at the end of the long lower hall, other servants in livery moved back and forth laden with linens or trays of china. "Is His Grace at home?" Philippa asked. "I need to speak with him."

"I will ask," Andrews said. He laid her things neatly on a side table, and disappeared up the stairs.

He was gone for some time. Philippa paced, smoothing her hair before a beveled mirror, unbuttoning her riding coat when she finally felt warm enough. When she came near the house-maid, the girl curtsied, and scurried off down the hall. Philippa turned on her heel, pacing the other way, wondering what had become of Andrews.

When he returned at last, and bowed to her a third time from the foot of the stairs, he avoided her eyes. "Lord William will receive you, Horsemistress."

Philippa paused. "No, Andrews," she said. "I came to see Duke Frederick."

"Yes, Mistress. I understood you to say so. But the Duke—" His eyes flickered to one side, back again. He cleared his throat. "The Duke is not well, Mistress Winter. And Lord—that is, I am told he can't have visitors this morning."

"Andrews—where is Lady Sophia?"

The steward let his eyes flicker up to hers, just briefly, and then he dropped them again. "The Duchess has been staying at the city house," he said, his voice weighted with sorrow. "Since they lost Pamella—Lord William says she can't bear to stay here in the Palace."

Philippa felt no surprise at that. Lady Sophia's predilections were well known, and they didn't include maternal devotion. She was famous for her affairs and extravagant entertainments, and had never shared Frederick's passion for the winged horses.

"And Francis?"

"Lord Francis is in Isamar, Mistress Winter. Lord William thought it best—that is, he sent him there, some weeks ago."

"That seems strange, just now," Philippa said.

Another voice spoke. "We needed a liaison with the Prince, of course." Philippa stiffened, and looked past Andrews at Lord William himself, who stood now at the turning of the stair, gazing down at her.

The old steward stepped aside, ducking his head in an uncharacteristically awkward fashion, and disappeared swiftly down the lower hall. William smiled down at Philippa.

"Mistress Winter," he said. His voice was light, like that of a young boy. He wore black and silver, the same hues as Philippa's own riding habit, though he affected a thickly embroidered scarlet and purple vest over his full-sleeved shirt. He came down the stairs, setting his feet with care on the polished oak. His soft boots made no sound. He stopped on the second step from the bottom, preserving the advantage of height.

He must have, she thought, the best barber in the Duchy. His cheeks and chin were smooth as a girl's, and his hair, the startling white-blond of all the Fleckhams, fell at a perfect angle to his shoulders. "It's always good to see you," he said smoothly. He leaned forward, ever so slightly, and Philippa, standing at the bottom of the staircase, had to resist the urge to lean back. He smiled again, as if he knew. "Tell me, Philippa. What can the House of Oc do for the Academy on this fine morning?"

How foolish a girl she must have been, Philippa thought, to have imagined herself in love with this cold man.

But she was no longer a girl, and she knew William for what he was. Tension tightened into a knot between her shoulder blades, and the familiar thread of pain lanced up her neck and into her skull. She regarded him gravely. "Rumors reached us," she said, "that His Grace was unwell. The Headmistress asked me to express her concern."

"Indeed." William spoke lightly, but Philippa saw the glint in his eyes. "How kind of Margareth to spare you from your duties to call upon my father. And when you have been so busy, dashing about the countryside. Pressing business for the Academy, no doubt."

A flare of anxiety added to Philippa's headache. Instinctively, she prevaricated. "Academy business, yes. Nothing of interest to you, my lord."

"You might be surprised."

Philippa gazed up at him, at his archly lifted brow, the expectant widening of his ice-blue eyes. "Why, no," she said. "I doubt I would." Her audacity was rewarded by a tinge of red creeping across William's pale cheek. She added, "In any case, I would not dream of burdening you with the small details of school business." She took a step forward. "And now, may I please go up to your father? It's been too long, and both Margareth and I are concerned for him."

Her movement forced William to either give in, or deliberately block her progress. He hesitated no more than a moment before he took a graceful step to his left, and indicated she should precede him. "Of course you may, Philippa. Now that I know how worried you are . . . but please, a short visit. My lord father is truly unwell." Maddeningly, he followed at her shoulder as she started up the steps. "But let me assure you, Horsemistress, that you may pursue your interests in any part of Oc without concern for your safety."

Philippa just prevented herself from hissing a swift breath. He meant, of course, that she was being spied upon. And there was nothing she could do about it.

William followed close at her heels, making it clear she would have no time alone with Frederick. Sophia, Francis, Eduard Crisp . . . William had done a thorough job. Frederick must be very weak, indeed, not to protest such isolation.

She didn't glance back at William as she made her way to the Duke's apartment. At her quiet knock, Frederick's valet opened the door. He bowed when he saw her, and held the door wide.

Frederick, her old friend and mentor, sat in a wing chair beside the tall windows. A blanket covered his long legs, and his spare figure slumped a little. The heavy drapes were pulled back, giving the Duke a clear view of his stables and courtyard, of the paddocks where winged and wingless horses grazed. As Philippa crossed to him, she saw a horsemistress in riding habit walk around the Palace from the south wing, and go into the stables.

"Your Grace," Philippa said softly. She drew even with Frederick's chair, and waited for him to respond.

His hair shone silver in the morning light, but his eyes, when they turned up to find hers, had gone dull, almost muddy. She sank into the nearest chair, pressed down by a terrible weight of sadness.

Now that she was close to him, she saw that he held something in his long white fingers. Even as he spoke to her, he caressed it, turning it in his hand. "Philippa," he said, a little hoarsely. "How kind of you to come."

"I'm so sorry to find you unwell," she said.

He turned the object again in his lap, and traced one finger across its surface. It was a framed miniature, a portrait. Philippa caught a glimpse of white-blond hair, a pretty face, the dark Fleckham eyes. Pamella. Frederick's lost daughter.

"Beautiful day for flying," he said vaguely. He turned away from her, toward the window. A winged horse rose from the far end of the park, and banked toward the White City. Frederick followed it with his eyes. When it disappeared beyond the trees, he dropped his gaze again to the miniature.

"Yes, it is," Philippa said. "I thought it was a perfect morning to come and talk to you."

Before Frederick could answer her, William was at his elbow, bending over him with a glass of water in his hand. "Father," William said. "Your doctors want you to drink more water." He encouraged Frederick to take the glass with a surprisingly gentle touch, and watched to see that he drank.

Absently, Frederick sipped from the glass. Philippa was alarmed to see how his hand trembled. When he handed the glass back, she waited for William to step away, but he remained where he was, holding the glass, leaning on the back of his father's chair to gaze out the window as if mesmerized by the sunshine. A long minute passed.

"Your Grace," Philippa said at last. She left her chair, and went to crouch beside the Duke's knee. She felt William's eyes on her, but she kept her gaze on Frederick's face, and put her hand on his. "I know you're grieving," she said. "And I'm sorry. But Margareth and I thought—"

"Please, Philippa," William said sharply. "My father can't be troubled about that now."

Frederick turned his attention to Philippa very slowly, as if having trouble focusing his eyes on her face. "About what?" he asked.

"A winged colt, Frederick," she said. "He was born out of season, in—"

Interest seemed to spark in Frederick's eyes, just for a moment, but before Philippa could finish her sentence, William overturned the glass in his hand, splashing the miniature with water.

Frederick gave a wordless cry, and there was a little flurry of apologies, of drying the little portrait, of fetching Frederick a fresh blanket for his lap. When these ministrations were complete, Philippa attempted to return to the subject of the colt, but William stood behind Frederick's chair, his arms folded, his eyes fixed on Philippa.

Frederick's brief flicker of interest had vanished. "Always taking chances," he said vaguely, caressing the miniature. "Always daring, the first one over a jump, the last off the dance floor, the most admirers . . ." His voice trailed off, and his head fell back against the chair.

"As I told you, Philippa," William said coldly. "My father shouldn't be troubled now."

"Trouble enough," Frederick said plaintively. "One son is too gentle, the other too hard."

Philippa was startled to see William's eyelids drop, his head turn away from his father. Was that pain that pulled at his mouth, that creased his brow?

"Dear Frederick . . ." Philippa began.

Harshly, William said, "I think Father should rest now, Philippa. Say your goodbyes. His doctors will be here soon."

Moments later Philippa found herself on the doorstep, with Andrews offering her cap and quirt, and Sunny awaiting her at the bottom of the steps. The efficiency with which William had managed this was impressive. Irritated, frustrated, she pulled on her gloves and her cap, marched down the stairs without answering Andrews's farewell wishes, and leaped into her saddle, ignoring the mounting block that had been set for her. She set Sunny to canter toward the park, and let her launch swiftly, even roughly, into the bright sky. It had been, she thought furiously, a fine morning. It was no more.

SIX

THE girl on the bed was willowy and fine-boned, if not pretty. Her brown hair clouded across her slender shoulders. William preferred her like this, her face turned into the pillow, her shoulders heaving with her sobs, bruises beginning to rise on her back and legs.

"Oh, by Zito's ass, desist your sniveling, will you?" he snapped. In truth, each of her pitiful cries gave him a fresh shiver of pleasure. It was all the pleasure he was capable of, and he savored it. He snapped his quirt against his thigh, and was rewarded by her squeal as she scrabbled through the bedclothes for something to cover herself.

William laughed. "No, no more, you little twit. I've sent for Slater, and he'll take you back to—wherever it is you came from. Come, now, get up and dress. It's late."

He turned his back on her, and went to stand by the window. A sliver of moon showed through shreds of cloud, but the stars were beginning to fade. He glanced at the silver clock on the mantel, and saw that it was almost four. At least his needs had been met—met, that is, as much as was possible for him. He would tell Slater to wake him at ten, and he could leave for the Uplands then. He could even, he thought, stop in Clellum while he was there, carry a little gift. He smiled at his dim reflection in the window. He felt better now. He had been so angry at Philippa Winter, at her interfering, her presumption . . . Naturally, it would have been more satisfying to use his quirt on Philippa herself. But Philippa was a horsemistress. Even the Duke's heir did not dare treat a horsemistress in such a fashion.

Thinking of this almost made him turn back to the cowering girl on the bed, but Slater knocked at that moment. The girl—if he had heard her name, he had already forgotten it—had pulled on her clothes and her hooded cloak, and she opened the door and slipped through before he could stop her.

Slater put his head round the door. He was a coarse-featured and thick-bodied man, none too clean, and his manner of address matched his appearance. William tolerated his rough ways because of his discretion, and his willingness to do any task, no matter how loathsome, that might be asked of him.

"M'lord," he said. "You be needing anything else tonight?"

"This morning, you mean," William responded. "And no. Wake me at ten."

"Aye, m'lord." Slater started to withdraw.

"Oh, Slater!" William said. He crossed the bedroom to his writing desk and fumbled in the drawer for a few coins. His valet stood in the open doorway. The hall beyond was deserted, the girl nowhere to be seen, probably halfway home already.

William jingled the coins in his hand as he crossed to the door. He dropped the money into Slater's rough palm. "I'll be needing more of old Notkin's brew tomorrow."

Slater grinned up at him as he dropped the coins neatly into the leather wallet at his belt. His teeth were stained brown by snuff. He dipped into a fold of his rusty black greatcoat, and pulled a brown glass bottle from an invisible pocket. "Thought you might be wanting this, m'lord," he rasped. "Naught else?"

William took the bottle with his fingertips. "No, excellent Slater. You have seen to all my needs magnificently."

Slater snickered at that, and turned with a sweep of his odorous cloak. William could hear him sniggering to himself all the way down the hall. With a grimace of distaste, he shut the door and barred it. Slater would hardly be his choice of personal servant, if matters were different. But choice, at the present moment, had little to do with it. Everything he did was governed by necessity.

He pulled the stopper on the little bottle to check the level of liquid inside. Notkin had cheated him once, sending half a bottle for the full price. This time, however, the bottle brimmed with noisome dark fluid, and William stoppered it again with a mirthless smile. Notkin had paid dearly for shorting him, and he doubted it would happen again.

He set the bottle on his dressing table. He took off his embroidered silk vest, and began to unbutton the linen shirt beneath. He paused with the job half-done, and stared into the oval mirror.

He let his fingers stray across his chest, lightly to the left, and then to the right. The half-light of early dawn glimmered in the glass, and he leaned closer to it, testing the texture of his jaw with his hand. How long since he had last needed a razor? Weeks at least, he thought. The skin of his face was as smooth and soft as—well, as that nameless girl's he had just sent packing. He picked up Notkin's product again, and cradled it in his hand. A necessary evil, this potion. Sacrifices were necessary if one were to accomplish one's goals.

Notkin had protested, saying that the concoction violated his apothecary's oath, that he couldn't vouch for the safety of such a recipe, that the Duke would hold him responsible if anything should happen to his eldest son.

William had persuaded him, of course. Such persuasion was, perhaps, unpleasant, but again—necessity drove him. Notkin protested no more after that, and William felt quite, quite certain he would tell no one of his special prescription. It helped that the old apothecary had a winsome granddaughter he doted on. She had not, as yet, been required, but it was always good to hold something in reserve.

That thought, oddly, brought Philippa Winter's face to mind, severe, controlled, with that air of authority that enraged him. What would she say if she knew that he was as celibate, in truth, as she was? He could imagine. Her lip would curl, and she would give him that familiar, scornful look, her eyes like blue ice. He should have dealt with her years ago, when she worked so hard to ingratiate herself with his father. She had pretended to like the books Frederick did, had feigned interest in the workings of the Council of Lords. He had made a grave error, and all because he could see that Frederick preferred Philippa and Pamella to himself and Francis. He should have foreseen that his father would bond Philippa to a winged horse, but by the time he realized it, it was done. Philippa Islington became Philippa Winter, a horsemistress, with her own privileges and power.

For a brief moment, William wished the girl were still in the room, so he could expend his fury on her white flesh . . . but no. He was tired. It was enough. There would be other nights, other girls, and he could think of Philippa at those times. And surely, before long, the Palace would be his. He would see to it then that the horsemistresses treated him with the respect he deserved.

He turned away from the mirror to strip off his shirt and trousers. He slid between the sheets, and lay on his back, staring at the ceiling. He was making progress, he must remember that. The foal from the Uplands proved that. He must let nothing stand in his way.

SEVEN

THE hesitant coming of spring in the Uplands became a stampede. Hillsides and fields and gardens exploded with color. The rue-tree burst into full leaf. Hedgerows bloomed and brightened, and mistle thrush and yellowhammers flitted around them, bearing fragile burdens of twigs and moss. Bobbins, the little round Uplands flowers, sprinkled the new grass of the pastures with pink and lavender and violet.

Tup seemed to blossom, too. Every morning, when Lark hurried from the farmhouse to greet him, he seemed taller. His head came to her shoulder now, and his rough baby fur had begun to slough away, revealing the sleek black coat beneath. His legs were stronger, his body rounder, his mane and tail growing. He soon preferred mash to Molly's milk, and he cropped the new grass in the barnyard with small, pearly teeth.

On the day the bloodbeet starts arrived, and a crew came from the village to help Brye set them out, the foal's wings opened.

Everyone in Willakeep had come, at one time or another, to see the marvel of one of the Duke's winged horses foaled at Deeping Farm. In the quiet way of Uplanders, they came alone, or in twos or threes, greeting Lark, standing at a distance as she moved about the barnyard with the colt at her heels. On this day, Brye's crew walked in through the gate just as Tup, with Molly in his wake, trotted across the barnyard after Lark. One of the laborers cried out, "Look! Look at his wings!"

Lark whirled, startled at both the voice and the words.

Tup startled, too, and shied, backing himself beneath the sparse cover of the rue-tree's branches. Lark stood on the kitchen step, staring at him.

His wings had loosened in the past days, but they had done that before, relaxing, lifting no more than a finger's width from his ribs, then clamping tight again. Lark, busier than ever with preparations, sewing to be done, linens to be assembled, arrangements to be made, had grown used to these exercises, and had given no thought to what they meant.

But now her lips parted in wonder. Her colt's half-spread wings stunned her anew with the unlikely miracle of his existence.

"Tup!" she breathed. "Oh, Tup!"

There were six of the work crew, brawny fellows in heavy boots and floppy hats. Two of them stepped forward to take a closer look at the marvel. Tup whimpered, and put his forefeet on the step, his head pushed into Lark's apron.

She held up a hand to the men. "Please, come no closer."

"Just wanted a blink at yon colt," one of them said softly. He took off his hat and held it between his hands. "Never seen such in the Uplands, miss."

"I know," she said. "But the winged horses . . . they don't like men . . ." Her voice trailed off as she gazed at Tup.

The ribs of his wings looked like the bones of a bird. The membrane that stretched between them was almost translucent, delicate as a baby's eyelid. Lark bit her lip, shaken by a sudden fear. Such fragile wings they were, no heavier than a fold of silk laid across the ribs of a fan! How were they ever to carry him, to carry them both, high into the air? She had watched Philippa Winter soar far, far above the barn, above the trees, above the hills! What if Tup were not strong enough? What if she made a mistake? They could tumble from the sky, both of them!

Tup, sensing her mood, whimpered again, and crowded against her.

"No, no, little one," she murmured. She looked up at the curious men, and shook her head. "He's just frightened. I'll take him back to his stall. Brye will be out in a moment."

She felt their eyes on her as she coaxed Tup across the yard. He tripped willingly beside her, his wings trailing, half-extended, pinions rippling above the ground. As she led him into the stall, he flexed his wings, making them rustle like a lady's silken skirts.

"There now, Tup," she said. "You just wait here. When they've gone to the south pasture, I'll come for you."

Molly bleated from the aisle, and Lark let the goat into the stall, stroking her bony back as she passed. An odd trio they made, she supposed, colt and goat and girl. Willakeep would buzz with it for years. At the end of summer, Tup would be eight months old, and they would be off to the Academy of the Air. It was a miracle. Kalla's miracle.

The men were still waiting. She nodded to them, and went into the kitchen, calling for Brye. Waiting for him, she trailed her fingers across the old oaken table where she had taken almost every meal of her life. She reached up to touch the skirt of the ancient Tarn where it hung above the sink, and a sudden wave of nostalgia swept over her, an ache of love for this plain kitchen, for the familiar feel of the worn stairs beneath her feet, for the very seasons of the Uplands. How would she manage among the finely bred girls of the Academy? She would be as out of place among such thoroughbreds as Tup was among the oxen of Willakeep.

Brye came stamping past her, and she shook off her black thoughts. There were workers to feed, cows to be milked, butter to be churned, eggs to gather. She followed her elder brother out into the fulsome sunshine, and watched the crew gather their tools.

Edmar had left before anyone, while the lanes were still dark, he and the other stoneworkers making the most of every hour of daylight. Nick was off with the oxcart collecting emptied milk cans. Lark had Deeping Farm to herself.

Tup and Molly trailed her as she moved about the barn and the yard. She poured out the fresh milk, skimmed cream from the milking of the day before, spilled it into the churn for later. She had to shoo the colt and the goat out of her way to get back up the steps from the coldcellar. She closed the slanted door against the rising warmth of the morning.

She knew it was time to start the joint on its spit, but the sunshine beguiled her. She went around to the southeast side of the house to lean on the blackstone fence and look out over the kitchen garden. Tup and Molly came with her, Molly nibbling at bits of grass growing against the stone, Tup leaning his head against her shoulder. She absently rubbed his neck, and gazed at the old raspberry canes, the dried pumpkin vines, the empty rows waiting for her to plant lettuces and carrots and potatoes. Who would till the garden when she was gone? This would be her last summer to plant the seeds, stake the tomatoes, tie up the runner beans. And she would be hard-pressed even this year, because she was to go to Dickering Park each week, to be tutored by the horsemistress there.

She turned, and put her back to the fence, lifting her face into the sunshine. The foal pushed his nose into her hand, and she hugged his head close to her. He smelled like sunshine and straw, like good clean earth. She buried her face in his silky fringe of mane.

When he threw up his head, the movement jarred her back on her heels. "Tup! What?"

His ears were pricked forward, his eyes wide. She followed his gaze.

A long-legged brown horse had come down the lane from the direction of the village, its hooves almost silent on the packed dirt. Lark watched a tall, slim man dismount and loop his horse's reins through the cast iron of the gate. He pulled off his hat, and his hair glittered, so blond it was almost white. Beneath his riding coat he wore the black and silver of the Duke's livery, but Lark was certain he was not the tithe-man. His boots shone with polish, and a worked silver belt circled his narrow hips. He wore a heavily embroidered vest, something she supposed must be an Osham affectation.

As the man crossed the yard, Tup sniffed, and laid his little ears back. Lark circled his neck with her arm, suddenly aware of how alone she was, how isolated the farm. The bloodbeet crew was in the south pasture, a fifteen-minute walk from the house. Neither Nick nor Edmar would return for hours.

But this was a finely dressed man, in the Duke's colors. Surely he was a gentleman, perhaps even a nobleman. Perhaps, as with the villagers, he had heard of her foal, had come to see the wonder for himself. She straightened her back, and stood as tall as she could, smoothing her milk-spattered apron and hoping her boots weren't too muddy.

He stopped beside the rue-tree. He knew, she thought. He knew the foal wouldn't tolerate him.

But Tup sniffed again, and his ears drooped sideways, as if in confusion. He made a small sound in his throat, not quite a cry, but not his welcoming whicker either. She patted him, and nodded to the man. "Good morning," she offered.

His pale lips curved in a faint smile. "A fine morning it is, Miss." He took another step, his glance flicking over Tup, the goat, herself. She noticed that he carried a small whip in his hand, the way Philippa Winter had done, holding it straight up and down in his closed fist. He took another step closer. Tup's ears flattened again.

"Ah," he laughed. "The colt doesn't like me."

"Not you, particularly," Lark said. "Men." She patted Tup once more, and again his ears fell to the sides in that curious position. She stared at him, wondering what it meant.

The visitor lifted his head to look around at the farmhouse, the barn, out to the north pasture, past Lark to the south pasture. "Are you alone here?" he asked.

Lark hesitated for half a breath. Then, briskly, she said, "My brother and a crew of six are just yonder." She nodded to the south pasture. "Setting out bloodbeet starts. Due back soon for their meal, as it happens."

He tilted his head, looking at her, one eyebrow quirked. "What are you called, Miss?"

"I'm Larkyn Hamley." She took her arm from Tup's neck, dusted her hands in businesslike fashion, and stepped away from the fence at her back. "And what are you called?"

He shrugged. "It doesn't matter. You wouldn't recognize my name."

The air was redolent with sunshine and growing things, but another, indefinable scent tickled Lark's nose. Her nostrils flared, testing it, wondering. She glanced down at Tup, and saw that he, too, was sniffing the air, his neck arching as high as it would go.

She said, "I suppose you came to see my foal, sir. Now you've seen him, you must excuse me. I've butter to churn."

"He's not your own foal, of course," the man said lightly. "But the Duke's."

Lark tossed her head. "Close enough," she said. "He's bonded to me. We're off to the Academy soon."

The stranger's smile vanished all at once, and now Lark saw how sharp his features were, his lips thin, his fine cheekbones gaunt, his nose long and narrow. "Bonded?" he said. "Who allowed such a thing?"

Lark took a breath and held it. There was authority in this man's voice, as there was in his bearing. There was also something menacing about him, though Lark could not have said what it was.

"When was he born?" he snapped. "Where's his dam? And who arranged for you to go to the Academy?" He leaned forward, his head tilting on his stiff neck. His eyes were night-dark, and just as cold. He slapped the quirt against his open palm, and behind him, in the lane, the chestnut whinnied, and pulled back against his rein.

Lark's own eyes narrowed. The scent around the man intensified—was it some sort of perfume? She had no experience with such things. "Excuse me, sir," she said swiftly. "I've work to do."

She set off at a quick pace, angling to her left to pass him by.

He put out his hand, and laid the quirt against her chest.

Lark froze where she was. The leather was thin, but it was hard and strong, a line of heat burning against her breasts.

Magicked. She couldn't move.

Tup had sidled to her left, not leaving her, but trying to give the man a wide berth. Now he whirled, forefeet planted, tail switching. Molly, trotting behind him, bumped into his hindquarters and fell back, shaking her scanty beard. Tup's ears went flat against his head, and his upper lip lifted to show his small, white teeth.

The man's eyes darkened till they were almost black. The cloying scent of him grew stronger as he leaned toward her. "Do you think you can thwart me?" he hissed. *"Me?"*

Lark whispered, through dry lips, "Who are you?"

He let the quirt slide a little lower, brushing the tips of her breasts, settling beneath them. She gasped a little, unable to stop herself, and he laughed.

His voice was too high, just as his perfume was too sweet. He said, lightly, "I am your lord, Larkyn Hamley. Your colt is my property. I can take away this farm—this house—and you, if I wish." He drew the quirt across her ribs, letting it linger on her body at the last moment, then lifting it.

She stumbled forward, as if she had broken through a fence. She turned on the man, fury burning in her cheeks. "Duke Frederick is my lord, sir," she exclaimed. "And I know you're not him, because he's an old man! And I'll let no one take Tup from me!"

She ran then, straight for the coldcellar. Tup followed at a stiff-legged canter, Molly bleating behind him. The chestnut stamped and nickered nervously. Molly skidded to a halt when she saw the big horse, but Lark pressed on, hurrying down the steps, throwing back the slanted door. Tup was close on her heels, and the two of them crowded in beside the milk cans. With an effort, Lark pulled the door closed, shutting them in the cool darkness. She threw the bar, and then stood staring at the wood, listening hard. Her chest still tingled where the magicked quirt had touched her.

She heard the stranger's soft boots on the three stairs. He must have leaned very close to the door, insinuating his light voice through the joins. "Larkyn Hamley," he said. "Remember what I said. You can lose everything, you and your family. It is no empty threat."

Lark didn't answer. She let Tup's clean smell wash the cloying perfume from her nostrils, and she didn't move again until the chestnut's hoofbeats faded from the lane, until Molly bleated at the top of the stairs. Cautiously, Lark lifted the bar and pushed up the door.

He was gone. The lane was empty, as far as she could see.

She went up the stairs, Tup behind her, and walked slowly around the corner to the kitchen door. The sun shone brightly as ever, but Lark shivered. Unconsciously, as she went into the kitchen, tied on her apron, rubbed the joint with garlic and pepper, she rubbed her hand across her chest, over and over, feeling the touch of the man's quirt as if it had been a brand.

EIGHT

LARK never told her brothers about the stranger's visit. More than once, she found herself about to tell Brye, to ask Nick for advice, to blurt it all out at dinner, but fear stopped the words in her mouth. She imagined Brye in a fury, rousing the prefect, the magistrate, hying himself to the White City to complain to the Duke's men about the treatment of his sister, and she shivered. She told herself she was too busy to dwell on it, with so much to think about, so many arrangements to make, plans to be laid. And in truth, nothing had happened, nothing real, anyway. The man had toyed with her, teased her, but he hadn't hurt her. Yet she remembered that day with frightening clarity, especially when she was alone on the farm, raking out last year's planting beds, churning butter in the coldcellar, grazing the goats and the milk cows in the north pasture. She remembered Philippa Winter's aristocratic accents as she informed the Hamleys that they could lose Deeping Farm. And the strange man, with his pale hair and odd voice, his smooth skin . . . he seemed the sort of man that had such power.

Summer trod hard on the heels of spring, bringing out the freckles on Lark's nose and causing the goats to shed their winter coats in great shaggy clumps. The bloodbeets sprouted fans of deep green in the south pasture, and the broomstraw began to show its feathery tops.

The months of preparation were almost gone. Tup's head now reached Lark's own, and he ate hay and grass as well as mash. Though Molly's milk had dried as the colt's appetites changed, the little she-goat still trotted faithfully by his side, and slept in his stall at night. The two of them followed Lark wherever she went, and stood beneath the rue-tree when she was in the kitchen, waiting for her to emerge.

"Yon goat will pine away when you're off to the Academy,"

Nick said one evening. The air was warm as bath water, and rich with the scents of growing things. The family had gathered for an outside supper on the weathered plank table built by some long-ago Hamley. On fine evenings, they often sat with their backs to the house, watching the yellow sunsets of summer or the red ones of autumn blaze beyond the roof line of the barn. The colt and the little goat were nibbling grass beside the garden fence.

Lark had spread a tattered cloth, and was arranging platters of early tomatoes and lettuce, a wheel of cheese, a fresh loaf, and a generous dish of her own sweet butter. She looked up at Nick, her mouth open in surprise. "Why—but, Nick. Surely Molly will come with us!"

Brye settled himself on the bench, stretching out his legs before him with a weary sigh. "Lark. Those fine stables are for horses. Not little Uplands she-goats."

Lark turned to her eldest brother. "But Tup needs her! And she's so attached to him!"

"Partings are hard. Sit you down now, and eat."

Lark sat facing her brothers, her back to the glories of the western sky. "Brye . . . at the Academy . . ." She swallowed. "I won't know anyone."

He said, "Mistress Winter."

"Well, yes, Mistress Winter. But not . . . I mean, none of the girls. Or the headmistress. I'll have only Tup and Molly for company."

Nick glanced up from slicing bread. "You'll meet the other students," he said. "And you and your colt will be busy, learning this and that! No time to be lonely."

"Learned a bit already." It was Edmar, who rarely spoke at dinner.

Lark smiled at him, but she shook her head. "Not much. The horsemistress at Dickering Park is . . . preoccupied, I suppose. She gives me books. Starts to lecture me, and then loses interest. I think she doesn't like me."

"Stuck-up cow," Nick said.

Lark sighed, and accepted a slice of bread. "Bit of a nob, yes. I'm afraid she is. But I expect they'll all be that way. Especially with a girl from the Uplands."

"Just remember who you are," Brye rumbled. "A Hamley of Deeping Farm. Nothing to be ashamed of."

"No," Lark said. "No." But she remembered the stranger's smooth face, and the cold, sickening feel of his little whip touching her body.

PHILIPPA had been a little late for dinner, and she had to hurry to finish her soup before the delicate china bowl was whisked away from her. She sat at Margareth's right, pleased to find that the Headmistress looked stronger tonight.

When the soup bowls had disappeared, Margareth turned to her. "Tell me, Philippa, how your flight was today. Irina had concerns about Prince."

"The flight went well, for the most part," she said. "We worked at Graces all morning."

"And Geraldine? Prince?"

Philippa scowled, wishing Irina had kept her thoughts to herself. A server with a platter of fish slipped between them, giving her a moment to frame her answer. When she had gone, Philippa said, with care, "I've spoken to Herbert, and to Rosellen. It's possible one of the fillies is in season, and they don't realize it. Prince is jittery, it's true. And Geraldine . . ." She picked up her fish fork, a slender filigreed piece of silver, and touched it to the delicate white fillet on her plate. "Geraldine must learn to settle him. I'll try to give her some extra time."

"Good." Margareth nodded, and turned to the woman on her left.

Philippa looked up and down the high table where the instructors sat. Below them, their students sat at long, narrow tables arranged in parallel rows. The hall sparkled with glass and silver, and bustled with servers moving in and out with platters and pitchers. The sounds of treble voices rang against the high ceiling, punctuated now and then by a girl's laughter. At the end of one of the tables, far from the high table, she saw Geraldine Prince, sitting in silence, an untouched plate before her. Unease trembled in Philippa's belly, and she set down her fork.

"Philippa. Eat," Margareth murmured to her. Philippa gave her a startled glance. "They'll take away the course, and you won't even have tasted it. You're too thin."

Philippa grimaced. "I know." She picked up the fish fork again, and took a bite of the delicately seasoned dish. When she had swallowed, she said, "I was just—distracted."

"Worry about it in the morning, Philippa. Nothing you can do tonight."

Again, Philippa agreed. "I know." She dropped her eyes to her plate, and set herself to finishing the fillet. But when the server came for her plate, her eyes drifted back to Geraldine.

The girl sitting next to Geraldine was younger. Hester, Philippa thought her name was, Hester Morning, a first-year girl, tall and bony, with a quite magnificent Foundation yearling. Hester leaned toward Geraldine, spoke to her. Geraldine shook her head, and the younger girl spoke again, her features drawn sympathetically.

Perhaps Geraldine was ill. Philippa thought for a moment of going to ask, but decided it was not a good time. It would be embarrassing for the girl and for everyone in her flight to press the point here in the Hall. She would talk to her in the morning.

After the meat course, Philippa excused herself to Margareth. "I'll go check with Herbert that a stall is ready for the Uplands colt," she said. "Have you spoken with Eduard?"

Margareth nodded. "Eduard tried to speak with Duke Frederick, too, Philippa. Like you, he was not allowed to be alone with him."

Philippa had half-risen from her chair, but she sank back, frowning. "William?"

"Of course."

"But why, Margareth?" She glanced around to be certain no one was listening to their conversation. "It's as if he's deliberately . . ."

"Everything Lord William does is deliberate."

Philippa rubbed her neck. It felt as if someone were pinching it between iron fingers. "Why cannot people leave well enough alone?" she muttered.

"Power," Margareth said. "Some people yearn for it like a drinker yearns for his ale."

"As if Klee doesn't give us enough problems, he has to stir up—"

"Shhh," Margareth hissed. "Don't say it."

Philippa met Margareth's gaze, and the thought passed between them, unspoken. Spies. William was a master of spying. It was an open secret in Oc that Lord William had eyes everywhere.

With a sigh, Philippa stood again. "Good night, Margareth. I'm off to the stables, then early to bed."

"Good," Margareth said. "And tell Rosellen to find a dog for the colt. He'll be lonely."

PHILIPPA found Rosellen at work in the tack room, a leather punch in her hand, a cinch across her knees. The stable-girl looked up at her entrance. The thong she had been holding between her gappy teeth fell to the dusty floor. "Good evening to you, Mistress Winter," she said cheerily. "I thought all of you were at your dinner."

"Why aren't you, Rosellen?"

"Oh, had mine an hour ago, in the kitchen. Good fish, that was." Rosellen put aside the cinch, and stood up, brushing crumbs of leather from her tabard. "Are you needing something?"

Philippa bent to pick up the dropped thong and handed it to Rosellen. "I hope Herbert told you we have a new colt coming," she said.

"He did," Rosellen said. She put the leather punch into its place above the work bench, keeping her gaze averted. "Odd time of year for it, isn't it," she said mildly.

"Indeed," Philippa said dryly. Rosellen knew perfectly well the situation was more than odd. A winter foal and his bondmate, arriving at the height of summer, would rouse everyone's interest. "Did you find a stall?"

"I'll show you," Rosellen said. She gave the tack room a quick glance, apparently finding everything in order, and then blew out her lamp, pinching the wick to be certain, and then muttering a charm over it for good measure. Philippa forbore to scold the girl. Fire in the stables was always a danger, and though she never resorted to smallmagics to prevent it, she had no objection to Rosellen taking extra care.

She followed the stable-girl's sturdy form through the wide door and into the stables proper. Her boots crunched on clean sawdust, and her nostrils tingled with the ineffable pungency of horseflesh. The winged horses put their heads over the stall doors as she passed, ears flicking forward. Three oc-hounds came to trot beside the women, sniffing at their tabards for treats, waving their plumy tails. Two of them dropped back when it was clear no food was coming, but Bramble stayed at Philippa's side. Philippa rested a hand on the oc-hound's fine head as they walked, and her tension drained from her, leaving her fatigued, but at peace for the moment. Winter Sunset, from her wide corner stall, whickered to her.

Philippa said, "I'll see you in a moment, Sunny. Just wait."

Rosellen stopped beside an empty stall in a quiet corner. It was already spread with clean straw, with a water bucket and feedbin waiting.

"Good," Philippa said. "Golden Morning is nearby. She's a quiet one, isn't she?"

"She is." Rosellen nodded at the palomino filly in the next stall. "And on the other side, Petra Sweet's gelding. Should be good company for the little one, as he's so young and all." She looked up from beneath an untidy fringe of hair, all freckled innocence.

Philippa knew she was burning with curiosity, and she would not be the only one. The other stable-girls, Herbert, all the instructors and students, would be wondering about the colt, and about Larkyn Hamley. Philippa said grimly, "I'll tell you what I can, Rosellen. What little I know. No one's happy about it."

Rosellen propped an elbow on the wall of the empty stall, showing her gappy teeth in a grin. "Not even the girl?"

Philippa gave a mirthless chuckle. "Well, yes. You're right, of course. She's thrilled. I only wish she weren't so . . ." She broke off, not knowing how to explain Lark to Rosellen.

The stable-girl waited, lips parted, to hear what was wrong with the new girl.

Philippa gave a shake of her head. "I shouldn't say that," she amended. "She's a plucky little thing, I'll give her that. A farm girl, used to hard work. Independent."

"So what's wrong with her?"

Philippa sighed. "Look, Rosellen. You know the Master Breeder chooses our girls."

A shadow crossed Rosellen's round face, but she only nodded.

"A wingless mare wandered onto the farm where this girl grew up. The girl and her brothers took her in, though they had never had a horse on their farm, or even in their district. They didn't know she was with foal, and when they discovered it, they just thought of it as good fortune. And then this little mare threw a winged colt. Surprise to everyone."

Rosellen frowned. "Hasn't happened in an awful long time."

"Two centuries, according to Margareth."

"Didn't they know, these farmers, that they should let the Duke's people know?"

"They told their prefect, and he sent a letter to the Academy."

Rosellen barked a laugh. "A letter! What a gammon!"

Philippa pursed her lips. "Precisely my thought, Rosellen. Precisely."

"So this girl . . . by the time you got there . . ."

Philippa eyed the plain girl with appreciation. Rosellen never lacked for wit. She could wish, indeed, that some of her students were half as quick. "You have it," she said quietly. "They were already bonded. The girl was sleeping in the foal's stall. Hadn't bathed in a week."

"What does His Grace have to say about all this?"

Philippa looked away from Rosellen's sharp gaze. With care, she said, "Duke Frederick is not very well at the moment."

"And Master Crisp?"

"He will have a look at the colt, see if he can deduce what bloodline he belongs to."

"If any."

Philippa brought her eyes back to Rosellen's, nodding slowly. "Neither Margareth nor Eduard seems to credit the random birth of a winged foal, not in these latter days."

"But from the Uplands . . ." Rosellen grinned again, and said in a stage whisper, "Could be descended from the Old Ones."

Philippa snorted. "I hope you're not spreading that nonsense to our girls, Rosellen."

Rosellen shook her head. "Not me. But where I come from, it's common."

"And where is that?"

Rosellen gestured with her head toward the north. "Marin," she said shortly. "A fishing village on the coast. I could see glaciers from my bedroom window."

Philippa's eyebrows rose. "So far north! And how did you come to be here?"

"Saw a flyer when I was twelve. A Foundation horse, I'm sure, patrolling the coastline. We didn't know what was required to become a horsemistress, and my mother and I thought, if I came to the White City . . ." She colored, and broke off. "Silly of us. Ignorant."

Philippa stared at her, wondering at how much she didn't know about the people who served the Duke. "But you didn't go back."

Rosellen took a deep breath, lifted her head, and smiled again. "I found work in the Duke's stables, mucking out, feeding, leading the winged horses about. And then here. I don't get to ride them, but I get to be with them. And they smell better than fish!" She laughed again, a hearty laugh that rang through the stables.

Philippa looked away from her, down the long aisle to the stall where her own Sunny stood with her head over the door, waiting for her to come and greet her. Bramble leaned against her thigh, and she absently stroked the silky fur. How would Rosellen feel about Larkyn Hamley, then? Larkyn's beginnings were as humble as Rosellen's, and yet she had achieved, without intending it, Rosellen's goal. Softly, she said, "It's going to be hard on her, Rosellen."

"That it is, Mistress Winter. I'll keep an eye out."

Philippa said quietly, "Thank you. She might need a friend."

The stable-girl grinned, ducked her head, and turned back to the tack room.

NINE

"NATURALLY I expected better than Dickering Park," Horse-mistress Cloud was saying, sniffing over her teacup and tucking a brackish strand of hair into its rider's knot. "I come from a very good family, in Isamar. Why, from our city house in Arlton we could see the Prince's Palace. My sister and I often had tea with the young Princesses, and the Princess Consort herself recommended me for the Academy!"

Lark shifted in her uncomfortable chair, crossing her ankles and then uncrossing them. She tried to comfort herself by remembering this was the last of her tutorial visits with Amberly Cloud. Not that there had been much tutoring going on—Mistress Cloud was apparently exceedingly lonely, and wished mostly to talk about herself and her family and her failed aspirations. Lark looked longingly at the door that led from Mistress Cloud's crowded parlor to the airy stable where her gelding waited.

"It will be different for you, of course, my dear." She put down her cup and chose a crook from the tiered plate before her. "As you have no breeding. I think you must expect to be assigned to some such place as this, but I—Kalla's tail, I never thought to work out my days in an Uplands village! Although I must say, I love these little biscuits they make here."

Kalla's tail was the only thing of interest the horsemistress had said all afternoon. Lark liked the epithet. Perhaps if you were a horsemistress, you could swear by Kalla, and it would be all right. It was surely more refined than swearing by Zito's ears all the time.

She sighed, yearning toward the stables. Silver Cloud was a lovely creature, with a brown coat. He was tall for an Ocmarin, according to Mistress Cloud. The sum total of her learning from

Mistress Cloud amounted to knowing that Ocmarins were the smallest of the bloodlines, prized for their speed and agility.

Lark glanced sideways at the bit of frumpery that was Mistress Cloud's clock. Everything in the horsemistress's residence seemed fussy to Lark. Miniature figurines crowded the shelves, and every surface was covered with some bit of lacy material. The tea set was delicate, with gold paint and vivid floral patterns. The clock was so heavily scrolled and crimped Lark could barely see its face, but she managed to deduce that the hour was coming four. Nick would be returning, and she had done nothing but listen to Amberly Cloud natter on about how little there was to do in Dickering Park.

Lark set down her cup with a sharp clink, hoping to move things along.

Mistress Cloud glanced up at her. "Don't fidget, Larkyn," she said. "One thing you must learn, and that is to comport yourself as one of the gentry, even if you aren't one. And remember, horsemistresses never, ever curtsy, not even to the Duke himself. We incline our heads, so." She demonstrated, her neck stiff, her lips pursed. "Now. Sit up straight, don't spill your tea, and try to improve that Uplands accent. You don't want everyone sniggering at you behind their hands!"

Lark was already sitting straight, and she hadn't spilled a drop of Mistress Cloud's tea, though the liquid was so weak and pale, no one would have noticed if she had. The tea needed a pass with a fetish, but then, Lark thought, perhaps horsemistresses disdained smallmagics. They ruled, after all, the one great magic.

"You're worried about my accent?" Lark said, impatience getting the better of her. "Aren't they more likely to laugh at me if I fall off my horse?"

Mistress Cloud scowled at her, making her round face look like a fractured moon. "Yet another problem for you! I can't imagine the Academy thought I alone should teach you to ride!" she exclaimed. "What an imposition! A nuisance! And a bore for poor Silver, rambling around the yard without using his wings!" She chewed the last of her pastry, crumbs falling down her chin and onto her tabard. When she leaned forward, her tabard folded in generous swaths around her middle. "Listen to me, my girl. I think this is a bad idea, from beginning to end. I wish you well, of course, it would speak ill of my breeding if I did not. But there has never been an Uplands farm girl at the Academy, nor do I think there should be one now! I'm doing my best by you, but I must say . . ." She leaned back into her chair again, and brushed at the crumbs that had fallen from her round bosom to her lap. "I must say, I find you a bit slow. I don't say it to offend you . . ."

Lark saw the oxcart round the corner of the street and trundle toward Mistress Cloud's door. She jumped to her feet. "Slow?" she said. "How would you know if I'm slow? You know nothing about me! Mistress Winter wanted me to learn a few things about horses, and tack, and . . . and things I'll need to know."

"My dear!" Mistress Cloud exclaimed. Her eyes were round, her full lips parted. She rose from her chair with a little grunt. "You must never address your betters in such a way!"

Lark could guess why there had been no riding involved in these tutorial afternoons. She eyed the older woman's plump silhouette in her voluminous divided skirt, but she swallowed the retort that sprang to her lips. She mumbled an apology instead. Irritating though the horsemistress was, she was right. The Academy would no doubt deal harshly with insolence in its students. And it would do no good to part with Mistress Cloud on bad terms.

Nick's little bell, the same he used to alert his customers to his arrival, sounded clearly through the hot afternoon. Amberly Cloud folded her hands. "Well, child," she said. "This concludes our sessions, I suppose. I will follow your progress at the Academy with interest."

In a pig's eye, Lark thought, but she dropped her gaze in a way that she hoped was ladylike, and said, "Thank you, Horsemistress."

"You're quite welcome." Mistress Cloud's lips made a prim little bow, and she turned to the door in a sweep of fabric. Her rear view looked more like one of the draught horses that pulled the mail coach than like that of her own Silver Cloud.

Too fat to fly, Lark thought. Living on memories. But she hid her rebellious thought, and only begged, "Could I just see Silver once again, before I leave?"

Amberly Cloud gave her a weary look over her shoulder. "Oh, Larkyn. It's so hot."

"You don't have to come outside. I'll just run to the stables, and then join my brother."

"Very well." Mistress Cloud fanned herself with one hand, and nodded to the door. "Be certain Master Hamley goes nowhere near the stables. I don't want Silver upset."

"He knows." Lark hurried to the door.

Nick looked up as she emerged, and smiled. "Climb you up, Lark! Let's be off."

"Just one moment, Nick, please." Lark grinned at him, and pointed to the stables. "I'm just going to say goodbye to Silver."

Behind her, Amberly Cloud stood in the shade of her little portico. Nick lifted his hat, bowing to Mistress Cloud and flashing his white grin. Even she, it seemed, could be affected by Nick's charm. She gave him a real smile, not the little pinchy one she saved for Lark, and waved a greeting. Lark seized the moment to dash around the corner.

The moment she reached the stables, Lark forgot about Mistress Cloud and even her brother. Silver Cloud's ears flicked forward at the sight of her, and he rustled his silken wings against their wingclips. He stretched out his nose for her caress.

The gelding's hide was faintly dappled, sleek and shining. Lark ran her hand over his smooth cheek and down his neck. "Poor thing," she whispered to him. "When was your last flight? If this continues, you'll be as fat as your mistress."

He lowered his head for her to scratch between his ears, and to run her fingers through the fine strands of his mane. "You're lovely fine, aren't you?" she said softly. "All slender bones and sweet temper." Silver bumped her with his nose, and blew through his nostrils. "Yes, yes, you are, lovely boy. Though you look nothing like my Tup! I wish I could have brought him along to give you a blink, but Mistress Cloud said not."

She patted the horse a last time, and stood back. Beyond his spacious stall, one of the flying saddles, with its high cantle and knee rolls, waited on its rack. Lark cast a glance over her shoulder to see if either Nick or Mistress Cloud had come around the corner to watch her, but they hadn't. She scooted around Silver's stall, and stepped up into the tack room.

It smelled marvelously of leather and saddle soap and polish. One entire wall seemed to be hung with straps and ropes and buckles, things for which she had no name. She put her hand on the cool surface of the saddle, admiring its finely tooled flaps, the pliable stirrup leathers, the steel-capped stirrups. She trailed her fingers across the wing-notch. She had never even sat in a saddle, not once.

Silver watched her intently. She turned back to hug his neck. Into the sweetness of his skin, she breathed, "Goodbye, sweet fellow. Good hap to you—and wish me and Tup the same! I hope to see you again." She stroked him one last time.

She found Nick leaning against the portico, chatting with Mistress Cloud. "Well," Nick said to Lark. "Are you ready at last? Said your farewells?"

"Yes," she said. "I'm ready." She turned to Mistress Cloud. "Thank you again, Horsemistress, for your time."

Amberly Cloud nodded. Lark and Nick climbed up into the oxcart, and Lark pulled her hat from beneath the seat and put it on. As the wheels began to turn, Mistress Cloud called after Lark, "Don't wear that awful hat to the Academy! You'll never hear the end of it!"

Lark sighed, and pulled off the hat to twirl it in her hands. It was the same as Nick's, as Brye's, as Edmar's, woven of good fresh broomstraw, flexible and cool, its wide brim keeping the beat of the mountain sun from its wearer's face. She supposed it did look bumptious next to the horsemistresses' elegant caps, but at least it covered her hopeless mass of curls.

Nick laughed. "Least of your worries, sweetheart. Anyway, you can take it off before you pull into yon Academy courtyard."

"I suppose." Lark replaced the hat on her head, which was already growing warm in the late sun.

"Any joy today?" Nick asked.

"No," Lark said. "More about Arlton, and the royals, and the importance of her family."

"Not much help to you, then."

"Not a bit."

They rode in silence for a few minutes. The air was so hot and heavy it seemed to Lark she could take a bite of it, chew it up, and swallow it. It was a relief to her when they escaped the steamy confines of the town and drove among the hedgerows where the clean scents of soil and shrub could cleanse her nostrils of the coaldust and sewer smell of Dickering Park. They turned into the lane that passed Willakeep, and drove between fields of ripening broomstraw and bloodbeets. Lark breathed in the essence of the Uplands, and found that her eyes stung with nostalgic tears. She turned her head to hide them, but Nick saw, and touched her arm.

"Not unhappy, surely, Lark?"

She swallowed hard, and blinked away the tears. "No, Nick. Not unhappy, but—" She turned abruptly to face him, making the bench seat creak on its springs. "I only wish I could have it both ways! Have Deeping Farm, and the Uplands, and have Tup, and the Academy! I wish—it's just that I will—"

Nick smiled at her, but his eyes were grave in the shade of his hatbrim. "Growing up, Lark," he said softly. "You're almost fifteen. Your friend Petal, now, same age as you—and already married, with a baby on the way."

"A baby is one thing I'll never have."

Nick was silent for a long moment, idly flicking his long whip to and fro above the ox. "Not looking like I will, either," he said.

At that, Lark flashed him a look. "Or you have a dozen in other men's homes!"

Nick chuckled. "What does a lass like you know about men's comings and goings?"

"I'm an Uplands girl, Nick Hamley," she said stoutly. "I know what causes babies!"

He laughed again, richly, and then drove in silence. Not until they could see the sloping roof of the farmhouse did he speak again. He said, "You could have chosen to marry, Lark. You've always been the prettiest girl in Willakeep."

"You just say that because I'm a Hamley."

"Just the same. Choose any lad you fancy. I suppose you could still change your mind."

"No, Nick, I can't. And I wouldn't if I could." She turned to stare blindly out over the field beyond the hedgerow. "I want to do this. I want to be a horsemistress, more than anything, to fly with Tup. But it's hard to leave my home."

"I know," he said. He circled her waist with his arm and squeezed her gently. "I know."

THE road to Osham from the Uplands ran from the northwest to the southeast, along the Black River until it spilled into the Grand River. Brye said they must make an early start, to reach the city before dark, and so they sat together in the old kitchen, breakfasting before dawn. Even Edmar had not yet left for the quarry when Lark climbed up on the bench seat of the oxcart beside Brye. Her little satchel of belongings fit beneath her feet. The back of the cart was empty.

A package had come by the mail coach from the Academy of the Air to Willakeep, and was carried personally to Deeping Farm by Master Micklewhite on the same day of its arrival. Micklewhite, Nick had snickered, was in trouble with the Council of Lords for delaying his report of the winged foal's birth, and was expending more energy than usual in carrying out his duties. Brye had accepted the package somberly, and sent the prefect on his way, much to Master Micklewhite's frustration. It was addressed, of course, to Lark. To Miss Larkyn Hamley, Deeping Farm, Willakeep, the Uplands, and it held a halter of fine leather, with tiny steel buckles and a braided lead rope, and a set of shining, intricate wingclips.

Tup wore the halter now, and Lark held the lead in her hand as they set out. She had puzzled and puzzled over the wingclips, but couldn't figure out how to attach them. In any case, Tup kept his wings tightly folded against his ribs. Molly pressed close to his flank as if afraid of being left behind.

Edmar stood in the gate, looking up at Lark, his battered hat in his hands. "Remember your kith," he said.

"Yes, Edmar." He nodded, as if everything had been said that needed saying, and started off down the lane toward the quarry.

"Edmar's talkative this morning!" Nick said. "But he's right. Remember who you are."

"Thank you, Nick. I will."

"Well, then." He cleared his throat.

"Best be off," Brye growled.

"Right. Good hap, little sister!"

Lark lifted her hand, unable now to speak. She took a last, long look at the farmhouse, the blackstone fence of the kitchen garden, the barn. Brye flicked the whip over the ox's head, and the cart began to creak down the lane. Nick stood waving from the gate, as their odd assortment moved out toward the road, Tup on his lead, Molly trotting alongside. The ox paid no attention to colt or goat, but plodded forward at his usual pace, as if the unaccustomed lightness of the cart made no difference to him.

Lark twisted on the seat to watch her home until a bend in the lane hid it from her sight. When she turned forward, she twisted her hands together in her lap. She wondered if girls going off to be married felt the same as she did at this moment, as if they were going through a door that would shut behind them forever. She could go home again, she supposed, but she feared she would be utterly changed.

"Brye," she said.

"Yes."

"You won't change anything, will you? Not Deeping Farm, the house, the barn . . ."

"Hasn't changed in three centuries, Lark."

Lark breathed a long, shuddering sigh. "No. And that's the best thing about it."

•

TEN

WILLIAM drove his horse hard on the road from the Palace, spurring her when she flagged, dashing past the sparse early morning traffic. Oxcart drivers, obviously not knowing who they cursed, shook their fists at him. A flock of pigs scattered before the gelding's pounding feet, but William paid no attention. Slater had brought him the news this morning with his morning tray, and he had leapt out of bed, ignoring the coffee and toast, thrown on his clothes of the night before, and dashed down the stairs and out to the stables. He had to stop that fool Crisp. There was no time to pretend to confer with his father. He would simply infer it, and be damned to the consequences. Crisp was hard to manipulate, though. He would have to think of something.

"Three days!" William muttered under his breath, jerking at the reins in his frustration. Someone would pay for failing to keep him informed. One more day's delay, and the deed could have been done! But he would think of that later.

Twenty minutes' gallop brought him to the gates of the Academy, where he slowed his gelding to cool him, and to disguise the haste with which he had ridden. The summer heat had not yet risen, and the Academy grounds were green and peaceful under a slight morning mist. William rode past the yearlings' pasture, where the winged colts and fillies dashed to the fence to watch him pass, and trotted along on their side, following his progress. When he reached the courtyard, he reined in before the stables and called, "Herbert! Herbert? Are you up there?"

Curtains twitched at the upper window, where the stable-man had his apartment, and a moment later the little man came clattering down the stairs. An oc-hound paced at his heels, and one of the stable-girls, a thickset, freckled young woman, put her head out from the tack room.

"My lord," Herbert said, with a shallow bow. "We wasn't ex-pecting you."

William swung down from his saddle, and tugged his vest into place. "I need Crisp."

"Not here yet, sir."

"Where's the new colt? The one from the Uplands?"

At this Herbert paused, his mouth a little open, his eyes dart-ing past William to the Hall. William felt a cold surge of fury. "Every horse here belongs to m—to my father, Herbert, and I act for him. If I wish to see the colt, I need no one's permission."

Herbert still looked doubtful. "Well, my lord. Rosellen can show you to his stall."

"And I want to speak to Eduard Crisp the moment he arrives."

"Expected any moment, my lord."

"Good. I'll breakfast in the Hall while I wait." William slapped his thigh with his quirt. "After I see the colt."

At a gesture from Herbert, the stable-girl, in boots and a well-worn tabard and skirt, stepped out of the shadows. She bobbed to William, keeping her eyes down. Heard of him, apparently. Well, good. A little fear would be useful today. Maybe this Rosellen had some connection with Crisp. He must try to find out. He could use that, if she did. She wasn't much to look at, but that didn't mean someone might not care about her.

He tucked his quirt under his arm, and followed her through the stables. The winged horses tossed their heads as he passed, and he kept a careful distance from them. No point in raising questions.

The stable-girl stopped beside a modest stall. Still not meeting his eyes, she mumbled, "Here he is, m'lord. The Uplands colt."

William took a half-step forward, enough so that he could see into the stall, not close enough to the colt to make the stable-girl curious. The colt lifted his head, and gazed at him through wide, intelligent eyes.

His chest was beginning to fill out, the muscles that supported his wings already ridging his chest. His croup was flat, his back short, his legs clean and fine. He was disappointingly small, his head barely reaching William's shoulder.

Mouse Queen had been small, of course, a plain little dun. She was one of those Ocmarin curiosities, born without wings for no apparent reason. But the stallion had been bigger, and known for throwing colts that matured early. Still, this colt was the first of his get with wings. And he had allowed William to get closer than any winged horse had ever done. Oh, yes, Isamar would be interested in this one.

He took another step closer. Something moved in the straw, and a little brown head poked up over the stall gate. It had drooping ears and a scraggly beard, and it eyed him with what seemed like suspicion.

William spat, "In Kalla's name—what is that doing here?"

"Goat, m'lord," Rosellen said in an offhand tone.

"I know it's a goat! I have eyes, girl! But why is it in the colt's stall?"

"Goat suckled him, kept him company. The young lady wouldn't leave her."

"Young lady."

"Yes, sir." For the first time, Rosellen's eyes slid up to his, then quickly away.

William gripped the quirt tighter in his fist, restraining his temper. "What 'young lady' would that be?" he said. He knew the silky quality had come into his voice, the tone that made Slater cringe. This stable-girl, apparently, was too stupid to notice.

"Larkyn Hamley, that would be, what's bonded to the colt."

"Hardly a lady," William muttered under his breath. "An Uplands farm brat." Rosellen slid him another glance, but did not press the point.

The sounds of treble voices carried across the courtyard as the door from the Hall opened. Breakfast must be over. Flights would be beginning, and Crisp would be here at any moment. William stepped back from the colt's stall, thinking furiously. The colt was small, it was true, but he wanted him intact. He had wings, and that was the whole point.

PHILIPPA stood beside Margareth's desk while Eduard Crisp was speaking. Larkyn Hamley stood opposite, glaring at the Master Breeder. Eduard, a stout, ruddy man with thinning hair, utterly ignored the girl.

"Margareth!" he snapped. "I hardly expected to be met with an argument this morning. The Master Breeder has been entrusted with these decisions since the days of old Duke Francis!"

Margareth rose stiffly from her chair. "Eduard. She has been here only three days, and has hardly had time to get used to our ways."

Lark repeated, "He's too young to be gelded!"

Eduard sputtered, "Margareth, since when are your students experts in these matters?"

Larkyn jutted her small chin. "I asked the man who drives the mail coach."

Without looking at her, Eduard said, "Even a new girl should understand that a winged horse is a very different creature from a coach cob!"

"Eduard," Margareth said. "I believe Larkyn thought, as I would have, that this decision wouldn't be made until the colt was at least a year."

"This colt's different," Crisp said. "Testes descended already, like a Foundation, though he's too small for that bloodline. Everything's wrong with him—his croup is too flat for a Foundation, he's black like a Noble, but he has the body of an Ocmarin. Nothing there we want to carry down the line."

"You're being a bit hasty, Eduard," Philippa put in. "There may yet be characteristics to develop . . ."

"No. Definitely not. I've called for the surgeon, and he'll be here within the hour."

Lark said, "And will you have a potion for the pain? We always give one to the goats."

Crisp still refused to look at her. "Margareth, I'm not having your students tell me my business! Why are you making me defend myself to a half-ignorant farm girl?"

Philippa began, "Come now, Eduard," but Margareth intervened.

"Eduard," she said quietly. "Our girls make great sacrifices, and they deserve respect."

"So do I," he snapped.

Through all of this Larkyn had stood, her cheeks burning. Philippa had seen the sunset and sunrise of Larkyn Hamley's color before, and she sensed an outburst coming.

"Eduard," Philippa said. "It's natural for us to feel protective of our horses."

"Well and good," he retorted. "But the bloodlines are my responsibility."

"As the winged horses are ours," Margareth said firmly.

"Philippa is right, Eduard. Larkyn's concerns are perfectly natural."

"I trust you," Crisp said dourly, "to tell Miss Hamley that I am not a cruel man."

"But Tup is—" Larkyn began.

For the first time Eduard spoke directly to the girl. "You will stop using that name!"

Lark leaned forward to force the Master Breeder to look at her. "My colt," she said, in her strong country accent, "will have a potion, or I won't let you do it."

"Let me!" Crisp whirled to face her. "You have no authority in this matter! And I'm telling you, young woman, it doesn't hurt that much!"

"Doesn't hurt?" the girl cried. Her back had gone ramrod straight, and her vivid blue eyes blazed. "And how would you be knowing that, sir? Perhaps you've had the experience?"

Eduard Crisp stared at the Uplands girl, his mouth agape.

Philippa snapped, "Larkyn!"

Margareth commanded, "Silence, girl!"

Lark stared at both of them, her lips gone white. She threw Crisp one last, agonized glance before she spun on her toes and stamped out of the office. The Master Breeder folded his arms and glowered at Margareth. Margareth coughed, and covered her mouth with her hand. Philippa looked at her curiously.

Eduard turned a grim eye on Philippa. "Not," he growled, "a good beginning."

Philippa shrugged. "Well," she said. "We have greater concerns than that."

"I demand an apology," he said.

Margareth dropped her hand, and her eyes narrowed. "Have a care, Eduard. We are not biddable sisters or dependent daughters. The Duke's bloodlines are worthless without riders."

He threw at her, "There are other riders."

"Not for these horses, Eduard. They are already bonded."

There was no denying that. Philippa, watching Eduard control his temper, felt a pang of sympathy. He looked at each of them for a speaking moment before he departed, stiff-necked and dignified.

Philippa, relieved, got up to close the door behind him. When she turned back, she found Margareth collapsed in her chair, her head in her hands, her shoulders shaking.

"Margareth! Margareth, my dear, are you all right?"

Margareth lifted her face, and Philippa saw that she was laughing.

"Why, Margareth—what is it? You're surely not laughing at poor Eduard?"

"It's that girl!" Margareth said, and then, for long moments, couldn't speak at all. She laughed till tears ran down her cheeks and she had to gulp for air. At length she managed to say, "I thought I would burst into hysterics watching a slip of a girl face down the great Master Breeder of Oc! Oh, Kalla's heels, what a sight!" She was off again, hiccuping with laughter. Philippa couldn't help chuckling, too.

When their merriment subsided, she said, "It *is* funny, Margareth. But we can't have Larkyn behaving that way. What a tongue the child has!"

"I know." Margareth's lips still twitched. She leaned back in her chair, and rubbed her eyes. "Oh, my very ribs ache!" she said. She took a shuddering breath, and shook her head sharply. "There now, that's enough."

"It does you good to laugh," Philippa said. "I only hope there will not be repercussions, for Larkyn and for us."

"Well." Margareth took one last deep breath, and laid her hands flat on her desk. "Well, I expect there will be. But we'll deal with them as we may. For now, we had better get to the stables and see that this is done right, if it must be done."

Philippa raised her eyebrows. "If it must? Don't you agree the colt should be gelded?"

"I think, Philippa," Margareth said, with no lingering trace of laughter in her voice. "I think Eduard is more concerned that this mystery colt doesn't breed than he is about where he came from. He should have stirred himself long before this, taken himself to the Uplands to assess the foal, tried—as you did—to speak to Frederick."

"He would not have been allowed."

"We don't know that." Margareth crossed to the door. "But I don't quite trust him to take proper care. He's an odd little colt, I grant you, but he's still one of Kalla's creatures. Every one of them is a gift. Let's be sure this is quick, and clean."

"Shall we keep Larkyn away?"

"I don't think so. I daresay the girl knows more about these things than any of us."

Philippa snorted. "And suppose she faints in front of Crisp and the surgeon?"

Margaret paused with her hand on the doorknob. "You know, Philippa, I would be surprised if Larkyn Hamley has ever fainted. Or ever will."

THEY found Larkyn in Tup's stall, staring over the gate at the surgeon and his array of murderous-looking knives. Rosellen stood just outside, ready with a basin and a pile of clean cloths. She had a coil of rope on her shoulder. The colt held his head high, neck arched in alarm at the nearness of Eduard Crisp and the surgeon. The surgeon was a skeletal man with graying hair and dirty fingernails. Philippa gritted her teeth at the sight of him. Crisp had repeatedly refused to teach a woman to do what was necessary. He was not the only one, of course, to believe that women were unsuited to such bloody work, yet here was young Larkyn, a calming hand on her colt's neck. Crisp eyed her as if she might bolt at any moment.

She was like a runty puppy, Philippa thought, tough because she had to be. She looked better now that she wore the uniform of the Academy, and had at least tried to tie her wild hair back. Only when she spoke did she reveal her country roots, and she was silent now.

These were never pleasant days. The proximity of men sent the colts into near-hysteria. They had to be tied down, and held there by whoever was available. Most of the girls hid themselves in the Dormitory, nearly hysterical themselves, sobbing and covering their ears against the frantic cries of their colts. All the instructors dreaded such events, and were giddy with relief when they were over.

The girls collecting their horses from the stables were quiet and subdued this morning. The word had spread, somehow, and they all seemed eager to be away from the proceedings. Philippa saw that Rosellen had already moved the palomino and the sorrel gelding outside the stables, away from the offensive scents that Herbert and Eduard Crisp brought with them. Philippa stepped closer to Tup's stall, and saw that the brown goat had pressed herself between the colt and the far wall, as far from the humans as she could get. Her wisp of beard trembled.

Trying to speak gently, Philippa said, "Larkyn, perhaps you should go to the Dormitory."

The girl's eyes didn't flicker from Crisp's face. "Tup needs me," she said.

Eduard sputtered something under his breath, and Philippa cast him a scornful look. "Eduard," she snapped. "Forbear, will you? You've given her no other name to call him by."

He opened his mouth, but his response died on his lips. Someone had come into the stables, and Crisp swung about to bow to him. Philippa, too, lapsed into a surprised and wary silence. Only Margareth had the presence of mind to greet their royal visitor.

"Lord William," she said. She inclined her head. "We had no word you were coming."

He gave her the shallowest of bows. "Headmistress," he said. "Your Hall was kind enough to give me breakfast, in the charming company of your students." His glance skimmed Philippa and Rosellen and came to rest on the Master Breeder. "Eduard."

Crisp stepped close to the stall, making the colt flatten his ears and shrink back, squeezing the little goat tighter against the wall. The Master Breeder pointed to him. "This is the foal from the Uplands, my lord," he said. "We're gelding him today."

"Bit premature, wouldn't you say, Eduard?" William said lightly. He smoothed the full sleeves of his shirt, and tugged at his embroidered vest. "Before we know who his sire was?"

Crisp's jowls trembled with indignation. "My lord," he said. "You can see for yourself the colt's breeding isn't true. He may be a throwback, for all we know."

"Nonsense," William said. "There hasn't been a throwback for centuries."

"Point is, my lord," Crisp said, with no sign of being intimidated, "we don't know where he came from, or why he was born to an unknown dam. My job is to protect the bloodlines of the Duke, and I am charged to perform it as I see fit."

Philippa dropped her head, watching the scene from beneath her brows. Eduard, apparently, had nothing to fear. The same stubbornness which so irked Margareth and herself served him well in dealing with William. She doubted there were many in Oc who could face down the Duke's eldest son so calmly.

William ran his quirt through his fingers. "His Grace, my father," he purred, "would like to know more about this colt before we take any steps. And so, I might add, would I." He turned and spoke to the surgeon. "We won't be needing you and your knives today, my friend."

Philippa felt, rather than heard, Larkyn's breath of relief, but she herself wasn't at all sure William could make this ruling stick. She doubted the Master Breeder would take his word for Frederick's wishes.

Eduard put out a hand to stop the surgeon from packing up his knives. "Wait a moment, Hemple." To William, he said, "My lord, I've heard nothing from His Grace. And it's quite clear to me that we don't want this colt passing along his dubious traits."

"Now, now, Eduard," Lord William said. His thin lips curved in his peculiar slanted smile. "Until he grows, we don't know that his traits are dubious at all, do we? All we know is that this . . ." He pointed the quirt at Lark. Philippa followed the gesture, and saw Lark, pale-cheeked and wide-eyed, tighten her arms around the colt's neck. "This farm girl found a mare wandering along the Black River, pregnant, as we now know, with a winged foal. Until we have gotten to the bottom of this little mystery, I propose we leave the colt intact. In fact," he added, forestalling the objection about to fall from Crisp's lips, "I insist upon it, Eduard."

"But the Duke—"

"I speak for my father."

Eduard squinted at him. "I don't know, my lord. The Council—"

"Let me deal with the Council of Lords, Eduard." William slapped the quirt against his palm, and nodded again to Hemple. "You won't be needed today," he repeated. "Unless Master Crisp has other work for you."

Eduard Crisp glowered. "We can postpone this for a few weeks, my lord," he said. "But it should be done. The colt fits none of the standards."

"None of *your* standards," William said, arching an eyebrow. "Keep in mind, Eduard, that the ultimate protection of the bloodlines falls to my father. And . . ." He favored all of them with a cool smile. "And, naturally, to me." He turned away in a clear dismissal. He inclined his head to Margareth, tucked the quirt beneath his arm, and departed from the stables with a murmured command to Rosellen to fetch his horse.

"Well," Philippa said softly. "What do you think the Council would make of this?"

"Damnably odd," the Master Breeder grumbled.

"You're quite right, Eduard," Margareth mused. "But it's wiser not to discuss it now."

Crisp looked around at Herbert, at Hemple, at Larkyn, and the colt. "Right," he said grimly. "But this won't be the end of it."

ELEVEN

LARK stood hugging Tup as the others left, the Headmistress and Mistress Winter together, then Herbert and the Master Breeder. The surgeon gathered his collection of ugly knives and walked away without a glance at either Lark or the colt. Only Rosellen stayed behind.

The moment the men were gone, taking their hated scent with them, Tup's ears relaxed. Lark stroked his forehead, and a moment later he and Molly put their heads in the feed box, nibbling at what was left of the morning grain. Lark leaned against the wall. She felt as if all the blood had suddenly vanished from her legs.

Concern creased Rosellen's freckled face. "Are you all right, miss?"

Lark stared at the freckled girl, and her heart fluttered in her throat. "I've seen him before, Rosellen."

"Who? Master Crisp?"

"Lord William," Lark whispered. "Only I didn't know it was him."

Rosellen leaned over the stall gate. "When? How?"

"He came to the farm." Lark shivered at the memory of that day. "I don't like him."

"Aye." Rosellen took a cautious glance over her shoulder. "We stays out of his way when we can, me and Herbert."

"What does he want with Tup?" Lark breathed deep. Her legs steadied, and she straightened. "It troubles me."

"Troublesome, aye," Rosellen said. "Though it saved your colt there a bloody morning's work."

"For the present, anyway." Lark slipped through the gate, and looked back at Tup and Molly. "It wouldn't be so bad if they'd let me do it myself, and properly, without scaring him half to death."

"Would you know how to do that?" Rosellen said in surprise. "Geld a colt?"

"I could figure it out."

"They'd never let you do it. Master Breeder thinks it's men's work, cutting and bleeding and all." Rosellen tugged at the thick, sandy braid that hung over one shoulder. "I always thought he had the right of it. Messy business, castration."

"I'm a farm girl, Rosellen. Animals are what I know, goats, cows, chickens. And vegetables. I'm better grubbing in my kitchen garden than mincing about the Academy." She sighed, and gestured across the broad courtyard at the Hall and the Dormitory. "Yon girls seem to think I came covered in farm dirt . . . they wrinkle their noses when I pass, and they giggle."

"Lot of nobs," Rosellen said, and spat liberally into the sawdust. "Give it time, miss. You'll see. The riding will make the difference."

"I don't know how to ride, either. Not properly."

"You'll learn. It's what the place is all about."

They walked together to the door of the stables, reaching it just as a flight lifted from the paddock, the horses launching themselves into the air, arranging themselves in one of the patterns—the Airs. Lark gazed up at them, open-mouthed with admiration. These were the third-level girls, their mounts already skilled. The winged horses swooped and turned, elegant as a flight of eagles. Their wings dipped in unison, and they sorted themselves into a long V, hovering there as if resting on the wind. Lark yearned to be one of them, to feel the breeze on her face, the flexing of great wings over her knees.

Rosellen said, "That's Open Columns."

"They're so beautiful, Rosellen! What could be more beautiful?"

"That." Rosellen pointed, and Lark followed her finger.

"Oh!"

It was Philippa Winter, circling above her flight. Winter Sunset's wings, gleaming scarlet in the sunshine, seemed barely to move as she coasted past the other flyers. Rosellen was right. Mistress Winter and her mare were so perfectly coordinated they were as one creature, as if they were created together, arms and feet and hooves and wings. Lark's breath stopped in her breast as the great V dissolved, and each flyer turned right around in the air, tails flying, necks bowing, riders leaning into the turn, their skirts belling around them.

Rosellen breathed, "Ah! Grand Reverses."

"It's magnificent."

"Aye, it is. It's also what they're to do if something is fired at them—"

"Rosellen! What would be fired at winged horses?"

Rosellen blew out her lips. "You'd be amazed. Arrows. Catapults. Stones. I saw one once at the Palace, had taken an arrow through her wing. She and her rider almost died, barely made it safely to ground. That mare never flew again, and a beautiful tall Noble she was."

"Zito's ears," Lark muttered.

Rosellen grunted assent. "War is one thing," she said. "But I don't understand attacking innocent animals."

Lark dropped her eyes to Rosellen's plain face. "We're the same, you and I, aren't we?" she said. "We love all animals. Farm folk."

"Fisher folk, in my case," Rosellen said. "And hardly the same, truth be told. You sleep in the Dormitory and me in a room above the stables."

"Nay, Rosellen. The only difference between us is my colt. Otherwise, no one would give a blink at a country girl like me."

Rosellen shrugged. "That's as may be. But I should tell you, Miss Hamley—best you not be seen with me unless needs be. Won't help you with the nobs."

Lark shook her head. "You're the only one who talks to me."

"What about a sponsor? All new girls're supposed to get 'em."

"I have one. Her name is Petra Sweet. She's not too pleased about it."

Rosellen tutted, and shook her head. "Who made *that* choice?"

Lark shrugged. "I don't know. But these three days have been the loneliest of my life."

"Give it time," Rosellen repeated. She lifted her hand to pat Lark's shoulder, and then seemed to think better of it. She gave her wry, gappy smile instead. "Give it time."

LARK hated leaving the stables for the stiff elegance of the Hall. She had been excused from morning exercises, but now she was due to meet with Horsemistress Strong. The other girls in the first level were well into their training, practicing canters and trots and lead changes on wingless horses in the dry paddock. Lark, knowing nothing of these things, was to have private instruction. And every other girl in her level knew it.

Lark went up the steps to the Hall, and through the big doors, but in the foyer she froze. She looked this way and that, her eyes still dazzled by the bright sunshine. She couldn't remember where she was to meet Mistress Strong. The Headmistress's office was off to her left, past the line of portraits, and the dining hall was to her right. She heard the clink of china and silver being laid. The classrooms were upstairs, but . . . what had the horsemistress said to her? The lounge? The reading room? Lark bit her lip, struggling to remember. So much had happened today, and the day before, and the day before that . . . the tears that had not threatened this morning, when she was so concerned about Tup, now stung her eyes. She stood in the very center of the tiled entryway, fighting them. One escaped to splash on her dusty tabard.

"Here, now," came a voice from her left. "Here, here."

Lark ducked her head to hide her brimming eyes, and found a lace-edged handkerchief held under her nose.

"No need for that," the voice said. Lark lifted her face to see a tall, broad-shouldered girl standing before her. "Take it," the girl said, waving the handkerchief. "And then let's fix what's troubling you."

Lark buried her face in the handkerchief, unable to speak for a moment. The other girl waited until she had blown her nose and snuffled back her tears. When she looked up again, dabbing at her wet eyelashes, the girl gave her a good-natured grin. "I'm Hester Morning," she said. "First-level, like you. Only I've been here six months already." She tilted her head and looked Lark up and down. "Surprised to find you blubbering," she said. "They say you're as tough as saddle leather."

Lark caught her breath, surprise overcoming her tears. "Who says that?"

"Oh, that idiot Petra Sweet," Hester said. "Never met a girl who talks so much. Is it true you're only fifteen?"

Lark sniffled, and nodded. "My birthday was just last week."

"You're two years younger than any other girl here! I can't

think whose idea it was to make Sweet your sponsor. She hates all us first-levels."

Lark shook her head. "I don't know. Her horse's stall is near mine."

"Well. Doesn't matter now." Hester took the wet handkerchief back, and jammed it into the pocket of her riding skirt. "So what's upset you? You look lost."

"I am!" Lark managed a small laugh. "Lost in almost every way, and now I'm supposed to meet with Mistress Strong, but I can't remember where."

"Ah! Well, I can show you. She likes to be in the reading room. Up this way." Hester turned toward the staircase, and Lark followed.

They were halfway up the stairs when the Headmistress's door opened, and the unmistakable voice of Lord William floated up to them. Hester put her finger to her lips, and both girls stopped where they were.

"I'll be back in a few weeks," he was saying, "to see how the colt is getting on."

Philippa Winter's voice carried sharply up the staircase. "We can't wait too long, William. If the colt matures the way Foundation foals do—"

"I'll tell Eduard to keep an eye on him," William said.

From the office, the Headmistress said something, to which Lord William responded curtly, "The Ducal Palace takes precedence over the Council, Margareth."

The girls shrank back against the wall as Lord William's heels clicked across the tiles. Hester and Lark stared at each other, wide-eyed, neither moving until the heavy door had opened and shut behind his lordship.

A heartbeat later, Mistress Winter's voice again rose up the stairwell. "I believe both you girls have duties?"

"Yes, ma'am." Hester grinned at Lark, and whispered, "Eyes in the back of her head!" before she led the dash up the stairs.

THE weary afternoon was almost over before Lark was free to return to the stables, and Tup. The second- and third-level girls were bringing their mounts in to rub them down, clean their feet, brush their manes and tails. The first-levels, like Lark, were currying their horses and gossiping between the stalls. Oc-hounds trotted here and there, and Bramble, Lark's favorite, came to sniff at Molly. The goat was just tall enough to poke her bearded chin over the gate, and the sight of the little brown goat nose to nose with the silvery-coated dog made Lark chuckle. Tup buried his nose in Lark's shoulder and whimpered over her long absence.

From her stall, Petra called, "Hamley! What *is* that noise your colt makes?"

Lark froze, the currycomb in her hand. Cautiously, she answered, "It's just his way. He's always sort of—cried, like that."

"Cried is right." Petra said scornfully. "You should make him stop. It's *odious*." She drawled the word, exaggerating the nasal accent Lark heard everywhere at the Academy.

There was something wrong with Petra's accent, though. It didn't sound quite right—not like Mistress Winter's, for example, or like Hester Morning's. Hester's pronunciation was precise, and she had a lifting intonation that gave her speech a musical sound. Petra's was just—nasal. Forced.

Hester spoke from Lark's other side. "Sweet! Kalla's teeth, leave Hamley alone."

"Mind your own affairs, Morning," Petra said. "I'm her sponsor. Her comportment reflects upon me."

Lark went to the gate. Hester's stall was just down the aisle from her, and she was brushing the mane of a tall, strong-looking palomino. She winked at Lark over her shoulder, and then called, "It's your own comportment that reflects upon you, Sweet. Better mind that!"

Petra sputtered some outraged answer, and Lark turned back to Tup, her heart lighter than it had been since the moment Brye left her standing alone in the Academy courtyard.

A few minutes later, Hester came to lean on the gate, watching Lark finish with Tup. "He's a pretty thing, isn't he? Black as midnight."

Lark smiled up at her rangy new friend. "Yes. I think he's perfect," she confided. "Though everyone keeps telling me he's too small."

Hester narrowed her eyes, considering Tup. "Yes. My own Golden Morning is already twice your colt's size. Her withers are as high as my head. She's six months older, of course. And . . ." Hester shrugged, and spread her hands. "She's a Foundation. I'm for the border patrols, no mistake about it." She looked down at herself, and gave a boisterous laugh. "But then, I was born for it! I'm twice *your* size!"

"Not quite," Lark said. She surveyed Tup's coat, turned to satin under her currycomb. His mane had grown, and it ran through her fingers like black water. She had combed his tail to perfection, and his fetlocks were wisps of black silk. If only she could manage her own hair!

Molly, too, had enjoyed a turn under the currycomb, and her light summer coat gleamed. Lark put the currycomb on its shelf, and turned to Hester. "You are a good bit bigger than me, though not twice! My brothers say I'm no bigger than a bobbin. But I think you're lovely tall."

"I like the way you talk," Hester said. "I've never met anyone from the Uplands." She opened the gate for Lark. "Now, tell me about this sweet little goat. What's her name?"

They chatted as they crossed the courtyard to the Dormitory and walked together up to the sleeping porch. Everything smelled wonderfully of horses and straw. The girls were changing from their riding clothes, washing their hands and faces at the basins at one end of the long room, brushing out their hair. Lark stood beside her bed, struggling as she had for the past three days to twist her hair into the proper knot. She had bent a dozen pins already, but nothing would hold her curly mop. Despairing, she threw the brush onto her cot.

Hester noticed, and leaned over to whisper, "We should get you a different hair clasp. In the city there are a hundred different shops that sell them."

"The city? Oh! I've never been to Osham."

"Yes!" Hester said, as if it were all decided. "We'll go. I'll get word to Mamá."

"Is that permitted?"

"If Mamá says so, it is." Hester grinned. "And we'll take Anabel. She loves to shop."

Lark hesitated. "Hester—I—I have no money, really. Just a few pence, that my brother left with me."

Hester chuckled. "Oh, we'll manage, Hamley," she said. "We're Academy girls. We have privileges!"

TWELVE

PHILIPPA led her students down the flight paddock at a canter, speeding into a hand gallop. The powerful downward drive of Sunny's wings lifted her surely into the air. Philippa felt the shedding of the bonds in her backbone, along her arms, down her thighs, the incredible freedom of flight. High clouds puffed in a hard blue sky, and she felt the heat on her neck. The wind of their flight cooled her somewhat, but the flight would have to be short, for the horses' sake.

Sunny hovered at Quarters while the flight maneuvered into Open Columns. The horses' chests and bellies darkened with sweat as their wings beat the heavy air. There were two Ocmarins, a roan and a brown. The three Nobles were dapple grays, and the Foundations were a chestnut and a bay. Their wings shone in the sun as they flew past Philippa, noses and tails aligned in the traveling pattern borrowed from high-flying birds. Columns were usually the responsibility of Nobles, but every pair that graduated from the Academy knew all the Airs, and all the Graces. Their training prepared them for whatever their careers might ask of them. Ribbon Day for these girls was a year off, but Philippa drilled them as if it were tomorrow. She knew, from experience, how crucial it was.

Her ears filled with the exhilarating sound of great wings beating. She signaled corrections, a tap of her quirt across her shoulder, a palms-down gesture, a leveled quirt. Elizabeth adjusted Chaser's angle, and Ardith dropped Feather's nose until it was inches from Chaser's tail. The leveled quirt meant that, for one precious moment, the pattern was perfect, the Open Columns for which the winged horses of Oc were famous. Frederick used to thrill to the sight of his winged horses performing Open Columns above his procession.

Philippa relaxed into her saddle, letting Sunny come out of Quarters to flank the moving formation. Thinking of Frederick caused her real pain. He was the father she had never had, the mentor who cared about her intelligence, her courage, her independence. Frederick had devoted his life to protecting the bloodlines, building on the legacy of his ancestors. The winged horses were the envy of every principality, every other duchy. Only Oc could send its nobility abroad escorted by Columns. When Isamar's Prince wanted such an escort, he had to request it from the Master Breeder. Any offense to Oc meant restricting the availability of the winged horses, and other dukes and princes knew it. The winged horses and their riders kept Oc strong.

Philippa's neck began to burn from the sun, and she thrust aside her grief for Frederick. She lifted her quirt to signal the change to Close Columns.

When a flight in Open Columns closed its ranks, it meant the procession beneath, or even the flight itself, was under attack. Philippa had employed Close Columns twice in her career. Both times she had blessed her instructors for drilling it into her and into Winter Sunset.

Philippa twirled her quirt, left to right, and the column began to close. Chaser's position didn't change, but Feather and Angel, Rose and Racer, Cocoa and Prince shifted the angle of their flight to narrow the distance between them, to tighten the formation until, from beneath, their extended wings blotted out the sky. Close Columns made a daunting sight, seven great winged horses flying like a many-shafted arrow. Should a weapon pierce their ranks, they were there to help each other. Should an enemy stand upon a battlement, the flight could smash through their line, scattering bowmen from their perch. More than one tower had thrown down its arms at the very sight of Close Columns.

For a moment, the pattern was perfect. Then Prince wobbled. His wings missed a beat, and the flyer behind him had to bank away to avoid a collision. Philippa wheeled Sunny about, urging her back with knees and rein, coming as close as she dared to Prince.

"Geraldine—pull Prince back into place, you're leaving a gap. Geraldine!"

It was clear that the rider and the horse were at odds. Prince's neck bowed, and his hooves clawed at the air, threatening to come out of their tuck. His wings fluttered, the membrane rippling. Sunny hesitated in her flight, unwilling to get close to an erratic flyer. "Geraldine!" Philippa shouted above the wind, irritated, and a bit frightened.

Geraldine, her face white and strained beneath her peaked cap, pulled on Prince's rein, trying to steady him. Philippa cried, "No! Don't yank him!" She lifted her arm above her head, and circled her quirt in the air. Elizabeth, the flight leader, signaled back that she understood, though Philippa could see her worry in the tilt of her head. She turned Chaser immediately, and gathered the flight behind her. The horses tilted, parted, dissolving Close Columns. They circled up and back, falling in behind Chaser for the short flight back to the Academy.

Anxiety dried Philippa's mouth, and she set her jaw to hide it. She urged Sunny alongside Geraldine and Prince. The girl cast her an anguished glance. Philippa read the awful truth in her eyes, but there was no time to think about it now. She would deal with it later. First, somehow, she had to get this pair safely on the ground.

She pressed Sunny in as close to Prince as she would go, hoping the older mare's presence might soothe the young gelding. They circled the Academy grounds, once, twice. For several awful minutes it seemed Prince might fall, his forelegs scrabbling at the air, his wings rippling erratically. Sunny kept a steady wingbeat next to him, and after a time he fell into her rhythm, tilting as she tilted, hooves curling beneath him. His eyes were wild with confusion, and Geraldine clung to her pommel, her back hunched, her chin on her chest, all the grace of her riding gone. Philippa saw her fearful glance at the ground beneath.

"Geraldine!" Philippa called, above the rush of the wind. "You won't fall. Give Prince his head, let him follow Sunny. I'm going to do the same—look, loosen the rein. Prince doesn't want to fall either! Sit deep in your saddle. Let Prince . . . yes, that's it."

Whether Geraldine could hear her, or she simply followed her example, the pair steadied. Sunny circled once more, and then angled toward the landing paddock, her neck long and graceful as she dropped. Prince followed in her wake. They glided in to land, one after the other, and the crisis ended. But it was, Philippa knew, Prince's last flight.

Half an hour later, she crossed the courtyard to the Hall again, her shoulders bowed with the weight of the news she must carry to Margareth. Geraldine could not be allowed to fly again.

Philippa trudged up the steps of the Hall, pulling off her gloves and her cap, tucking them into her belt. She stood a moment in the shadowed coolness of the foyer, gathering her strength. It was not the first time such a thing had happened, but nothing could soften the ghastly event that was to come. Only the death of a rider was worse, and Philippa had seen that, too.

LARK had seen no one except Petra and Rosellen and Mistress Strong all day, and she was glad when Hester Morning took a seat beside her at dinner. Lark offered her a smile, and Hester nodded in return, but she looked strangely grim.

Little bowls of consommé were put before them, a pale broth that made Lark long for the thick pottage of her own making. She tried to eat slowly, imitating Hester's use of the little round soup spoon, but she was so hungry! It seemed the soup disappeared on its own. When the server came to take her empty bowl, she lifted her head. For the first time she noticed the silence in the dining room, and she looked about, wondering what had changed.

The next course was a tiny, elaborate salad, with baskets of yeast rolls the size of Lark's thumb. She ate the salad in three bites, and did the same to a slice of poached fish. When a roasted squab was set before her, she picked up her knife and fork with reluctance. She was no stranger to squab, but at home she would have dismembered it with her fingers, the practical utensils she was born with. Here she must use flatware. She watched Hester to see how it might be done.

Hester picked up her knife, and then laid it down again, shaking her head.

"Hester," Lark murmured. "What is it? Why is everyone so quiet?"

Hester spoke in a low tone. "Didn't you hear?"

"Hear what?" She followed Hester's slight nod to the long table where the third-level girls sat. One of them, at the very end, was eating nothing. She sat with her head low, her shoulders slumped. Lark whispered, "Who is that? What's wrong with her?"

Hester picked up her knife again, and gave the squab on her

plate a halfhearted stab. "That's Geraldine. In their flight this morning, Geraldine lost control of Prince . . . Mistress Winter had to help them in. They almost fell."

"Fell?" Lark pressed a hand to her throat.

Hester sat back. "Yes," she said heavily. "The rest of the flight was terrified."

"Is that why everyone's upset?"

Hester leaned forward, and picked up her fork again. "Eat, Hamley. I'll explain later. This isn't a good time."

Lark struggled with the squab, leaving most of its meat shredded among the bones on her plate. She ate two rolls, and plucked a third from the basket just as it was being taken away. The table was cleared again, and an ice served. When the Headmistress rose, signaling the end of the meal, the girls filed out in near-silence. They dispersed, some to the Dormitory, some to the stables, some to the yearlings' pasture to bring their colts and fillies in for the night.

Lark paused on the steps. "I have to go to the library," she told Hester. "Mistress Strong set me to memorize ten generations of the Ocmarin line."

Hester didn't speak for a moment. She stood on the step below Lark, gazing out across the courtyard to the quiet pastures. To the east, the spires of Osham glimmered white. To the west, the sky still glowed with sunset light.

Lark touched her arm. "Hester. Won't you tell me what's wrong?"

"Let's talk in the library."

Hester led the way down the steps and around the side of the Hall to the tiny, lamplit library. They found it empty, the books neatly shelved, a small fire crackling in the fireplace. Hester pulled down a book and laid it on the study table. Lark took a chair and pulled the book to her, but she didn't open it. She looked up at Hester, waiting.

"Of course you know our horses can't stand the scent of men," Hester said. Lark nodded. "If a rider's scent changes . . . the horses become confused."

"Is that what's happened to Geraldine?"

Hester gave a great sigh, and sat down opposite her. "There were rumors about Geraldine. She comes from a baron's family, I think, and I've heard she was wild." Hester's brow furrowed. "It may all be gossip, but they say her family was relieved to bond her with a winged horse." She sighed again, gustily. "And now she's in trouble."

"She's breeding," Lark said.

"Yes."

Lark rested her chin on one hand. "On Deeping Farm, I always knew when the she-goats or the cows had caught. They smelled different. Richer, somehow. Stronger."

"Whatever it is, the horses know it. They know other things, too, like—if a girl uses one of those potions the witchwomen sell, to stop conception, or to abort a pregnancy. And you know, Lark, once a woman has a baby, her body is changed forever. The horses can't bear it."

"Oh," Lark breathed. "New Prince . . ."

"Yes. New Prince." Hester gave a gusty sigh. "I know what Mamá would say. Men can do almost anything, and there are no consequences. Women are the ones who pay the price."

"In the Uplands . . . when this happens, we have quick weddings."

"In Osham, girls who get pregnant are sent away."

"That seems unfair."

"So Mamá says. But just because it's unfair doesn't change anything." Hester sat shaking her head, her eyes bleak. "I don't know how she could do it, knowing what could happen."

"What will happen to Geraldine now?"

Hester shrugged. "She'll never escape the disgrace. She'll have to leave her family, the Academy . . . I expect they'll disown her. And no one will want to marry her."

"Then what will she do?"

Hester only shrugged again. "But I can tell you this! I could never, never risk losing Goldie!"

"Will they really do it? Will they put Prince down?"

"They have to." Hester fixed Lark with a hard gaze. "A winged horse goes mad if it loses its bondmate. It's already started with Prince. He'll destroy himself, in the end, and he could hurt other horses and even people in the process."

"Oh. How terrible." Lark stroked the book, thinking how precious each winged horse was, trying to grasp how Geraldine could have taken such a risk.

"And we have to witness it," Hester said bleakly.

Lark felt a wave of cold sweep up from her belly. "Watch?"
"Yes."
"Have you seen this before?"
Hester shook her head. "No," she said. "Nor did I ever expect
to. But it's part of the discipline—so that we understand, each of
us. So we don't make the same mistake."

Lark thought of Tup, the prick of his ears at her approach, his
shining eyes so full of trust. Like Hester, she would never do anything to put her horse at risk. The very thought turned her blood
to ice.

She pushed the book of the Ocmarin line away from her. There
was no point in opening it. She would be able to learn nothing this
night.

THE Headmistress spoke to the students at breakfast, her voice
dry and even as if she was announcing a change in schedule. The
girls stared at their plates as they listened to her explanation. Mistress Morgan finished by saying, "Our work often involves life-
and-death matters. In your service, you will see many things, and
this one, hard thing you must witness, so that you will remember,
and understand."

No one made a sound as they left their half-eaten breakfasts
and straggled across the courtyard. Hardly knowing she did it,
Lark noted the hills to the west beginning to rust in the heat. In
Willakeep the peak of the growing season would have passed, the
early mornings and late evenings just starting to cool, the farmers
beginning preparations for harvest.

The horses tossed their heads as the girls circled the stables.
Several whickered to their mistresses, and Lark heard answering
sobs, quickly muffled. She was grateful that Tup, for once, did
not cry out for her. With the others, she trudged to the dry paddock, and she and Hester leaned against the pole fence. Hester
stared straight ahead, her profile rigid. Lark felt the grief of the
students around her, their hearts aching as one, unified for the
moment by tragedy. No one whispered, no one giggled, no one
spoke at all. Even Petra Sweet was silent.

Rosellen led New Prince out of the stables, and Lark's heart
turned over. The gelding had already been dosed with some potion. His head hung low, and his wings dragged in the dirt. He was

tall and deep-chested, with the muscular legs of a Foundation horse, but his eyes were dull and his ears drooped.

Rosellen coaxed the drugged horse forward. Geraldine, standing inside the dry paddock, drooped against the fence as if she, too, had been drugged.

Philippa Winter stood beside her. Mistress Winter put something into Geraldine's hand, and guided her across the paddock toward her bondmate. Geraldine walked as if in a daze, her face a mask of anguish, her eyelids swollen and red. Mistress Winter's face was set in hard lines that made her look ten years older. When Geraldine sagged against her, she forced her upright, and propelled her forward with an unyielding arm.

As they came close, Prince roused from his stupor, pulling back against his lead, his hoofs scrabbling in the dry dirt. Geraldine began to weep, her mouth open, her face blotching. Lark could see a small glass vial in her hand. Geraldine tried to press it back on Mistress Winter. Grimly, Mistress Winter pushed it away, and drew a white cloth from her pocket.

"Geraldine," she said, her voice sharp in the painful silence.

The girl muttered something through her tears.

"No," Philippa said evenly. "No one can do this for you. It is your duty."

Geraldine dropped the cloth, and tried to cover her eyes with her hand, but Philippa pulled it away from her face. Rosellen, her freckles standing out in her pale face, bent to pick up the cloth. Prince rustled his drooping wings, and shook his head from side to side, all his movements muddy and uncoordinated.

Lark bit her lip till it stung. There were soft sobs around her, and Mistress Winter raised her head and fixed the students with a hard gaze. Silence settled over the paddock again. The only noise was Prince's harsh breathing, the scuffing of his hoofs in the dirt as he tried to put distance between him and his bondmate.

"Swiftly, now," Mistress Winter said. "For kindness' sake."

Geraldine's hands shook as she unstoppered the little bottle, and poured its contents onto the cloth. She stepped up to Prince, as Rosellen dug in her heels to hold him in place. Sobbing aloud now, Geraldine held the cloth out to the horse's nose. He jerked back, lifting Rosellen off her feet. Geraldine cried out, and dropped both cloth and vial. She turned to flee, and Mistress Winter's strong arms stopped her.

But Prince had a whiff of the potion now, and he backed across the paddock, energized by some instinctive understanding. The watching students gasped. "Rosellen!" Philippa snapped. "Can you hold him? Geraldine, stop! Hysterics won't help Prince!"

But it was clear that Prince, terrified now, would not go easily. He dragged Rosellen backward until his hindquarters struck the pole fence. Geraldine began to struggle in Philippa's grasp. From a distance, the Headmistress called, "Someone fetch Herbert!" There was a rustle as one of the third-level girls pushed through the crowd into the stables.

Lark saw how the poor gelding's eyes rolled, saw the foam that flecked his muzzle, saw the sweat dripping from the jointure of wing and chest. She couldn't bear it. Rosellen was at the fence with him now, pulling with all her might on the rope. Prince reared, his wings flapping against his wingclips. The near clip popped off, and spun across the paddock. Without thinking, Lark leaped up on the bottom pole of the fence.

Hester cried her name, but Lark had already pulled herself up to the top pole. She swung her legs over, and jumped lightly down inside the paddock. She was beside Prince in a moment, pressing herself against his near wing, twining her fingers in his mane. His other wing was trapped against the fence. Rosellen gritted her teeth. Perspiration ran down her cheeks as she fought to hold his head.

Lark said softly, "Prince, Prince. Poor Prince. Settle down, now, lovely boy, settle down. It will all be over soon."

He was far taller than Tup, of course, and more than once he pulled her off her feet as she clung to his neck. She kept talking to him, all the while trying not to be stepped on. His near wing battered at her thigh, and he gave a choking neigh. Lark crooned, "Come now, Prince, poor lovely boy. Come now. Poor thing, poor lovely boy."

Just when it seemed both she and Rosellen would exhaust their strength, the horse gave one last, halfhearted leap, and subsided. The wing beneath Lark's thigh went limp. Prince's brief burst of energy was spent.

— "Them fools gave him half a potion," Rosellen muttered. "Might as well have me do it right in the first place."

Prince began to sag to the ground, unevenly, first one foreleg and then the other crumpling beneath him. He fell to his knees, his pinions spreading in the dirt, his hind legs folding. Rosellen loosened the lead, and Lark stepped around the stable-girl and knelt to cradle the gelding's head, soothing his forehead with her free hand. A moment later, Philippa Winter crouched beside her. In one swift motion, she covered Prince's muzzle with the potion-soaked cloth, held it there with a firm hand as his eyes glazed and his breath rattled.

The smell of the potion stung Lark's nostrils and made her eyes water, but she held the horse's head throughout. Even after Philippa withdrew the cloth, and touched Prince's throat to see that no pulse still beat in it, Lark stroked his smooth cheek, watching the spark of life fade from his eyes like the flame of a candle guttering and dying.

After the wildness of the struggle, the tension and drama of the scene, the end seemed unnaturally quiet. It was as if, Lark thought, Prince had given in. Had given up.

Philippa touched her shoulder. "He's gone now, Larkyn. Thank you for helping him."

"Aye," Lark whispered. "It had to be done."

"Indeed it did."

Philippa put out her hand to help Lark to her feet. Lark gently laid Prince's head on the ground, smoothing his forelock, palming his eyelids closed. Behind her she heard Geraldine's wild weeping, and someone trying to quiet her. The other girls were silent, and when she straightened, their collective gaze on her seemed weighted, like the breathless summer heat. Lark saw Petra move, and mutter something, but Hester Morning stepped in front of her, blocking her from Lark's gaze.

Lark looked back at the beautiful horse lying in the dirt. His right wing was folded beneath him at a bad angle, and his left lay stretched across the ground like a fold of ruined silk. Those wings would never carry him high into the air again. His shining hooves were splayed uselessly, his graceful neck twisted at an impossible angle.

Bitterly, Lark said, "What a waste."

Mistress Winter gave her an odd look. "Indeed it is, Larkyn," she said in a low voice. "A terrible waste indeed."

THIRTEEN

"**HOW** useful it will be for Rosellen," Petra Sweet said, "to have a goat-girl in the stables." Her tone was just loud enough to carry through the sleeping porch. A few titters followed her remark, quickly hushed as Hester Morning abruptly stood up to glare down the row at Petra.

"What are you talking about, Sweet?" Hester demanded. Lark hastily pulled her nightshift over her head to hide her burning cheeks.

"Not that I need to explain to you, Morning," Petra sneered, "but after all . . . how fortunate that Hamley there doesn't mind scrabbling about in the dirt to do a stable-girl's job."

Hester put her hands on her hips. She made an imposing figure, tall, broad-shouldered, stiff-necked. "Prince should have done it," she snapped. "It wasn't Rosellen's duty."

"She's not Prince any longer," someone said. Lark poked her head out of her nightshift to find the speaker. It was another first-level, Anabel Chance, a fine-featured girl with a voice as soft as the straight blond hair that fell past her shoulders. "But I don't remember her surname." No one answered Anabel.

Hester kept her hard gaze on Petra. "If you ask me, one of you second-levels should have stepped into the breach instead of mooning around like a bunch of weepy maidens."

Petra stalked to the end of her cot to face Hester. "You listen to me, Morning, and you, too, Hamley. There are proper ways to do things here, and you'd best learn them."

Lark yanked her nightshift down over her shoulders and jumped up. She could fight her own battle. She, too, stepped out from between the cots, and faced Petra. All the girls were watching, the first-levels agape, the second-levels grinning, a few of the third-levels frowning.

"Yon horse was suffering!" she said loudly.

"*Yon* horse?" Petra Sweet repeated, imitating Lark's Uplands accent. Someone laughed, and someone else shushed her.

Hester said, in her perfectly cultured voice, "It's pronounced 'horse,' Sweet." She pinched her rather long nose and said, in perfect mimicry of Petra's forced accent, "Not 'hoss.'"

Petra's face darkened, and her hands clenched. She took a step forward, and someone seized her arm. Hester's hands, too, had curled into fists.

Hastily, Lark said, "No matter how you say it, Prince was in agony, and there was nothing to do for him. My accent isn't the only thing I brought from the Uplands."

"No," Petra snapped. "You brought the stink of goat!"

Lark responded tartly. "I may stink of goat—and cow, too, for that matter—but I know better than to stand idly by while an animal suffers!"

"Are *you* telling us our business? A goat-girl?"

Hester sniffed loudly. "I believe you carry your own stink, Sweet," she said. "What is that fragrance that follows you . . . cured leather? Bootblack? You make shoes, I believe."

Petra's face went scarlet, and she sputtered, "I've never even been in the manufactory . . . Don't be an idiot, Morning!"

Hester shrugged. "In any case, Sweet, we all smell of horses. All the time."

"Don't be vulgar," Petra spat. She pointed to Lark. "I'm warning you, Goat-girl. In the future, you wait for orders."

One of the third-levels—Elizabeth Chaser, Lark thought—said, "Sweet! That's enough! It's been a terrible day for everyone, and you're making it worse."

Petra swung around and stalked back to her own bed. Lark sank onto her cot, and Hester stood beside her, arms folded, as if daring anyone else to say anything. One by one, the curious faces turned away, and the girls began to slip into their cots.

"Why does she hate me?" Lark whispered. "I know I don't fit in . . . but I haven't done anything to hurt her."

"She was just waiting for someone to pick on," came a soft voice.

Lark and Hester both turned, and found Anabel standing before them, a hairbrush in her hand. She flushed under their regard. "She would have picked on me, I expect, as I'm so slow in my classes, and I have such a bad seat. But my father is an earl, and hers is only a boot merchant." Her voice grew smaller. "I thought what you did was wonderful, Larkyn," she said. "I wish I had your courage."

"Good common sense," Hester said. "Made everyone else look foolish."

"Oh!" Lark said. "But that wasn't why I—"

"Oh, no, of course not," Anabel breathed in a rush. "You didn't do it on purpose. But that poor horse!" Her eyes filled with easy tears, and they spilled over to shine on her porcelain cheeks. "I'll never forget it! I've never, ever seen anything so terrible."

"Nor have I," Hester said. She sank down next to Lark. "I've never seen anything die."

Lark stared at them, mystified. How could they have grown to such an age—Hester was at least eighteen, and Anabel must be almost that old—having never seen death? Of course she knew they would not have herded goats, or milked cows, or delivered a foal. But death was so much a part of life. How sheltered their lives must have been! How different the life of an Uplands farm girl from the lives of these highly bred daughters of Oc. She despaired of their finding any common ground.

Except, of course, for their winged horses.

THE next morning, Philippa was leaving the Hall with Margareth and the other horsemistresses when she saw the tall, slender figure of Lord William just entering the stables. His brown gelding had been turned loose in the dry paddock. Bramble, the oc-hound, stood in the center of the courtyard, watching William with her hackles raised high.

"Do you see, Philippa?" Margareth murmured.

"I do. I suppose I had better—"

"Yes. I'm afraid so."

Philippa sighed. It always fell to her to deal with the Duke, and by default, the Duke's son. Her history dictated it. She pulled her cap from her belt, and as she fitted it on her head, she called to one of her riders. "Elizabeth!"

Elizabeth left the little group of girls, and came to Philippa. "Yes, Mistress Winter."

"Will you see that everyone tacks up and assembles in the flight paddock? I'll be there as soon as I can."

Philippa saw the girl's eyes flicker to the stables, and back to her, and she knew that the third-level girls were all aware of Lord William's visit. Philippa spoke sharply. "And Elizabeth—no gossip. If you girls need to know something, we'll tell you."

"Yes, Mistress. The flight will be ready."

"Thank you." Philippa watched Elizabeth stride back to the group waiting for her on the cobblestones. Her step was long and lithe, her back straight, her cap tilted gaily over one eyebrow. She looked every inch the horsemistress she would become. With another sigh, Philippa turned to cross the courtyard to the stables. She wished her girls would not have to deal with politics, with undercurrents of power and poison and danger. But Elizabeth, like Philippa herself, rode a Noble mare. She would work for and with the nobility, whether or not they deserved her talents and her discipline. She would be manipulated, paraded, exploited. Her idealism and energy would mature into acceptance and pragmatism. Indeed, they must. If they didn't, her life would become unbearable.

Philippa walked into the stables, and turned left without hesitation. There was no doubt in her mind about why William was here. He had come to see Larkyn Hamley's little black. She supposed it was too much to hope that he might explain why. An ache began to spread up her neck and into the base of her skull.

She rounded the corner that led to Tup's stall, and stopped.

William was leaning over the gate, staring at the colt. Tup stared back. His ears drooped oddly, one on each side, and he whimpered uneasily. But he hadn't backed away. His nostrils flared, but he stood in the very center of the box stall, looking utterly confused.

Philippa froze where she was for a long moment, as mystified as the colt.

"My lord!"

It was Herbert, hurrying toward the stall from the opposite direction. William leaped back from the gate as if it had burned him. Philippa took one quiet step, and then another. William had not yet noticed her approach.

His back was to her as he greeted the stable-man. "Herbert," he said smoothly, as if nothing unusual had happened. "Will you find Eduard, and send him to me?"

Herbert's mouth opened, and his gaze shifted from William's face to the colt's puzzled eyes and drooping ears. He took a noisy breath. Philippa strode swiftly forward, and Herbert caught sight of her with obvious relief. "Y-yes, my lord," he stammered. "Of course. Of course. I'm off now, and—and here's Mistress Winter." He backed up a couple of steps, and then turned to hurry away, still muttering. "Yes, yes. Master Crisp, yes. Right away."

William turned to greet Philippa with icy composure. If he suspected she had seen him leaning into the colt's stall, closer than any man should be able to get to a winged horse, his demeanor betrayed nothing. He said lightly, "Philippa. How kind of you to take time out of your busy day."

"Not at all," she said. She hoped she hid her puzzlement better than Herbert had. She resorted to small talk. "What news of Duke Frederick?"

"My father is no better than when you saw him last," William said.

"And your lady mother? She must be grieving, too."

William gave her his humorless, slanting smile. "My mother is . . . more resilient," he said. "She busies herself with society and friends."

Lady Sophia had been a famous beauty in her youth, and admirers still trailed after her in her rounds of card parties and musicales and country weekends. It was said she was openly unfaithful to Frederick, but the Duke had never complained of her to Philippa. He had, however, been unashamedly adoring of his pretty and reckless daughter Pamella, boasting to Philippa of her frequent escapes from her governess and her chaperones. Her loss had broken him.

Philippa leaned her elbows on the wall of Tup's stall. The colt extended his nose to her, and she stroked his satiny muzzle with her fingers. His head now came to her chin, and the membranes of his wings were beginning to thicken. His back was still short, but his tail plumed nicely behind his croup, very like Sunny's. "If I didn't know how unlikely it is," Philippa mused, "I would say the little one had a Noble sire."

"As you say."

Philippa turned to see the Master Breeder approaching the stall. As Eduard stepped up beside William, Tup gave a sudden toss of his head, and backed sharply away, his head high, his ears laid back. He gave his wings a hard shake, and then clasped them tightly to his ribs, the pinions flaring with distaste. Eduard, too, gave William a curious look, and stepped back from the stall to give Tup his distance. The colt's behavior bemused Philippa so that she hardly heard William and Eduard greet each other. When she brought her attention back to them, they were already in a heated discussion.

The heat was all on Eduard's side. William revealed his anger only in the droop of his eyelids over his dark eyes, the silken quality to his voice.

"My lord," Eduard said, a little too loudly. "Oc takes pride in the purity of the three bloodlines—none of these by-blows that have cropped up in the past! Your great-grandfather went to great expense, as your lordship knows, to acquire every winged horse throughout the principality. If we allow even one of the lines to be corrupted, we endanger our reputation—*your* reputation, my lord, as you'll inherit! You must see that—"

"Eduard," William said with deadly lightness, "we would not like to have to replace you. But authority over the winged horses rests with us. The final decision is ours."

Philippa frowned, noting the plural pronoun. When had "we" replaced "my lord father" in William's vocabulary?

Poor Eduard paled under the threat, but he stood his ground. "Lord William," he said more quietly. "Please consider. It has been a terrible week here at the Academy—"

"Yes. We heard the news." William rounded on Philippa so quickly she took an involuntary step back, bumping her elbow on the wall of Tup's stall. His hooded eyes reminded her of something, some image she could not quite place.

But she would not be intimidated by William. They had far too much history for that. And she was almost his equal, by birth and by profession. She lifted her head to look down her nose at him. "I can assure you, William," she said, deliberately omitting his title. "That it did not happen here. The girls go home to their families for holidays, funerals, weddings. You know that. Duke Frederick knows it." She angled her body away from him, and leaned over the low wall to gaze at the black colt.

Despite her unease at William's behavior, and his threat to Eduard, she thought a case could be made for waiting to see how the colt grew before gelding him. She understood Eduard's concerns, and as an instructor, she didn't want one of her students having to deal with an uncut stallion if it weren't necessary. But Tup, if one put aside the expected conformation and coloring of the bloodlines, was a lovely creature. His short back and flat croup gave him a graceful line through the hindquarters, and his neck, though also rather short, curved above a well-muscled chest. His wings were narrow, but long. She looked forward to seeing him fly.

"Eduard," she said abruptly, still watching the colt. "What is the latest date the colt can safely be gelded?"

"We always geld Foundations by eight months," Eduard said. She heard the tension in his voice, and felt a brief spasm of sympathy for him. He was, after all, doing his job, though he irritated her often in the process.

"The little black was a winter foal. He will be eight months next week," she said.

"He's not a Foundation colt," William said.

"Testes descended," Eduard snapped. "That's a Foundation trait."

"What other traits do you see, Eduard?" Philippa asked.

"Been watching him," the Master Breeder answered. "I'd guess his dam was an Ocmarin, and with that back and tail, the stud was probably a Noble. How an Ocmarin mare came to be bred to a Noble, I can't imagine, but that's the look of it."

William stroked his smooth chin with a long forefinger. "All the more reason, Eduard," he said softly, "to postpone gelding the colt."

"I disagree, my lord," Eduard said stubbornly. "His dam was a wingless mare, and that's just the tendency we're trying to breed out of the line."

"But she threw a winged colt. That's what we're trying to increase."

Eduard glowered, but said no more. William was gone a moment later, calling for Herbert to fetch his horse. Philippa and Eduard stared after him.

"Bad business for Oc," Eduard growled. "The Duke being so ill."

"Yes," Philippa said.

"One bad generation could ruin everything."

Philippa nodded to Eduard in silence, and started out of the stables. It was better—safer—not to ask which generation Eduard meant. The power of the Ducal Palace was too great, and if Frederick died, they would all have to answer to William. Philippa could not persuade herself that William's motives would be as selfless as Frederick's had always been. Frederick himself had known that since William's boyhood, and therein lay the great problem of the succession.

As she walked toward the flight paddock, pulling on her gloves, the image she had been trying to recall sprang to her mind. Frederick kept an old, old painting in his library at the Palace. No one remembered the artist anymore. The paint had gone dark and obscure with the passage of time. It was a huge canvas depicting a flight of the legendary Old Ones, nostrils flaring red, scaled wings stretched wide above a mountain glacier.

It had been the eyes that held Philippa, narrow, black eyes, their glitter still evident in the fading paint. William's eyes.

FOURTEEN

LARK glared at Herbert. "Zito's ears, I'm not riding *that*!"

He stared back at her, his weathered face impassive. "My orders, Miss. A pony for you, until you learn some skills."

The creature in question was piebald, splashed with brown and white, with pale eyelashes and thick pinkish lips. He was nearly the fattest animal Lark had ever seen, his belly as round as one of the cows in calf, his hindquarters thick and his neck wide. "Pony?" she cried. "He looks like a hog ready for market! Our own cart-ox would be better to ride!"

She walked around him, noting his thick hooves, his splayed hocks. A flying saddle perched on his withers, high-cantled, with a tall, thin pommel. It looked miserably uncomfortable.

The pony laid his ears back, and he twisted his head, baring his teeth. Lark yelped, and jumped out of his reach. Bramble, the oc-hound, came racing around the stables, dashing toward the back paddock with her ears up and her tail stiff.

Herbert nodded at the dog. "Bramble don't like your tone, nor me neither," he growled.

Lark glanced down at the dog. "Nay, it's not me upsetting the dog!" Bramble proved she was right by stepping between her and the pony.

Herbert ignored this. "I've saddled P—I've saddled the pony, got him all ready, and I expect you to take a turn around the paddock on him, as ordered."

"I don't see what good it will do." Lark stuck her chin out. "I want to ride a real horse."

Herbert scowled at her. "Now, listen to me, Miss. If you want to catch up to your level, best do as you're told. Come on, now. Mistress Strong wants you to ride. Might as well get the feel of the saddle."

Lark took one more look around, relieved at least to see that no one was watching. She approached the pony again. It would be nothing like riding Char, with her sweet mare's scent, her neat hooves clipping along the packed dirt of the lane, her dainty ears flicking back and forth, listening to Lark's voice.

It had been, she realized, a year now since she had come upon the little mare in the shallows of the river. Even here, near the White City, the ripeness of autumn was upon the land. At home, the broomstraw would be coming in, the bloodbeets piled in carts to carry to market. She could smell the char in the air from the burning of straw and cornhusks. She felt the change in the slant of the sun on her face. Autumn. She had been at the Academy for three months. Tup would soon be nine months old.

Herbert bent to turn out the stirrup for Lark. The pony reached for the stable-man's rear pockets with his teeth, and Herbert smacked his nose with the back of his hand.

Lark kept her distance from this display. "What is he called?"

Herbert twisted the stirrup, keeping an eye on the pony's head. "Call 'im Pig, Miss. I don't know why. Someone bought him at the Osham stock fair, and he was already called that."

Lark stared at the old man for a moment, and then she giggled. "Really? Pig?" She approached the pony with care, from his left hindquarter, and gingerly fitted her left boot into the stirrup iron. Pig tossed his head, and shuffled away from her, almost spilling her to the ground. Her foot popped out of the stirrup, and Bramble growled.

Herbert gave the bridle a vicious yank. "Sorry," he muttered.

"No need," Lark said. "Yon Pig is an unhappy beast."

"That he is, Miss, and always was."

Lark took a step closer to the pony. He was, she thought, like one of the he-goats on the prod, anxious and angry. Once one of them had bitten her arm, a deep bite that left a circle of tooth marks that never completely faded. Brye had threatened to slaughter the billy on the spot, but Lark had spotted the nasty bit of blackstone embedded in his forefoot. When she had soothed him into letting her pull it out, he gave them no more trouble. That billy was devoted to Lark from that day forward. She could do anything with him she wanted to. Whenever she saw the scar on her arm, she reminded herself to look carefully at her animals. She didn't believe an animal could be evil by nature. Beasts behaved as they did with cause.

"Herbert, who rides Pig?"

"Rosellen, mostly."

"Is she such a fine rider, then?"

"I don't know about that. She rides him bareback, off to the market or out to the Ruins on her off day."

Lark came close to Pig again. The saddle seemed to sit oddly upon the fat pony's broad back. "Herbert," Lark ventured, "maybe he's better-tempered without the saddle."

Herbert shrugged. "Don't matter, Miss. You're supposed to be trying the saddle. Can't ride a winged horse without it." He glanced over his shoulder. "We should hurry."

"Let's try it once, Herbert. Take the saddle off, and let's see if he's happier."

It took a few moments, but Herbert managed to get the saddle off without being bitten. Lark waited at a safe distance, on Herbert's insistence, but when the saddle lay on the ground, its cinches and breast strap sprawled around it, she asked for the reins.

It took some persuading, but at last Herbert collected both reins in his hand, and held them out to her. He said doubtfully, "Careful of them teeth, now."

Lark took the reins, and stood facing Pig. He had stopped tossing his nose and shifting his feet. Bramble, too, relaxed. Her ears came up, and though she stayed close to Lark, pressing against her thigh, her feathery tail began to wave again. "The saddle hurt him, Herbert."

"Could be," Herbert allowed grudgingly. "Guess he's too fat for it."

"He needs exercise."

"No one has time for a bad-tempered pony, Miss. Winged horses to think of."

Lark sidestepped, and approached Pig at the point of his shoulder. She tightened the reins as she moved, keeping a close watch. His pink lips stayed closed as she pulled his head gently to her. His chin dropped into her hand, and she stood a moment, letting him sniff her palm.

"Poor old Pig," she said. "Silly old Piglet. Bad saddle, wasn't it? But it's gone now. Just you and me, Piglet, you and me and Bramble. We'll have a little jaunt, shall we?" She ran her hand up his withers and scratched, where she knew the goats liked to be scratched. His withers came only to her shoulders, and a moment later, she shinnied herself up on his back. She sat still, stroking his thick neck, hoping he wouldn't choose to throw her right back off.

The pony quivered, but otherwise stood still. Lark let the rein out, bit by bit, until his head lifted. She said softly, "Let's go, Piglet. Let's walk."

It was only the dry paddock, and it was only a fat pony with a back like an enormous roll of broomstraw, but Lark was glad to feel a horse beneath her once again. She wasn't aware of guiding the pony, or even of Herbert standing guard in the center of the paddock, but it felt lovely. Pig lumbered more than he walked, but she didn't care. It simply felt right, the warmth of horseflesh beneath her thighs, the coarse mane under her palms. She didn't bother with the reins, letting them fall loosely from her hands. She didn't think about how she let Pig know what she wanted him to do, but it happened, just the same. It had been like that with Char, and the memory brought nostalgic tears to her eyes.

"What in Kalla's name are you doing?"

Lark startled, and twisted on Pig's back to look at the entrance to the paddock. She expected Mistress Strong, was ready for her irritation at finding Lark riding bareback. Instead, she saw Petra Sweet, her hands on her hips, her head raised high. Herbert stood uncertainly, the saddle in his hands, its cinches trailing in the dirt. Bramble, pacing beside Pig just where Lark's ankle hung down over his wide girth, whirled, and made a noise in her throat.

Lark took a deep breath, and lifted the reins, whispering, "Stop now, Pig."

The pony stopped. Lark lifted her right leg over his withers, and slid to the ground. As she faced Petra, she brushed at the seat of her riding skirt, sure it was covered with brown and white pony hair. "I—I was told to ride P—the pony," she said.

"With," Petra drawled, her voice dropping in disgust, "a *saddle*, Goat-girl. Not bareback like some Uplands peasant."

Lark lifted her chin, and said sharply, "I *am* an Uplands peasant, and the saddle doesn't fit poor Pig. I couldn't magick it, so I did what I could."

"Magick it? What are you, some kind of witchwoman?" Petra laughed. "Better not let the horsemistresses hear you talk like that. No one holds with smallmagics here."

Herbert cleared his throat, and came up to Lark to take Pig's reins. "Exercise was good for him, Miss," he said quietly, his back to Petra. "I'll look for a better saddle, shall I?"

In a clear and carrying voice, Lark said, "Aye, Herbert, I thank you. I'll try to work some of that fat off him."

"It's perfect," Petra said. "The Pig and the peasant."

Lark turned on her heel, and set out across the paddock for the stables. Bramble trotted beside her, her silky head brushing her arm, her tail waving. Petra called something, but Lark pretended not to hear. Her snappy tongue had already gotten the best of her. There was no need to make things worse.

PHILIPPA'S reduced flight was a somber group. They adjusted their patterns to cover for the loss of Prince and Geraldine, but there was little joy in their flying. It would return, Philippa hoped, as time healed their sorrow and shock. For the moment, as she drilled Graces, her heart, too, was heavy. She had dreamed, the night before, of Alana Rose, seeing her once again spinning out of control, her Ocmarin filly screaming as she fell, Alana's terror silent and horrible. Philippa had been the flight leader. It fell to her to go to them first, to come upon Alana's limp and broken body, to see her filly's mangled legs. She had to order someone to bring a knife so that she could put an end to Summer Rose's suffering. She thought her nightmares of the raid on the South Tower had been vanquished years before. Some memories, she supposed, never die.

Philippa signaled, and the flyers reformed Open Columns. Alana's loss had at least been honorable, a death in the service of the Duke, a sacrifice made to preserve the Duchy and its winged horses. And now? William threatened to poison it all, to tarnish the honor and the reputation of the bloodlines, and Philippa didn't understand why.

William of Oc had been a dark presence throughout her life, it seemed, since she was sixteen years old. The conflict had begun then. It had been a confusing time for her, when she didn't understand his resentment of her closeness to his father, when she was wounded, as only a young girl can be, by his rejection of her. Frederick had erased all her pain and confusion by bonding her to Winter Sunset, but now, as Frederick grew weaker, William grew stronger. He was up to something, but she couldn't guess what it was. She hoped the Council of Lords could rein him in, if necessary.

She signaled to Elizabeth to lead the flight in. Sunny hovered at Quarters while she watched them land, experienced riders all, skilled horses soaring down over the treetops to land nimbly in the soft grass. The midafternoon sun glowed on the whitewashed stables, the tiled roofs of the Domicile and the Hall, the beech trees turning autumn gold along the lanes.

On an impulse, Philippa laid the rein on Sunny's neck and shifted her weight. The mare, freed from Quarters, surged to her right, her wings driving downward with a joyous burst of energy. Skeptic though Philippa was, such a moment was full of magic, Kalla's magic, that needed no fetish nor icon nor spell nor potion. In such a moment, she and Sunny owned the sky.

An hour, Philippa thought. She would give herself, and Sunny, an hour away, to fly above the hills. For an hour she would not think about Prince, worry about Margareth, fret over her difficulties with her colleagues, or about Larkyn Hamley and her crossbred colt. She loosened Sunny's rein, and gave herself up to the perfect accord between bondmates.

Sunny wheeled to the west, her wing muscles swelling beneath Philippa's thighs, her mane streaming back over Philippa's gloved hands. At this moment, Philippa felt as she had when she was a student, with no care except the mastery of the Airs, the strength of her mount, the future before her as rich a landscape as the one that swept beneath her now.

They flew over newly mown fields, above work crews harvesting their crops of fruit and grain, above twisting lanes marked out by leaves of flame. Philippa's saddle felt as much a part of her as her own boots, and the wind in her face was as sweet as perfume.

For fifteen minutes Sunny winged to the west, and then to the north. To the east, between their flight path and Osham, lay the Ducal Palace. As Philippa glanced over her right shoulder, she saw two flying horses lift from its emerald paddocks and bank toward the White City. Their horsemistresses were slender specks of black against the slanting rays of the sun. Couriers, perhaps. She had loved flying for Duke Frederick, working for the betterment of the Duchy. How smug her brother Meredith had been, believing he had succeeded in strengthening the family's position! Frederick had trusted her with the most confidential messages and tasks. It had driven Meredith mad when Philippa would tell him nothing, and refused to support his schemes. The rift between Philippa and her brother had grown so wide she doubted it could ever be bridged.

Philippa brought Sunny around to the left, to make a wide arc back toward the Academy. She glanced down once more, and recognized the broad, low outlines of Fleckham House, William's private home. To think that she might be dwelling there even now as William's wife, chained to the ground, locked into a role she must surely have come to hate! The thought gave her a spasm of sympathy for the poor lady who lived that life, and fresh joy in her own freedom.

She saw that the estate had expanded since her last visit, with an extra stable added on its western border, shielded from the house and the road by a grove of beech trees. A small band of wingless horses cropped grass in a long, fenced pasture. Philippa wondered who rode them. She had never seen William ride anything but his speedy brown gelding, and it was said that Lady Constance lived in seclusion, rarely stirring out of doors.

What fools we are when we are young, she thought. And how easily hurt. William's laughter, when she had professed her desire to be his wife, had cut her to her soul, and Meredith's scorn had been salt in the wound. Twenty years had passed since that day, yet still she remembered William and Meredith speaking of her figure and her face as if she were an ox on the block.

Or a winged horse to be assessed for the bloodlines.

Sunny slowed as they neared the Academy grounds, and stilled her wings. As they dropped toward the return paddock, Philippa felt the weight of her responsibilities return, as if intensified by the pull of the land.

Sunny landed with a few running steps, and cantered easily across the grass, her wings floating beside her. Rosellen came out to greet them.

"Had a nice flight, Mistress Winter?" she asked.

"Yes, very nice, Rosellen." Philippa handed over Sunny's reins. Rosellen touched the mare's shoulder, and waited for her to fold her wings before she started toward the stables.

Philippa let herself out of the return paddock. Stripping off her gloves, she turned, and was startled to see the oxcart waiting in front of the Hall, the tall man just climbing down from its driving seat.

Philippa tucked the gloves into her belt as she crossed the courtyard. "Master Hamley," she said. She stepped around the ox, who stood flicking his tail against buzzing flies.

"Mistress Winter." Brye Hamley took off his hat and bowed to her, a very creditable gesture of courtesy. She had almost forgotten what an impressive figure he made. He wore country clothes, a collarless shirt of openweave linen and canvas trousers with a wide, much-worn belt of leather, but these simple garments seemed only to enhance the breadth of his shoulders, the depth of his chest, the ridged muscles of his thighs. His one concession to traveling garb, she noted, was a pair of worn but well-polished boots.

"I'm surprised to see you," Philippa said. "I hope nothing is amiss?"

"I've learned something," he said bluntly. "Thought you lot should know."

FIFTEEN

PHILIPPA raised her eyebrows. "This is not about your sister? I assure you, we are taking good care of her."

"I'll see her while I'm here."

Philippa nodded toward the Hall. "Come inside, Master Hamley. I will introduce you to the Headmistress."

"My ox?" he said.

"Ah." Philippa glanced over the oxen's broad back to the stables, where both Rosellen and Herbert stood in the doorway, goggling at the cart and the beast in its traces. Philippa beckoned, and Herbert came trotting across to her. "Herbert," she said. "This is Master Hamley, of Deeping Farm, the Uplands. He is Larkyn's eldest brother."

Herbert bobbed his head at Brye, and Brye nodded in return.

"Perhaps you could find a spot in the shade for his cart-ox," Philippa said. "And some water, and a bit of hay."

"Very good, Mistress," Herbert said. Brye Hamley deftly unhitched his animal, letting the yoke drop to the cobblestones, neatly coiling the traces over it. He attached a lead to the ox's halter and handed it to Herbert, who led the beast away.

"Now," Philippa said, with a gesture toward the Hall. "Come and tell me."

Brye waited until Philippa had shown him into Margareth's office and made introductions. Margareth looked as weary as if the hour were far gone, instead of only midafternoon, but she welcomed the Uplands farmer, and called for someone to bring refreshments. Their guest took the chair she offered him, lowering himself into it with caution, as if afraid his bulk might break it. Philippa watched this, bemused, rather charmed by his care.

"Took two calves to market," he said without preamble. "At

Mossyrock, in the hills. Small market. Farmers round about, village-folk from Clellum, a few merchants."

The maid came with a tray of cider and biscuits, and laid it on Margareth's desk. When she had gone, Brye set his hat on the floor beside his feet, and accepted a glass of cider. "Do go on, Master Hamley," Margareth said.

"A saddle was for sale in the market. Nice piece of work, stamped leather, brass fittings."

"Is that unusual?" Margareth asked.

"No horses in the Uplands," Brye answered. "Except for the mail cob. And such a saddle would never fit a draught horse, even if someone wanted to ride it."

"It wasn't a flying saddle, then," Philippa said.

"Didn't look like yours," was the answer. "Didn't have that high back on it, and there was no . . ." He tried to show his meaning with his big, work-hardened hands.

"Breast strap."

"Aye. And no notches for wings."

Philippa began to follow where his logic led. "And so, Master Hamley, you thought . . ."

Brye leaned forward, and the chair beneath him creaked. "Char had no saddle when we found her," he said.

"Char?" Margareth asked.

Philippa told her, "The mare that foaled Larkyn's colt."

"A strange name."

"Uplands word," Brye said, with a dismissive wave of his hand. "Smoke from the autumn fires, leaves and straw." Margareth nodded her understanding, and Brye continued. "Seemed strange. Last year a lost mare, and this year a saddle for sale in Mossyrock."

"An odd coincidence," Philippa murmured. Brye Hamley flashed her a skeptical look. She didn't know whether to be amused or offended. All the Hamleys, apparently, were a hardminded lot.

"Did you buy the saddle?" Margareth murmured.

"No need for such," the farmer answered. "The fellow was asking a deal of money, though why he'd expect a buyer in the Uplands I can't say. But I thought you should know."

"And what became of it?" Philippa asked.

"Still there when I left," he said. "Sold my calves early." He drained his glass of cider, picked up his hat from the floor, and stood. "I thank you for the drink, Mistress."

"Must you leave so soon?" Margareth asked.

"Harvest crews at the farm," he said. "But I'd like a blink at Lark before I go."

Philippa glanced at Margareth, who rose slowly, staring at Brye Hamley with an unreadable expression. "I believe she is in a tutoring session with Mistress Strong," she said. "But I will excuse her for the moment."

Brye said merely, "Good," which made Margareth's lips twitch.

Philippa went to the door to send word. When the maid had gone scurrying up the stairs, Philippa beckoned to Brye. "This way, Master Hamley, if you please. Larkyn will meet you in the reading room."

She was prepared to lead the way in silence, but as they mounted the stairs, Brye spoke. "Mistress Winter."

"Yes?" she answered over her shoulder.

"Is Lark doing well in her studies?"

"She is far behind the other girls in her class, but we expected that."

"Riding?"

"I believe she has begun with a pony we keep here. So that she can get used to a saddle, and learn some of the basics."

They had reached the reading room. Philippa opened the door, and found it empty. The curtains were drawn against the late-afternoon sun, and the room was pleasantly dim and cool. "Larkyn will be here presently," she said.

She stood aside. Brye walked to the middle of the room, and stood looking about him, turning his hat in his hands. "How's the colt?"

"Growing quickly," Philippa said. "Our winged horses mature early."

"What does the Master Breeder say about him?" The farmer lifted his eyes to hers. She saw no diffidence in him, no sense that he was out of his depth.

She answered bluntly. "Eduard thinks he's crossbred, as I do. He's too small for a Noble, and he has a Foundation's coloring. He's small, like an Ocmarin. He might be a throwback."

"Is that possible?"

"It has not happened for two centuries."

"Something's afoot, then."

Philippa drew a careful breath. "It could be. Or it could be an accident."

"No blame to our family."

"Of course we don't believe so, Master Hamley."

"And the Duke?"

At this Philippa paused again. Brye Hamley was too straight-forward and too intelligent a man to be deceived. These were difficult matters, though, issues of politics and power.

"You hesitate, Mistress Winter." He enunciated the words so clearly that the Uplands inflection dropped from his voice. The blue eyes, so vivid in Larkyn's face, were cool as forged steel in his.

Philippa pulled the door closed behind her. "Master Hamley, the colt's very existence is a problem. And I will not disguise from you that the Ducal Palace has taken an interest in him."

"Duke Frederick?"

"No. In truth, His Grace has not been well for some time."

"So they say. Lost his daughter, didn't he?"

Philippa pulled her gloves from her belt and pleated them between her fingers, avoiding those Hamley eyes. "He did," she said quietly. "She disappeared without a trace. The Council of Lords has had to take up a good many of his duties." She looked up. "It is Lord William who has been here to see the colt. Twice. He and the Master Breeder disagree about what should be done with him."

"But this doesn't affect Lark?"

Philippa made a slight gesture with the gloves. "If the colt is left intact, Larkyn will be taught how to work with a stallion. Eduard—the Master Breeder—thinks he should be gelded. Lord William disagrees."

"Is Lark upset by that?"

Philippa gave a short laugh. "On that account, Master Hamley, I think you may rest easy. Your sister seems unaffected by the dispute other than to protect her colt!"

The door opened, and Larkyn, her riding cap askew on her untidy hair, boiled into the room, and threw herself into her brother's arms with a glad cry. Her hat flew to the floor as Brye wrapped her in a huge embrace, and held her there for a long moment.

Philippa averted her gaze. Silently, she withdrew, and closed the door behind her.

"OH, Brye!" Lark breathed, disentangling herself from her brother's arms. She smiled up at him a bit mistily, moved by the scents of Deeping Farm that clung to him.

"You look well in your fine clothes," he said.

She smoothed her riding jacket. "It's called a habit," she said. "The riding coat and the divided skirt . . . and look at these wonderful boots."

"Aye. And your peaky cap, there."

Lark bent to pick it up from the floor. "It's a problem," she admitted. "My hair is hopeless. Everyone ties theirs into a riding knot, but mine won't go. I don't know what to do about it." And then she laughed. "But never mind that! How I've missed you! How is Nick, and Edmar? The cows? Do the goats miss Molly?"

Her brother laughed. "One question at a time, Lark! But all is well at home. Nick made the blackberry jelly, in your absence." He handed her a string-wrapped parcel. "And he sent some crooks, and a bit of cheese."

She unwrapped the present with delight, bringing out a wax-sealed jar of ruby jelly, a packet of the long, crisp cookies, and a thick triangle of yellow cheese wrapped in oiled cloth. "Oh, thank you, Brye. You would not believe how hungry I am! They serve such tiny meals. Now tell me, how does Nick get everything done?"

"Hired a girl," Brye said. "Peony. She comes in to milk and to cook for the crew."

Lark nodded. "I know Peony." She grinned, remembering the plump, pretty girl flashing her dimples at Nick. "She must be pleased."

Brye's eyes sparkled, though his face had settled into its usual grave lines. "Seems so."

"Are the bloodbeets in? Are you harvesting broomstraw yet?"

"Bloodbeets were early this year. We're cutting broomstraw now."

Lark, with the cheese and the jelly in her hands, stood still. "Now, Brye? Then how—why are you here? Should you not be at home?"

"I should," he agreed grimly. "But there was something I thought your Mistress Winter should know." He told her about the market at Mossyrock, and the saddle.

Lark felt a wave of unease. She had told no one, yet, that Lord William had been in the Uplands, had come to see Tup—and had behaved strangely. It was on her lips to tell Brye now, but she remembered that magicked quirt, and the threat to Deeping Farm . . . and she did not dare. She only said, "Char's saddle."

"Aye. It makes sense."

"The Master Breeder doesn't know where she came from even now," Lark said. "And they don't like the name I gave Tup. Or anything else I've done, for that matter!"

Brye eyed her closely. "Are you unhappy, Lark?"

She hesitated. "It's hard. I have to study things like history, and geography—Master Micklewhite knew so little. And there are lists and lists of names to memorize."

"The other girls?"

Lark looked away, afraid he would read the pain in her eyes. "They find me—different, I think." She thought of Hester. "But I have made a friend." She looked back at him, and smiled. "It will be all right. As soon as I start to ride!"

"You're not riding yet?"

She made a face. "Oh, I am to ride a great fat pony called Pig, so I can learn the saddle and the stirrups and the reins. Poor Pig hates it as much as I do!"

"Shall I speak to yon Headmistress for you?"

"Nay, Brye, thanks just the same. I have to handle this myself."

AN hour later, a knock sounded on Margareth's door. Philippa and Margareth had been puzzling over Brye Hamley's news, debating what was to be done about it. At Margareth's nod, Philippa rose and went to the door, to find Larkyn standing without.

She had removed her flying cap, and was struggling to scrape back her unruly hair. She gave it up, letting the strands fall over her shoulders, and looked from Philippa to the Headmistress. "Do you know if the saddle was Char's?"

"Do come in, Larkyn," Margareth said in a wry tone.

"A little more formality with the Headmistress, please,"

Philippa said as Larkyn stepped past her. The girl's blue eyes rose to hers. There was something of her brother's wisdom in them, Philippa thought.

"We don't know anything yet," Margareth said.

"But someone needs to find the saddle, don't they? Won't that tell us Tup's breeding?"

"Larkyn," Philippa warned. "Speak to the Headmistress in a respectful tone."

"But, Mistress Winter," Larkyn blurted. "If we wait—it could be gone!"

"We know that. But we can't simply rush off to the Uplands without consideration."

"I'll go!" Larkyn cried.

"And fall further behind your class? Don't be foolish!" Philippa's voice sounded harsher than she had intended. Still, she spoke the truth. Larkyn had a lot of ground to make up.

Margareth's tone was kinder. "Larkyn," she said quietly. "This may tell us something of Tup's background, or it may not. But you can't take a winged colt into an Uplands village, and you know you can't leave him for a journey of two days. We will handle this, Mistress Winter, the Master Breeder, and I."

Margareth stood up, a gesture of dismissal. "Return to your studies now, Larkyn. You must leave this to us."

Philippa watched as the little chin jutted, and telltale spots of red flamed in the girl's cheeks. Margareth, however, was not an easy person to defy. Larkyn departed moments later, her boots clicking a resentful rhythm on the tiles.

When the door had closed behind her, Philippa said, "I suppose we must tell Eduard."

Margareth nodded. "Yes. I think he will want to see that saddle."

"Larkyn is right, though. It could be gone."

"You will have to fly to the Uplands, Philippa. If we send someone else . . ."

"Indeed. Word will get out. But Irina will not be pleased with me."

Margareth's chuckle was weary. "That can't be helped. Leave her to me."

"This time," Philippa said with resignation, "I think I had best do that. I'll go in the morning, then." She moved to the door, but paused with her hand on the latch. She looked over her shoulder at Margareth. "Kalla's heels, where *is* Mossyrock? I've never heard of the place."

SIXTEEN

THE next morning dawned bright and clear, the perfect day for a long flight. Philippa rolled the map she had found in the library, and tied it behind her saddle with the packet Matron had prepared for her. She led Sunny out to the flight paddock early, before the rest of the Academy had left the Hall. Sunny danced with pleasure in the morning, the sunshine, the freedom of a solitary launch, but Philippa wished she could have chosen a different day. Today the yearlings were to fly.

One by one, the young horses' wingclips would be removed, and their mistresses would lead them to the flight paddock, and then remove their halter leads. Philippa knew well the anxiety the girls would feel as they released the colts and fillies to the monitors. It was no small thing, this first attempt at flight. There was reason for the girls to be anxious. Though the instructors would keep a close eye on the young horses, and the monitor horses would set careful examples, it was a great thing—exciting and terrifying—to fly for the first time.

Philippa loved seeing the colts and fillies shake their wings to full length, flutter them experimentally, flick their ears in wonder at their bondmates. She thought that watching your colt fly for the first time must be like watching a beloved child take its first steps, a mix of pride and anxiety and even regret. The colts would never again be the dependent creatures they had been. The oc-hounds who had kept them company since their foalings would part from them, one by one. The colts could separate from their bondmates for a day or two, even three if necessary. The first flight was their first taste of freedom and power.

Sunny didn't share Philippa's mixed feelings. She stretched her neck eagerly, her wings quivering joyously as she banked to the west, toward the mountains. Philippa dropped one gloved hand lightly on her neck, remembering Sunny's first flight.

Sunny had been a quiet filly, her movements restrained, her temper even. But on that day, when her monitor cantered down the length of the flight paddock, Sunny had dashed eagerly behind her. Her wings had stretched in perfect imitation, beginning to beat in instinctive rhythm with the older horse, and she rose from the flight paddock like a young bird, swerving slightly, dipping, then ascending as she found her balance, discovered the power of the wind above and below her wings, the incredible strength of the wing muscles that ridged across her chest.

Philippa had stood below, hardly breathing, hugging her elbows. It seemed an hour before Sunny returned, though it was really no more than a few minutes. Yearlings began with short flights, increasing the distance each time they flew, gradually adding a flying saddle, then sand weights, strengthening their wings, building their endurance.

Philippa glanced over her shoulder. She could see the gambrel roofs of the Academy stables, the morning sun brilliant in the east. She squinted against its brightness, and thought perhaps she could just make out the flyers rising into the air. Hester Beeth's Golden Morning would be first, the most reliable of all the yearlings. Though she was a Foundation filly, she reminded Philippa of Winter Sunset at that age, steady and quiet, strong, confident. After Golden Morning would come Little Duchess, a Noble filly; then another Foundation, Dark Lad; the Ocmarins Sweet Spring and Sea Girl; and last, Isobel Burleigh's Sky Heart, a rambunctious Noble stallion. Eduard expected Sky Heart to throw great colts one day, but when the day came for the girls to fly, Isobel would have her hands full.

Philippa turned her face forward, to where the sunburned hills of the Uplands marked her destination. Perhaps, today, she would find out something that would help them determine the future of Larkyn's colt.

"SHE should have waited for me." It was Eduard Crisp's grating voice.

Lark had just lifted a forkful of soiled straw from the floor of Tup's stall. She stopped where she was, the pitchfork suspended over the wheelbarrow. Master Crisp was coming down the aisle with the Headmistress, and Lark knew he was talking about Mistress Winter and the discovery of a saddle in the Uplands.

Hastily, she put down the pitchfork and backed away from the gate. Mistress Morgan said, "And you can fly, now, can you, Eduard?" Lark's eyebrows lifted at the edge in the Headmistress's tone.

"No need for sarcasm, Margareth," Master Crisp responded. "I'm weary of all this."

They were coming closer. Lark grabbed the currycomb and bent behind her colt as if busy with a tangle in his tail.

"Tracing the colt's lineage has been impossible," Mistress Morgan said. "But blame for that can't be laid at my door, or Philippa's. Or yours. We felt haste was essential, because the saddle could be sold and gone by now."

"Even if she finds it, it may not mean anything."

Lark heard the exasperation in Margareth Morgan's tone. "Master Hamley felt it was unusual enough that he took time away from harvest to come all this way. In his oxcart."

"Kalla's teeth, he's a farmer! What does he know of what is unusual or not?"

"I think, Eduard," Margareth responded stiffly, "that if you do not open your mind, we may never know the colt's parentage."

Lark straightened, and faced the two of them across Tup's back. The Headmistress's eyebrows rose at the sight of her. "Larkyn. I thought you were having a riding lesson."

"Yes, Headmistress. In half an hour." Lark was on the point of bobbing a curtsy, but she caught herself just in time. Mistress Strong, like Mistress Cloud, had been very clear that horsemistresses never curtsied. And she had learned, since coming to the Academy, that they never wore their riding caps indoors, nor did they ever—no matter how dirty the task—wear aprons. Aprons were, Petra had told her condescendingly, for servants.

"Ah." Mistress Morgan let herself into the stall, and crossed to Tup. She ran her hand down his hind leg, and he obligingly lifted his foot as she reached his fetlock. She traced the shape of his hoof, and set it back in the straw. "You see that, Eduard?" she said.

"You mean, the hoof?"

"I do." With a little exhalation of breath, as if bending had pained her, the Headmistress straightened her back. "That is a Foundation foot, though small," she said decidedly. "And a Noble croup, with the arching tail. And of course, there's his color."

"Only an Ocmarin would be so small at nine months," Crisp growled.

"Ten," Lark said.

"Perhaps you have the day wrong, Miss," the Master Breeder said.

"I do not," she said firmly. " 'Twas just after Erdlin. Four months before the goat kids were born, or the calves. Ten months last week."

Margareth Morgan's gray eyes twinkled at Lark across the colt's back. "Did you see the yearlings fly this morning?" she asked.

Lark turned her back on Master Crisp, and threw her arms around Tup's neck. "Oh, Headmistress!" she cried. "It was—it was wonderful and terrible, all at once! I couldn't believe Hester was so calm. Anabel, and Beryl, and Grace and the others . . . I would be just as nervous as they were, I'm sure! But the horses were marvelous, weren't they, and none fell, not even on landing, and every horse followed its monitor—I'm so glad I was there!"

The Headmistress smiled, a web of wrinkles spreading across her face. "I watched from my window," she said. "I never miss it." She patted Tup, and turned to the Master Breeder. "Eduard. Have you spoken with Frederick about this colt?"

His heavy features drooped with real sadness as he answered. "His Grace has taken to his bed, Margareth. They're saying he may die."

"You spoke to William, then."

"I tried. He's adamant."

"He wants Tup to breed?" Lark asked.

"As if he understood the bloodlines," Crisp muttered.

"Eduard! Careful." The Headmistress glanced about anxiously, but there was no one to hear. The second- and third-level flights were in the paddocks, the yearlings restored to their pasture. Lark waited, hoping to understand something more, but the Headmistress and the Master Breeder only gazed at each other in a heavy silence.

"Well," the Headmistress said after a moment. She let herself out through the gate, and gestured to Master Crisp to follow her out of the stables. "Whether we geld him or not, it's time to give the colt a proper name. Perhaps it would be best . . ." Her voice dropped as they walked away, so that Lark could barely hear. "Perhaps you should simply declare the colt a throwback, and leave it at that."

"Can't do that if Lord William wants to breed him," the Master Breeder said. "We'll have to choose a name to fit the bloodlines."

Mistress Morgan made some response, but Lark couldn't hear what it was. She laid her cheek against Tup's neck. "It doesn't matter," she whispered. "They can call you whatever they like. You're still my Tup."

PIG plodded across the dry paddock behind Herbert. True to his word, Herbert had found a saddle that fitted the pony better. It was not a flying saddle, but a clumsy, elaborate thing with a broad cantle, a thick flat-topped pommel, rings and ties everywhere, and a double cinch. The cinches stretched to their maximum to reach around poor Pig's girth, and the stirrups were of hammered iron. Lark eyed the whole thing with distaste.

"Looks a misery to sit in."

Herbert said, "I wouldn't know. Not a rider, meself."

As Lark came closer, Pig laid his ears back again. It made him look even more porcine, with his eyes too small and his haunches so swollen. Lark sighed, and took the rein. "Aye, Piglet," she said. "Neither one of us is happy about this."

"Could wait for Mistress Strong," Herbert offered.

"That won't improve the saddle."

Bramble came racing around the side of the stables to leap the pole fence in a flowing streak of silver. Lark was glad to see her. The oc-hound came close, pressing her shoulder against Lark's hip, curling her lip and growling over Pig's flattened ears.

The pony rolled his eyes, but his ears released. He stood stiffly, legs splayed. The cinch cut into his flesh, creating piebald rolls on either side.

"Teeth," Herbert muttered.

"Aye," Lark said. She kept an eye on Pig's muzzle as she approached, shortening the rein as she moved closer. Bramble came around to her left, and Pig's eye shifted to the dog. Swiftly, Lark seized a handful of mane. She didn't bother with the stirrup, but swung herself up and over until she perched on the pony's wide back.

It was like straddling a rock. The leather was rigid beneath her. She found the stirrups with her boots, but they, too, were hard. When she moved her legs, the leathers creaked.

"Well, here's your instructor," Herbert said dourly. "Luck to you!"

Lark looked up to see Irina Strong's broad figure just coming through the gate. Her pale hair was neatly smoothed under her cap, and her habit was, of course, immaculate. Lark felt her cheeks warm as she looked down at herself. Her tabard was creased, her belt askew from the leap upon Pig's back. And her hair, of course—as always—was more out of its clasp than in.

At least she was in the saddle. She lifted Pig's reins, and whispered, "Piglet. Help me here, will you?"

Pig rattled his bridle with an irritated shake of his head. Bramble's lip curled again, but Lark murmured quickly, "It's all right, Bramble. Poor old Pig can't help it."

"Well, Larkyn," Mistress Strong said as she strode forward. The pony took a step backward, making Lark clutch at the pommel. Mistress Strong stopped where she was, and eyed the fat pony and his off-balance rider with an expression full of doubt. "Well. Let's see if we can teach you to ride."

PHILIPPA flew north and west for two hours, until she felt Sunny should have a rest. She scanned the hills beneath her for a meadow where the mare could safely descend. She found a long, narrow clearing, and was glad to find, when Sunny had cantered to a stop, that a little blue stream ran at one end. Already the air seemed cooler here, the breeze tinged with the smells of burning straw and browning leaves. Philippa let Sunny drink her fill and then graze a little while she unrolled the map and spread it on a black boulder. She traced the path with one gloved finger. Another hour's flying, she guessed, would bring her to Mossyrock. A glance at the sun, quartering from the east, told her that she would arrive before midday.

Philippa ate the cheese and biscuits in Matron's packet while Sunny ambled about grazing, her tail switching at flies. The sight of her red coat gleaming in the sun, her delicately flared nostrils, her intelligent eyes, moved Philippa, even after the eighteen years of their bonding. She called her close, and then leaned against her shoulder, warmed by the autumn sun, comforted by the sweet smell of horseflesh. "Oh, Sunny," she murmured. "My faithful girl. Wouldn't it be nice to simply fly away from everything?" Sunny blew a noisy breath, and tossed her head, making Philippa chuckle. "No, you're right," she said. "Duty first. And always."

Soon they were in the air again, and within the hour, the blackstone butte given by the map as a landmark came into view, dividing the mountain valley into two. The village of Clellum was to the north, beyond a narrow, untilled pasture. To the south of the butte was the hamlet of Mossyrock.

It was tiny, perhaps twenty houses flanked by cottage gardens and wooden byres. The lane leading to it would surely accommodate only one cart at a time, and the market Brye Hamley had spoken of must have been small indeed. She guided Sunny in a circle above the peaked roofs. Just to the east of the village was a space of packed dirt, shaded by cottonwoods and aspen. The market square, Philippa guessed, empty now, and broad enough for Sunny to come to ground.

She made another circle, and then came down at a steep angle beneath the cliff. Sunny cantered a few strides, trotted, and came to a stop at the edge of the houses. By the time Philippa had dismounted and pulled off her gloves, a little troop of children had already raced out of their houses, and stood staring at the winged horse with eyes wide in dirty faces. As Sunny folded her wings, rib by rib, they gaped at her.

Philippa eyed them, too, and decided that a tall boy in the back, wearing a broad-brimmed straw hat very like Brye Hamley's, must be the eldest. "Will you take me to your prefect?" she asked him.

He only stared at her, his mouth hanging open. A smaller boy stepped in front of him. "I will, Mistress," he said. "If you'll let me pet your horse."

A repressive answer sprang to Philippa's lips, but she pressed them tight and didn't speak it. For a moment she looked down at the boy. He had dark, curling hair and a freckled face that reminded her of Larkyn, and he was too young to be a problem for a winged horse. A chuckle found its way up her throat, surprising her. She pressed that back, too. "The prefect first, please," she said crisply. "And you may hold Sunny's reins while I speak with him."

The boy grinned, and spun about to trot down the narrow lane between the houses.

Philippa followed, with Sunny pacing beside her. The children trailed after like a gaggle of goslings, chattering to each other, calling out to their mothers as they passed their homes. By the time Philippa stood before a narrow, two-story dwelling with a sign proclaiming the prefect's residence on its door, most of the village seemed to be gathered in the lane, watching her.

As she handed Sunny's reins to the boy, admonishing him to stand exactly where he was, the door opened, and a wizened man with bent shoulders and sparse white hair appeared on the doorstep. Philippa murmured a command to Sunny, tucked her quirt under her arm, and crossed the meager bit of grass between the lane and the house.

The old man bowed from the waist. Philippa nodded to him. "Good day. Are you the prefect here?"

"Aye, aye, Mistress," he said. "I am he. What an honor, to see someone in the Duke's colors here. A horsemistress! Welcome to Mossyrock!"

"You had a market here recently," Philippa said without delay.

"Aye, aye," he answered her. He negotiated the two steps from his door to the grass with care. He looked as fragile as if he might blow away in a puff of dust. His eyes were rheumy and vague, and she wondered if he could see much. "We had a market last week. Lively, it was. Village full of people." He peered up at her through his filmy eyes. "I don't believe we've ever had a horsemistress here before. Would you like some refreshment? Come in, sit you down! Dickon, tell your mother to bring some cider for the horsemistress!"

Dickon, holding Sunny's reins, looked as if he would burst into tears at being robbed of his special role. Philippa hastily said, "No, no, thank you, Prefect. Don't send for anything. What I need is information."

The prefect indicated his cramped dwelling. "Would you like to come in?"

"No." Philippa looked around at the people watching and listening. "There was a saddle," she said in a carrying voice, doubting that this aged and fragile man would be of much help. "A saddle for sale in the market. The Duke would like to know what became of it."

The prefect looked confused. "Saddle?" he said.

Philippa made a gesture that included all the villagers. "Did any of you see this saddle? Do you know who was selling it?"

The villagers, mostly women and girls, murmured together, shaking their heads. The children whispered. Only young Dickon seemed to have an idea. He said, "Horsemistress! The man with the saddle came from another village, up the mountain. He let me touch it, and I asked him where it came from."

Philippa looked down at the boy. He stood holding Sunny's reins carefully, his hand raised to shoulder level.

"What village?" Philippa asked.

Dickon's chest swelled with importance. "It came from Clellum," he said. "Up the mountain." He pointed north, beyond the blackstone butte.

"Ah. Is it far?"

"You just have to ride around the butte, there, Mistress," the prefect quavered.

"But the saddle's not there," Dickon piped. "Not anymore."

Philippa stiffened. "It's not? How do you know?"

"A man bought it." Dickon's grin creased his grimy cheeks. "I had a blink at him."

"What man?" Philippa's voice sharpened, and the boy's grin faded. "Do you know his name?"

Dickon shook his head. "No, Mistress. But he wore the same colors you do, black and silver." He considered, scratching his scalp with a dirty forefinger. "He had a horse, too, a lovely fine brown horse. It didn't have no wings, though. Oh, and he wore a—" He shook his head, not finding the word, and instead sketched a gesture over his scrawny chest. "Lovely rich, it was, sewn all over with blue and green and red. Never saw such in the Uplands."

"I slid around like a fish on a rock!" Lark cried to Hester. She tossed her gloves and cap on her cot, and turned her palms up in despair. "Mistress Strong thinks I'm hopeless!" She collapsed onto her cot with a groan of pain.

Hester chuckled. "A bit sore, are we?" she asked.

"My bones ache! It makes no sense. I was never sore when I rode Char. Of course, I never fell off her, either."

"It's the saddle," Hester said with a grimace. "You just have to get used to it."

"It's so hard! It's like it's made of wood."

"Bits of it *are* wood, I'm afraid. Mistress Strong will make you learn all the parts."

Lark moaned, rubbing her thighs. "I wish she would just let me ride bareback. It's so much easier! Mistress Strong says it's all in the thighs, but mine slip on the saddle skirts and the stirrups fly out at all angles! It was nicer when I rode Char, when I could feel her, muscle and bone and hide."

Hester sat down next to her, shaking her head. "It wouldn't be easier for me."

"Really? But it's just—it just seems natural. The balance, the—"

"Natural?" Petra Sweet's drawl interrupted her. "Maybe for a goat-girl."

Lark sat up, and found her sponsor standing at the foot of her bed, arms akimbo, lip curled. "Stop calling me that!" Lark snapped.

Petra's nostrils flared. "Listen to me, Hamley. Riding bareback could get you killed."

"What do you mean?"

Petra gave a humorless laugh. "You're going to *fly*, you little fool. You need something to hold on to! You want to come crashing down from fifty rods above the ground?"

"I'm more likely to fall out of a saddle," Lark muttered. "As I did this very afternoon!"

"Listen, Hamley," Petra persisted. "If you fall off that little crossbreed and die, the whole Academy will look bad."

Lark leapt to her feet, sore bottom forgotten. "I would never fall off Tup!" she cried.

"Take it easy," Hester murmured. "You're just giving her what she wants."

Lark turned her back to Petra, and drew a slow breath, trying to cool her flare of anger. Petra hissed at Hester, "You should stop interfering. She needs to learn."

"She's doing fine," Hester said lightly. "None of the rest of us could ride Pig without getting bitten or kicked."

"Pig!" Petra laughed. "I suppose flying her little Crybaby is going to be just like riding that fat piebald pony!"

At that, Lark whirled, her cheeks ablaze. Hester took a quick step forward, putting herself neatly between Lark and Petra.

Petra snapped, "And by Kalla's tail, Hamley, do *something* about that hair!"

Lark put a hand to her head. As usual, her mass of unruly hair was falling about her cheeks and over her neck. Petra was right about that. Her hair would not stay in its knot no matter what she tried.

"No need to worry, Sweet," Hester said smoothly. Lark glanced at her in surprise, hearing how she deliberately exaggerated her patrician accent. She waved one hand, a gesture somehow both casual and elegant. "My mamá is coming tomorrow with the carriage, to take Hamley shopping."

Envy stiffened Petra's features. "Lady Beeth?"

Hester said lightly, "Oh, yes. I told my mamá we simply *must* find a decent hairclip for my friend." She gave the last word the tiniest, most subtle inflection.

Petra's face reddened, and she turned swiftly away. Lark watched her stalk away to her own cot, and a feeling of sympathy almost drowned her temper.

Hester whispered, "I'd better send a message to Mamá. I haven't actually asked her yet."

"Will she mind?" Lark whispered back.

Hester grinned. "Oh, no. Mamá loves to shop. And we'll ask Anabel, too. We'll make a day of it!"

SEVENTEEN

STARS pricked the black sky as Sunny stilled her wings to glide down onto the broad lawns of Fleckham House. It had been a long flight from the Uplands village, and the heat of the day had given way to a chill clear night. Philippa felt sunburned and irritable. She would have much preferred to go home, to relax in the reading room with her boots off and her feet up. But she was angry. She wanted to speak directly to William, and to do it while the fire of her temper still burned hot and clean.

The Fleckham grounds appeared exactly as they had when she was young, the new stables hidden from the house by the grove of beeches. As a girl, Philippa had often visited Fleckham House for riding or dancing parties with William and Pamella and the gentle, bookish Francis. In those days, the windows had blazed with light far into the evenings, and Frederick had always been present, smiling at the young people.

Though Duke Frederick had inherited his title before Philippa was thirteen, he had always found a few moments to spend with her, to lend her a book he found interesting, to ask her opinion about a point of politics. Her own mother had tried to persuade her from all things intellectual. Meredith had called her pretentious. Only Frederick encouraged her, and had proved it by bonding her to Winter Sunset, foaled in his own stables.

Philippa led Sunny across the white-gravel courtyard beneath dim, shuttered windows. She realized, with a little shock, that she was almost as old now as Frederick had been then.

A stable-man came out to apologize for having no stable-girl. Philippa had to lead Sunny to a stall herself, slip off her saddle, give her a rubdown. The stable-man had left a bucket of water and a measure of grain waiting outside the stall. Philippa paused a moment, watching Sunny nibble her feed. Then, with a conscious straightening of her back, firming her resolve, she let herself out of the stall, and turned toward the house.

A steward bowed her through the doors and into the wide foyer. Fleckham had always been an open, generous house, brilliant with lamplight, its fine old furniture and oaken floors polished till they shone. It seemed rather dismal to her now. Only one lamp glowed in the entrance, and every door leading off the foyer was closed.

"Horsemistress," the steward said. "I'm afraid Lady Constance is not receiving visitors."

"I've come to see Lord William."

"I see." He held out his hand for her riding coat and cap. "Fortunately, his Lordship is here this evening. I'll call him for you."

Philippa nodded her thanks, and stood alone in the center of the foyer as the steward laid her things on a side table and then made a dignified progress up the stairs. She turned in a circle, feeling the loneliness, the lifelessness, of Fleckham. She must visit Frederick again as soon as possible. Perhaps she could persuade him to come back here for a time, where he had spent happy years before his succession.

"Ah. Philippa. Such an honor."

She faced the staircase, and saw William standing several steps above the foyer. He was dressed, much as the ragamuffin Dickon had said, in black and silver, and an elaborate vest. His white-blond hair gleamed silver in the lamplight. "My lord," Philippa said. She inclined her head, and saw the irritated look that passed over his face.

"If you've come to call on Constance, I'm sorry to tell you that—"

Philippa made an impatient gesture. "William, I barely know your lady wife. I've come to see you."

His smile was icy. "Indeed," he said. "I thought perhaps my steward had misunderstood. You have business with me?" He descended the last few stairs, and led the way into the study, opening the double doors and then closing them when Philippa had passed through. There was no fire, and the oil lamp was dark. William struck a match and bent over a candelabra. The candlelight softened the gloom a bit. William rested one elbow on the mantelpiece, his back to the cold fireplace, and waved his other hand languidly at a chair. "Would you care to sit down?"

"No, thank you." Philippa gazed at him, feeling utterly exhausted, fed up with postures and pretense. She saw lines around his mouth and eyes, lines she had never noticed before. She supposed she must have them, too. "William. What do you know about the little black that you haven't told Eduard?"

Though he didn't move, she sensed the stiffening in his lean body. The gelid silence was broken only by the ticking of the great clock in the foyer.

"My dear Philippa," William finally said, lifting his arm from the mantel, tugging his vest down with both hands. "You presume upon old acquaintance, and I understand that, so I will try not to take offense at your tone."

"I'm too tired for games, William," she snapped. "Save us both some time. I know you went to Mossyrock, and I know you bought the saddle. What do you know about it? Who had it, and how did they get it?"

His voice went very soft. "Do you not think," he said, "that if I thought you needed to know, I would have told you?"

"Why did you go to the Uplands?"

His lips curled slightly. "Every district of Oc is important to us," he said.

Philippa snorted, and yanked her gloves out of her belt so she could pleat them with her fingers. She paced, left and then right, pulling at the gloves. "I'm no longer the naive girl you laughed out of this house twenty years ago, William," she said. "You're up to something, and knowing you, it's something nasty."

His eyes narrowed. "Careful, Philippa."

"Careful be damned," she said evenly. "Why should you travel all the way to an Uplands village you probably never heard of before this?"

He left the fireplace, and crossed the room to stand very close to her. He leaned forward, so that she could feel his breath on her face. Odd, that when she was young, she had wanted just such proximity. Now it turned her stomach.

"Philippa," William said softly. "Do not cross me. It's not wise."

She took a step back, and glared at him. "You cannot intimidate me as you do so many others, William. You have no leverage."

"Oh, but I do," he said. He smiled, and folded his arms across his chest. "The girl who came to the Academy with the little black—what's her name? Larkyn, I believe. Ah, yes, Larkyn Hamley. Whose brothers own a fine farm in the Uplands . . . a family farm. A shame to lose it after so many years."

"You wouldn't dare." Philippa put her hands on her hips. "Frederick would not allow it."

"My lord father is too ill to interfere."

"The Council, then. They will protect the family of a flyer."

"The brat's unworthy of riding a winged horse," he snapped back at her.

"I don't agree, but it doesn't matter. She is bonded."

William sneered at her. "She has a peasant's accent and a laborer's manner."

"And a way with horses you'll never understand!"

William's color rose in his pale skin so that even in the candlelight she could see the patches of scarlet on his cheekbones. "You know nothing about it, Philippa!" he said, his voice rising to shrillness.

"Why, William," Philippa said softly, feeling the beginnings of a smile on her lips. "You're jealous. Jealous of a mere girl."

"I warn you, Philippa!"

"Oh, nonsense. You can't touch me, and you know it! Because I fly a winged horse, and you can't. That's it, isn't it? That's always been the issue!"

He drew himself up, and his eyes glittered like black diamonds. "Philippa, you overstep yourself. I will not forget this, upon my succession. I will naturally be making changes, and that will include the Academy."

"Why did you buy the saddle, William?"

He glared at her. She stared back at him, and they stood in a frozen tableau for a long moment. At last, he shifted his gaze to the ceiling, and said with feigned weariness, "You would be well advised, Horsemistress, to stay out of our affairs."

"The genealogy of a winged horse is an Academy affair," she said tightly. "As is everything to do with the winged horses."

William's eyebrows drew together, then, deliberately, apart. "Come, now," he said. He made a limp gesture with one hand. "We are simply taking an interest in our people. Even those of the Uplands."

"You won't tell me."

William had moved to the door, and opened it. He held it ajar, and said in an icy tone, "Thank you so much for coming, Mistress Winter. I will convey your greetings to my lady wife."

Philippa saw, through the open door, that the steward stood in the foyer, and with him the hunched figure of Slater, William's man, dressed as she had always seen him in a caped greatcoat. As she passed through the door, and accepted her riding coat and cap, Slater bowed low, peering up at her from beneath ragged eyebrows. She turned her back on him, and went out into the night.

"FOLLOW her," William said to Slater, when the doors had shut behind Philippa and the steward had gone below stairs.

Slater grinned, showing his long yellow teeth. "Can't fly, me lord," he said.

"Don't be a fool," William said. "Just see that she leaves directly. Stop her if she begins snooping."

"She'll never find it," Slater said with confidence. "Hid it right there in the tack room, amongst all the others. No one'll know the difference."

"Philippa will have noticed the new stables. She's no beauty, but she's no fool, either. I don't want her wandering around."

"Nothing to see, is there?" Slater said. "Not yet, anyway."

"Just do it, man. And then come back to me. Work to do."

"Aye, me lord."

Slater turned to pass under the stairs, to use the servants' entrance. "Slater," William said. "One more thing. Who is our man at the Academy?"

Slater gave a throaty, greasy-sounding laugh. "We have a man, me lord. Peebles, in the kitchens. We also have a woman."

"Excellent Slater," William purred, pleased and surprised. He smoothed his vest with his palms. "How did you manage that? And when?"

"One of them horsemistresses was . . . what you might call impatient, me lord. Thought when she came back from the borders, she ought to be senior. A word in her ear was all it took."

"But do we have—an assurance?" William asked.

Slater nodded, and tapped his nose with a none-too-clean finger. "Her family has been in some trouble of recent years," he said. "Only thing kept her father out of prison was having a daughter in the service of the Duke."

William nodded satisfaction. "Most helpful, Slater. Good work. And what's her name?"

"Strong. Irina Strong."

"Ah. Useful." William ran a hand thoughtfully over his smooth chin. "Of course—once my lord father dies, she won't be necessary."

Slater shrugged. "Backup, me lord. Backup."

EIGHTEEN

HESTER caught Lark's arm after breakfast, holding her back from the tide of girls pouring out into the sunshine. "Mamá's here," she said. "That's our carriage in the courtyard."

Lark laughed. "Hester, you always get what you want, don't you?"

Hester grinned. "No point in being Lord and Lady Beeth's daughter if you can't pull a few strings now and again."

They stood in the doorway as the other students moved to the stables, or around the Hall to the classrooms. "But, Hester . . . what about Mistress Strong? I'm supposed to be studying etiquette with her this morning."

Hester waved a hand with blithe unconcern. "Oh, never mind that," she said. "Mamá is having a word with the Head. Everything will be taken care of."

"And Tup?"

"You left the little goat with him, didn't you? Molly?"

"Yes, of course."

"And my Golden Morning has her oc-hound. They won't miss us before tonight!"

Lark looked down the broad steps at the fine equipage awaiting them. Two dappled draught horses, with enormous hooves and tufted fetlocks, stood patiently in the traces. A driver in scarlet livery perched on the high bench, the reins loose in his hands. Another liveried man lounged beside the carriage door, which was open to show piles of thick cushions.

Petra and a companion were just passing the carriage. Petra looked up at Lark and Hester standing side by side, and the look in her eyes startled Lark. She looked jealous, of course, but she also looked—confused, Lark thought, as if she couldn't quite make sense of the situation. The Headmistress came out of the

Hall with a tall, elegantly dressed woman beside her. The woman smiled at Hester, and kissed her cheek. Petra spun about, and stalked away toward the stables.

Lark was introduced to Lady Beeth, whose large features and easy grin reminded her very much of Hester. The girls, of course, wore their Academy habits, but Lady Beeth was dressed for town in a girdled tabard and a rope of pearls that hung to her waist. She regarded Lark for a long moment, then nodded, and murmured to her daughter, "Yes, indeed, I do see the problem." Lark touched her unruly hair, blushing with embarrassment.

Anabel shook hands prettily with Lady Beeth, and then climbed up to nestle among the cushions next to Lark. Hester and her mamá began to chat as the horses set up a heavy, steady trot. The liveried man stood on a running board outside, visible through the curtained window. Lark turned to the opposite window. The hedgerows passed with surprising speed. She would have liked to sit up with the driver, to watch the action of the horses' great haunches, the bobbing of their heads, to see how he managed the reins, but she supposed that would be considered unladylike. She wanted to ask a dozen questions about the feeding and grooming and dispositions of draught horses. She turned to ask Lady Beeth, and was surprised to find Hester and her mamá speaking seriously of some matter to do with the Council of Lords.

"Isn't it a lovely carriage?" Anabel murmured in her ear. "My parents' isn't half so fine."

Lark laughed. "Ours is an oxcart!"

Anabel's eyes widened. "Truly?" she breathed. "You ride in an oxcart? Oh, that sounds wonderful fun!"

"If you like your bones jounced about, it is," Lark said. She waved at the landscape flowing past the carriage windows. "And of course, you ride slowly enough to see everything!"

The two great horses covered the distance between the Academy and Osham more swiftly than Lark would have believed possible. Along the way, Hester pointed out the turning that led to her family home, less than an hour's drive from the Academy. A signpost stood at the corner where a lane ran between neatly trimmed hedgerows, proclaiming the road to Beeth House. Lark was speechless before this evidence of Hester's status. A sign, just for your family home! She could hardly wait to point it out to Nick or Brye when they next came to the Academy.

Before another hour had passed, Lady Beeth and the girls were handed out by the liveried servant, and Lark stood gazing up at the turrets and spires of the White City. Bright awnings shaded the dozens of shop windows that lined the street, and the paving stones were laid out in patterns of black and white.

"Blackstone!" she murmured, caressing one of the black squares with her toe.

"Does it interest you?" Lady Beeth asked, her eyebrows raised.

"My brother Edmar . . ." Lark began, and then stopped, a little abashed. Her brothers could hardly be more different from her present company.

"What?" Hester demanded. "What about Edmar?"

"Hester, dear," Lady Beeth said mildly. "You mustn't press your friend."

"Never mind, Mamá," Hester said gaily. "She understands me. Don't you, Hamley?"

Lark smiled. "Aye," she said. She gestured to the paving stones beneath their feet. "Blackstone comes from the Uplands," she told Lady Beeth. "And my brother Edmar works in a quarry, cutting it out of the ground."

"How fascinating," Lady Beeth said warmly. "On the ride back, Larkyn, you must tell me all about your family." She adjusted the little jeweled cap she wore on her smoothly coifed brown hair. "And now . . ." She indicated the row of shops before them with a gay wave of her gloved hand. "Let's see what the White City has for us today."

Lark's experience of shopping had been limited to a rare excursion into Dickering Park each fall for winter necessities. When she outgrew or simply wore out her clothes, Nick usually bartered with the seamstress in Willakeep for replacements, and each new set looked exactly like the previous one.

To wander in and out of the elegant, colorful establishments of Osham was at first delightful, and then overwhelming. Lady Beeth turned over hair clips and brushes and jeweled pins with her fingers, assaulted clerks with questions, rejected item after item without hesitation. From time to time she twisted Lark's mass of curls and tried to clip them into place, then tossed the inadequate bauble back into its tray, and led her little troupe off to the next shop.

Hester winked at Lark behind her mother's back as they exited one shop and crossed the street to another. "I told you," she whispered. "Mamá loves this. She is meeting a great challenge, like telling Papá what to say in the Council of Lords, or like a warrior doing battle with one of the Old Ones!"

"I'm afraid," Lark murmured, "that my hair is beyond even your mamá's powers!"

Anabel, it turned out, was as tireless in their mission as Lady Beeth, exclaiming over scarves and pins, and suggesting this method or that of restraining the offending tresses.

By the end of two hours, Lark felt there had been no progress at all. Everything she looked at seemed pointless. She would have felt guilty about the whole excursion if Anabel and Lady Beeth had not made several purchases that delighted them. Hester rolled her eyes as the two chose yet another shop to try. "Here we go again," she muttered.

Lark started to follow Hester across the street to the latest discovery, but paused with her foot still on the walkway, her eye caught by an herbalist's shop. A little fetish hung in the window, reminding her of the Tarn at Deeping Farm. Had their own Tarn, when it was new, ever possessed such a vivid yellow skirt, such shining bead eyes? Theirs was ragged and faded, but still, this bright new one conjured a vivid image of her old kitchen, with its dented pots and worn curtains, its rich smells.

"Hamley! Are you coming?" Hester called.

"I'll be there in a moment." Lark waved, and then, on an impulse, went into the shop.

It was a tiny space, crowded with merchandise. There were a dozen fetishes she had no name for. There was one shelf full of smallgods, even one of Zito, his great ears and phallus rendered in painted clay. There were at least a dozen images of the twin gods Erd and Estia, entwined in their traditional embrace. A cabinet with glass doors held vials and jars and bunches of dried herbs tied together with string. The shop seemed to vibrate with dark energy. Lark fingered a small, fox-faced icon, feeling a delicious shiver through her fingers.

She thrust the icon back onto its shelf when the proprietor emerged from a curtained space at the back of the shop. She was a tall, ribbony woman with gray hair skinned back from her sharp-nosed face. When she saw Lark, she tipped her head to one side, looking like an elongated bird. Even her smile was beaky.

"Welcome, Miss," she said. "I'm always glad to see a flyer in my shop. You need an image of Kalla, perhaps, for your horse's stall?" Lark shook her head. "A simple, then?"

"Oh, no," Lark said. She looked at her boots, embarrassed. "I just—"

The herbalist tipped her head to the other side, and dropped her voice. "Ah. I see. Perhaps you need a potion for—for a bit of trouble you might be having."

Lark's head came up. "Of course I don't need a potion!" she snapped.

The woman held up a hand. "Now, now, only asking." She ran her hand down her stained apron. "Just as well you don't, Miss. I hear them winged horses can smell a potion as well as they can smell a man."

Lark took a step back toward the door, wishing she hadn't come in. "I was only curious," she said stiffly. "You have a Tarn in your window. It reminded me of the one we keep at home."

"A Tarn?" The woman's eyebrows rose to little points. "A Tarn, indeed. Few calls for a Tarn here in Osham. You're from the Uplands, mayhap?"

Lark hesitated, but before she could decide whether she wanted to tell this woman anything about herself, the curtain swept aside again, and a stooped, heavy-bodied man emerged. Lark's nostrils twitched at the miasma of herbs and sweat that surrounded him. He peered around the herbalist to see her clearly.

"I'll be with you in a moment, Slater," the woman said.

He nodded, but he stayed where he was, eyeing Lark.

"Excuse me," Lark said. "I don't think I need anything here after all."

"No, wait, Miss," the woman said. "Let me give you something to take back to school with you . . ." She crossed to a shelf with an assortment of icons. She plucked a small one out of the jumble, and pressed it into Lark's hand.

Lark tried to hand it back to her. "No," she said, but her protest was weak.

It was a lovely little thing, an image of Kalla done in some kind of gray stone. Kalla's tail swept up and over her shoulders, and her horse face had been carved with tiny, delicate features, the ears small and pricked forward, the eyes widely spaced.

Lark said, "No, I can't take it. I have no money."

"It's a gift," the woman said. She backed away, leaving Lark holding the bit of carving. "When you ride your winged horse, you'll remember me."

Lark, confused and unsure of the propriety of accepting the icon, mumbled a hasty thanks, and made her escape. She hurried across the street to the milliner's shop where Lady Beeth and the girls had gone. The stooped man stood in the doorway of the herbalist's, and as she went in search of her companions, she felt his dark gaze on her back. Unconsciously, she held the figure of Kalla to her breast for protection until the shop door had closed behind her.

"Larkyn? Are you all right?" It was Lady Beeth, holding out a hand to her, urging her to a chair before a tall mirror. "You look a little pale, dear."

"What's that?" Hester pointed to the icon Lark had clutched to her chest.

"Oh, the—the herbalist . . ." Lark pointed back the way she had come. "I wasn't going to—I mean, I didn't ask her—she insisted I take it."

"Yes, of course she did," Lady Beeth said. "Now she can say she is patronized by the students of the Academy of the Air."

Hester snickered. "Told you, Hamley. Privileges."

"I didn't like the shop," Lark said frankly.

"Why?" Anabel asked. "It's a pretty little icon."

"Oh, aye, I like the statue, but . . ."

Hester was standing by the window, staring out. "Who's that man?" she asked.

Lady Beeth laid down the handful of ribbons she had been sorting, and went to stand beside her daughter. Lark stood behind them. The stooped man was standing just inside the doorway of the herbalist's, as if hiding in the shadows.

Lady Beeth drew a sudden, noisy breath. "Step back, girls," she commanded. There was an edge to her voice, and an air of authority Lark hadn't noticed before. She understood, now, where Hester came by her self-confident manner. "Move away from the window, please," Lady Beeth repeated. "We want nothing to do with that—that *gentleman*." Her tone made it clear she considered the stooped man to be nothing of the sort.

"Why, Mamá?" Hester said, even as she did as her mother bid. Her mamá turned away from the window, and Lark saw the glance she exchanged with her serving-man. "In a moment," Lady Beeth said, "we will go to lunch, and I will explain." She glanced over her shoulder. "When he has gone."

When they were all seated at a table in the handsomest inn Lark had ever seen, with an order placed for an ample lunch, Lady Beeth leaned forward to address the girls in a low voice. "The man you saw," she said, "works for Lord William."

"But, Mamá," Hester began. "Then why—?"

Lady Beeth put up her hand, and shook her head with a decisive motion. "I don't like speaking of such things to you girls," she said. "You're in the Duke's service, and one day Lord William will be Duke." She glanced around to be certain no one was approaching their table. "He has a reputation," she said grimly. "And that awful man has something to do with it. Your father and I, Hester . . ." She patted her daughter's shoulder. "We took care to keep you away from William's company. And most parents of our acquaintance did the same. Since he was a young man, his behavior has been . . . well, less than honorable. And in recent years, ever stranger stories about him, and about his man, reach our ears. You are young to be thinking of such things, but they are real, and they are dangerous. I would be remiss if I did not warn you."

Lark sat back in her chair, her arms wrapped around herself, all her pleasure in the day evaporating. Lord William . . . the magicked quirt, dragged across her body so she couldn't move . . . She wished she dared tell Lady Beeth all about that day, and how odd it had made her feel. But her brothers, and Deeping Farm . . . She did not dare risk it.

She dropped her hand to her pocket, and held the little icon of Kalla in her palm. Surely, she thought, Kalla's magic was stronger than whatever smallmagic Lord William employed. Surely an icon of the horse goddess had power over a magicked quirt. But did Kalla have power over the Duke of Oc?

"Larkyn? Aren't you hungry?"

Lark looked up, and realized that their meal had been served, a big platter of hot meat pastries, with brimming cups of cider and a bowl of crisp vegetables. Lady Beeth's concern made her feel much better and she found herself smiling up into those strong features, so very like Hester's. "Oh, aye," she said. She saw that Hester and Anabel were already attacking the pastries, and she reached for two herself before they should disappear. "Oh, aye, Lady Beeth, I'm starving!"

Hester's mamá nodded approval. "And so you should be, you young things. Eat, now. It won't hurt you to be full for once!"

More shopping ensued after the excellent lunch, and Lady Beeth's manservant made several trips to the carriage to stow their purchases, though Lark kept her little image of Kalla in her tabard pocket. Still, when the slant of the sun's rays told them the day was coming to a close, they had not solved the problem of Lark's hair.

As they all rode home, drowsy with heat and good food and fine company, Lady Beeth shook her head kindly at Lark. "I don't know what to recommend, dear," she said. "You have wonderful hair, and anyone but a horsemistress would envy it. How you are to restrain it under your cap I have no idea."

Hester said sleepily, "Cut it."

"What?" Lark turned to her, startled out of her own sleepy state.

Hester put her head back against the cushioned seat, smiling. "You'll have to cut it, Hamley. I don't see what else you can do."

Reflexively, Lark put a hand to her head. A chaos of curls met her fingers, and she tugged at them ruefully.

"It would be unusual . . ." Lady Beeth began.

Anabel said, squinting a little at Lark, "It will look marvelous. With your skin, and such brilliant eyes . . . I'll do it for you."

Lark giggled. "What will my sponsor say?"

Hester spoke with her eyes closed. "Tell her it was Lady Beeth's idea. She won't have a word to say against it."

NINETEEN

PHILIPPA returned from visiting Duke Frederick on a cool afternoon when the last of the beeches had turned to gold. It would be the final flourish of color before the sere shades of winter set in. The air aloft held the sharp bite of fall. To the north, the Ocmarins glimmered with early snow. The grass in the Academy paddocks was the only patch of pure green, its emerald hue protected by careful watering.

Philippa handed Sunny's reins to Rosellen and walked slowly toward the Hall, weighed down by worry over her old friend. Frederick had roused barely enough to nod to her. His eyes were dark in sunken sockets, and his cheeks, always lean, seemed to sag from the bones as if there were no flesh left to hold them up. Andrews had confided in her that his lord ate almost nothing, and sat staring out of his window, hour after hour. In times past, he would have been watching his winged horses fly. Now, it seemed, he watched for the daughter who would never return. William had been absent. That he no longer felt a need to be present at Frederick's interviews was an evil harbinger.

As she left the return paddock and started across the courtyard, Margareth came out of the Hall and down the steps. Students dashed here and there, finishing last chores before dinner, one or two stopping to bob their heads to the Headmistress. Margareth smiled at them before she spoke to Philippa.

"Did you see him?" she asked in an undertone. "Did you speak to him?"

"I tried," Philippa said. She glanced around to be sure no one was close enough to hear. "He's dying, Margareth. I doubt he heard a word I said."

"So William will win this battle with Eduard. The little black will go uncut."

They had reached the steps, and started up them. Philippa gave Margareth a wry look. "We're going to have to stop calling him that, Margareth. He needs a name."

Philippa took off her riding cap as they passed through the foyer, and smoothed her hair. Margareth signaled to a serving-girl to bring tea to her office. Once they were settled, Philippa said, "Even when I was young, Frederick always seemed lonely. Francis was at school, and William . . ." She shrugged. "William challenged his father even as a boy. When Pamella came along, late in Frederick's life, he doted on her." She sighed, and rubbed her eyes. "His father's decline suits his purposes, I'm afraid."

Margareth said heavily. "The day Frederick dies will be a dark day for us."

"Indeed. William will make changes, and I doubt they will be in our best interests."

A knock at the door interrupted Margareth's answer. She called a response, and a maid put her head around the door. "Headmistress, one of the girls wants to see you."

"Fine," Margareth answered. "Show her in." The maid curtsied, and turned away. A moment later, the student stood uncertainly in the doorway.

"Why—Larkyn!" exclaimed Margareth.

"Kalla's teeth," Philippa said. "What have you done?"

Larkyn took a hesitant step into the room. "It was . . . it was Lady Beeth's idea."

Philippa stood up abruptly. "Since when does Lady Beeth dictate Academy dress?"

Larkyn's cheeks were already red, but her color deepened. Her hand rose, almost involuntarily, to touch her hair.

Margareth stood up, and moved around her desk. She came to stand before the girl, tipping her chin up with her fingers and turning her head this way and that. "Hmm," she said. "Well. It will grow, I expect."

"It will never grow like yours, though, Headmistress!" Larkyn said. "It's such an awful tangle of curls, and Pe—I mean, my sponsor is always scolding me about it. We couldn't find anything in Osham that would work, and so—I mean, Lady Beeth tried so hard, and then we gave up, and she suggested—"

"I think I like it," Margareth said. "It's trim, and it's neat. It will probably save you no end of hours brushing and pinning."

Philippa pursed her lips, but she could see Margareth's point. Lark's black hair now curled tightly to her scalp, just grazing the tips of her ears, framing her forehead and her cheeks. The close silhouette dramatized her eyes and her full lips. Still . . .

"If any other girl imitates her," Philippa said sternly, "we shall have to have a rule."

Larkyn's laugh was short and hard. "Mistress Winter, no one wants to imitate me. My hair only sets me more apart than I already am."

Another warning came to Philippa's lips, but died unspoken. She understood what it was to feel different. At Larkyn's tender age, such a distinction must be even more painful.

Margareth said, in a gentler tone than Philippa's, "Larkyn, did you come only to show me your hair? Or is there something else?"

The girl's eyes brightened, and she thrust a hand through her newly shorn tresses in a gesture Philippa could wager would become habitual. "Yes, Headmistress, there is something else." Her gaze slid warily to Philippa, and then back to Margareth. "Yes," she repeated. "It's Tup. Mistress Strong doesn't think so, but I—I think he's ready to fly!"

IT was always a relief to Lark to come into the stables. Straw and horseflesh filled her nostrils with their comforting scents, and Tup's little whicker greeted her as she hurried to his stall and he thumped at the wall of his stall with one heel. "Tup! Stop that!" He had already splintered one board, and Herbert had scolded her for it. It was because he was restless, though, she knew it. Though she took him every day to the yearlings' pasture, so he could canter to and fro with the older colts and fillies, it wasn't enough.

She let herself in, and went to hug his neck with one arm, dropping the other hand to pet Molly. Tup had grown so that Molly's poll tucked easily under his chin.

"Kalla's teeth, I swear he's grown taller since yesterday," Mistress Winter said. She and Margareth Morgan stood in the aisle, gazing over the wall at Tup.

"How old is he now, Larkyn?" the Headmistress asked.

Lark stroked Tup's gleaming shoulder with pride. "Ten months," she said. She urged Molly to one side so the horsemistresses could admire Tup's straight, fine legs, his arching neck, the silky fall of his tail. "Autumn is a month old now, and Tup was born one month to the day after Erd's Festival."

Mistress Winter leaned on the low wall of the stall and eyed Tup with a practiced eye. "Eduard has still made no judgment, I gather."

"He has nothing to go on," the Headmistress responded.

Lark ran her hand down Tup's neck and tickled the jointure of wing and chest. Obligingly, he lifted his wing and opened the pinions, showing the silken membrane.

"Ah," murmured the Headmistress.

Mistress Winter fixed Lark with a hard look. Lark knew the horsemistress understood what she had done. But Tup was ready! It was time, and past time, for him to know what flying felt like, to begin to strengthen his wings—to be ready to carry his bondmate.

"You must follow our judgment on these things, Larkyn," Mistress Winter said sharply. "Our colts fly at twelve months. When you come back, after the Festival of Erd, I will take him up with Sunny."

"But, Mistress Winter! He's almost as big as the yearling Ocmarins, and he—"

"Not yet," the horsemistress said. A glance passed between Mistress Winter and the Headmistress, heavy with knowledge Lark couldn't share. She wanted to stamp her foot, to insist, to explain . . . but the older women had already turned away.

Lark turned back to Tup and pressed her forehead against the sweet warmth of his neck. Tears of impatience stung her eyes. "They don't understand," she whispered to Tup. "They just don't understand."

TWENTY

THE cold white stars of impending winter glittered above William's head as he hurried across the sloping lawn of Fleckham House, his fingers fumbling with the buttons of a heavy woolen shirt. He wore little else except boots and a pair of narrow trousers, picked up in haste from where he had dropped them hours before. His stable-man trotted ahead of him, the oil lamp in his hand swinging wildly. One of the oc-hounds barked, but at William's hissed command, the dog whined, and slunk back into its kennel.

The stable beyond the grove still smelled of new paint. Three mares put their heads out of their stalls, and the lamplight glimmered in their eyes. William ignored them. What he wanted, what he had been awaiting for months, was in the last stall on the left.

"Stand back, Jinson," he said harshly. "Leave this to me."

"M'lord," the stable-man said anxiously. "I don't think he'll stand for it . . ."

"Is it a colt, then?" William said eagerly. "A stallion?"

"Oh, aye, m'lord, a fine one. But I don't think he'll allow you to—"

"Never mind, Jinson. It's different with me, you understand? It's going to be different."

The stable-man, little more than a youth, lifted his lamp high, but kept his distance from the stall. William approached, deliberately slowing his steps, savoring the moment. It was like wanting a woman, this desire. He craved it. It made his mouth dry and his loins stir in a way no woman now could do. This achievement represented his triumph over the constraints of tradition. The foal in the stall meant freedom from an old man's slavish devotion to the past, of the dominance of the horsemistresses in Oc . . .

"Hang the lantern on the hook, Jinson. Go back to the house, and get me some bedding. A nightshirt, and a bottle of brandy. I'll be sleeping here tonight."

Jinson, with a doubtful look on his face, did as he was bid. When he had vanished into the darkness, William stepped into the vague circle of light, and peered into the stall.

The foal was so pale he glimmered in the dimness, as if stars shone on his hide. His sire was a fine dapple gray, known to Eduard, like the other had been, for getting winged foals on wingless mares. And this foal—this trembling, secret creature of silvery hue, still wet with afterbirth—this one had neat little gray wings clamped to its sides.

William sidled in through the gate, and leaned against the inner wall, watching. The foal was intent on finding its dam's udder, and the mare was busily licking her little one clean. Absorbed as they were, they hardly noticed William, though the mare's ears flicked his way, and then relaxed.

William knew how it was done. He had lurked about, curious and resentful, as Philippa Winter—Philippa Islington, then, sixteen years old—had bonded with her newborn filly on a chilly spring night in the Duke's own stables. Duke Frederick, William's own father, had watched with pride, as if Philippa were his own daughter. He had ignored William, as always, in favor of anything to do with the winged horses. And that ass Meredith, Philippa's brother, stood by smirking, pleased with himself at this connection to the Duke. William swore to himself that Meredith Islington would never step foot in the Ducal Palace again, once he assumed the title.

His own plans would come to fruition at last. He would be free of Eduard Crisp's meddling, free of his father's criticism, free of those cursed horsemistresses' lording it over everyone, including even the Duke himself. And he knew, he remembered, what he needed to do. The last one had gotten away from him, but this one was right here, in his own stable. It was in his control.

Carefully, moving slowly, he lowered himself to his knees in the straw, and began to murmur to the colt.

PETRA, as Lark expected, sneered over her shorn hair. But she had little free time to torment her. The girls of the first level, all except Lark, were preparing to fly for the first time.

Mistress Strong stopped at Tup's stall to suggest Lark should be in the flight paddock to watch the momentous event. "Your own day won't come for some time, Larkyn," she said, in her lifeless way. "Your colt is only—what is it, eleven months now? And he should be eighteen months before he carries weight in the air. But you should observe this, and perhaps you'll understand why your drills with the pony are so important."

Lark only said, "Yes, Mistress Strong." Rosellen stood in the aisle outside Tup's stall, and Lark studiously avoided her eyes.

In their free time, she and Rosellen had been galloping Pig around the back paddock, each taking a turn while the other kept an eye out for any girl or instructor who might come near. Herbert knew, of course, and rolled his eyes at Rosellen. But Pig was the better for it, his muscles beginning to emerge from their layer of fat, his legs trimmer, his neck leaner.

"No pride in a fat pony around the place," Herbert muttered. "So I'll keep your secret. But if Mistress Strong finds out, I won't defend you."

Mistress Strong's objection, of course, would be to the manner of Lark's riding. The moment the instructor departed the dry paddock, the girls slid the saddle from Pig's wide back.

Lark felt like a completely different creature without the rockhard saddle tree beneath her, without jouncing against the restraining pommel and the stiff cantle. Her heels tucked neatly around Pig's ribs, and her seat seemed to mold to his back. More than once, as she persuaded Pig to some feat of coordination or flexibility, Rosellen would demand to know how she did it. Lark couldn't explain it. It was something instinctive, as natural to her as herding a flock of goats to graze, or as coaxing a flighty hen into its coop. It was as easy a thing for her to ride the pony without tack as it was hard to suffer the cumbersome saddle.

Worried the flight might launch before she could reach the flight paddock, she hurried to put Tup's new halter on. The one they had arrived with had grown far too small, even with the straps let out as far as they would go. Tup now measured twelve hands at the withers, and his legs and chest had filled out. He was still small, but he had begun to look like the mature horse he would one day be. His mane and tail flowed long and full, and his eyes twinkled with intelligence and mischief. Lark touched his nose with affection as she slipped the halter over his head. "Tup," she murmured.

"You're the most beautiful horse at the Academy, make no mistake!" He tossed his head, making the halter jingle, and she laughed.

With the short lead in her hand, Lark led him out of the stables toward the flight paddock. Once in the crisp air, Tup threw up his hind legs in a gesture of sheer exuberance, and she scolded him to behave himself. Molly trotted behind them, faithful as any oc-hound. The other colts were already outgrowing the company of the dogs. The oc-hounds, one by one, retreated to their kennels to wait for new foals to foster. But Molly had only Tup's stall to sleep in. The little she-goat followed Tup and Lark everywhere.

As the three of them processed to the flight paddock, they passed Petra on her way into the stables. "Oh, look," Petra said to a companion. "The goat-girl and her flock."

The companion snickered. Lark kept her eyes on the ground, gritting her teeth to stop the retort that sprang to her lips. Bramble bounded to her side, and Lark stroked the oc-hound's sleek head with her free hand. "Aye, Bramble. Lovely wise, you are," she whispered.

The dog laughed up at her, tongue lolling, and then twisted her neck to cast a glance back at Petra.

Petra called, "Hamley! See that your Crybaby keeps quiet! This is an important day."

Lark made no answer, but Bramble swung about, tail and legs rigid. She glared at Petra. Lark glanced back to see Petra staring at the dog in wide-eyed surprise.

"Come along, Bramble," Lark murmured. "Best ignore her." She pressed on, but Bramble stood for another moment before she spun about, and trotted after Lark and Tup. Lark grinned at her, and tugged her ears. "Fine judge of character, aren't you?" she said. Bramble's tongue lolled, and her tail began to wave again.

Lark's nostrils flared in appreciation of the tang of winter in the air. The hand of the year was opening, as they said in the Uplands, opening to release the seasons. The girls of the Academy would soon return to their homes for the Erdlin holiday, and Lark and Tup and Molly would go to Deeping Farm for ten precious days.

The first-level girls were already mounted in the paddock when Lark and her little following arrived. A knot of older girls and a few instructors gathered near the gate. The first-level instructor, Mistress Dancer, was speaking in a carrying voice.

"This will be short," she said. "Let your horses try their strength, but we don't want to tire them. I'll lead with Dancer, and you will follow . . . Hester first, then Beatrice, Lillian, Beryl, Isobel, Grace . . . Anabel. Anabel, are you all right?"

Anabel's slender figure hunched over her pommel, and she looked as if she were about to be sick. Her gray gelding fidgeted, and Anabel, with obvious effort, pulled her spine straight. Lark saw her throat work as she swallowed, but she lifted the reins to calm Take a Chance. Her voice trembled, but she managed to say, "I'm fine."

All the girls were pale and wide-eyed. The sleeping porch had been restless last night, girls tossing and turning, moaning in their dreams. And Anabel—she looked ill with fear. Lark felt a sudden wave of anxiety for her.

Only Hester looked confident, even eager. She twisted in Golden Morning's saddle to grin at her classmates. "Come on, girls," she called. "Goldie can't wait, and neither can I." Her filly thumped the ground with her forefeet, and there were a few half-hearted chuckles.

Mistress Dancer trotted Sky Dancer briskly to the foot of the flight paddock, wheeled, and began to canter. Hester came behind, and the girls lined out in order. Anabel, at the end of the line, seemed out of balance to Lark, jouncing against the cantle of her flying saddle.

Four rods from the grove at the end of the flight paddock, Sky Dancer broke into a hand gallop, and then leapt into the air with a powerful downward thrust of her wings. Golden Morning followed in perfect imitation, her tail streaming in the breeze, her breath pluming in the cold air. And Hester—Hester, so plain and angular on the ground—was magically transformed in the air. Her tall figure swayed in gentle synchrony with Goldie's beating wings, and the reins lay lightly in her hands. She looked as slender as a willow branch, as light as a feather. Hester looked as if she had been flying all her life, and Lark beamed with pride.

The others lifted from the ground with somewhat less grace. The horses' wings spread, membranes rippling, pinions shivering with effort. Several teetered as they left the ground, as horses and riders strove to feel this new balance. When it was Anabel's turn, Lark found the little icon of Kalla in her pocket and gripped it till her fingers hurt. Anabel sat too straight, she thought, making it hard for Chance to lift—and then, as they ascended, Anabel slipped in the saddle, and Chance's wings lost their rhythm. Lark felt her thighs clench in sympathy, and she knew from the little gasps around her that others, too, were following Anabel. Lark didn't breathe again until Chance found his rhythm, and Anabel found her seat again, put her heels down, and lifted her head. The pair banked to their left, and took their place behind the others.

The young horses dipped this way and that, striving for a straight line. When a pair faltered, the watchers muttered among themselves. Lark pulled her icon out of her pocket and pressed it to her chest. It seemed to her that the flight, all at once, steadied. They flew in a long, almost even line, making a great arc above the Academy grounds.

Molly gave a plaintive bleat. Lark turned, and found that Tup was no longer beside her. In her fear for Anabel, she had dropped his lead.

She whirled, and tripped over Bramble, catching her balance just in time to see Tup, head high, ears forward, leap the fence. He raced down the grass, past the crowd of watchers, and dashed toward the grove at the end of the flight paddock, the halter lead flying out behind him. When his wings opened, Lark cried out. Not only had she dropped his lead—she had forgotten his wing clips!

His feet twinkled over the grass, faster and faster, with no sign of slowing as he approached the grove. As he neared the trees, his hindquarters bunched and drove, and his wings swept up and out. He lifted smoothly into the air, his narrow wings seeming to beat without effort. Lark stared with a dry mouth and thumping heart as he circled up after the flight. His slender neck stretched, and his hooves curled into a perfect tuck. The halter lead flew sideways in the wind and tangled in the flow of his mane. Around Lark, the instructors and older girls cried out in alarm. Lark didn't hear them. She was lost in the wonder of Tup's flight.

He was so beautiful. Achingly, inexpressibly beautiful. She should not have lost control of him, but all she could think of at the moment was how right he looked in the air. It was his natural home, the environment for which Kalla had created him. She clutched the icon, and watched her bondmate's slender black figure arrow through the blue sky after the others.

Tup's wings tilted, and he dropped his nose close to Take

a Chance's tail. Anabel looked back. Her mouth opened in surprise, and she gripped her pommel, but she didn't slip again. The flight curved up and around in a long loop, led by Mistress Dancer. Tup followed, wings beating with joyous ease.

Mistress Dancer, on the return side of the loop, saw him. Her mouth opened, too, and she shouted something. She lifted her arm, pointing her quirt at him in a commanding way.

Tup faltered, interrupting the rhythm of his wings. His forefeet clawed the wind. Lark cried out, clutching Kalla to her breast. Tup, with that toss of the head she knew so well, arched his neck. His wings stilled, and he dropped, a rod, two rods, three, until he was well back of the flyers. When his wings began to beat again, their tempo was faster than before. He climbed, flying higher and higher, rising above the flight of horses and girls until he could circle above their heads. Lark saw laughter in the flash of his teeth, the ripple of his tail. He darted in playful circles above the flight, swooping down in little rushes toward the other flyers, then lifting up and away at the last moment, intoxicated with his own energy and strength, his newly discovered freedom.

It could only have been moments, but the length of the flight was a lifetime to Lark. Mistress Dancer, her face set with fury, led the horses in their descent. Everyone in the watching crowd turned to the return paddock to see them come to ground.

Sky Dancer hovered aloft as Mistress Dancer called orders. Hester and Golden Morning came to ground as smoothly as if they had done it a hundred times, gliding in over the copse of trees, cantering down the paddock toward the stables. The next horse stumbled, but caught himself, and Beatrice, though she clutched at his mane, recovered her poise by the time he cantered to the end of the paddock and stood, breathing hard, beside Golden Morning. The next three also had uneasy moments, a slight wobble before finding the ground, a jolt that threw Lillian back against the high cantle, a high, jerking trot, that must have rattled Grace's teeth. Anabel and Chance were the last pair. As Chance descended, Anabel bent too far forward over the pommel. Only at the last moment did she bring herself upright. For a bad moment, it seemed Chance might overbalance and come to his knees, but his forefeet touched the ground firmly, his hind legs collecting just in time. As he cantered up the return paddock, Anabel looked almost faint with relief.

And then Tup, riderless, ribbon of tail floating behind him, soared in over the grove. His forefeet reached, touched, his hind feet following in perfect coordination. He galloped, then cantered, dancing to a stop before Lark, blowing and proud, eyes alight.

"Oh, Tup," Lark whispered. "Oh, Tup! We're going to catch it, you and I." She opened the gate, and as he came through, belatedly took his halter strap in her hand. She kept her eyes on her boots, vainly hoping to lead him away before anyone could scold her. It was, of course, Petra Sweet who caught her first.

She dashed up to her, hissing, "Hamley! Your Crybaby could have killed someone!"

Lark muttered, "I know. I'm sorry."

"Sorry?" Petra's voice rose. "How does sorry help? You're a disgrace! You can't do anything right, you talk like a peasant, and you look like some sort of street urchin. If I were Head, you'd be sent down on the spot!"

Lark tried, she really did, to swallow the flare of anger that warmed her cheeks. But at that moment, Molly came trotting up, bleating her relief.

Petra exclaimed, "Oh, by Kalla's heels, now the damn goat cries! It's like being in a bloody nursery!" Several girls snickered. Bramble growled, and Lark lost her temper.

She stopped so abruptly that Tup almost trod on her heels. She lifted her chin, and stared into Petra's face. "Seems to me it's you making all the noise, Sweet," she said. "Clack like a duck, don't you? Nasty dispositions, ducks."

Petra's sharp features reddened. "How dare you!" she began, but another girl caught her arm, and whispered something to her. Petra turned her head to look over her shoulder, and then took a step back. Lark saw, with sinking heart, that she began to smile. Petra looked back at her, her smile widening. She hissed, "Good luck, Goat-girl. I wouldn't be you for anything at this moment!"

It was not Mistress Strong approaching, but Mistress Winter. She strode toward Lark and Tup with purpose, pleating her riding gloves between her fingers. Bramble trotted to meet her. Molly pressed herself against Lark's thigh. Tup whickered as Mistress Winter came near.

"Larkyn," Mistress Winter said coldly. "Stable your colt and come to the Hall. Meet me in the Head's office."

Lark nodded without speaking. She tried to feel penitent. It had been her fault, after all, and whatever came, she had earned it. But oh, to watch Tup fly like that, in the wake of the other horses . . . it had been magnificent! She led him into his stable, and pressed her cheek to his neck. "I'll come and brush you later," she promised. "Whatever happens. But you looked so beautiful, Tup! So perfect! I only wish I could have flown with you!"

Tup tossed his head, and his closed wings shivered with excitement.

"Oh, I know," Lark murmured. "And you should be proud. It was marvelous!" She slipped out the gate, saying, "I'll be back. As soon as I can. Here's Molly, now, and Bramble is in the aisle. You won't be alone."

Still, she heard his little cry as she left the stables, and she knew he wanted her there beside him, to help him shed the nervous energy created by his adventure of the day. A great day, for Tup. And for her, too, she decided, despite the dressing-down she was about to receive.

She tried, as she walked across the courtyard to the Hall, to think of some defense. She had, after all, warned Mistress Winter and the Headmistress that Tup was ready to fly. And she had been right! But Tup could have hurt himself, or another horse, there was no denying that. And she hadn't helped matters by insulting her sponsor. And cutting her hair, and failing to learn to use the flying saddle . . .

Her steps dragged, but she reached the Hall just the same, and stood looking up at the double doors, steeling herself. She put her foot on the bottom step, promising herself she would simply take her scolding, and control her snappy tongue. She had caused enough problems for Mistress Winter already. This one time, at least, she would try not to make things worse.

TWENTY-ONE

BY the evening of the next day, William was in a towering temper. He had slept in the straw, or tried to, and his back hurt. The stable-man had brought his meals, but they were cold by the time he wended his way out of the kitchens and through the grove to the stables. The coffee was tepid and the brandy was gone. His clothes were foul with bits of straw and muck.

And despite these sacrifices, the foal would not respond to him. It quivered at his touch, shrank into a corner trembling and whimpering, and refused to suckle. If William had believed in the horse goddess, he could have believed she was playing a cruel trick on him.

William no longer recalled how Philippa's Winter Sunset had looked as a newborn. When he had seen the little black at Deeping Farm, the colt was several months old, clean and shining, well groomed and well fed. But this foal—

William didn't know if there was something wrong with it, or if newborns simply looked this way. Its fragile legs shook like willow saplings in a breeze, and its ears drooped to the sides of its head, giving it a stupid look. Its eyes rolled, showing the whites, and it drooled from slack lips. Its dappled coat was dry, thanks to the ministrations of its dam, but it was coarse to the touch. William could find nothing attractive about it, nothing that promised the breathtaking beauty of a flying horse.

"M'lord," Jinson said. He stopped outside the stall gate, eyeing the trembling foal with an uneasy expression.

William was sitting on the little nest of blankets, his back against the wall, glowering at the cowering bit of horseflesh in the corner. He shot the stable-man an irritated glance. "Well, what is it?" he demanded.

Jinson swallowed, and spoke with obvious reluctance. "M'lord—if the colt don't suckle, he'll die."

"Oh, yes?" William snapped. He got to his feet, groaning at the pain in his back. "Well, do something about that, damn it! I've tried everything I can think of." He took a step toward the gate, and the foal stumbled back to the wall and fell to its knees. William whirled and glared at it. "There's something wrong with it!" he expostulated.

"He—he—" Jinson's response broke off, and he stood back from the gate, avoiding William's gaze.

William gave a gusty sigh. The foal struggled to its feet again, and the mare stepped between William and her offspring, her ears laid back. "Go ahead, Jinson," William said with exasperation. "Say it."

"It's you, sir," Jinson blurted. "Sorry, but the foal won't suckle with you there."

"How in Zito's hells am I supposed to bond with him if he won't tolerate me?" William hissed. The mare twisted her head around to eye him balefully. The foal stumbled again, and fell to the straw. This time he didn't rise.

William put his back to the gate and stared at the mare and the foal. "I don't care," he said. "Either he bonds, or he dies."

"M'lord!" Jinson breathed. "He's—m'lord, he's a *winged horse*!"

William gave Jinson a cool look over his shoulder. "Don't be a fool, man," he said. "Of course he is. That's the whole point. But he's no damned good to me if he won't bond."

Jinson's mouth opened and closed again, like a fish out of water. When he found his voice, he stammered, "But m'lord . . . the Duke . . ."

William allowed his lips to curve, ever so slightly. "I'll be Duke soon enough, Jinson," he purred. Jinson stiffened, and seemed to shrink within himself. William chuckled. "That's right," he said. "You don't want to cross me, and neither should this misbegotten colt."

Jinson dropped his eyes and stared at his boots.

William considered the foal, lying flat now in the straw. The mare nosed it, and whickered to it, trying to get it to rise. "Take the mare out," William finally said to Jinson. The stable-man came into the stall and put a halter on the mare. He cast William one last, despairing glance, but William only pointed, and Jinson led the mare away.

When they were gone, William went to the foal once again, and squatted beside it in the straw. "Too bad," he said. "The other one throve from the beginning."

He hooked his blanket toward him, and folded it around the colt's face and nose. He pulled the ends tight around its head, and held them there.

The tiny thing had grown weak, and it was all over in moments. It gave a feeble kick, and then another. Its spidery legs stiffened, trembled, and then subsided to lie limply in the straw. Its ribs no longer rose and fell, and its stub of a bristly tail lay still, as lifeless as a handful of broomstraw. Its little folded wings seemed to shrivel and dull.

William stood, dusted his palms, and pushed the blanket away with his booted foot. He let himself out of the stall, and called, "Jinson! Come take care of this mess. And fetch Slater."

THE last days before the holiday were hard ones for Lark. She hardly saw Hester, or Anabel, except at meals and on the sleeping porch. All her waking hours were spent drilling on Pig, with Mistress Strong snapping orders in her flat voice, or helping Rosellen muck out stalls as part of her punishment for losing control of Tup. Lark didn't mind hard work. She had shoveled plenty of wet straw before she came to the Academy. She did mind falling out of her saddle every day, and she minded the pitying glances of the third-level girls, the poorly hidden mirth of the second-levels, the sympathetic murmurs of some of her own classmates. And she hated the triumphant look on Petra Sweet's face. But true to her promise, she kept her peace. She held her head high, and went about her extra chores with a will.

The only happy moments in those cold days came when Tup flew, with Winter Sunset as his monitor. Lark had been afraid it would be forbidden, but Mistress Winter was firm about it.

"He's tasted it now," Mistress Winter had said severely. "If you have to keep him on the ground, he'll be restive. It's best to let him have as much exercise in the air as possible. Sunny and I will see to that."

"Thank you, Mistress," Lark said, in as demure a voice as she could manage.

The horsemistress was not deceived, and her look made that clear. "But, Larkyn," she added, and her voice grew hard. "When you're away for the holiday, you must keep his wing clips in place. Do you understand? It's only a few days, and he will have the distraction of travel. Your colt wouldn't fly away from you deliberately, but without a monitor, anything could happen. He could get confused, or get into trouble, and not know how to get back to you."

Lark grew cold at the very idea that she could lose Tup. "Aye, Mistress Winter," she said in a rush, and there was no pretense in her compliance. "I'll be careful. I promise!"

And so, every day, she stood in the flight paddock and watched Tup launch himself into the air after Winter Sunset. Each time, Lark's own muscles tensed, as if she could do it for him. Sometimes, her arms ached afterward, as if she were the one who had circled and swooped after the Noble mare, who had skimmed the treetops and pierced the low clouds, who had sailed down at a daringly steep angle until her feet grazed the grass, found the ground firm beneath them, pinions stretched wide.

Tup seemed to grow before her very eyes. Once, she even found Mistress Winter measuring him with her palm and outstretched fingers, murmuring to herself as she counted.

"How tall?" Lark asked.

The horsemistress didn't look at her, but ran a practiced hand over Tup's croup. "Thirteen hands," she said shortly. "It's time to start him with a saddle, just for ground work. He's growing so fast it's affecting his balance in the air. We must be careful."

"Oh," Lark said faintly. "I didn't know. I didn't see it."

"How could you, when you haven't been there yourself?" Mistress Winter said sharply.

Lark bit her lip. She was learning that Philippa Winter spoke most harshly when she was most worried. She waited to discover what it might be that troubled her on this day.

The horsemistress left off examining Tup, and faced Lark. "We have met with Eduard once again," she said. "There is now, apparently, no question of gelding your colt. Lord—that is, the Duke has decided he wants to know what sort of colt he'll throw."

Lark breathed, "Oh. And does that mean—they know what line he is?"

"No." Mistress Winter set her jaw, and stared past Lark to the east, where the spires of the White City glimmered in the dusk. The nights were drawing in, and Lark often finished her chores and studies only after full darkness settled over the Academy. "No, Larkyn. It means the Palace has chosen to ignore Eduard's advice, and he is unhappy about it. It also means we may never know Tup's lineage."

Lark hesitated a long moment, absently stroking Tup's neck with her hand. "Mistress Winter," she said at last, softly. "Does it matter so much? We can serve, Tup and I, whether he's Ocmarin or Noble or Foundation . . . or a throwback. He's a wonderful colt. Must we know which bloodline he belongs to?"

Mistress Winter returned her gaze to Lark. She looked at her for a long moment, and the angular lines of her face softened in the gloom. "You're right, Larkyn. He's a fine colt, strong and agile and spirited. Not unlike his bondmate."

Lark dropped her eyes to hide the pride that must kindle in them.

"It's not about Tup, really," Mistress Winter went on. "It's about Oc, and all the winged horses." She stroked Tup again, her hand tracing the line of his hindquarter. "It's about Duke Frederick's life work, preserving and protecting Kalla's creatures, making certain that they are the best they can be. They are prized throughout the principality—throughout the world—and they protect Oc in many ways. But for Duke Frederick, the horses themselves have always been the point, the purity of the bloodlines, the strength of their heritage. He loved them for their beauty and spirit and . . . well, all the things we love them for."

She lifted her hand from Tup, and dusted it lightly against her thigh. "I like your colt, and I have no doubt that you and he will serve the Duchy well. But if someone has violated the bloodlines—then someone has committed treason. And to keep your colt intact implies further breeding violations." Her voice dropped very low. "You must not speak of this, Larkyn, but you should be aware of it."

"Yes, Mistress." Lark hesitated, and then blurted, "But the saddle? Was it not Char's?"

Mistress Winter's face hardened again, all at once. "I don't know. I never found it."

"Char was an Ocmarin," Lark said with confidence.

"You can't know that for certain."

"I can, Mistress. I know the bloodlines now. Her color, her conformation, her size . . . she was an Ocmarin. A wingless one, of course."

"Perhaps."

"But Tup—his color is that of a Foundation, but he has Noble traits."

"You think you've figured all this out?"

Lark laughed aloud. "It's obvious! Who could miss it?" Then, suddenly, she caught herself, wondering if she had given offense.

But Mistress Winter seemed to be in a mellow mood. "Indeed," she said quietly. "Who could miss it, indeed." She straightened her tabard, and picked up her quirt from the stall shelf. "Well, Larkyn. The point of all this is your colt's name."

"Has Master Crisp—have you decided?"

"Margareth decided," she answered. "She felt some decision should be made, and Eduard agreed. He is to be called Black Seraph. Seraph is an honorable name, one of the earliest of the bloodlines."

"Black Seraph," Lark repeated, a little dazedly. "'Tis a bit hard to say, isn't it?"

"No winged horse has ever had a name like Tup. It's not appropriate."

"I—to me he'll always be Tup, I think."

"Your situation is unique, Larkyn. The question that remains is what you'll be called."

"They mostly call me Hamley, in the Dormitory." And Goatgirl, but she didn't say that.

"Such names tend to develop on their own. I was pleased to change my name to Winter. And you could be Larkyn Black, if you find Seraph difficult."

"I like Hamley, though. And my brothers are so proud."

Mistress Winter tipped her head to one side, and regarded Lark with an odd expression. "Are they, indeed?"

"Oh, aye, Mistress! What other Uplands family has a horsemistress to bear its name?"

ROSELLEN, forking soiled straw from the stall of one of the horsemistresses' mounts, looked up as Lark came into the stables, a pitchfork in her hand. "Lark!" she exclaimed. "I thought your punishment was finished."

"It is," Lark said. "But I thought I'd give you a hand, one more time. Tomorrow we all go off for the holiday, and you'll be on your own. I . . ." Her cheeks warmed, and she bent to lift a forkful of straw. "I'm afraid you'll be lonely," she finished, not meeting Rosellen's eyes.

"Heh," the stable-girl said. "Maybe a mite. Me and Herbert will have a bit of a holiday, too, though, with all the flyers gone."

"I suppose it's too far for you to go home to your village."

Rosellen grunted. "Haven't been back in five years," she said. "Letters sometime, that's all." They worked in silence for a bit, and then Rosellen straightened, leaning on her pitchfork. "Bit far for you, too, isn't it? The Uplands?"

"It takes most of a day, in the oxcart," Lark agreed.

Rosellen tapped her nose, and grinned. "Thought you'd be going off with one of the swells, Goat-girl."

Lark laughed. Only from Rosellen did Goat-girl sound affectionate. "I can't wait to see my brothers," she said. "Although Lady Beeth did invite me, which was so kind. You should meet her. She doesn't seem like a Lady at all, just a mother."

They finished the stall, and Lark helped Rosellen empty the wheelbarrow, then trailed after the stable-girl as she made her final check of the tack room and the water buckets. "Thanks, Lark," Rosellen said, when everything was finished. "I'm sorry you got in trouble, but it was nice having company."

"I'm used to chores," Lark said. They paused beside Tup's stall, and Tup and Molly ambled over to them for a pat. Lark was startled to realize she had to reach up to touch Tup's cheek. He was still slender and coltish, though, and he would never be as tall as Hester's Golden Morning, or even Anabel's Take a Chance.

"Mind you remember them wing clips," Rosellen said. She gave Lark her gappy grin.

"Kalla's heels," Lark said fervently. "I'm not likely to forget again!"

TWENTY-TWO

PHILIPPA sat by her window in the Domicile, a book on her lap, watching girls depart from the courtyard. Her own flight had left early in the morning, flying off to their own homes on their own mounts, exhilarated at the taste of independence that would be theirs after Ribbon Day.

And now the families of the younger students had come to collect their daughters. Their carriages filled the courtyard. Philippa leaned forward to watch Hester climb up beside her mamá and her plump little father. Hester waved at her departing friends, calling farewells. The perfectly matched draught horses paced away, and Golden Morning, wing-clipped and blanketed, trotted alongside, shining gold and silver in the frosty sunshine.

Petra Sweet's father had sent a phaeton, with a uniformed driver and a footman. Petra climbed up on the high seat, and looked down at the other girls with an expression of smug satisfaction. She was right to feel proud, Philippa thought. The phaeton was a beauty, sleek and high-wheeled, drawn by a fine pair of grays. Every head turned as it wheeled away, with Sweet Reason trotting beside it.

The courtyard emptied, bit by bit, as servants finished hefting luggage, girls ended their farewells, a few parents greeted each other. Everyone made their way out of the courtyard in their turn, until a colorful procession wound toward the road, each carriage trailed by a winged horse. And just coming in, working its stolid way through the traffic and around the cobbled courtyard, was the Hamley oxcart.

Philippa laid her book aside, and stood up for a better view. She was vaguely disappointed to see that it was not Brye Hamley driving this time. It was the youngest brother—what was his name? Ah, she remembered, it was Nicol. Nick. The handsome, laughing one. He seemed unaffected by the curious glances he received as he pulled up before the Dormitory, even lifting his wide-brimmed hat to one or two other drivers, shamelessly flashing his white teeth at the well-dressed ladies of Council Lords. Larkyn dashed out to meet him, her worn carpetbag in her hand. She tossed the bag into the cart, and then dodged the last of the equipages to cross the courtyard to the stables. By the time she emerged with Tup on a halter, all the carriages were gone, and the courtyard was empty.

Philippa was tempted to check the colt to make certain he was wearing his wing clips beneath his blanket, but she refrained. Larkyn would never again forget. She had worked too hard to show her penitence, and never a word of complaint. She had learned that lesson, at least.

When the odd party started out of the courtyard, the slow but steady ox, the prancing near-yearling colt, the little brown bearded goat, Philippa smiled to herself. She sank back into her chair, and picked up her book once more. For a time, she need not worry about Larkyn Hamley and Black Seraph. Brye and the other Hamley brothers would watch over them.

Ten days of peace lay ahead, and she welcomed them. Her mother and brother had invited her—well, summoned was perhaps the better word—to Islington House, but she had declined. If she went, Meredith would talk of nothing but the Duke's illness, and how Philippa might mend fences with William. Her mother and her sisters and their husbands would talk of children, society, clothes, finance, none of which interested Philippa. She much preferred the quiet of a half-empty Domicile, meals in the kitchens, aimless flights with Sunny. Erdlin, and Estian in the spring, were a time of respite.

There had been a time when Philippa spent all her holidays at the Ducal Palace. This would be the second year in which there was, evidently, no Festival celebration at the Palace at all, no lavish banquet, no dancing, no midnight bonfire. Idly, as Philippa allowed her eyes to close and a rare afternoon sleepiness to overtake her, she wondered what Lady Sophia, and Francis, would do on that day. And William, William with his oddly affected embroidered vests, his smooth face . . .

And the Hamleys? Would they feast, or visit neighbors, or dance in the village square? Brye Hamley did not seem the type, but perhaps, once a year, when the flutes and harps began to play, he would take some apple-cheeked girl into his embrace and dance . . .

Philippa yawned. Her book slid to the floor, and with a sigh, she slipped into a drowse.

"So thin, you are, Lark! As if you have birds' bones under your skin!" Nick exclaimed as he lifted her down from the cart.

She gazed around at the familiar buildings of Deeping Farm, and answered absently, "Oh, aye. Meals are small at the Academy! Flyers must be light—and I'm the lightest girl there."

"Well," her brother said with a laugh. "We'll soon put some meat on you."

"Oh, no, Nick," Lark said swiftly. "I'll be flying soon, and though Tup has grown so much, he's still not very big. I don't want to be too heavy for him to carry!"

Nick handed her bag to her, shaking his head. "Can't imagine that, little sister. I could carry you myself, in one arm." And laughing, he demonstrated by lifting her and twirling her around so her skirt flew out around her ankles.

Moments later Brye came around the corner of the barn, and the girl Peony came up the steps from the coldcellar. Lark hugged her brother, greeted Peony, and allowed her bag to be carried away while she led Tup into the barn. Molly trotted at her heels, bleating with pleasure as she caught sight of the other goats. It had been a long day, and the early darkness already enfolded the farm by the time Lark finished stabling Tup, and crossed to the house.

She paused at the kitchen door to touch the bare skeleton of the rue-tree. It had been in full leaf when she departed. The fields beyond the house, the kitchen garden, had all been in bloom, but now lay empty. She felt as if she had one foot in Osham, and one in Willakeep. She felt divided between the girl she was and the girl she had been, and it gave her an odd sensation of being out of balance, as if the ground beneath her feet might shift at any moment.

She stepped into the kitchen and looked around at the old, familiar room. She tried to see it with affection, but she found herself noticing that the counter had crumbs on it, that the butter dish had a coat of old grease on its rim, that the sink needed a good bleaching.

Peony was waving the Tarn over a garlicky pottage. She looked up, and grinned at Lark, her round cheeks dimpling. "Here you are at last!" she said. "Sit you down! Soup and bread."

She hung the Tarn on a hook by the close stove. Lark picked it up again, and moved it to its proper place over the sink. "Thank you, Peony," she said politely. "I would love some of your soup, but I can't eat too much bread. Flyers have to be thin."

"You're more than thin, Lark," Peony said in a motherly way. "Skin and bones, you are!"

Lark flashed her a look of resentment. Peony was only a year older than she, after all. But she sat down, and began to slice cheese from the wheel, biting her lip to keep herself silent. Peony, all unaware, bustled about, ladling her pottage into the bowls, pouring glasses of milk, running to the kitchen door to call to the men.

Lark thought the milk a bit blue. No doubt Peony had skimmed it too finely. She would let Brye deal with it, though, or Nick. She didn't want to be like Petra, criticizing every detail, picking away at the poor girl.

Lark looked around the old kitchen as she waited for her brothers to join her. It seemed darker than it had in her memory, smaller and dingier. Deeping Farm hadn't changed, of course. It was she who was different, her eyes dazzled by fine china, sparkling crystal, white tablecloths, high ceilings.

When Brye and Edmar came in, with Nick following, tears pricked her eyelids. Her two older brothers looked so tired, and so begrimed from their day's labors. Their cheeks and noses glowed red from the cold. Though they scrubbed their hands for long minutes at the sink, farm dirt clung to their fingernails. They began their meal in silence, with nothing like the chatter that filled the Dining Hall at the Academy.

Lark dropped her eyes to her soup bowl, not wanting anyone to ask her what was amiss. How could she explain? She was no longer Lark of Deeping Farm. But she was not really Larkyn Hamley of the Academy, either. She fit nowhere. Her throat closed so she dared not take a spoonful of pottage in case she couldn't swallow it.

"Now, Lark," Nick said gaily.

She blinked, hard, and lifted her face.

"Tell Brye and Edmar—and Peony—all about why you cut your hair. The whole story!"

Lark touched the icon that hung round her neck, and thought of Lady Beeth and Anabel and Hester. She began to tell the story backward, beginning with the Headmistress, but Nick stopped her and made her start again from the beginning. By the time she finished, everyone was laughing, including herself. They asked a dozen questions about Hester, and Lady Beeth, and the shops of the White City. By the time the soup was eaten, the bread polished off, and the dishes cleared and washed, Lark felt at home again. When she went upstairs to her old bedroom, and tucked herself in beneath the worn quilt, she felt whole at last. She lay awake, relishing the feeling that, at least for the moment, all the parts of her were in their rightful place.

As Mistress Winter had warned, Tup became restive after only one day of confinement at Deeping Farm. He complained when she left the barn, chewed on his feed bucket until its edges were splintered, kicking at the wall of his stall. Brye scowled over the indentations in the planking and threatened to hobble him.

Lark took him walking in the fields, with Molly trailing behind. Tup pranced sideways, threatening to step on Lark's feet. He tossed his head, and flexed his wings against the clips. She took him up to the north pasture to walk along the riverbank. The current swirled with clots of ice, reflecting the blackstone of the riverbed. A dusting of snow had fallen before dawn, turning the ground crisp and gray. Lark unclipped the halter lead to let Tup race back and forth. Molly bleated her anxiety, but Lark soothed her. "Don't worry, Molly. He won't leave us. But he needs exercise, and neither you nor I can run that fast!"

Moments later, Tup returned to stand before her, blowing, ruffling his pinions beneath the wing clips. "No, Tup!" Lark said. "You can't fly, not alone. It's not safe!"

He whickered, and pushed at her with his nose, and when she wouldn't comply, he dashed off again, racing to the river's edge and back, whinnying now, stamping his feet. Lark gave up trying to explain it to him. She replaced the lead on his halter, and led him and Molly back to the barn.

* * *

THE next day, she blanketed Tup against the chill, and took him with her when she went to visit Amberly Cloud. She found Silver Cloud almost pitifully eager for company. She turned Tup into the little paddock behind Mistress Cloud's small stable, and let the two spend time together. She would like to have stayed with them, or even better, let Tup fly with Silver Cloud as monitor, but Mistress Cloud had an elaborate tea ready, and had no interest in coming out into the cold. Hours later, it seemed, Lark set out for home, with Tup beside her. Nick and the oxcart were to catch up with her on the road.

Tup cried piteously as she led him away from Silver Cloud, and Silver Cloud was no happier. "I'm sorry," Lark said. "Sorry for both of you."

Tup bobbed his head as if he understood, but the moment they reached the open road, he pranced, and tugged at the halter lead. His wings rustled beneath the blanket.

Lark glanced behind her, hoping to see the oxcart trundling toward them, but the road was empty as far back as she could see. It was a frigid midafternoon, too early for the workers to be walking back from the quarry, from the silos, or from the various shops. She peered ahead, and there was no one coming toward her, either. Tup turned his head to follow her gaze, as if he understood what she was thinking.

"Oh, no, Tup, it would be silly, wouldn't it? I mean, I've never . . . and you've never . . ."

He whickered. It sounded, to her ears, exactly like a laugh.

"No flying!" she said sternly. "Do you understand? The clips remain!"

He shook his head to make the halter jingle, and nosed her at every step. She went on a little, torn by indecision. If she was too heavy . . . or if she should fall off . . .

But she only fell from saddles! And she knew the sand weights he'd been carrying weighed half again what she did. Laughing, feeling deliciously reckless, she looped the halter lead in her hand, turned to Tup's left side, and took a handful of his glossy black mane.

His withers, at thirteen hands, were at the same level as her nose. In fact, Tup was only slightly taller than the redoubtable Pig, and Lark never needed Rosellen's assistance when she climbed up on Pig. Tup twisted his nose around to watch her. His ears pricked forward, and his eyes gleamed with anticipation.

"Rascal," she said. "You think this is your own idea, don't you?" She took a deep breath, stretched her right arm around his spine, and jumped.

She teetered on her stomach for a moment, before she could swing her right leg across. Tup trembled, once, at the surprise of her weight, but he steadied immediately. She sat astride him, her legs fitting over the jointure of his wings, his folded pinions like the ribs of a fan beneath her calves. She looked ahead. Tup's ears rotated toward her, waiting for a signal. His arched neck and the slope of his shoulders in front of her knees were, she thought, the most beautiful and natural thing she had ever seen. Her seat fit him perfectly, as if she had been made just for this. She caressed the icon of Kalla she now wore around her neck. Indeed, she had been made so, by Kalla's design.

She lifted the halter rope, and pressed her heels ever so slightly to his ribs. "Let's go, Tup," she said. "Let's go home!"

He stepped out willingly. She watched carefully for any sign that her weight affected his stride, that he was uncomfortable beneath her, but she found nothing. Unlike Pig, who lumbered from side to side as she rode him, Tup's stride was even and effortless. After a few moments, she sensed his desire to go faster. She snugged her thighs tighter over his barrel, and let the halter lead swing loose. Tup broke into a trot, a smooth, ground-eating gait. Lark kept a firm grip on his mane, but she felt no anxiety about slipping off. This was easy! She could feel every action of his muscles, every movement of his joints. She knew as soon as he did where he would put his feet, how long each stride would be. His rhythm was her rhythm, the slight bob of his head as much a part of herself as the flex of her spine. Oh, if only Mistress Strong could see her! Of course, if she did, she would only scold her, first for riding Tup before she had permission, and second, for riding bareback!

Lark laughed aloud into the gloom of early twilight, and Tup, ears flicking back and forward, lengthened his stride. They would reach home before Nick did.

When they drew close to Willakeep, Lark drew up the halter lead and shifted her weight back. "Whoa, Tup," she said. "I'll get down now. This will be our secret."

Obediently, Tup slowed his trot, and stopped. Lark slid down from his back, and threw her arms around his neck. "Tup!" she cried. "A lovely fine boy, you are!" He blew through his nostrils, in obvious agreement, and she released him, laughing. She dusted the back of her skirt as best she could with her hands before they started up the road again. When they turned into the lane, they were walking demurely side by side. Tup, at last, seemed calm.

The oxcart caught them there, halfway down the lane. Nick said, "Lark! Either you left Mistress Cloud's early, or you walk faster than I could."

Lark laughed and shrugged as she climbed up onto the seat beside her brother. Tup whickered at the ox, flicked his tail with what seemed like obvious pride to Lark, and settled into a quiet walk beside the cart.

Nick eyed him. "Yon colt has settled down a bit."

Lark blushed, and stammered a moment. She wouldn't lie to her brother, ever, but she didn't want to be scolded, either. She had been scolded enough in the past weeks! Finally she said, "Oh, aye. He spent a bit of time with Mistress Cloud's gelding."

Nick's eyebrows rose and fell, but he made no further comment.

TWENTY-THREE

THE windows of Willakeep danced with candlelight as the Hamleys' oxcart rolled into the cobbled square and took its place among the others. The bonfire blazed, and torches burned at every corner, driving back the chill darkness that marked the season of Erdlin. The farmers and villagers crowded the square, wrapped in woolens and wearing brightly embroidered caps pulled down over their ears. The women's braids fell from beneath their caps, decorated with ribbons and sprigs of ivy. The men were scrubbed and shaved. The doors of both taverns stood open to the night, and a steady stream of revelers flowed in and out, tankards and cups in their hands. Music came from each open door, the tunes competing with each other in the center of the square.

Lark climbed down from the cart, and followed Brye through the crowd, working their way toward the bonfire. Nick and Edmar hurried off to the nearest of the taverns, laughing over their shoulders at their sober elder brother. People greeted Brye as he passed, and nodded to Lark. She knew every face, every name, but they had grown shy with her since the change in her fortunes. Even the girls she had known in school kept their distance. Petal, only months older than Lark herself, balanced a baby on her hip. She, too, was shy, lifting one hand in greeting, and then turning away to join another group. Only Peony came dashing up to Lark without hesitation, crying, "Lark! Brye! At last. Where's Nick?"

Laughing, Lark pointed at the open tavern door, and then went to stand beside Brye, her back to the warmth of the bonfire, her gaze on the faces of people she had known since her girlhood. It seemed she barely knew them anymore, though she had been gone a scant six months.

A dance began in a little cleared space off to her right, one of the Uplands rounds that meant arms in the air, legs kicking high, couples spinning about with skirts and coats flying. Lark climbed the rail fence surrounding the firepit so she could watch. Everyone began to sing, Lark included, remembering the words to the old tune:

> THE HAND IS OPEN,
> RELEASING THE YEAR
> SWING YOUR SWEETHEART,
> ERDLIN IS HERE.
> WINTER'S FIST WILL CLOSE SOON ENOUGH
> AND THE BOOT OF SPRING IS SWIFT AND ROUGH,
> SUMMER IS SHORT AND AUTUMN IS LONG,
> BUT FOR NOW, ONCE AGAIN, WE SING ERDLIN'S SONG.

The dance ended in general hilarity, and as the song died away, the celebrants were washed in the clash of music from the taverns again. It was all sweetly familiar, and Lark, her back now toasted by the bonfire, pulled off her heavy coat. Brye spread it on the top rail, and she perched there to watch the next dance, the toes of her riding boots hooked through a lower rail to steady herself. Nick and Edmar returned from the tavern. Peony trailed at Nick's heels, making Lark think of Molly tagging after Tup. Nick grinned up at Lark, and handed her a mug of something hot and fragrant. She sipped it, and found it to be strong red wine, sweetened with honey and steeped in cinnamon. She wrinkled her nose, and Nick laughed.

"If you don't like it, sweetheart, just hold it for me!" he said.

"Come and dance, Nick!" Peony pleaded. Her dimpled cheeks were flushed, her eyes bright in the light from the bonfire. She shrugged out of her coat to reveal a scarlet tabard and a wide, flowing skirt. Her braids were woven with scarlet threads.

Nick glanced up at Lark, and she shrugged, laughing. "Your other admirers won't like it," she said.

"Ah, well," he cried. "What better way to begin Erdlin than by breaking a few hearts?" He seized the delighted Peony's hand, and pulled her through the crush to join the dancers.

Lark, truly warm now from the fire, pulled off her cap and ran her fingers through her short curls. Brye leaned against the fence next to her, content, it seemed, to simply watch, and sip the tankard of beer Edmar had brought for him. Edmar, to Lark's astonishment, had drained his own tankard and plucked a plump woman from the crowd to dance with. Lark pointed this out to Brye, and he turned one of his rare smiles up to her. She smiled back, and returned to gazing around her at the festive scene. Surely, she thought, her classmates in their fine houses could have no better celebration, no higher spirits, than these country folk of Willakeep.

"Missy? Oh, aye, aye, you're the flyer, aren't you, Missy?"

Lark looked down to see a much-wrinkled woman standing beside her feet. Her gray braid was twisted around the crown of her head, and her tabard and skirt were a rusty black. She squinted up into the firelight. "Aye, aye, that's an Academy habit."

"It is," Lark said. She unhooked her feet, and slid down from the rail, nodding politely to the older woman. "I'm Larkyn Hamley."

The woman nodded, the skin of her neck pleating against her collar. "Oh, aye, I've heard about you," she said, tapping her temple with one brown finger. "The girl from Willakeep. Winged foal. Academy."

"Yes," Lark said. For courtesy's sake, she added, "We haven't met before, have we?"

"Oh, no," the woman said, shaking her head the other way. She grinned, showing small yellow teeth. "No, no, I'm from the hills. Clellum, it is, beneath the butte of blackstone." Her grin sharpened, and she leaned toward Lark. "You ever need a potion, you come to see me! You come and see old Dorsey!"

Lark drew herself back with a spasm of distaste. The old woman cackled. "Nay, nay," she cried. "Of course not, not Larkyn of Willakeep! Never!" She leaned in again. "Never say never, that's the wise thing."

"I have no need of potions," Lark said stiffly. She wished she hadn't come down from her perch, but she could hardly clamber back up again now without being rude. She wondered what Hester would do if an old witchwoman approached her in a public place. Hester always knew what to do.

"Nay, nay," the old woman said again, shaking her head so gray strands flew out from her braids, gleaming silver in the firelight. "But if you ever need a simple, or a smallmagic—do you come to Clellum! I'll take care of you, like I did that other!"

Despite herself, Lark bent a little closer to the witchwoman.

She was no taller than Lark herself, and her skin looked dried on her bones. "What other, Mistress?" she asked.

"Oh, that other girl from Osham! At least . . ." The witch-woman put her head to one side, and her eyes, black and small, gleamed like a bird's. "At least I feel sure she was from Osham. She doesn't speak, that one."

"What would a girl from Osham be doing in Clellum?"

"I gave her a potion, a good potion," the woman said, as if she hadn't heard. Her gray wisps of eyebrows drew together in distress. "Didn't work. Or she didn't take it. Nay, nay, never mind, never mind." She shrugged, and grinned again. "Where's your horse, Missy? Old Dorsey would like a blink at a winged horse, for once!"

"He's stabled for the night." A cold feeling stole through Lark, and she absently took a sip from the mug in her hand. The wine had cooled, and its sweetness cloyed in her mouth. Nick came reeling back, Peony in tow, and took the mug from her, shouting something she couldn't understand. Brye turned to her, and asked if she wanted anything. By the time she had answered him, and pointed out Edmar's clumsy but energetic dancing to Nick, the old woman had disappeared. Slowly, Lark climbed back to the top rail of the fence, and settled herself to watch the revelers. But throughout the long, loud evening, she bridled over the old witch-woman's nonsense. Silly woman, she thought. Never say never was such a stupid saying.

"THEY'RE going to call you Black?" Brye said, staring at Lark across the breakfast table. "Larkyn Black?"

Peony had come early and cooked a lavish holiday breakfast, and wouldn't let Lark help her. Lark sat at one end of the table as if she were a guest, feeling restive and frustrated.

"Stick with Hamley." This pronouncement came from Edmar, who didn't look up from his plate as he gave it.

"I want to," Lark told him. "But horsemistresses take their surname from their horse's name . . . and Tup is now officially Black Seraph."

"Oh, that's beautiful!" Peony cried. "I love it! Don't you love it, Lark?"

"I don't know yet. I'm just used to calling him Tup."

Brye leaned back in his chair, and folded his arms. "Just because they put Black Seraph in their book," he said, "doesn't mean you have to use it."

"You know about the book?" Lark asked. "The one on the Headmistress's desk?"

"Saw it," he answered. "When I went to tell them about the saddle."

Nick said slyly, "That did a lot of good, didn't it, Brye? You drove all that way during harvest, and no one did anything! They still don't know where Char came from."

"I wish everyone would let it go," Lark said plaintively. "Tup is Tup, and he's the best colt at the Academy. What difference does it make?"

Brye unfolded his arms, and picked up his knife and fork. "It matters, Lark," he said. "Because Oc matters."

"I still don't see—"

Nick surprised her by taking up Brye's point. "Listen, little sister. We may think we're independent, here in the Uplands, but we're not. We may grumble about the Duke's tithe-man, and turn up our noses at the high-and-mighty ways of the White City, but we need them as much as they need us. Isamar protects Oc in large part because of the winged horses. If they didn't, there are kingdoms—Klee, for one—who wouldn't hesitate to come ashore in Eastreach or Marin and help themselves to what little Oc has!"

"It's about power," Brye said. "And Oc has little enough of that. The old Duke knows his job. And he and the Council of Lords, though they tax us white, are of one mind."

Lark stared at her brothers, amazed. She had never, in all her life, heard them say anything political. She had never heard them discuss anything at all beyond the world of Deeping Farm and Willakeep and the occasional news from Dickering Park.

Nick said, "It's business, Lark. We're out in the marketplace, Brye and I both. When Oc is in trouble, business suffers."

"Then I should go to Mossyrock myself," Lark declared. "I should find out whose saddle it was, and who left Char to wander along the river."

"Why would you have luck where yon Lady Lackbosom had none?" Nick said.

"Don't call her that, Nick," Lark said. "She's—she seems hard, I know, but she's—"

"An intelligent, hardworking woman," Brye said.

Everyone stopped eating, and stared at him. He laid down his fork, and stared back. "You don't like her, Nick, because she talks like a nob. Got my back up, too, at first." He reached for the mug of tea beside his plate. "Know better now. So leave be."

Nick gave a bark of laughter. "Zito's ears, Brye! Sweet on Lady Leanshanks?"

"Nick!" Lark exclaimed.

Brye glowered at his brother, and didn't answer.

Nick chuckled. "All right, I'm sorry. Fine woman and all that. But my question still stands. Horsemistress Winter had no joy of Mossyrock, so how do you think you would?"

"Mistress Winter gave up as soon as she knew the saddle was gone. I would ask more questions—ask the people."

"You don't know the people."

"I'm an Uplander, and so are they. They would talk to me." Like the old woman had, last night, Lark thought, but she didn't say it. She didn't want to speak of the witchwoman and her talk of potions.

"Hard journey to Mossyrock in winter," Brye said. "That track is full of ice."

DAWN came late in the week of Erdlin. Though the calendar would not proclaim true winter until after Erdlin, in the Uplands it was already at hand. The hours of darkness outlasted those of light by four at least. Lark rose before the weak sunshine reached her window, and dressed in wintry gloom. Tup nickered from the barn, sensing her waking.

Her holiday was almost over. It had passed all too swiftly. She had postponed her visit to Petal in her new home, with her new baby, but it could be put off no longer. She would have preferred to slip off with Tup, up to the snow-filled meadow by the river, to walk, to ride a little, to dust snow from the cottonwood branches and toss stones at the chunks of ice floating down the Black River. But Nick had chided her, and she had promised to go to-day. She would go to the village first to find a trinket for the baby, and then make the hike out to Cutbank Farm, where Petal lived with her husband's family.

When she reached the barn to feed Tup and Molly, Peony was

already milking. Lark measured grain for Tup, and listened to the music of the milk squirting into the tin pail. She tried not to dislike Peony. The girl was doing well at Deeping Farm, really, and her presence freed Lark from the guilt that might otherwise have haunted her days at the Academy. It was just that she wanted it both ways! She wanted the farm still to be hers, but she wanted the Academy, too, the company of winged horses and oc-hounds. She missed Hester, and Anabel, and even the lean, graceful horsemistresses, though they looked at her with such doubt.

She watched Tup and Molly at their feed, running her fingers through her cropped curls. "I'm of two minds, Tup," she murmured. "And that's truer than true."

He flicked an ear toward her, and she patted him. "I'll be back this evening," she said. "We'll get a little exercise then." He left his feed bucket to follow her to the gate, and put his nose over as she left, whickering.

Nick was just leaving on his rounds, so she caught a ride in the oxcart as far as Willakeep. There she bade her brother farewell and trudged down the cold stones of the street to the woollery, where Mistress Cateliss sold sweaters and scarves and socks, and had a shelf displaying stuffed dolls with knitted faces and hands. Lark had remembered to beg a few coins from Nick so she could buy her present.

She nodded to several people she knew, and exchanged greetings. She passed the tea shop, where Master and Mistress Bickle sold cut tea and served brewed tea and crooks to their customers. She was just walking by the door to the meat-shop when she stopped as if her feet had frozen to the cobblestones.

A man stood in the door of the woollery. He was no Uplander, in his sweeping greatcoat with its caped layers. He was a large man, but stooped about the shoulders. He had left a horse tethered to a post in the street, and he was just opening Mistress Cateliss's door.

Lark knew this man. She had seen him in Osham, peering out of the door of the apothecary shop where she had received her icon of Kalla.

She remembered the four of them gathered in a shop window, looking out, she and Hester and Anabel and Lady Beeth. And Lady Beeth had drawn the girls back, warned them not to go out until the man was gone. And then she had told them about Lord William, and the stories, and cautioned them . . .

This was Lord William's man, with his greasy dark hair and small eyes, his air of disrepute and danger. Lark could not fathom why he should be in Willakeep, why he should be visiting a woollery shop in an Uplands village in the winter . . . By Kalla's heels, what was Slater doing *here*?

She ducked inside the meat-shop. The butcher greeted her, and she was forced to ask him for something. She chose some oddment she felt certain he wouldn't have, and then dallied, making pointless conversation until she saw the man Slater emerge once again from the woollery, mount his horse, and ride off. Only then, frowning and uneasy, did Lark go back out into the street.

TWENTY-FOUR

PHILIPPA strolled slowly between the hedgerows in the waning afternoon. It was her last day of freedom, and she meant to savor every moment of it. Tomorrow they would return, the girls laughing and full of tales of parties and dances, the horses capering, brimming with unspent energy. The horsemistresses would trickle in, as well. Even Margareth had gone to Eastreach, to her family's estate.

Bramble trotted beside Philippa, occasionally darting to one side to investigate some scent or sound beneath the dry hedgerows. The snowfall of the morning glistened on the branches, and glittered on the stones along the lane. The sky had cleared at mid-afternoon, and the sun was already descending toward the towers of the White City. True winter had begun.

Bramble padded ahead of her into the stables. Philippa spent a few moments changing the water in Sunny's bucket and carrying a fresh flake of hay for her, then turned toward the Domicile. There was an hour still before dinner, when the few of them remaining at the Academy would gather for a quiet meal in the big kitchen of the Hall. Until then she could relax in the reading room, build up the fire, read something.

She was surprised, when she opened the door, to find Irina Strong already there, kneeling on the hearth. Irina tumbled a log onto the embers, and stirred the coals into flames with the poker. She stood, dusting her hands together.

"Good evening, Irina," Philippa said. "Did you just return?"

Irina nodded. "An hour ago."

Philippa took one of the armchairs near the fire, opened her book, and stretched out her feet to the warmth. "I hope you found your family well."

Irina didn't answer for so long that Philippa looked up, her brows raised. The other horsemistress stood staring down into the fire, her square jaw flexing. At last she said, in a colorless tone, "My family lost their home last year. I spent the holiday in Osham, with a friend."

Philippa caught a breath. "Irina. I'm sorry—I had no idea."

Irina folded her arms and turned to look down at Philippa. "No," she said. "You wouldn't, would you? No one knows anything about a junior instructor. Or cares to."

"That's hardly fair," Philippa said.

"Fair," Irina said, in her odd monotone. "Nothing that has happened to me is fair."

Philippa suppressed a sigh. She closed her book, trying not to wish that Irina would take her moods elsewhere. "What do you mean?"

Irina stared into the flames again, and was quiet for so long that Philippa began to hope she would drop it. But after taking a deep, noisy breath, Irina said, "My father's business was ruined. I was serving in the Angles, flying daily reconnaissance over the Straits." She glanced up again, and the bitterness in her face startled Philippa. "You Nobles wouldn't know about that, would you? You and your processions, your fancy shows and games."

Philippa laid her book aside, and stood up. "You should know better than to say that, Irina," she said crisply.

"The borders are hard," Irina responded. "We met the enemy almost every week."

"But you have no idea the kind of service Sunny and I have done."

"I know Sunny's a Noble and my Strong Lady is a Foundation. The Prince never asks for a Foundation unless there's danger. No one wants Foundations in their fairs or expositions."

Philippa snorted. "What a foolish thing to be bitter about, Irina! You sound like a first-level girl complaining about her assignments. You're too old for such nonsense."

"What do you know about it? You'll be Headmistress one day, and I'll still be teaching first-level girls to change leads and clean their horses' feet." Irina turned her back, and stalked away to the window seat, where she sat down, gazing outward across the snowy courtyard. The darkness had closed in around the Academy grounds, and a faint sliver of moon showed above the stable roof.

Philippa stood where she was, staring at the other woman's broad back. She had no idea what to say, or whether she should say anything. Margareth would know what to do, but . . .

"Listen, Irina," she said. She strode across the room to stand at Irina's shoulder. "Fourteen years ago, Sunny and I were at the South Tower of Isamar when the raiders came. We were flying beside Alana when Summer Rose took the arrow. It was a great, thick, horrid thing like a bolt on a knife, and they never had a chance. It could as easily have been Sunny, or me. There have been too many dark nights I wished it *had* been me, but these events are in Kalla's care, not ours—like being bonded to a Foundation instead of a Noble."

Irina blew out a breath that seemed to Philippa full of scorn and disgust.

"Well," Philippa said quietly. "I'm of the belief we can choose to be content. If you prefer being unhappy, that's up to you. If I were you, I'd rejoice that my bondmate and I survived our border service."

"I could choose," Irina said dully, "to wish that my family were as close to the Duke's family as yours. That I would be appointed a senior instructor at the Academy right off, as you were. Everyone knows your brother Meredith and Duke Frederick are—"

"That's enough," Philippa snapped. "Self-pity wins no ribbons, Irina. If you don't like your position here, ask to be reassigned."

Irina swiveled in her seat, and stared up at Philippa with narrowed eyes. "Just wait, Philippa," she said softly. "Just wait until the old Duke dies. We'll see what happens then."

Two days later, Philippa and Sunny led an eager Tup on a flight before morning classes. The air aloft was ice-cold, the sky clear and pale. Larkyn stood in the paddock, watching, with Bramble at her side, the little she-goat just behind her. Philippa gave the colt an extra ten minutes, watching the strength of his wingbeats, the ease with which he followed Sunny's patterns. Experimentally, she dropped Sunny in a Grand Reverse, and Tup, after only a moment's confusion, dipped his left wing and followed. Philippa glanced over her shoulder at him, and almost laughed aloud at the utter joy in the set of his head, the prick of his small ears. He stretched his long, narrow wings with the grace and confidence of

an older horse, and pushed their speed so Sunny had to fly faster
to stay ahead of him.

Tup's landings, too, were deft, with none of the awkwardness
yearlings often showed, not even slipping on the thin layer of
snow that covered the grass. He cantered beside Sunny, head
high, wingtips shivering with exuberance, tail a proud, fluttering
flag. He passed Sunny, racing to the end of the paddock to where
Larkyn waited, and skidded to a stop on his hind legs, his hocks
almost touching the grass. Philippa and Sunny, more sedately,
trotted after. Bramble leaped the fence and came to meet them,
her tongue lolling happily.

Philippa slid down from Sunny, and handed her reins to the
waiting Rosellen. "I should have suggested before the holiday,
Larkyn, that you begin putting more weight on Black Seraph.
Should have sent a saddle with you. He's more than ready."

Larkyn had slipped a halter over Tup's head, and was fitting
the clips over his wings. She asked in an unusually demure voice,
"Should I start now, then, Mistress Winter?" Philippa cast her a
suspicious glance. The girl kept her head down, fiddling with a
wingclip that looked perfectly secure already.

"Yes, please," Philippa said dryly. Larkyn glanced up at her
from beneath her lashes, and then quickly away. Philippa sighed,
and turned away. Her flight would be assembling soon, and their
drills would begin to intensify this very morning. Their Ribbon
Day loomed in the coming summer, the culmination of their six
years of study and practice. The first- and second-level girls
would also be tested, of course. Philippa had debated with Margareth about what Larkyn should do. It hardly seemed possible
she could pass the first-level Airs and Graces. Irina had reported
to Margareth that Larkyn could not even handle the pony without
falling.

Philippa led the way through the gate, and Rosellen and
Larkyn followed, leading the horses. They parted at the corner of
the stables, as Philippa turned toward the Hall.

Bramble paced at her side, but as she reached the center of the
courtyard, the oc-hound stopped, and whined, twisting her head
back toward the horses.

"Bramble," Philippa said, touching the dog's silken head.
"You can go with them. Go ahead! I have a flight, anyway."

Bramble's tail stood straight back, away from her body, and

she whined again, but she didn't move. Philippa looked toward the stables, trying to discern what was troubling her.

What she saw was the stocky figure of Irina Strong standing just within the shadow cast by the gambrel roof. She seemed not to notice Philippa or the oc-hound, but was watching Black Seraph intently as Larkyn led him out of the cold sunshine.

Philippa laid her hand on Bramble's neck. "I see her," she murmured to the dog. "I don't know what that's about, either, Bramble, but I see her. Go, now. Keep your eye on them." Bramble gave one short bark, and bounded off toward the stable.

Soberly, frowning, Philippa crossed the courtyard and went up the steps to the Hall.

"HEH," Rosellen said cheerily to Lark as they measured out feed for the winged horses. "Good Erdlin? Them Uplanders know how to celebrate?"

"Oh, aye," Lark said, grinning. "Even my brother Edmar danced."

"And that one gave you no trouble, not flying?" She pointed her chin at Tup.

Lark grimaced, and shook her head. "Oh, he gave me trouble, Rosellen. Nearly kicked a hole in the side of our barn."

"So what did you do?"

"Well, I walked out with him, and let him run in the pasture, but . . ." Lark leaned close to Rosellen, about to confess to her friend that she had ridden Tup.

"Larkyn?" It was Mistress Strong's voice. Lark straightened quickly, and touched a finger to her lips. Rosellen nodded.

"Yes, Mistress," she called. She ducked out of the feed room and into the aisle of the stables, where she found the horsemistress leaning over the wall of Tup's stall, assessing the colt.

"Black Seraph's filled out," Mistress Strong said. "Legs and chest."

"I know," Lark said, coming to stand beside her teacher. "Mistress Winter says he should begin to carry more weight."

"Well, then. I suppose he should."

Lark dropped her eyes, afraid her secret would be plain on her face. Tup whimpered at her, and she took the excuse to slip inside the stall and pour the grain into his bucket.

Mistress Strong said, "I'm going to fetch a saddle. We'll try it now."

"Yes, Mistress." Lark leaned against Tup as the horsemistress went to the tack room. She pressed her cheek against his shoulder, and felt the ridges of muscle that flowed across his chest, the muscles that powered his wings and centered his strong small body. His haunches rose in an elegant arch from his short back. Even his legs, though slender, were corded with muscle.

Mistress Strong came back with a flying saddle on her hip, a silk blanket in her other hand. She handed the blanket across the wall, and then let herself in the gate. Tup snorted, and backed away from her, making Lark blink at him in surprise. "Tup," she murmured. "Stand still. It's only a saddle."

She spread the silk blanket over his back, smoothing it down his ribs, tucking it beneath the points of his folded wings. But when she moved aside to let Mistress Strong approach with the saddle, he laid his ears back. Molly bleated and retreated to a corner of the stall. Lark heard a rustle in the sawdust of the aisle, and glanced out to see that Bramble had come pacing around the corner to put her forefeet on the gate, her eyes fixed on Mistress Strong.

Mistress Strong spoke heavily to Tup. "Here, now, son. No nonsense from you." She walked closer, and Tup backed all the way to the wall, ears tight against his head. The horsemistress unhooked her quirt from her belt, and flourished it.

Abruptly, Tup whirled, presenting his hindquarters. He lifted one hindfoot as if to kick, but held it poised in the air, watching Mistress Strong from over his shoulder.

"Tup!" Lark cried. "No!"

Mistress Strong dropped the saddle in the straw, and lifted the quirt as if she were about to lash Tup's rump. Lark sprang forward without thinking, and stopped the quirt from falling by seizing it with both hands.

Mistress Strong almost lost her hold on it in her surprise. She glared down at Lark. "Back away," she said, with more energy than Lark had ever heard her use. "I know how to deal with a bad-tempered colt."

"But he's *not* bad-tempered!" Lark cried. Mistress Strong pulled on the quirt, but Lark didn't let go. She was vaguely aware that Rosellen had come to the gate, drawn by the excitement. She said, "Let *me* do it, please, Mistress! He won't kick me. I'll let him smell it, let him get used to it."

"Nonsense," Mistress Strong said.

Tup stamped his hind foot on the floor. He made a good strong bang, and Mistress Strong took a step back.

"Take care," she warned, as Lark bent to pick up the saddle. "You wouldn't be the first girl to get kicked by her horse."

Lark barely heard her words. She heard Tup's rapid breathing, saw the flinching of his ribs and the stiffening of his pinions. As she drew close to him, she *smelled* the change in him, the sweet peppery tang of his flesh deepening to the acid of fear. It made no sense. Tup wouldn't be afraid of a saddle, a mere collection of leather and wood and metal.

"If you can't get it on him," Mistress Strong said, "we'll get him out to the dry paddock and tie him to a post till he gets used to it."

"We will not," Lark muttered under her breath. She lifted the saddle as she walked around Tup's hindquarters and approached his shoulder.

The saddle was half the weight of the one she used on Pig. It was still rigid and slick, though, and hung all over with ties and cinches and a wide, stamped breastpiece. She leaned against Tup's shoulder, the saddle on her right hip, and she caressed his neck with her fingers. "Here, Tup," she crooned. "Here, lovely boy. Look what I have here! Let's just take a moment to see what it's like, shall we? There, lovely boy, there, just a saddle. You see them every day. Just a saddle."

Tup whimpered, and she shushed his complaint. She stepped back, and held the saddle under his nose, letting him sniff the slender pommel, lip at the high cantle, nose the breast strap. In moments he relaxed, and lifted his head as if to ask what would happen next. Lark folded back the right stirrup and cinches, and lifted the saddle onto his back, murmuring to him all the while. He accepted the weight without tremor.

Mistress Strong stood with her arms folded, watching. When Lark brought Tup's head around, and coaxed him into taking a few steps around the stall carrying the uncinched saddle, Mistress Strong harumphed. "Well. Worked this time, Larkyn. But you'll have to take a firm hand with that one. They're still horses, wings or no. They have to know who's in charge."

Other girls and horses were starting to come into the stables. Mistress Strong, distracted, turned to see who had arrived. Girls called to each other, and their horses whickered.

"Leave it on him for fifteen minutes," the horsemistress said, not returning her gaze to Lark. "Again tomorrow. Try the cinches, but have a care. Black Seraph has a black temper."

Mistress Strong sidled out past Rosellen and the oc-hound, and Lark stared after her, mystified. When she was gone, Rosellen whispered, "Tup doesn't have a bad temper. Strong Lady does, though. Terrible for kicking if you're not careful, and the kick of a Foundation is nothing to sneeze at! I'll wager Mistress Strong has felt the bite of those heels more than once."

"Tup doesn't like her," Lark said, shaking her head. "I don't understand it. He seems to like everyone else at the Academy. He just doesn't like her."

TWENTY-FIVE

TRUE winter slowed activities at the Academy of the Air. It seemed to Philippa that horses, hounds, even the girls walked slower. The long nights and short days limited the amount of work that could be done, and tempers frayed. Snow glittered in the return paddock and frosted the bare branches of the hedgerows, and the cobblestones of the courtyard were treacherous with ice. Each morning, Rosellen and Herbert had to break a thin glaze of ice on the oc-hounds' water trough.

The winged horses grew impatient from lack of exercise, but there were some days simply too cold to be in the air for more than a few minutes. This was one of those days, and Philippa had decided to drill her flight on the ground. She watched from the side of the dry paddock as Elizabeth and Chaser circled slowly at a collected canter. The air was so cold it seemed one could take a bite of it, and all the horses were restive. When Elizabeth cued a lead change, Chaser's wings unfolded impatiently.

"Elizabeth, use your quirt. Don't let Chaser open his wings. There will be times flying is not possible."

Elizabeth tapped Chaser on the point of each wing. He shook his head from side to side, and his canter grew a little rough, but he obediently refolded his pinions. Before the next girl made her round, Philippa reminded them all of the importance of practicing each command. As she spoke, her breath curled from her lips in the still air.

As she released her flight to go back into the warmth of the stables, Larkyn came out, leading the old piebald pony. Bramble trotted beside her.

"Larkyn," Philippa said. "Surely you're not still riding Pig?"

The girl's vivid gaze came up to her face, and she flushed.

Not, however, as hotly as she once had, Philippa thought. Larkyn was gaining some composure.

Larkyn said, "Mistress Strong says I must ride Pig until I can hold my seat in the saddle." She added, a bit mournfully, "I fall off. Every time I canter. I have a terrible seat."

Philippa pursed her lips. Absently, she put out her hand to take the pony's bridle, and he bared his teeth. Startled, she snatched her hand back. Bramble growled, and her hackles rose.

"Oh, I'm sorry!" Larkyn said hastily. "I should have warned you. Pig's a biter."

"Kalla's heels! Has he bitten you?"

"Oh, no. He wouldn't bite *me*. But Herbert, several times, and Rosellen, once."

Philippa folded her arms. "Larkyn, I don't know if it's possible for you to catch up with your class by Ribbon Day. But if there's even a chance, you must not only ride, but fly. You can't do that on a pony."

"I know." Lark stopped where she was, and Pig's heavy feet stopped, too. The snow had worn off the dry paddock, leaving a sort of icy mud. Not, Philippa thought, a surface one would want to fall on.

"Mistress Winter," the girl began, and then faltered.

"What is it?" Philippa saw Irina Strong crossing the courtyard, and she felt a sudden rush of impatience. Her own temper was not helped by the restrictive weather.

"If I could only ride Tup . . . instead of Pig . . ."

Philippa had no chance to answer. Irina had arrived at the pole fence, and was unlatching the gate and coming through. Philippa nodded to her. "I'm going to watch Larkyn ride today."

"You and the Head don't trust me, I suppose."

"It's not a question of trust, Irina." She could have explained further, but the very thought of putting it all into words gave her a sense of ennui. She leaned against the fence, and watched through narrowed eyes as Larkyn struggled to turn the stirrup toward her foot while still keeping an eye on the piebald's teeth. Irina snapped Pig's rein, making him jump, and Larkyn dropped the stirrup. The girl cast Irina a wary glance, and Philippa had no doubt that had she not been there, Irina would have said something cutting to the girl.

Philippa sighed, and let her eyelids close. She listened to the creak of saddle leather, the familiar jingle of bit and bridle. The pony's footsteps plodded around the paddock, approaching her and then receding. Irina gave commands, and Philippa opened her eyes to see how Larkyn responded.

The girl, unfortunately, had been right. She had a terrible seat. She hunched over the pommel as if she had no balance at all, and she clutched at the reins with her left hand, the pommel with her right. There seemed to be no coordination between her hands and her feet, and Pig labored around the paddock in a sort of confused waddle. Irina, instead of correcting Larkyn's posture, commanded her to trot the pony. Philippa wanted to close her eyes again, but she forced herself to follow the scene.

Larkyn jounced in the big saddle like a dry pea in a cup, only saving herself from falling by standing in her stirrups. The pony's gait was rough and irregular, and Philippa had to clench her jaw to keep from snapping commands of her own.

And when Irina ordered Larkyn to the canter, the girl tilted to one side, lost her left stirrup, then lost her rein, and then, as Pig stepped on the dropped rein and tripped, Larkyn lost her seat entirely.

With a grunt, the girl fell to the frozen ground of the paddock. The pony lurched to a halt, and whirled as if he might step on his fallen rider. Bramble, sitting at Philippa's side, leaped forward, curling her lip, but Irina at least had the presence of mind to seize the piebald's drooping rein. She kept it at a good length, Philippa saw, no doubt aware of those teeth.

Irina looked up at Philippa. "You see?" she said dully. "I have nothing to work with."

"If I didn't know better, Irina," Philippa said crisply, "I would think you have deliberately sabotaged a young rider. Start again at the beginning. Help Larkyn with her posture, and check the stirrup lengths. I'm going to have a word with Margareth."

She turned, her back stiff with anger, and left the paddock. She glanced back once through the rank of poles to see Larkyn, like a redfaced, curly-haired urchin, dusting the seat of her skirt and approaching the pony once again. Sympathy did Larkyn no good, but she felt it anyway. It was no wonder Irina had never been made a senior instructor. She showed, as far as Philippa could tell, absolutely no aptitude for the job.

* * *

LARK made her escape from the dry paddock as soon as she possibly could. Her bottom ached from falling on it, and her calves burned from struggling to stand in the stiff stirrups. She crept into Tup's stall, and crouched beside him, her back against the wall, her head buried in her sleeve to muffle her sobs.

She wept for only a few moments before Tup's velvet muzzle found her cheek. He lipped at her tears, and whimpered at her. Molly butted at her, trying to push her arm away from her face, and under these awkward ministrations, Lark began to giggle.

She lifted her face, still wet with tears, and laughed at the colt and the little she-goat. "Aye, rascals," she said. She swiped at her running nose with her hand. "Crying won't help, will it? If it's hopeless, it's hopeless, and they'll just have to send me away. As long as you both come with me, I swear I don't care!"

She clambered to her feet, and took Tup's halter from its hook. "Come along, my lovely boy. It's exercise time." She checked his wingclips, and slipped the halter over his head. He already was wearing his blanket against the cold.

Every afternoon he was allowed to run in the yearlings' pasture. They were in the middle of the two-year cycle, and there were no yearlings at the moment except for Tup.

She led him out of the stables, past the other girls working with their horses. Molly trotted beside her, and as she emerged from the stables, Bramble loped across the courtyard to lead the way. The whole little entourage moved through the gate and into the pasture. Lark unclipped Tup's halter lead, and he cantered down the length of the pasture toward the stand of spruce trees that marked its far end. Lark strolled after him, glad to stretch sore muscles. Molly and Bramble followed, each at their own speed, Bramble stopping to sniff every shrub, Molly snuffling at the snow in hopes that a blade or two of grass had survived the cold.

When they reached the grove, Tup came galloping up to Lark, snow flying from his hooves. He skidded to a stop before her, and bumped her chest with his nose.

She rubbed his forehead. "I'd love to have a ride, Tup," she said. "But I don't dare. Not here! What if someone saw us?"

Tup snorted, and dashed away from her again to make a circuit of the pasture. When he came back, he nosed her again, then offered her his side in clear invitation.

Lark glanced back at the Academy buildings. No one was in the courtyard at the moment. Everyone was either in the Hall, out of the cold, or working in the stables. The early evening already shadowed the pasture and the lane, and a ghost of moon showed above the western hills.

Bramble stood beside Tup, laughing up at Lark. Molly was contentedly pawing at the snow. Lark looked back down the length of the pasture, and seeing no one, sprang to Tup's back. Surely, she thought, her standing mount was as good as anyone's. She tightened her riding cap on her head, and said softly, "Let's go, Tup. But through the trees. The grove will hide us."

What a relief it was to ride him again! Her calves snugged easily beneath the points of his wings, her feet curling around his ribs. Her seat conformed to his spine, his short back and fine withers a better fit for her than any saddle could be. She had only the halter lead, but she didn't need even that. With one hand on Tup's mane, the other on his neck, the two of them were in perfect accord.

Surely, she thought, to canter through the grove was almost as marvelous as flying. Tup's gait on the snow-covered grass was like flowing water beneath her, without jolt or bump or break. He responded, it seemed, to her every thought. He changed leads, and swept around the farthest tree. She leaned into the turn, balancing easily, thighs tight on his barrel as if they were glued there. Tup's ears turned forward, and his breath and hers mingled to rise in frosty spirals. They were both, for the moment, supremely happy.

PHILIPPA found a moment, late in the afternoon, to talk with Margareth about Irina Strong's failure to help Larkyn progress. "There's nothing worse than a stubborn woman who's also stupid," Philippa said.

"Now, Philippa," Margareth responded. "Perhaps she's not so much stupid as unimaginative."

"I can't think how she ever learned to fly herself!" Philippa snapped. "She hasn't taught her anything, except to fall on her country backside every time the pony changes gaits!"

Margareth rubbed her eyes, and Philippa immediately regretted her temper. "Never mind, Margareth," she said more quietly. "I'll deal with it. I'll—I'll take over her training myself."

"Kalla's teeth," Margareth said. "Irina will be unbearable if you do that."

"Then things will hardly be different than they are now!"

Margareth stroked the leather-bound genealogy on her desk with her fingers. "It's difficult to like Irina," she said quietly. "But I try. Her father was in some sort of trouble, and for a time there was talk he might be imprisoned. I don't know how he got out of that."

Philippa sighed. "I'll try to have more sympathy for her. But it won't be easy."

Margareth gave her a tired smile. "Thank you. Now go, spend some time with Sunny. Put it out of your mind for a bit."

Philippa nodded, and took her leave of the Headmistress. She shrugged into her riding coat as she went down the steps of the Hall, and pulled it close against the cold as she crossed the courtyard. No one was about. The sky was as gray as lead, the pallid sun invisible behind snow-laden clouds. When Bramble trotted from the flight paddock to greet her, her silvery fur made her almost invisible against the gray and white background.

Philippa reached to stroke the oc-hound, but Bramble dodged her hand, leaping to one side as if about to run off, then standing still, tail high, fixing her with an expectant black gaze.

"Bramble!" Philippa said. "What are you up to?"

For answer, the dog came close again, and then dashed a few steps off, turning to stare at her. Philippa laughed, and moved toward the oc-hound, her hand outstretched. Bramble waited until she was within arm's reach, and then ran a few more steps.

"Kalla's heels, Bramble," Philippa said. "I'm tired, and all I want is to give Sunny a brushing and go sit by a warm fire."

The dog's tongue lolled as she stared at Philippa. She backed away two more steps and then sat, waiting. Philippa clicked her tongue, and gave in.

The moment she moved forward again, Bramble whirled, and trotted purposefully toward the yearlings' pasture. Philippa followed. As they reached the fence, Bramble leaped over it, and stood waiting, tail waving, while Philippa came through the gate.

"If you're just trying to get me to play, I'm going to be very cross with you," Philippa warned her. Bramble grinned up at her, and trotted off. Philippa pulled on her gloves, and walked after the dog.

In truth, the fresh air felt sweet in her lungs, and her eyes were soothed by the pale landscape and muted sky. Philippa walked faster, braced by being out-of-doors, by the crunch of dry snow beneath her boots and the sweet silence of the deserted pasture. She drew breath to call out to Bramble, who had dashed ahead of her to the spruce grove. She released the breath, the call unvoiced. Bramble had reached the trees, and sat down in a clear spot beneath one of them, her task accomplished.

Philippa stood where she was, and watched, amazed, as the girl and the horse dashed between the trees, cutting in and out, changing leads every three or four strides, whirling at the end of the grove and galloping back. They moved as one, as beautifully as Philippa had ever seen a rider and a horse work together. Larkyn's slight form seemed melded to the winged horse's back. Her spine was straight, swaying easily with the horse's movements, and her hands were low, invisible in the flying strands of his mane. Tup ran without effort, every step full of the joy of being young and strong. He carried no tack except a halter, its lead swinging in a loose arc beneath his neck.

Philippa turned her back on the scene. She should scold the girl, of course. She should inspect the colt for injury, issue an ultimatum to Larkyn. She should report to Margareth, and take the whole matter in hand.

But she wouldn't.

As she walked, Bramble came bounding after her, apparently satisfied she had done her duty. Now she let Philippa stroke her head, and walk along with her fingers twined in the oc-hound's silky fur.

Philippa pondered what had just happened. Larkyn weighed so little. She couldn't possibly hurt Black Seraph. And though, obviously, this was not the first time she had ridden the colt, he glowed with health. If Philippa reported their infraction, that fragile ecstasy she had just witnessed—the perfect joy of bondmates in movement—would be extinguished, would be buried under rules and orders and discipline. Irina Strong would be delighted.

But, Philippa thought, as she trudged back down the paddock

toward the Hall, Irina was right in one thing. Larkyn could not fly bareback. It wasn't safe. The challenge was going to be convincing the girl of that.

Philippa thought of a struggling student slipping from Pig's saddle, falling like a sack of oats to the ground, an object to be pitied. Then she remembered Larkyn and Black Seraph dashing through the spruce grove as if they had not a care in the world.

Had she ever, she wondered, looked or felt so utterly free?

TWENTY-SIX

WILLIAM eyed Irina Strong with a slight feeling of revulsion. It was not that the horsemistress was ugly, exactly. There was nothing particularly amiss about her features, though they tended to be large, a substantial nose, rather thick lips, heavy eyelids. It was, he thought, the way she used them—or didn't use them. The monotone of her voice grated on his nerves, and she had a stolid air about her, giving an impression of weighty dullness, rather like one of the magistrates he sometimes had to deal with, or the prefect of a large, prosperous, utterly uninteresting town.

He smoothed his vest with his hands, and kept his face turned to the window. Cold sunlight glittered from the smooth blanket of snow that stretched over the grounds of Fleckham House. "Would you like a cup of tea, Horsemistress?" he asked, forcing courtesy into his voice. "It must have been a cold flight."

"I did not fly, my lord," she answered. "It would draw attention. I came by carriage."

He let his gaze flick over her, and then return to the window. "I would have thought," he said lightly, "that there would be nothing exceptional in a horsemistress calling upon her lord."

"You are not my lord," she said.

He turned to face her. "I beg your pardon?" he said, letting his voice go very soft.

"Duke Frederick," she said. She could have been reading a shopping list, he thought, for all the emotion she showed. "I am in the service of the Duke."

William lifted his chin, and looked at her through hooded eyes. "Take care, Horsemistress," he said with exaggerated lightness. "At any moment—quite, quite literally, I assure you—I could become the Duke."

"When that happens, our business will be easier," she answered

him. She seemed to feel no anxiety, though Slater, standing beside
the door, had hunched inside his dilapidated greatcoat as if he
wished he could disappear.

William commanded, "Get on with it, will you? I have other
business."

"I came to tell you that the girl will never learn to ride. She's
stupid, and uncooperative. The Academy is wasting its time
with her."

William arched one eyebrow. "I met her once," he said. "On
her farm. She seemed anything but stupid to me."

Mistress Strong shrugged. "Perhaps that's because the farm is
where she belongs. I tell you, she can't ride. And she has made no
improvement in all these months."

"Does Margareth Morgan agree?"

"She may not be aware of how badly the girl is faring.
Philippa Winter knows, though."

William opened his eyes wide. "Philippa? Indeed," he purred.
"What is her opinion?"

"She tried to blame the girl's failure on me."

"Ah." William turned back to the window, taking pleasure in
the blinding glare of sun on snow. "That sounds like Philippa."

"You should also know, my lord, that the colt is evil-tempered.
I doubt he'll be worth much, even if Larkyn learns somehow to
fly him."

"Odd, that he should have a bad temperament," William said.
"His dam and his sire were both spirited, but known for their
manners. My own gelding is their get."

"This one is going to be trouble."

William stroked his chin with one finger. "What are you re-
commending?"

"It's a waste, my lord. You might as well take the colt now, and
be done with it."

"Hmm." William thought for a long moment before he faced
his caller again. "If, as you assure me, the girl will fail on Ribbon
Day—then I could take the colt with impunity, I believe."

"Why wait?"

"Well, Mistress Strong, as you have pointed out with such
subtlety . . ." He paused, and noted with amusement that Slater
shrank against the door once more. What did the fool think, that
he would harm a horsemistress, right here in Fleckham House?

"As you have pointed out, I am not yet the Duke. I must tread carefully, and with some discretion."

"Yes, my lord. But I thought you should know."

He allowed the corners of his mouth to curve. "Quite right. I have taken note of it." He nodded to Slater, who opened the door, and held it wide for the visitor.

Irina Strong eyed the door, and then William. "Is that all, then, my lord? You're . . ." For the first time, it seemed that some emotion flickered in her eyes and her voice. "Are you satisfied, then? My father . . ."

"I am satisfied for the moment," he said.

"Best be present on Ribbon Day," she said. "Before the Headmistress takes action."

"Of course," he said. "I never miss Ribbon Day."

She inclined her head to him. He stood rigidly, arms folded over his vest, watching her depart. Even after all these years, it galled him. Only the horsemistresses believed themselves too important to curtsy to a scion of Oc.

William snarled, "You know, Slater, when my day arrives, things will change."

"Oh, yes, me lord?" Slater gave him an ugly grin. "The Council of Lords?"

"The Council, yes." William threw himself into a chair, and tipped his head back, closing his eyes. "That collection of foolish old men stands in the way of progress. I will deal with them. And I swear to you, those damned horsemistresses will learn to curtsy to their Duke, or I'll know the reason why."

"Lovely idea, me lord," Slater agreed. "Only right and proper."

William murmured, "I grow mightily tired of waiting, too."

"Well, me lord," Slater said, coming close and speaking in a confidential tone. "You know . . . we could hurry things along. We have a man at the Palace. There are ways . . ."

William opened his eyes and, without moving his head, fixed Slater with a bitter gaze. "How dare you suggest such a thing?"

Slater took a step back. "Oh, well, me lord, I only meant—"

"I know what you meant," William said. He closed his eyes again, and smoothed his vest with both hands. "Do not mistake me, Slater. Everything I do, I do for the future of Oc. I draw the line at patricide."

TWENTY-SEVEN

THE weeks of winter slipped past almost without Lark's noticing. She fell into her cot each night exhausted in brain and body, and rose each morning determined to renew her efforts.

She had learned the bloodlines for ten generations past. She had memorized the succession of the Dukes of Oc and the Princes of Isamar. She could draw the coastline of Marin and Eastreach and name the principalities poised beyond the sea to invade Isamar for control of the shipping lanes. She knew all the parts of a flying saddle, down to the smallest panel. She kept Tup brushed smooth, currying out his winter coat, polishing his ebony hooves. She submitted to endless lectures by Mistress Strong about the proper care of a stallion, and the precautions she must take to keep him away from fillies in season. She put a flying saddle on him each day and led him around the dry paddock, avoiding Herbert's eyes when he counted out the sandweights to hang from the pommel.

"Build up them muscles," Herbert would say. "You should be riding Black Seraph soon, let old Pig go back to pasture."

Lark obediently hung the weights on the saddle, and said nothing. By the time there were four of them, she knew the saddle and the weights together weighed twice what she did, and any lingering worries she had about Tup carrying her evaporated.

It was, of course, not the weight Tup minded, but the tack. He nipped at the cinches and tried to rub the saddle against fence poles, whimpering at her. "I'm sorry, lovely boy," she murmured, scratching his ears in apology. "It seems we both have to get used to it."

And despite her most determined efforts, she despaired of ever satisfying Mistress Strong that she could ride. Over and over she struggled to sit Pig at his heavy trot, to grip with her thighs and drop her heels as he broke into his lumbering canter, to feel his rhythm at the gallop.

At the end of one of their lessons, Lark—who had managed at least not to fall that day—dismounted from the old piebald pony, and stood with her hands on her hips, her temper worn to nothing. Beyond the paddock the snow had melted from the fields and roads, and the air carried the sweet hint of early spring, but she was only remotely aware of it.

"Mistress Strong," she said. "I want to ride my own colt."

"No." The horsemistress shook her head. "How are you going to teach Black Seraph what he needs to know when you know nothing yourself?"

"That's not fair! I can teach him, we understand each other!"

"Put the pony in his stall," was all Mistress Strong said. "Feed him and brush him. And don't forget to clean his feet."

"You don't need to tell me that," Lark muttered, as she turned to lead Pig away.

"No? I need to repeat everything else a hundred times," Mistress Strong said.

Lark stopped, and looked over her shoulder. The horsemistress stood like a pillar of stone in the center of the paddock. Pig pulled on his rein, eager for his feed bucket. Lark said, "No, Pig, wait." She turned about, and lifted her chin at her teacher.

"I know you don't like me, Mistress," she said. "But I'm not stupid."

Mistress Strong's eyes flickered. "Liking has nothing to do with it," she said. "I don't want to see a winged horse wasted."

Lark felt the rush of heat in her cheeks. "Wasted? What does that mean?"

"It means," the horsemistress said in a sour tone, "that if you can't learn to ride, you can't learn to fly. And if you can't fly, Black Seraph will be of no use to the Duke."

Lark's mouth opened, but no words pushed past the shock that tightened her throat. Tup wasted? The very thought stung her soul. He would never, never be wasted! How could this rock of a woman even say such a thing? Even Mistress Winter had more heart!

She watched helplessly, Pig tugging at the rein, as Mistress Strong turned her back, went through the gate, and disappeared around the corner of the stables.

"Now that," said a voice behind her, "is a stupid woman."

Lark whirled, and found Hester leaning against the jamb of the stable door. "Hester!" Lark cried. "She just—Mistress Strong said . . ." Her voice broke, and she sobbed. "She said—Tup—wasted . . ."

"I heard," Hester drawled. She straightened, and came to Lark, relieving her of Pig's rein, and putting her free hand behind Lark's back. "Come on, Goat-girl," she said. "Let's go groom this fat pony and we'll talk."

Moments later Lark had dried her tears, and Pig was munching oats while she combed out his tail and Hester ran the currycomb over his broad back.

"My mamá tells my papá," Hester said, "that when you deal with stupid people, you have to work around them. If you can't get rid of them, that is. She advises Papá about his work on the Council all the time."

"You don't think she's right, then? That I'm hopeless?"

Hester shrugged. "Doubt it very much," she answered. She tossed the currycomb and caught it, then twirled it between her fingers. "Someone like Mistress Strong just isn't very—creative, I think would be the word my mamá would use."

"Lovely kind you are, Hester," Lark said in a small voice. "But I don't know how I can work around her. And I certainly can't get rid of her!"

Hester rested her elbows on Pig's back and looked across at Lark. The pony shifted his feet and chewed with noisy contentment. "My Goldie is such a great sweet thing," Hester said. "And you don't weigh any more than a sack of feathers. If you're not afraid of her . . ."

"I'm afraid of no beast," Lark said with confidence. "Least of all a winged horse."

Hester smiled. "I thought not. So let's take our horses out for a walk. Your Seraph needs to carry his weights around, doesn't he?" Lark nodded. "Goldie and I will join you."

It was not quite so simple an enterprise as Hester made it sound. Herbert made no demur as they left the stables, Tup laden with a flying saddle and four sandweights, Golden Morning saddled and bridled, both horses wearing their wing clips. Mistress Strong spotted them, though, and came out of the tack room, her brow furrowing with suspicion.

Hester had learned well from her mamá. She smiled pleasantly at the horsemistress, and spoke with an air of aloofness Lark was certain she must have cultivated in childhood. "Good afternoon." She started past her.

"Where are you going?" the horsemistress said.

"Why," Hester said, brows up, head held high in the unmistakable manner of a born aristocrat. "Exercise, of course! Just as we've been instructed."

"Black Seraph is intact, you know, Hester. You must not let him and Golden Morning . . ."

Hester's lip almost, but not quite, curled. "Thank you *so* much, Mistress Strong," she said in her precise accent. "I learned that lesson quite well at Beeth House stables. I have been riding since the age of four."

The horsemistress set her jaw. Hester lifted her filly's rein and pressed on. Lark hurried after, Tup at her heels.

Bramble trotted around the corner of the stables, and stood watching, tail waving gently, as Hester and Lark led their horses off to the yearlings' pasture and through the gate.

"Hester," Lark said as they moved down the long pasture toward the grove. "Why did that work?"

"It's quite sad, really," Hester said. "Or it would be if Strong weren't such a dim-witted ox. Her father cheated Duke Frederick on a shipload of silk and linen, and his lands were confiscated. The family lost everything, and Mamá says only having a daughter in the Duke's service kept him out of prison."

"Your mamá knows everything, doesn't she?"

Hester nodded. "She's the brains in the family."

"What is your father like?"

Hester smiled. "Papá is sweet . . . quite a nice man, really. And wise enough to let Mamá manage things."

"I barely knew my father," Lark confided. "And I never knew my mother."

"That's a hard thing," Hester said. "I've been fortunate."

They had reached the grove. As they threaded through the trees, Tup began to stamp his forefeet and whimper, eager for his run. Hester turned to Golden Morning and adjusted the stirrups and checked the cinches. The tall palomino picked up Tup's impatience, shaking her bridle, bending her neck around to see what was keeping her bondmate.

"There," Hester said. "I think those are short enough. Ready to try?"

Lark looked up at the saddle. Suddenly the palomino seemed like a cliff, her withers towering over Lark's head, her legs and feet enormous.

"Here, I'll boost you," Hester said. "Give me Seraph's lead."

A moment later, lifted up by Hester's strong arm, Lark found herself perched in the flying saddle, her knees tucked beneath the points of Golden Morning's folded wings, her boots settled in the narrow iron stirrups. The ground looked very, very far away.

"Zito's ears," she breathed. "She's enormous."

Hester grinned up at her. "Scared?"

"No," Lark lied. "Not a bit."

Hester chuckled, and handed her the rein. "She's like riding a rocking chair," she said. "Give her a try."

Obediently, Lark lifted the rein. She squeezed Goldie's ribs tentatively with her calves, and the filly's ears flicked toward her inquiringly.

"Bolder than that," Hester said. "She's used to my great long legs." She laid a hand on Goldie's sleek neck, and murmured into her bondmate's ear. The filly tossed her head, once, and when Lark squeezed her again, she set off at a brisk, ground-eating walk.

Lark thought that either she truly had learned a thing or two in her struggles with Pig, or Golden Morning was worlds easier to ride. Goldie's big body moved nimbly, smoothly, and her head bobbed nicely as they moved between the outer edge of the grove and the hedgerow at the end of the paddock. The saddle still felt hard and slippery, but as Goldie extended her stride into a swinging trot, Lark felt the rhythm of the post for the very first time. She balanced in her stirrups, rising and sinking in time with Goldie's steps.

They reached the end of the narrow ride, and Lark felt the filly collect beneath her to turn. She slid across the saddle, but the cantle caught her before she could slip too far. She tried to sense Goldie's intention as the horse settled into her hindquarters and reversed her direction. This was the hardest part, she thought, finding the balance point, centering herself over the movement, feeling the horse through the layers of leather and wood and iron.

Goldie, though, was already beautifully schooled, though she was not quite two years old. She slowed her pace, as if sensitive to Lark's fear, and then eased back into her trot.

"You lovely, lovely girl," Lark breathed, beneath the beat of hooves on the bare ground. "Lovely, lovely girl!" She became gradually aware of the cool sparkling sunshine, the fragile blades of new grass, the first fuzz of spring green on the hedgerows. Ahead her friend Hester stood, holding Tup's halter lead. The palomino filly increased her pace, and Lark leaned forward as Goldie broke into a long-legged canter.

She turned her head to smile at Hester as they passed. Hester grinned back, and waved.

Tup, at that moment, reared, tearing the lead free of Hester's hand. With a squeal that Lark had never heard from him, he broke away, and tore after Goldie. Lark cried out, and Goldie, hearing the hoofbeats behind her, broke into a gallop. Lark clutched at the pommel, and called over her shoulder, "No, Tup! No!"

Hester, too, was shouting, something Lark couldn't hear. Tup was coming after Goldie at a dead run, ears back, tail high and streaming. Lark had no idea what to do. The end of the paddock was ahead, where the grove met the hedgerow. Desperate, not knowing whether to be most fearful of falling beneath the galloping hooves, or of what Tup would do when he caught up with Goldie, she held on tight, and shouted, "Whoa!"

The filly, obedient to the urgency in her voice, skidded to a rough stop. Lark lost her grip on the pommel and the reins, and flew in an arching somersault over Goldie's head, landing on her back with her feet in the branches of the hedgerow. The fall drove the breath from her lungs. She heard Tup's squall, and she closed her eyes tightly, dreading what she might see when she opened them.

Even as she struggled to breathe again, every warning of Mistress Strong's about a stallion's behavior ran through her mind. What if Tup hurt Goldie? What if he tried, Kalla forbid, to mount her, saddle and all? Or if Goldie kicked him, broke his wing or his rib or . . .

Something like prickly velvet touched her forehead, and then her cheek. She felt a rush of warm, oaty breath, and she heard Tup's familiar, comforting cry. Her own breath returned in a sudden flood of welcome air, and she opened her eyes.

Her bondmate stood over her, lipping at her face, whimpering at her to get up, to tell him she was all right. Beyond him, Goldie loomed, reins dangling, a look of puzzlement in the tilt of her ears.

Hester came running, breathlessly crying Lark's name. "Are you all right? Lark, say something! Are you hurt?"

Lark wriggled her shoulders. She reached up with her arms to Tup, and found that everything still seemed intact. With some difficulty, she extracted her feet from the hedgerow. "Oh, damn. Look at my boots!"

Hester, pale with anxiety, bent over her to pull her up. "Kalla's heels, Black, I'm *so* sorry! He just got away from me! I know better, with a stallion, but I . . . oh, tell me you're all right!"

Lark started to laugh, a little weakly. "I'm fine, though I'll be buffing scratches out of my boots half the night . . . but, oh, Tup, you bad, bad boy, what am I to do with you?"

Tup whickered, and nuzzled her hair.

When Lark was on her feet, and both horses in control again, Hester began to regain her color. She leaned against Goldie, shaking her head. "Your cap is gone," she said, "and you may have torn your skirt."

"I don't care," Lark declared. "I'm not hurt, and neither are the horses."

"He was jealous, wasn't he?"

Lark circled Tup's neck with her arm. "Yes, he was. I should have known."

"Why should you have known? I rode other horses all the time at Beeth House, before I was allowed to ride Goldie. It didn't seem to bother her then."

Lark bit her lip for a moment. "Hester," she said. "I haven't told anyone, and you mustn't tell either . . ."

Her friend arched an eyebrow. "What have you done now, Black?"

"I've been riding Tup. Since Erdlin."

Hester stared at her. "Riding? But then why—"

"We ride bareback. It's so easy!"

"But, Black, you can't—when you fly, you can't ride without a saddle!"

"But without a saddle, I can *feel* Tup's movement. I know just what he's going to do, and when, and he seems to know just what I want!"

Hester shook her head and clicked her tongue against her teeth. "Asking for trouble, Black," she said gloomily. They turned the horses and started through the grove, back toward the stables. "Ribbon Day is only six months off, and you have to fly to pass the Airs. You're asking for trouble."

TWENTY-EIGHT

There was something special, Philippa thought, about the way the spring sunlight glittered on the towers of the White City, and turned the twists of the river into shining silver ribbons. It was like the light of early morning, bright with promise and energy. Spring should be a season of joy, the anticipation of new life. It was a terrible time to be preparing for a death.

Yet death was now preoccupying all of Oc, from the highest born to the lowliest of servants. Word had come to the Academy, by way of one of the horsemistresses in residence at the Ducal Palace, that Duke Frederick's doctors believed the end was near.

Philippa had been aloft with her flight when an Ocmarin gelding angled beneath them toward the Academy grounds. The horsemistress, Marielle Star, one of Philippa's former students, was now in service at the Palace. Philippa looked away from her flight to watch Marielle and Star glide down into the landing paddock, and she felt a chill that had nothing to do with the cool air aloft.

She held Sunny at Quarters while Elizabeth and Chaser led the flight into the first segment of a relay. It was a tricky maneuver, and not all the flyers had mastered the intricacy of a baton passed from one to the other. It required precise timing, and careful spacing so that one flyer's wings would not interfere with the movement of another's. Elizabeth and Chaser performed it perfectly, but the next pair had some trouble, and the baton, which in actual service could be a scroll or a package, or even a weapon, went spinning into the clear air, out of reach. Philippa sighed, watching it fall. She had an extra on her saddle, of course, but she was distracted by Marielle's arrival, and the news she must bring.

She signaled the end of the flight, and Elizabeth and Chaser swooped to the head of the line to lead the flyers back to the

Academy. Philippa and Sunny followed, above and a little behind the others. Sunny seemed to have caught Philippa's anxiety, and her approach was efficient, a straightforward landing, a hard canter to the end of the paddock. Within fifteen minutes of Marielle and Star's arrival, Philippa was hurrying up the steps to the Hall, pulling off her gloves and cap as she went.

It had been as she feared, bad news carried swiftly. And now, only a few hours later, she was on her way to the Palace for what must be her final farewell to her old friend.

Sunny's wings shone red against the white stone turrets of the city and the circle of the Rotunda in the middle distance. As they passed the dome of the Winter Tower, Philippa felt a stab of nostalgia for the days when her family would join the Duke's for the Estian Festival, she and her sisters and Pamella dancing in the brick plaza with Meredith and William and Francis and even Frederick himself, showering each other with dried, perfumed flower petals, preserved from the previous spring. The priests sold those petals in tiny baskets, promising Estia would endow long life to those who received them. Estian had done Frederick no good, but then, Philippa had never expected it would. She placed no faith in such things, not even as a girl.

There had been no magic in her life until Kalla brought her Winter Sunset. Kalla's power, at least, was demonstrable. It carried her even now to the deathbed of the old Duke, and the bitter dawn of a new era for his Duchy.

Jolinda, grim-faced, was waiting for her. Philippa slid down from the saddle, touched Sunny's wingpoint gently with her quirt. As Sunny folded her wings, Philippa said, "She's had a busy morning, Jolinda. Would you take her saddle off, give her a rubdown? A half-measure of grain, and some water, please."

"I'll see to it, Mistress Winter," the elderly stable-girl said. "You best get on, now. Them doctors been scurrying around like ants this morning."

A brown riding horse with a black and silver saddle put his head out of one of the stable stalls as Philippa passed. William's horse, if she remembered correctly. Of course William would be keeping the deathwatch. She pressed her lips together as she stripped off her gloves and reached up for her riding cap. William's ambitions were about to be fulfilled.

As she moved into the foyer of the Palace, a slender blond

man stepped from the library to her left. "Philippa!" he said softly. "How good you are to come."

She stopped in the act of smoothing her flyer's knot. "Why—Francis! It's been years."

Francis, Frederick's younger son, came to her. Presuming on their childhood friendship, he pressed his cheek to hers, and she smiled at him. "I'm sorry, Francis, that we don't meet again under happier circumstances."

His eyes, dark like all the Duke's progeny, were heavy with sorrow. "It won't be long, I'm afraid, Philippa. It's good you're here. Come, I'll take you up to see Father myself."

As they climbed the stairs, she asked, "How did you come so quickly from Isamar?"

"I was already on my way," he said. They reached the landing, and he paused. Two servants passed them, hurrying downstairs with basins and towels, their faces grave. Francis watched them go, and Philippa had a chance to look at him. He was younger than she by almost ten years. He looked superficially like his older brother, but his eyes were warm and his mouth full and gentle.

He said, "I had a wild letter from Father, raving on about Pamella and saying no one cared, not even Mother. He must have written it himself. His secretary would have edited out half of it. He sounded so . . ." Francis's voice trembled. Philippa thought how deep his voice was in comparison to William's. "He sounded like a foolish old man in his letter, Philippa. Nothing like the father I knew."

"His heart is broken, Francis."

"Yes." Francis gestured to the stairs, and they continued climbing. "I know. She was the repository of all his affection. Neither William nor I . . ." He let the words trail off, and she knew he found them too painful to speak aloud. She put a sympathetic hand on his arm. She knew how it hurt to love someone who did not love you in return.

They met Andrews outside the door of the Duke's apartment, and he bowed them inside.

Philippa had expected a darkened room, hushed voices, hovering doctors. Instead, she found spring sunshine pouring through the window, the velvet curtains tied back, the sash up. Francis said, "He likes to see his horses." Philippa glanced out the window, and saw that the winged horses were turned out to graze in the grounds.

Their wing clips were in place, but they roamed freely over the grass.

The doctors, it seemed, had been sent away for the moment. Only William sat beside the Duke's bed.

He rose when Philippa and Francis entered, and nodded to them both. He was dressed, as he had been every time Philippa had seen him of late, in narrow black trousers and a full-sleeved white shirt, with the embroidered vest. His hair was perhaps not quite so neat as it usually was, but his cheeks and chin were smooth-shaven. "Philippa," he said gravely. "I'm glad you're here. My father wanted to speak with you."

Philippa nodded, and crossed the room to the high bed to look down on the sunken face of her old friend. He lay propped, half-upright, on scattered pillows. She hardly recognized him in the skeletal profile, the wisps of white hair. His breath rattled in his chest, and his eyes were closed. She found his hand among the layers of blankets, and pressed his fingers. "My lord Frederick," she said quietly, but clearly. "It's Philippa Winter. Philippa Islington. I'm much grieved to find you so ill."

Francis stood opposite her, watching, his mouth drooping. Frederick's eyelids lifted slightly, but fell again. He took a noisy, shallow breath, and then another. It seemed he had to gather his energy to speak. "Philippa," he rasped. "Good. Thank . . ."

There was a long pause. William leaned against the head of the bed, and Philippa, glancing up, saw that he watched his father with an odd expression. He did not appear as pleased at his father's imminent passing as she would have expected. His mouth twisted, and she wondered if, now that the moment was at hand, he might be remembering the affectionate parent of his boyhood, or feeling some sorrow for the end of a distinguished career.

She held Frederick's cold, dry hand in both of hers. "Dear Frederick," she said. "You have done so much for me, and for all of us who fly. Margareth wanted me particularly to tell you that."

Hoarsely, he whispered, "Please . . ."

She waited for him to go on, but a long pause stretched while he struggled to breathe. At last she bent closer to him. "Frederick? Can I do something for you?"

His fingers moved feebly in hers, and his eyelids struggled to rise. For one moment, they succeeded, and Philippa had one last look into his dark eyes, bright with intelligence and determination.

He said, with a rush of breath as if exhausted, "Pamella. Please." And then his eyes closed again, his fingers went limp, and his chest sagged. Long seconds passed before it rose again with another ragged breath.

Philippa stayed where she was, waiting, hoping he might say more. She looked up at William. Did he know what Frederick wanted of her?

Francis bent forward from his side of the bed, and said urgently, "Father. Philippa doesn't understand. What is it about Pamella? What do you want Philippa to do?"

There was an agonizing pause, and then Frederick said, "Remember."

Philippa met Francis's anguished gaze. She shook her head slightly, and he lifted one slender shoulder. For a long time they stayed where they were, listening to the rattle of Frederick's breathing. William, after a time, moved to the window, and stared out. One of the doctors came back, put his hand on Frederick's forehead, and then left. Andrews came in a moment later to stand at the foot of the bed, his head bowed. Philippa's back began to ache from bending, and she pulled a chair to the bedside and sat down. Another doctor came in, and took a chair near the door, where he dozed, snoring lightly. In this tableau, this moment frozen in time, they waited.

It was midafternoon when Frederick drew one last gravelly breath, released it, and didn't take another. The doctor bent over him, straightened, and shook his head at Andrews.

Andrews turned to the window, to William, and bowed. "Your Grace," he said solemnly. "Your lord father is dead. Long life to the new Duke."

William turned slowly from the window. His eyes swept the still form on the bed, and then rested on Francis and Philippa in turn, and then Andrews. Philippa thought she had never seen an expression of such complexity. There was real grief in the twist of his mouth. There was also, unmistakably, a gleam of triumph in his eyes.

"Andrews," he said, in his high-pitched voice. "Take word to my lady mother, and tell my father's secretary to write the pronouncement."

Andrews bowed again, and withdrew. The doctor also bowed to the new Duke, and followed Andrews out of the apartment.

"And now," William said. He stood very straight, and pulled down his vivid vest with both hands. Philippa imagined that it was to her his words were addressed. "Now, it begins."

EDUARD Crisp was relieved of his duties within three days of Frederick's death.

Philippa and Margareth were assembling the second- and third-level students to fly above the funeral cortège. The first-level girls, whose horses were not yet old enough for a long flight, would be taken into the White City by carriage, to follow the procession on foot. They stood admiring the older girls and their horses as they prepared for their first ceremonial function.

Black ribbons twined in the manes and tails of every flyer, Foundation, Ocmarin, or Noble. Their saddles bore black and silver streamers, and the girls wore silver armbands over their black riding coats. As the flyers moved out to the flight paddock, Margareth said quietly to Philippa, "The new Master Breeder is someone named Jinson."

Philippa sighed. "Poor Eduard. And his son! It has always been an inherited position."

"No longer, I'm afraid."

"Is there any sign that this new man knows anything about the bloodlines? About the dangers of inbreeding, about promoting strengths, diminishing weaknesses?"

Margareth gave an expressive shrug. "All I know is that this Jinson is the new Duke's private stable-man." She sighed. "And there is something else."

The flyers were all in the flight paddock now, and Rosellen stood in the courtyard with Sunny, waiting for Philippa. Philippa and Margareth walked down the steps. "What else?" Philippa asked.

"I received an order this morning," Margareth told her. "Directly from His Grace."

"Did you, Margareth?"

"I did," Margareth said lightly. "On a fine piece of paper with the Ducal seal. Irina is to be made senior instructor."

Philippa stopped where she was, one foot on the cobblestones, one on the bottom step. "That seems very odd. Why would William care about what position Irina holds?"

"The order spoke of her service in the Angles."

"What are you going to do?"

Margareth looked past Philippa to the ranks of winged horses, their horsemistresses, the students and instructors in her charge. "I'm going to obey the order," she said. "I've been in the Duke's service more than forty years, Philippa. Obedience is my duty."

LARK, like the other students, was dressed in her best tabard and a clean riding skirt, boots polished, gloves clean, her hat carefully pinned onto her short curls. She tried hard to feel solemn, but the hills to the west blossomed in vivid shades of green, and birds twittered from the hedgerows. The freshly whitewashed pole fences shone in the sun. More than a hundred flyers assembled in four lines in the flight paddock, fluttering with black and silver ribbons. Wings rustled, restless hooves scuffed in the new grass. Two horses, a chestnut Noble and a brown Ocmarin, squealed, and their horsemistresses wheeled them out of the line to trot in tight circles, necks arched, chins tucked. When they had calmed, both returned to their places.

From the stables, Lark heard Tup whinny, and then bang his heels against the wall of his stall, piqued at being left out of the excitement.

Hester murmured in her ear, "All our horses wish they could be part of this."

Lark said ruefully, "But only Tup complains so loudly everyone can hear him!"

Hester started to grin, and then remembered the solemnity of the day. She forced a grave expression onto her long face. "He'll outgrow it, Black, don't worry."

"He wants to join the rest of you in your ground drills," Lark said. "And so do I!"

Hester nodded. "I'd say it's past time for that."

They heard a clatter of hooves on cobblestones, and turned to see Philippa and Winter Sunset pass through the paddock gate in a high trot. "Oh!" Lark pressed her palm over the icon she wore under her tabard. "They're lovely fine, aren't they, Hester? Mistress Winter . . . surely she's the finest rider in all of Oc!"

"They say she defended in the battle for the South Tower of Isamar."

"Oh! Did she?"

"Yes. Alana Rose was lost there, with her horse. I think they teach us all this in the third level." Hester put a hand under Lark's arm, and they moved toward one of the carriages. "They try not to frighten us too early in our training," she added under her breath. "But Mamá told me the whole story."

They climbed up into the carriage with four other girls between them, and the conversation ended. Anabel was in the carriage behind them. She waved as she stepped inside. The carriages, draped in black and silver bunting, began to move. Lark leaned from the window to watch as the flights of winged horses launched from the flight paddock, seven by seven, assembling themselves into Open Columns. Mistress Winter and Sunny led the whole, great red wings driving them up, banking toward the White City in a long arc. It was the most magnificent sight she had ever seen. She gazed upward, her lips parted in wonder, as the third-level Academy students and then the second-level also launched.

The girl next to her, Grace, pressed close to Lark. "Have you ever seen anything so magnificent?" she breathed.

It was the first time Grace had spoken directly to her, and for an uncomfortable moment Lark wasn't sure it was she being addressed. But Grace smiled at her, and nodded toward the spectacle aloft. "Nay, Grace," Lark said hastily. "Never in my life."

"And how terrifying," Grace said, "to fly with all those other horses! What if you make a mistake? What if you bump someone, or drop out of the line, or . . ."

Lark didn't know how to answer. She wasn't terrified at all, but eager and impatient. She thought if Mistress Strong made her ride poor old Pig one more time, she would throw herself on the floor and bang her heels like Tup. They must, they simply *must*, learn to deal with the saddle. They could fly together, she was certain they could, if Mistress Strong would only release her, let her join Mistress Dancer and her own class. The next time there was a grand occasion like this one, she and Tup would fly with the others.

TWENTY-NINE

LARK and Hester and Anabel stood together in the sloping brick plaza of the Tower of the Seasons. The Academy girls mingled with the lords and ladies of Oc, the merchants and shopkeepers, other students released from their studies for the day, and even a few maids and serving-men who could escape their duties to attend the funeral procession of the old Duke.

Black and silver ribbons and armbands were everywhere, and faces were solemn, but nothing could dispel the air of festival that hung about the White City. The scents of roasting meats and baking puddings wafted from every inn and tavern, and the fragrance of yeast and cinnamon and sugar tantalized the girls from the shuttered tea shops surrounding the plaza. They would not go into the Tower for the funeral itself, but would stand as an honor guard as the coffin was carried out to the caisson. Until that happened, they were free to roam the plaza, to stare up at the aged copper dome, the latticework surrounding the top of the tower, the priests in their forbidding undyed woolen hoods and ropes of wooden beads, filing in and out of the Tower in twos and threes.

"Look, there's Lady Beeth!" Anabel said. She started to lift her arm to wave, but then remembered the occasion.

"She has to go inside for the service," Hester said. "That's Papá with her. And Grandmamá and my older brother Graham."

"Your brother is a fine-looking man," Anabel said.

Lark stood on tiptoe, trying to peer over the heads of the crowd. "I want a blink at your brother," she complained. "But everyone is so tall!"

Hester grinned at Anabel. "What do you think, Chance? Shall we give the goat-girl a boost?"

Anabel laughed, and took Lark's left arm. Hester seized her right, and the two girls lifted her up above the heads of the crowd around them. Lark giggled, and people turned, frowning until they recognized the girls' habits. One or two smiled, then nodded indulgently. No one spoke to them. Lark, braced on the arms of her friends, looked across the plaza and found Lady Beeth just going up the steps into the Winter Tower, a small, chubby man in her wake, a tall, broad-shouldered young man after that. "Oh!" she said. "Is that Graham, in the tall hat?"

"Yes. That's my brother."

"Oh, aye, he's lovely handsome, Hester!"

"That he is," Hester said wryly. "Graham got all the beauty in our family."

Lark was about to protest this statement, but another face caught her attention. Surely she had seen that crone before, an old woman with wisps of gray hair coming out from her battered straw hat. But where? Lark puzzled over it, distracted from admiring Graham Beeth. Somehow she associated the old woman with the Uplands, with home, but she couldn't remember.

A moment later, the girls set her back on her feet. The crowd had begun to exclaim in low voices, and turn their faces up to the sky. When Lark followed their gaze, she forgot all about the old woman.

From the west, the direction of the Ducal Palace, a double line of winged horses flew toward the Tower of the Seasons. All three girls tipped their heads back, gripped their hands together, struck with envy and pride at the beauty of the sight.

A path cleared from the street to the steps of the Tower. An empty caisson, drawn by a single black draught horse, wearing blinkers and his harness wound with black and silver, rattled up over the bricks. Black and silver pennants fluttered from the corners of the caisson. The flyers, in two great double Columns, slowed their wingbeats to soar above the plaza. They circled the dome at a stately pace. A breathless silence spread over the crowd.

"Oh," Lark whispered. "Only look at Winter Sunset!"

The sorrel mare hovered at Quarters at the highest point, just at the center of the copper dome. The movement of her wings as she held her position was elegant, her neck and head outstretched in a perfect line. The slender black figure of Mistress Winter sat so still upon her mount that she might have been a statue. Lark's heart swelled at the sight. They were too high for her to see details, but she imagined Mistress Winter's sharp profile serenely still against the clear blue sky, her gloved hands steady upon the reins, her back straight and her head high. Tears of admiration filled Lark's eyes, casting the whole scene into a golden haze.

When Mistress Winter signaled with her quirt, the entire company of flyers executed a Half Reverse. The watching crowd gasped as the great circle of flying horses dissolved, opening like the petals of a multihued flower, each horse winging out from the Tower, then wheeling, finding its place again in the re-formed Open Columns. The whole body of them turned back toward the Ducal Palace. They would alight there, and rest until the end of the service, when they would return to escort the funeral cortège from Osham to the Palace cemetery, where for centuries past the Dukes of Oc had been laid to rest.

A collective sigh swept the crowd as the winged horses left the city. Anabel said, "Imagine! One day we will be part of that."

"We have to remember," Hester said, "how marvelous it looks from below."

When the last horse disappeared to the west, murmured conversations began around the plaza, and the crowd began to disperse. Hester said, "It will be hours now."

Anabel pulled a little purse out of her pocket. "My uncle sent me some money," she said. "Let's find a tea shop."

They chose a place with flower-patterned curtains and cushioned chairs, and were served cups of pale tea and plates of sugared scones. When Anabel tried to pay the hostess, the woman smiled, and waved off her coins. "No, no, young ladies. You just remember me when it's your turn to fly for the Duke."

The girls thanked her, and went out to wander through the throng, passing the hours until they were needed.

Just before they were to take their places beside the caisson, Lark saw the old woman again, and this time she remembered where she had met her.

She stood in the shadow of the dome, her gray hair bristling, a goat-hair cloak wrapped around her. She peered up from beneath the hatbrim, and grinned fiercely when she caught Lark's eye. "Oh, aye, aye, you remember me, don't you, Missy? You remember old Dorsey!"

"You're the witchwoman," Lark said. She saw Hester and Anabel watching her curiously, and she gestured for them to go on without her. "You're from Clellum."

"Aye, aye, that's me, that is!" The woman shook with a cackling laugh, and nodded rapidly. "Missy wanted none of old Dorsey's potions!"

"No," Lark said. The witchwoman's scent had reached her now, and her nose twitched with distaste. Dorsey of Clellum smelled of herbs and beer and unwashed flesh. Horses, Lark thought, no matter how tired or dirty, never smelled as bad as this old woman did. The thought gave her a pang of compunction, and so she tried to say something courteous. "I'm glad to see you well, though, Mistress." She took a step away, to follow her friends.

"Oh, aye, aye," old Dorsey cackled. "I'm well enough. That other one isn't, though!"

Lark nodded politely, and tried to edge away, but the witchwoman seized her arm with bony fingers. "You know that other one?" she asked, her eyes fever-bright in her wrinkled face. "You know her?"

"I told you before," Lark said. "I don't know anyone in Clellum."

"Aye, aye! But this one, she's from Osham! She's had visitors!"

Lark pulled her arm free. "I don't know her."

"Nay, nay, a pity. She's that lonely, poor thing, only her baby for company. No voice, no one to talk to. Sold everything to buy a potion, and now she has no money, neither."

"I'm sorry," Lark repeated. "I don't have any money."

"She wasn't supposed to have the baby," the witchwoman whispered. "I gave her the potion. Gave her a good potion." She leaned close to Lark again, and the wave of sour breath made Lark shudder. "Never says a word, that one."

"It's nothing to do with me, Mistress," Lark said. She firmly disengaged the old woman's hand from her arm. "If the girl needs help, you must go to your prefect."

"Don't have such in Clellum."

Lark paused, looking down at the woman. "Well, then. What's the nearest town?"

The witchwoman grinned again, as if the name were going to mean something to Lark. "It's Mossyrock!" she said gleefully. "Mossyrock, where they have the market!"

At that moment, the crowd in the plaza hushed, and every head turned up to the sky. Lark looked up, too, and saw that the great company of flyers was on its way back, approaching from the west. She would be late, and Mistress Strong would scold her.

Without bidding old Dorsey farewell, she began to squeeze her way through the crowd. By the time she found Hester, lined up with the other Academy students, the coffin had appeared in the great double doors of the Tower of the Seasons. Men in the Duke's livery carried it down the broad steps to the waiting caisson. The new Duke followed, and stood on the steps watching.

Everyone stood in a somber silence. Lark slipped quickly into her place beside Hester, and turned to watch the great carved coffin being gently laid in the caisson. The draught horse shifted in his traces, and the jingle of his harness was the only sound in the crowded plaza. As the driver picked up the reins, and the caisson began to creak forward, the winged horses above flew in a slow, elegant circle, a formation Lark supposed must be one of the Graces. They dipped and turned, their wings catching the sunlight, the slender black-clad riders swaying with their wingbeats.

Duke William walked on foot behind the caisson, alone, elegantly tall, his white-blond hair gleaming, his face set in cold lines. The quirt hung from his belt, and Lark stared, lips apart, as he passed her.

As if he could feel her gaze, his head turned. He found her there, among the others, and his eyes narrowed.

Later Lark tried to tell herself she was wrong, that she had imagined it. But it wasn't imagination. The new Duke's expression changed as he looked at her. The stiffness relaxed from his face. His narrow lips curved in a mirthless smile, and something dark and frightening gleamed from his eyes.

WHEN the first-level girls returned from the White City, tired and thoughtful after the day of solemn ceremony, the older girls and the horsemistresses were already back, grooming their mounts, feeding them, making their way in twos and threes to the Hall for a late supper. Rosellen and Herbert were busy finding stalls for the visiting horsemistresses, who had flown in for the funeral from Isamar and Marin and the Angles. Lark caught a glimpse of Amberly Cloud just leaving Silver Cloud in a stall at one end of the long row. She couldn't remember seeing her in the formation today.

Lark and Hester and Anabel hurried to the stables to see to their horses, and then followed the others to the Hall. Tea and cold sandwiches were laid ready on the long tables. Conversation was scattered, and quiet. Lark, despite the feast of pastries in Osham, was hungry again, and ate three of the thin sandwiches and drank two cups of tea.

As she finished, she looked up at the head table where the horsemistresses sat. "Hester," she whispered. "Did you notice Mistress Strong?"

Hester followed her gaze. "Look at that!" she murmured. "She's been made senior."

Anabel sat near them. "What is it?" she asked. "What do you see?"

Hester said, "Irina Strong. She has the senior's insignia on her collar."

"When did that happen?" Anabel asked. "Did someone leave?"

"I don't think so. They're all there," Hester said, scanning the faces that flanked the Headmistress and Mistress Winter.

The senior instructors always sat in the center seats, the juniors at the ends, or even with the students. And it was true, Lark saw, that Irina Strong now wore the jeweled wings of a senior instructor. "Now I'll never be allowed to ride Tup," she said miserably.

"Or she'll have bigger worries than making you ride Pig," Hester said.

"What flight will she teach?" Anabel wondered.

Hester shook her head. "I don't know. Let's hope it's not ours."

They rose when the Headmistress did, and Lark saw then that the visiting flyers had a table of their own, near the front of the big room. Amberly Cloud was there, looking plumper than ever.

"Hester," she whispered. "Do you see that horsemistress there—just by the door?"

Hester looked over Lark's head. "You mean the fat one?"

"Well—yes. She's the horsemistress from Dickering Park. She was supposed to teach me to ride, but all she did was bend my ears about how hard her life is!"

"Kalla's tail," Hester said in hard voice. "She's the one who missed the flight today. I heard Mistress Dancer say she barely made it here, and no wonder! What winged horse could carry her?"

"It's so sad. Her Silver Cloud is the sweetest gelding."

Anabel said, "I will never, never get fat, never."

Hester said tartly, "Not on Academy food, you won't!" and Lark and Anabel giggled as they made their way across the courtyard to the Dormitory.

Lark went up to the sleeping porch with the others, but after she had washed her face and folded away her cap and gloves and coat, she wasn't sleepy. It had been such a long, odd day. The old witchwoman's face floated through her mind, and then Duke William's cold smile.

Some girls were already in their cots. Hester and Anabel were both yawning, pulling on their nightdresses. Lark took off her boots, and sat on the edge of her cot. She thought of poor, gentle Silver Cloud, having to watch all the other horses fly off without him. When she had left Dickering Park for the last time, he had looked after her with such longing. Today had to have been hard for him, even worse than it was for Tup and all the other first-level flyers. Cloud could have expected to fly the Airs and Graces with the others.

The other girls fell asleep quickly, without even murmuring last bits of gossip to each other. Lark pulled her boots on again, and unfolded her coat. She tiptoed out of the sleeping porch and down the stairs.

She found the courtyard deserted. Most of the windows of the Hall and the Domicile were dark, their panes reflecting the light of a nearly full moon. In the reading room, a single lamp gleamed through the window. The apartments above the stables were also dark and lifeless. Lark felt as if she had the entire Academy to herself. Not even an oc-hound rose to greet her as she crossed the courtyard.

She stopped in the feed room for a bit of grain, and then found Silver Cloud's stall at the end of one of the long aisles.

The gelding put his nose over the wall, and Lark stroked his cheek. "Cloud," she murmured. "Was it hard for you today? Poor lovely boy! Maybe Mistress Winter or Mistress Morgan will speak to her, make things better."

She offered him the grain. Cloud lipped it delicately from her palm, and blew a warm breath over her cheek. "Ah," she said, "you recognize me, do you? Yes, lovely boy. It's good to see you, too."

She rubbed the gelding's ears, and breathed in the familiar smells of horses and hay and sawdust. After ten minutes or so she began to feel sleepy at last. She murmured a good night to Silver

Cloud, and turned to go. Just one glance at Tup, she thought, and then, at last, her bed.

She wandered back down the aisle between the quiet stalls. The winged horses nodded drowsily at her. One or two whickered, and she spoke to them in soothing tones. As she rounded the corner, she glanced across the courtyard and saw that the last lamp had been turned out in the Domicile. She was, she thought, the only person awake in all of the Academy. The thought made her smile, and even though now she felt truly tired and ready to sleep, she hated to give up this moment.

She turned toward Tup's stall.

When she first reached it, she thought the moon must have already set. She couldn't see her colt at all. "Tup? Where are you?" She opened the gate.

Molly came stumbling forward, bleating with misery. Bramble suddenly appeared behind Lark, a growl growing in her throat.

Lark pushed past Molly, and peered into the shadowed stall. She saw nothing.

With a strangled cry, she turned about, stretching her hand out into the darkness. She found nothing.

Bramble's growl grew louder, and Molly bleated again and again. But there was no sound from Tup. The stall was empty.

Tup was gone.

THIRTY

PHILIPPA felt as if her very bones ached with exhaustion. Margareth had needed to rest, and it had fallen to Philippa to confer with Herbert, to speak to Matron about beds and trays, to greet returning flyers. She had rubbed Sunny down, and given her extra feed, and then toured the stables, making certain every winged horse had the same comforts. She had stood in the doorway to the Hall, pointing out the visitors' table, welcoming the horsemistresses she knew, introducing herself to the few she didn't.

Irina Strong wore a triumphant expression on her heavy features, but Philippa was too distracted and weary to bother with her. She simply, mutely, pointed to the head table, and then turned away to greet a horsemistress from Eastreach.

The evening seemed as endless as the day had been. When at last she was free to trudge up the stairs to her own apartment, she felt edgy and restless. She put on her nightdress, and then, as she often did, wrapped herself in a quilt from the bed and sat beside her window, watching the lights wink out around the courtyard, the Dormitory first, then the Hall, the two windows above the stables, and the last lamp in the Domicile.

Still she sat on, as her eyelids grew heavy. It felt good to have her feet up on the windowsill, her head supported by the cushioned back of her chair. The moon shone its silver light over the stables and the paddocks, and peace settled over the Academy of the Air.

When a slight figure in a black riding coat crossed the courtyard, Philippa almost didn't notice. She had just been thinking of rousing herself enough to get into bed. The slender wraith moved quickly, with the agility and ease of youth. One of the girls, then. Why was she not in her own bed?

Philippa put her feet on the floor, and leaned toward the glass. The girl slipped into the stables, out of her sight.

Rarely, if a horse were ailing, a student might have permission to leave the Dormitory at night to check on her bondmate. But if a horse were ill, Philippa and Margareth would be the first to know.

Philippa stood, hesitating. Hope for sleep had fled, all at once, though she would be exhausted in the morning. Slowly, keeping an eye on the stable door, she reached for her boots and her clothes. She had an uneasy, premonitory feeling that something was about to happen.

She had had that same uncomfortable presentiment the night before the raid on the South Tower, that nagging twinge beneath her breastbone. She wished she could banish it, erase it so she could rest. But she knew from experience such an attempt would be pointless.

The small figure of the student came dashing back from the stables toward the Domicile barely ten minutes later, an oc-hound pacing beside her. Philippa swore, and hurried out of her room and down the stairs. The girl pounded on the locked door only seconds before Philippa shot back the bolt and threw the heavy door open.

She was not at all surprised to see that it was Larkyn Hamley on the doorstep. The girl's face was a pale blur in the moonlight. The oc-hound at her side gave an urgent whine.

"Mistress Winter!" Larkyn cried. "It's Tup—they've taken him!" And she started to sob.

"Shush, shush, child," Philippa said, stepping outside and pulling the door shut behind her. "He must be there somewhere. Come, let's not wake the women. Everyone's exhausted. Let's get Herbert, and a lantern, and we'll see what's happened."

She spoke with a confidence she did not feel. The quivering in her belly foretold trouble. She put her hand on Lark's shoulder as they hurried back to the stables, feeling the shudders of the girl's weeping. She climbed the stairs to Herbert's apartment and thumped on his door, then went to the tack room for a lantern without waiting for him. By the time she had found matches, lighted and trimmed the lantern, Herbert was on his way down the stairs, his hastily donned shirt misbuttoned and flapping over his trousers. Lark led the way down the aisle to Black Seraph's stall, stifling her panicked sobs as she went.

Philippa held the lantern high, and looked over the wall.

Only the little goat looked back at her, eyes glowing in the lamplight. Molly caught sight of Larkyn beside Philippa, with Herbert on her other side, and gave a single, desolate bleat.

"Kalla's heels," Philippa gritted. "Do you have any idea, Herbert?"

"None," he grunted. "And Rosellen's not in her room."

Philippa turned to stare at him. "She's not? Do you think she might have had something to do with this?"

Larkyn snuffled, "Rosellen? She would never . . ."

Herbert shook his head. "Right you are," he said. "That girl would never be part of anything hurtful to a horse."

"Let's look." Philippa turned on her heel, and marched back toward the tack room. She swept the light over the inside of the tack room, and then the feed room next to it. She gazed down each aisle, and winged horses put their noses out to see what was happening, but she saw nothing amiss. "Outside," she said. Herbert and Larkyn followed her out of the stables, where she turned left, toward the flight paddock. Herbert swore steadily under his breath, and Philippa could feel Larkyn's struggles to keep her panic under control.

"Larkyn, Black Seraph is a winged horse. No one would dare hurt him."

The girl's wide eyes rose to hers, and then turned away, searching. She didn't answer, and Philippa didn't blame her.

They circled the stables, past the closed gate to the flight paddock, past the return paddock, on around the side of the stables to the dry paddock. It was there that they found her.

"Rosellen!" Larkyn cried, and ran to kneel beside the stable-girl.

Rosellen lay facedown on the ground, a dozen paces from the rear door of the stables. Philippa handed the lantern to Herbert, and crouched beside Larkyn, her hand on Rosellen's back. She felt the movement of her breath through her thin shirt.

"She's alive," she said in a low tone. "But she must have been on her way to bed. No jacket, and . . ." She scanned the girl in the lamplight. "And no boots." She moved to Rosellen's other side, and with a nod to Larkyn, the two of them gently turned the stable-girl, Philippa cradling her head and shoulders on her knees.

Rosellen's freckled face was smudged with dirt, and her hair, undone as if for sleep, straggled over her shoulders. "Rosellen," Philippa said firmly. "Rosellen. Do you hear me?"

The girl groaned, and her eyelids flickered. A great knot already swelled on the back of her head. It was hot to the touch. "Herbert, we need ice. Could you go to the Dormitory and ask Matron, please? Leave the lantern with Larkyn. And ask Matron to return with you."

"Best call a doctor," Herbert said in a shaky voice. "She looks that bad."

"No," Rosellen moaned. "No, please."

Larkyn bent to Rosellen, and peered into her half-open eyes. "Rosellen, can you open your eyes? It's Lark."

Rosellen's eyelids fluttered again, and then lifted. Weakly, she said, "Oh, Lark! Lark! I tried to stop them, but—"

"Never mind that now," Philippa said.

Larkyn said with confidence, "Her eyes look all right. I don't think she needs a doctor. The ice should do it."

Philippa gazed at her with some doubt. "How would you know that, Larkyn?"

"I'm a farm girl, Mistress. People get hurt on a farm, or in the quarry. If she was bad off, her eyes would be funny."

Rosellen heaved a great sigh, and said, "Zito's ass, my head hurts, Lark."

"I know," Larkyn said softly. She stroked Rosellen's freckled forehead. "Herbert is fetching ice, and Matron. You'll be better soon."

"What happened, Rosellen?" Philippa said, knowing her tone was sharp, but too upset to modulate it. "Can you remember?"

"They took him," Rosellen said. Her eyes, still a little bleary, but focused, found Larkyn's face. "They took Black Seraph, and I couldn't stop them!" Fat tears began to run over her cheeks. "I'm sorry, Lark!"

"Who was it?" Larkyn asked. Her eyes were terrible, the pupils enormous.

"I didn't know him," Rosellen sobbed. "A little man, youngish, fearful."

"But Tup would never go with a man!"

Rosellen started to shake her head, and then cried out with pain. "Nay," she said miserably. "Nay. It was Mistress Strong was leading him. And this man with a lantern. I tried to stop them, I said, Mistress, what are you doing? But then . . ." She winced, and touched the back of her skull. "Oh, aye, and then someone hit me from behind. Went down like a broken mast, I did! Don't remember hitting the ground at all."

"It was William!" Larkyn breathed.

"Larkyn!" Philippa snapped. "Take care! You're speaking of the Duke."

The girl's stricken face turned up to her, full of horror. "He's the Duke now, and he thinks he can get away with it! He's stolen my horse!"

PHILIPPA had feared they would have to carry Rosellen up the stairs, but by the time Matron and Herbert returned with ice wrapped in a cloth, and pressed it to her injury, she was able to stand, and walk with steady enough steps, leaning on Larkyn. Both girls were weeping, but silently, clinging together. Waiting, and expecting, Philippa thought grimly, that she could do something.

Rosellen told her story in bits and pieces, Philippa asking questions, Larkyn listening with streaming eyes and fingers pressed to her trembling lips. Apparently Rosellen heard someone in the stables when she had just taken off her boots and coat. Herbert's light was already extinguished, and she assumed he was asleep. She had hurried down to investigate, and found a strange man standing in the aisle near Black Seraph's stall, a lantern in one hand. And in the stall—here Rosellen blinked, as if she could hardly believe her own account—in the stall was Irina Strong, putting a halter and lead on Black Seraph, leading him out.

"And Bramble, Bramble was growling, and the man kicked at her, and she slunk back into the shadows. And then I tried to take Seraph's lead from her, but he—he had this quirt, and he put it on me, right across my neck, and I couldn't move a muscle!"

"Smallmagic," Larkyn breathed. "Zito, or some such."

"Nonsense," Philippa said firmly.

Larkyn's violet eyes, glistening with her tears, came up to her again. "It was the same for me, Mistress Winter," she said in a shaking voice. "Duke William did it to me, at Deeping Farm. Froze me where I was."

"I don't blame you for being frightened, either of you," Philippa said. "But that kind of magic is only real to those who believe in it."

She saw the girls' eyes meet, and she knew she had not persuaded them, but that was not her main concern at the moment.

She left Larkyn and Matron ministering to the injured girl, and she rose and strode to the window of Rosellen's cramped apartment. Surprisingly, no one else had been roused by Larkyn's knocking on the Domicile door, or by Herbert's wakening Matron. Of course, everyone was tired, including herself.

Dawn would come all too soon. Philippa had to think what to do.

"If this man and Mistress Strong were in front of you, Rosellen, do you have any idea who might have hit you?"

Rosellen frowned, and then grimaced at the pain that caused her. "I—I followed them out of the stables, Mistress, and I started to call out for Herbert. I heard footsteps behind me, heavy ones, and then—there was a smell, like of someone who doesn't wash—and then that's all. Whoever was behind me hit me, and I fell, and then—then you were there."

Herbert said glumly, "Didn't hear a thing."

Larkyn stood up, and came to stand beside Philippa. "Mistress Winter," she said in a low, intense voice. "Can we go after him? Can we get Tup back?"

Philippa's throat tightened. She felt the child's misery as if it were her own. She forced herself to meet Larkyn's eyes.

"We have to discover who took him."

"Who dares steal a winged horse except the Duke?"

"I don't know." Philippa found herself hoping, almost violently, that it wasn't William who had abducted a winged horse. The political implications were staggering. Eduard, certainly, would have laid down his life before he would have let such a thing happen. But this new Master Breeder, clearly, was in William's pocket.

Would the Council move against the new Duke? She didn't know what the law might say. Or what leverage William might have.

Fresh tears welled in the violet eyes, but Larkyn did not sob. "Why do they want him, Mistress? Do you know?"

"I don't, Larkyn. But I will ask, I promise. I'll go to the Palace tomorrow, and I'll ask."

"Take me with you!"

Philippa, her heart aching, shook her head. "No, child," she said softly. "I think not. I know it's hard, but it's best you wait here. Black Seraph will be all right without you for a day."

She watched Larkyn wrap her arms tightly around herself, and press her trembling lips together. The girl gave a single nod, and then turned back to Rosellen's bed.

Philippa folded her own arms, and glared out into the fading night. It was as she and Margareth had feared. She didn't want to admit to the girls that she thought they were right, that it was William who had arranged for Black Seraph to be stolen. The new Duke had his own intentions for the winged horses, and for Oc, and he must feel some need for hurry.

Whatever William's scheme, it would be in his own interests, and not those of the horses or their riders. And there was, it seemed, very little any of them could do to stop him.

THIRTY-ONE

"HE wants to breed him, of course," Margareth said. "That's why he stopped Eduard from gelding Black Seraph, why he removed Eduard from his position. He wants to breed a colt who is already crossbred. He must have a mare in season somewhere."

"I'm going to the Palace, Margareth. Someone will have to take my flight—but someone else, please, not Irina!"

Margareth gave her a grim smile. "Irina is not here," she said. "She was 'called away on the Duke's business,' according to the note I had on my desk this morning." She rose stiffly from her chair, and trailed her fingers over the genealogy before her. "I cannot run the Academy this way," she said, her eyes and her voice full of bitterness. "I wish you would tell William so."

Philippa stood, too. She pulled her riding cap on above her rider's knot and began to draw on her gloves. "We may both lose our posts, but I will tell him that, and more."

"I've sent for Larkyn. We'll need her to be circumspect."

"I warn you, Margareth, she's upset. Just as you or I would be, in the circumstances."

"Yes, I'm certain she is."

"We'll need to devise some explanation for Black Seraph's absence."

Margareth said tiredly, "I suppose we must."

"It would be wise, Margareth. Rosellen and even Larkyn are at risk. I fear Larkyn is in danger in any case, if William wants her colt enough to steal him right from our stables."

"That is my fear, too, Philippa. You know William better than I. I've heard him described as a devious man, but I've never heard that he was an evil one."

Philippa smoothed her gloves over her fingers. "He has a cruel nature. I learned that as a girl. And he is ambitious. But I never thought he would commit treason."

"Perhaps you should talk to him before you draw your conclusions."

"I will try. And as to the other girls . . . you could put it about that the new Master Breeder wanted to examine Black Seraph."

"That should suffice." Margareth glanced at the old brass-encased clock on the mantelpiece. "Larkyn should have been here by now."

"It was a late night. Let's hope the child was able to sleep in a bit."

"I'll check with Matron."

"I'm going to leave that to you, Margareth, and be on my way. I saddled Sunny myself—Rosellen is having a lie-in, too. Perhaps Matron could check on her later."

"I wish you luck with the Duke, Philippa."

"Thank you. I have no doubt I'll need it."

THE Ducal Palace, not surprisingly, was abuzz with activity. Philippa and Sunny soared gently in, Sunny's wings fluttering in the cool spring morning. They trotted up from the grounds to the courtyard, passing a line of laden carts busy moving the new Duke's household from Fleckham House to the Palace. A carriage was drawn up before the door and three ladies were being handed down from it by Andrews even as Philippa dismounted, ordered Sunny to fold her wings, and handed the reins to Jolinda.

"Good Duke Frederick barely cold before it started," the elderly stable-girl grumbled.

"I suppose you can understand it, Jolinda," Philippa said. She took off her gloves and tucked them in her belt, eyeing the hubbub around the steps of the Palace. One of the ladies was William's wife, the reclusive Constance. She didn't recognize the others. "Little point in postponing the move." A line of servants began unloading a cart, hauling trunks and boxes around to the side door, carrying armloads of linens up the steps to the foyer. A supervisor called orders, and the servants shouted to each other. It all had an air of cheerful industry.

"That's as may be," Jolinda said tartly. "But them horses could have waited a day or so, give us a chance to get stalls ready." She pointed with her chin to a little band of horses.

Philippa turned to give them a curious look. A mixed lot gazed back at her above the whitewashed paddock fence, ears pricked forward. Sunny nickered, and one or two of the watching mares whinnied back. "What horses are these, Jolinda?" Philippa asked. "They look like wingless Ocmarins . . . and that's a Noble, isn't it? That bay in the back?"

Jolinda cast a dark look up into Philippa's face. "Heh. Bit odd, isn't it, the new Duke having such a collection, him what hardly ever rides but one horse? We have to give over a wing of the stables to them. And unload an entire cart full of their tack."

"Jolinda . . ." Philippa hesitated, wondering if she should entrust her worries to the old stable-girl. Of course, chances were good Jolinda would hear from Rosellen in any case. "Jolinda, did a new horse come last night to the stables? A new winged horse?"

Jolinda peered at her, the wrinkles around her eyes deepening. "A winged horse? Nay, Mistress. I mean, we have a flight of them here, with their horsemistresses living in the Palace. Not a new one."

Philippa looked across the cluster of carts and carriages at the Palace. Its windows gleamed back at her, the spring sun sparkling on clean glass and white stone. "I'm sorry to add Sunny to the chaos, Jolinda. It won't be for long."

The stable-girl stroked Sunny's neck with affection. "That's all right, Miss," she said. "Sunny and I are old friends. I'll find a quiet corner for her, and a bit of grain. The rest of that lot can just wait."

Philippa left Winter Sunset in Jolinda's care, and worked her way through the traffic in the sunwashed courtyard.

An unfamiliar butler, a small man of middle years, bowed her in through the open doors of the Palace. "Good morning to you, Horsemistress," he said.

"Good morning," she answered. She took off her cap and smoothed her hair, looking about her at the bustle of labor. "Where's Andrews?"

The new butler held out his arm for her things, and she gave them to him. "I don't know Andrews, Mistress," he said. "His Grace engaged me last week, just after the death of his father. I took up my duties yesterday." He bowed again. "Parkson, at your service, Horsemistress."

"Parkson." Philippa looked into his eyes, but saw no deceit there. "I'm Philippa Winter. Of the Academy of the Air."

"Of course," Parkson said smoothly. "You're the assistant to the Headmistress."

Philippa inclined her head. "I need to see Duke William without delay. Is he here?"

"I believe he is, Mistress. His breakfast tray came down perhaps an hour ago. His man Slater is with him, and his secretary, but I will find out if he can see you."

Parkson turned and pattered up the stairs, moving twice as fast as Andrews could have. Still, Philippa expected to wait for some time. William would cast about for some way to avoid seeing her. She went to the tall mullioned windows and stared through the polished glass at the comings and goings outside. As she watched, two flyers circled the grounds and settled into the paddock. A young stable-girl she didn't recognize came out to take the horses. The two horsemistresses, carrying courier bags, circled the courtyard toward the south entrance. Philippa watched them until they disappeared, wondering who might have her old apartment. Suddenly, she missed Frederick and his orderly reign with a poignancy that made her chest ache.

She was surprised when Parkson returned within only a few moments, and bowed to her yet again. "Mistress Winter," he said. "His Grace invites you up to his apartment, and asks if you will take coffee with him."

Philippa raised her eyebrows. "Coffee, Parkson? I'm surprised the Duke has time."

"Most generous of His Grace," he said. "But of course, you are one of his horsemistresses. I expect he will always make time for you." He turned away before he could see Philippa's skeptical look. "This way, if you please." He led the way back up the stairs, walking more slowly this time, looking over his shoulder once to be certain she followed. William's secretary passed them on his way downstairs, and behind him came the unpleasant Slater. He peered at Philippa from beneath his heavy eyelids, and nodded his head. She gave him a cold glance as she passed.

She braced herself, before entering what had so recently been Frederick's rooms, for more change. But when she stepped through the door, she found that everything was as it had been. The same velvet and damask furniture, the long curtains, the windows thrown open to the bracing air of spring, welcomed her with their familiarity. Only the occupant was different.

William stood alone by one of the windows, looking down into the courtyard. The noise had quieted somewhat, and Philippa, crossing the apartment, saw that the carriage had gone, and only two carts remained. William turned from the window, and gave her a cool smile.

"Philippa," he said. "What a pleasant surprise for us."

She pressed her lips together to stop herself asking who might be in the room she couldn't see. William was, after all, now her liege lord. She would have to try to see him that way, for the sake of the winged horses. "My lord," she said, with only a hint of irony in her voice. "Thank you for seeing me."

"A tray is on its way up," he said. "It's time I had a break. My secretary insisted I dictate a dozen letters this morning."

"It's all happening quickly, isn't it? You have not yet had your investiture."

"Well," William said, smoothing his vest with both hands. "There is a Duchy to be governed, Philippa. Business cannot wait on ceremony."

She eyed him. He had changed nothing in his appearance, either. He still wore the narrow black trousers, polished black boots, the full-sleeved shirt, and the vest that was now, apparently, habitual. His white-blond hair was tied neatly back with a bit of black cord, and his cheeks and chin were smooth as if he had just been shaven. He carried a quirt in his left hand, and rubbed the braided leather with the fingers of his right hand.

"Do I look like a Duke, Philippa?" He smiled without humor. "It will be good for Oc, don't you think, to have a leader who is young and vigorous. Who knows the uses of power."

"Power," Philippa said, "is a dangerous thing. Your father respected it."

William chuckled, a sound like a rattling of pebbles. "Do you not think I respect it?"

"I think you longed for it. Whether you know how to use it we have yet to learn."

William's eyes narrowed, and his lips thinned. "I caution you, Philippa. You too often presume upon old acquaintance."

"Ah." She regarded him for a moment, her head tilted to one side. Her patience stretched thin at the thrust and parry of polite conversation. The old thread of pain worked its way up her neck. "Tell me, my lord," she said tightly. "Did you steal one of our horses last night?"

His face didn't change, nor his eyes flicker. "They are *our* horses," he said in a silky tone. "You should remember that."

"You don't deny it, then."

He drew the quirt through his fingers, then tapped it idly on his palm. "I have no need to deny anything," he said. "I am your Duke, and I don't have to answer to you."

"You have to answer to the Council of Lords."

His lips curved. "For what, Philippa? Can you truly accuse me of anything?"

"We know you had an unusual interest in Black Seraph. And now he's gone."

"You're going to carry that to the Council?"

"I will if we don't find him soon."

"The winged horses are the Duke's concern, Philippa."

"Without us, William, they are useless to you."

His smile faded, and his eyes seemed to harden to stone as he gazed at her. "Are you certain of that?"

A knock at the door, and a formal, "Your pardon, my lord Duke," interrupted them. Parkson held the door for a maid with a coffee tray.

A few moments passed as the coffee was laid, a tray of biscuits set out, cups poured. Philippa stood in rigid silence, watching this ceremony, shaking her head at the maid's offer of cream and sugar. When the servants had left, and the door closed, she put her hands on her hips and stared at William.

"Irina Strong sold herself to you, didn't she? For promotion, and to keep her father out of prison."

William sat down beside the coffee tray, crossing his long legs. He laid his quirt on the seat beside him, and picked up a cup. He sipped from it, watching Philippa over the rim. When he set it down, he was smiling again. "Sit down, Horsemistress," he said. "Rest a moment. You flyers work too hard."

"Precisely, William," she said, deliberately omitting his new title. She stayed where she was. "We work far too hard to have time for politics and intrigue. Margareth asks me to tell you she cannot run the Academy under these conditions. And I think—"

"What, Philippa?" William asked lightly. "What is it that you think?"

Philippa put her hands on the back of the chair before her, gripping it until the knuckles whitened. "I think, William," she hissed, "that you are committing treason. That's what you will answer to the Council for!"

He stood up awkwardly, bumping the low table with his shin, dropping his cup into its saucer with a clatter. "How dare you," he said. His voice sounded thin and high. "How dare you speak to me—to us—that way!"

"I dare because they are our horses, too, William Fleckham!" she said, biting the words. "Because someone came into the Academy stables in the night, like a thief, and used a horsemistress—a *flyer*—to steal one of our own! Do you think we won't report this?"

"If you do, the Hamleys will lose their farm. How long has it been in their family? What a shame if the loss of it were laid at your door!"

"How long has the Ducal Palace been the protectorate for the winged horses?" Philippa snapped. "Will you destroy that in the first year of your succession?"

She raised her chin, and leaned forward over the chair, wishing almost that they could come to blows, that they could have it out, this tension that had built between them for years. "You can do nothing to me, William. I'm a *horsemistress*, and you simply can't forgive me, can you? I fly one of Kalla's creatures, a creature you can't even get near!"

"You just wait!" he shrilled, and then put his fingers to his mouth, as if to stop any more words from escaping him.

"For what? Wait for what, William?" she taunted.

He clenched his jaw, and for a long moment there was silence in the room. The sounds of the last cart trundling away carried up to them from the courtyard, and from somewhere in the park, a horse whinnied.

Then, with deliberation, William bent and picked up his quirt from the couch. He strolled around the low table, and came to stand close to Philippa. She stepped back from the chair, but her calves struck another small table, trapping her. His heeled boots gave him a slight advantage in height. He had recovered his composure, and he looked down at her with a paternal expression. "Don't you worry about it, Philippa," he said. "The future of Oc is in our hands now. We do what we think is best."

"Don't give me that 'we' nonsense," Philippa snapped. "I know you for what you are."

She was close enough to hear the breath he sucked in at her words, and to watch his eyes narrowing, his neck stiffening. He raised the quirt in his left hand, and laid it against her right arm. It felt oddly cold through the fabric of her tabard. She tried to pull away from it, but his right hand came out and gripped her left shoulder.

"I think," he said almost conversationally, "that Irina Strong would make a very good Headmistress. Don't you?"

"Perhaps as good a Headmistress as you a Duke," Philippa said.

"You—you *bitch*!" William exclaimed. He lifted the quirt, and she felt certain he meant to actually strike her.

"Don't you dare!" Her arm, suddenly released, came up, and she thrust against his chest with the flat of her hand.

He cried out, wordlessly, and reeled back away from her, the quirt falling to the floor. She stared at him, at his embroidered vest, and then at his smooth, pale face again. Slowly, slowly, she dropped her hand to her side.

"William," she breathed. "William, what in Kalla's name . . ."

"Get away from me," he said hoarsely. "Get out! And don't you dare—don't you ever—touch me again!"

"But William, what is it? What has—is something the matter with you?"

He pointed at the door, his outstretched arm shaking with fury. "Get out, Philippa!" he shouted, his voice strained and high. "I tried to be polite to you, tried to show you respect, because of the Academy, because my father cared for you. You've always thought you were better than everyone else, and I don't have to put up with it anymore. Get out of my sight, and don't come back!"

THIRTY-TWO

BRAMBLE bent her long nose to the ground, sniffed, and growled deep in her throat.

"Do you have it, Bramble? Do you still smell him?"

The dog whined, and angled off to her left. Lark followed close behind. The trail led them away from the road, down a tree-shaded lane too narrow for carts or carriages. They had been moving since long before dawn, and Lark's boots were meant for narrow stirrups, not long walks. Her feet burned, and the high tops chafed her calves beneath her divided skirt. She carried her riding coat over one arm, now that the sun was high. The swiftly moving clouds of spring fled across the sky, but fortunately no rain threatened. Rain would wash away the scent, and all would be lost.

Bramble stopped again, briefly, to touch her nose to the dirt lane, and then trotted on. Lark, exhausted but determined, struggled to keep up. "Good girl," she murmured to the oc-hound. "Keep on, Bramble. We'll find him."

She had no idea what Mistress Winter or the Headmistress would do when they found her gone. Would they expel her? She didn't know. She didn't care.

Mistress Winter had said to wait, but she couldn't. The need to find Tup made her mind spin and her chest ache. And what must Tup be feeling? He knew Mistress Strong, he might have trusted her for a time . . . but to find himself far from his bondmate, lost and alone in . . . alone where? That was the question. And that was what she and Bramble were going to discover.

Of course Mistress Strong had had to lead him away on foot. She could hardly have flown him, as her Foundation had never monitored Tup. By the look of the trail they had made, Irina had led both horses. Lark doubted Duke William would have walked all this way, but perhaps that third, mysterious assailant who had hurt Rosellen had tramped along after Mistress Strong, adding to the trail of scents Bramble now followed.

Lark had to put her trust in the dog. The oc-hound had not left her side since she discovered Tup to be missing.

Even Duke William, it seemed, had not had the temerity to lead a winged colt down the main road without his bondmate. Bramble had picked up the scent behind the stables, and followed it through the fields to a lane Lark had never seen before. One lane led to another, and then another, each narrower than the one before, more shaded by ash and spruce and oak. As they pressed on, farther and farther from the Academy, the moon glowed like a great lamp, casting leaf shadows on the ground.

Lark twined her fingers in the oc-hound's long coat, walking close beside her. When the moon set, and dawn painted the eastern horizon in shades of rose and gold, she let Bramble go, and the oc-hound loped ahead, sniffing the ground this way and that. When she got too far from Lark, she waited, and then started off again.

Lark wondered how far they had come. They were three, perhaps four hours behind Tup. Surely no more than that. Had she waited to sleep, or for Mistress Winter to fly to the Palace and return . . . who knew how far away Tup might be? Or if she might ever find him again?

She was doing the right thing, she felt certain, tired though she was, impossible though it seemed. Surely Duke William, with his cold smile and that wicked quirt, would feel no compunction about keeping Tup from her until he went mad. She couldn't let that happen, and she couldn't trust that Mistress Winter was a match for Duke William and Mistress Strong together.

Bramble stopped again, sniffing the ground, growling, trotting in circles.

"Oh, no, Bramble," Lark whispered. "You haven't lost it, have you?"

Bramble growled again, and stopped, snuffling hard at the packed dirt. She whined, and then spun about, dashing away from the lane and into the woods. Lark followed, crashing through underbrush, having lost all sense of direction or distance. She had no idea where she was. She could only trust the oc-hound.

They traveled now through thick stands of ash and oak, where only the narrowest of paths must have allowed Tup to walk. Hazel catkins brushed Lark's sleeves and sprinkled Bramble's coat with pink and yellow pollen. Lark glanced up past the treetops, and saw that the sun had passed the zenith and begun to sink into the west. She had had nothing to eat since the night before, and only stream water to drink. Her mouth felt dry as dust, and Bramble's must feel the same. But perhaps, if they were leaving the lane, they were close to their goal.

She swallowed, and tried to moisten her lips with her tongue. Bramble, ahead of her, had reached the edge of the wood. She paced back and forth, whining over her shoulder at Lark.

"I'm coming, Bramble," Lark said. Even her voice felt dry and worn out. "I'm right behind you."

"WAS there any sign of Black Seraph?" Margareth asked. She had come out to meet Philippa, and she braced herself against the wall as Philippa rubbed Sunny down.

"None." Philippa laid down the cloth. "Jolinda hadn't seen any winged colt. I took a turn through the stables at the Palace, and there were just the seven flyers assigned to the Duke. And the wingless horses William brought from Fleckham House, of course. They're still preparing stalls for them—nice horses, Nobles and Ocmarins, one Foundation."

"Sounds like a busy place."

"It was today."

"And Irina?"

"I didn't see her. And William told me nothing I didn't already know." Philippa patted Sunny, and then paused, resting her cheek against her mare's sleek neck. Quietly, she said, "I think, Margareth, that when it comes to our new Duke, I am no asset to the Academy."

"You have a complicated history, I know," Margareth said. "But surely, for the good of the Duchy . . ."

"There's something strange going on with him." Philippa straightened, and rubbed at the pain in her neck.

"We already knew that, of course," Margareth said. "I only wish you could have found out why he—"

Philippa turned to face her. "Margareth, it's something else. Besides Black Seraph. I—I touched William, inadvertently. We were arguing, and I thought he was going to strike me. I put out my hand to stop him, and I . . ." She shook her head. "I can hardly believe it. If I hadn't felt it myself . . ."

Margareth frowned. "What is it, Philippa? What did you feel?"

Philippa touched her own chest with her palm, and then, on impulse, she reached for Margareth's hand, and pressed the flat of it against her own thin bosom. "Do you feel that?"

"Feel what?"

"William's chest . . ." She dropped Margareth's hand. "He has reason to affect those embroidered vests. You'll think I'm mistaken. I can hardly believe it myself, in fact, but . . . but William's chest swells like my own. Like yours." Her voice cracked, and she touched her throat with her gloved hand. "Like a woman's."

HESTER called out to them just as they were going up the steps into the Hall. "Mistress Winter," she said, "Headmistress. Please excuse me."

They turned together and watched her dash up the stairs. She was a plain girl, angular and rangy, but Philippa had seen her grace in the saddle. Hester had an indefinable air of confidence and authority, no doubt learned at her mother's knee. It would stand her in good stead in her career.

"What is it, Hester?" Philippa asked.

"It's Black," Hester said, her tone low and urgent. "She wasn't in her cot this morning, nor in the stables. Do you know where she is? Could she be with Mistress Strong? She's missed breakfast, and lunch, too."

"Are you certain, Hester?" Margareth said.

"I've looked everywhere, Headmistress," she said. "Library, sleeping porch, the tack room . . . She's gone. And so is her colt."

"Kalla's teeth," Philippa grated, looking past Hester's worried face to Margareth's.

Margareth's eyes narrowed, and her mouth tightened. "Come with us, Hester," she said. She led the way on up the stairs and into her office, shutting the door when they were all inside. She crossed to the window, and pulled the curtains back, letting the sunshine stream in over the dark furnishings, and then sank into her chair. Hester stood near the door, biting her lip.

Philippa paced, stripping off her gloves and pleating them with her fingers. "She's gone after him," she said to Margareth.

Margareth turned, standing with her back to the light, her hair a gray nimbus, her face furrowed with worry. "How would she know where?" she said. Her voice thinned. "If we don't know where . . . or who . . ."

Hester spoke. "Mistress Winter, what's happened? Does Lark need help?"

"We don't know, Hester." Philippa tucked her gloves into her waistband. "Has anyone else noticed she's missing?"

"Everyone assumes she's with Mistress Strong. We haven't seen her today, either, or her mare. Everyone knows she's been giving Black a hard time."

Philippa gave a sharp nod. "Very well. We'll keep it that way if we can. We knew Black Seraph was missing, because someone took him, and injured Rosellen when she tried to stop them."

Hester looked at the Headmistress, and then back to Philippa. "Mistress Strong took him?"

Philippa stopped pacing. "Why would you say that?"

Hester shrugged. "Mamá knows all about Strong's family, and her troubles. It had to have been a woman, to take a winged horse. And I assumed, when she was made senior instructor . . . There's some connection with Duke William, isn't there." It wasn't a question.

Carefully, Philippa answered, "There may be, Hester. We're not certain."

"Someone took Black Seraph," Hester said, frowning. "And now Lark's gone after him, just as I would do if someone stole Goldie. This could be dangerous, for both of them! We have to do something."

Margareth said, in a shaking voice, "We were just trying to decide. I can't think . . . I don't know . . ."

Philippa said gently, "You can leave this to me, Margareth."

"And to me," Hester said firmly.

Margareth gave a sigh of acquiescence. Philippa turned to the girl. "I see you understand, Hester, that discretion is necessary."

"Of course."

"I can only guess where Black Seraph might have been taken."

"And why?" Hester asked. "What good is he to the Duke without his bondmate? And how would Lark know where to find him?"

Philippa shook her head. "I would only be guessing at any of it, Hester. Let's see if we can find him first. And stop Larkyn before something awful happens."

LARK took hold of Bramble's fur to stop the oc-hound from dashing out into the open. The dog whimpered, but she sank to her haunches under the pressure of Lark's hand. Her gaze was fixed on a low-roofed building on the opposite side of a wide, sloping meadow. Lark knelt beside her, and tried to understand where they were.

It was growing late, she knew. The sun already skimmed the western peaks. Could Tup be in those stables, on the far side of the broad meadow? Who would be with him?

She put her arm around Bramble's neck, and watched for signs of movement. A single horse, wingless, dappled gray, grazed in a grassy pasture. Another horse was tethered to a post. A little copse of beech separated the stables from a park. Above the treetops Lark could just see the roofs of a great, sprawling house. In the distance, a broad lane ran to the main road. Carts, drawn by oxen, came and went on the road, and a carriage or two bowled along behind a trotting horse. The great house itself seemed oddly quiet, as if it were abandoned. The afternoon had that suspended, pregnant quality of early spring. Not even a bird sang in the woods, nor did Lark hear the usual barking of dogs or bleating of sheep.

And then, in the hush, she heard a familiar sound. A whimper, then another. And immediately following, the hard, sharp thump of neat black hooves on a stable wall.

"Tup!" she breathed. He had sensed her presence.

Bramble whined, jumping to her feet, tugging to be free of Lark's restraining hand.

"Yes, Bramble, you've done it!" Lark said. "Lovely smart, you are! But it's not safe for us to go rushing in there. We have to wait to see if—"

But the oc-hound was already off, a streak of silver-gray racing down the slope, arrowing across the field. Lark struggled to her sore feet, and stumbled after her.

* * *

WILLIAM spent his bad temper in whipping his borrowed horse into a lather, making him run full out down the hard dirt of the lane to Fleckham House. What he wanted, craved, was to take his quirt to Philippa Winter, to wipe the sneer from her face, to make her fall to her knees and look up at him with fear and respect instead of glaring at him as if he weren't now her liege lord!

They were all like that, those horsemistresses. Philippa was the worst, but Margareth Morgan had known him since he was a baby, and had never accorded him the respect he deserved. All of them made him furious. Thinking of the two of them, Margareth and Philippa, conspiring to thwart his plans, made him cut the mare again with the quirt. The horse ran faster, breathing hard, and her hoofbeats jolted William against the cantle. He gritted his teeth against the dust that rose from the lane, and regretted leaving his own swift brown gelding with Jinson.

His temper had not yet subsided when he reached the courtyard of Fleckham House. He dismounted, and found that his legs were a bit shaky from the ride. His stable-man came out to meet him, frowning over the dripping horse, but wise enough to keep his damned mouth shut. "Are you alone, my lord?" was all he said.

"I don't need an escort to ride ten miles," William snapped at him.

"Of course not, my lord." The man took the mare's reins and disappeared with cautionary swiftness into the stables.

William took a deep breath, looking around him at the deserted courtyard, the blank windows of Fleckham House. Only a skeleton staff remained. There would be a housekeeper, a cook, a gardener, a few maids and footmen. Everyone else had removed to the Palace. The Fleckham family home might remain empty for some years, but William would not sell it. He needed it. Now that his household had left, there would be no danger of visitors interrupting his privacy. He and Jinson could go forward with his plan, and bring in Slater or Irina Strong when they needed an extra pair of hands. The simplicity of it all was perfect.

As he strode toward the beech grove, his bad mood began to lift. He had what he needed now. Just let one winged horse bond to him, one he could train and fly himself. The shock and disgust on Philippa Winter's face would no longer matter. The changes of his body would be worth that triumph, worth the feeling of looking down on the Academy from the air. Centuries of the female monopoly of winged horses were going to come to an end. Duke William of Oc would be the agent of change, and neither Philippa nor Margareth nor any other cursed horsemistress could stop it. And by Kalla's tail, when that day came, horsemistresses would curtsy to their Duke like proper females!

He slapped the dust from his trousers and shirt, and hurried through the trees.

THIRTY-THREE

THE closer Lark got to the stables, the louder the ruckus sounded from within. She crept past the small paddock that ran along the back, and sidled along the fence. The horse in the paddock, the dappled gray, was a young mare, perhaps four or five years old. She flung her head up, her ears flicking toward Lark and then toward the racket from the stables. The other horse was a long-legged brown gelding, wearing a black and silver saddle. Lark had a vague feeling she should recognize him, but the noise distracted her.

She knew it was Tup, whinnying, pounding walls with his hooves, stamping his feet. Her heart raced with fear and with relief.

The rear door of the stables was hooked back, open to the afternoon air. Lark ducked beneath its long latch, and flattened herself between the door and the wall. Someone was coming, clattering down the stairs from the upper level. Lark peered through the crack left by the door's iron hinges.

It was no stable-girl stamping down the aisle. Lark knew Irina Strong's heavy tread, and her voice as she snapped at Tup, "Quiet, Crybaby! Enough of your nonsense!"

There was a smacking sound, as of a leather strap applied to a horse's hindquarters. Tup squealed, and Lark had to press her hands to her mouth to stop herself from crying out, too. Tears sprang to her eyes, but she blinked them away, trying to think what to do.

When she flattened her cheek to the door, she could see two stalls, part of the sawdust-strewn aisle, and a door opening into a small tack room. Strong Lady put her head out of one of the stalls, her ears twitching nervously. Lark couldn't see Tup, or Mistress Strong.

Lark drew a breath and held it. If she couldn't see Mistress

Strong and Tup, perhaps they couldn't see her, either. She hesitated only a moment, fearful of losing her chance. Then, under the cover of another flurry of noise and banging of hooves, she slipped around the door and dashed for the tack room.

She ducked inside, and squeezed herself between a saddle rack and a wall hung with ropes and halters. Tup kicked the wall again, and there was the distinct sound of wood breaking. A new voice, one she didn't recognize, stammered a string of curses. Not a stable-girl, then. A stable-man. Tup would never stand for it.

"Get back, Jinson, you're making it worse!" Mistress Strong snapped. "Give me a minute to get him settled."

"He broke the gate!" the man said. He sounded rather young, Lark thought, and a little frightened. "Watch his wing, there, those splinters—"

Lark almost sprang out of the tack room then. If they hurt Tup, or allowed him to hurt himself . . .

And then there was another voice, one Lark knew well. As soon as she heard it, she knew where she had seen the brown gelding before.

"Jinson," Duke William said. "Irina. What in Zito's hells do you think you're doing?"

Lark pressed back against the wall, a braided rope catching at her hair, the buckle of a hackamore digging into her hip.

Tup whimpered, and the noise of his hooves ceased. He had reacted to William this way before, his ears flopping sideways, his little cry sad and confused.

She bit her lip, and listened.

"My lord," the man called Jinson said anxiously. "The mare's ready, she's right there, but—I did tell you, sir, I said you couldn't take a winged horse from its bondmate—"

"You mean it's not done? Why did we go through all this, then?"

"My lord, the little stallion is going crazy! He could hurt the mare, or worse, he could hurt himself, and he's a winged—"

"That's enough, Jinson." Duke William's voice was so light Lark could barely hear his words. "Irina should have been able to handle this."

"I told you he was bad-tempered," Irina said.

"I don't know why that should be," William said smoothly. "His dam was as mild as they come, and his sire was steady enough for a child to ride."

"My lord," Jinson said in a shaky voice. "Maybe it's mixing the bloodlines does it, ruins the temper? Master Crisp used to say—"

There was a sharp cracking sound. Lark thought William must have whipped something, a wall, his boot, perhaps even this man Jinson. A moment of tense silence passed before William said, "Eduard Crisp had no vision. I do. You have his job, Jinson, because I expect you to share my goals."

Jinson answered meekly, "Yes, my lord."

"I don't give a damn if he hurts the mare, and if he hurts himself, that's too bad. But we have to get him back, or I'm going to have to explain all of this to the Council. I don't want to do that."

Mistress Strong said, "Let's try again, then."

"I'll get a halter," Jinson began.

"Do that," William said, and then added in an offhand manner, "Irina tells me he's useless anyway. He'll never make a flyer."

Mistress Strong exclaimed, "Your Grace! If something happens to him—"

"No one can prove anything. If he won't cooperate, we'll put him down."

Lark gasped, and pushed herself away from the wall. The halter that had been biting into her hip fell to the floor with a clank of metal.

She heard William exclaim, and then Mistress Strong's boots came stamping down the aisle. Lark cast about for someplace to hide. It was a simple box of a room, smelling of leather and straw and oil. There were only four saddles on the rack, and a small stack of oat sacks, not high enough to conceal her.

There was nothing she could do but face them. Just as Mistress Strong reached the tack room, Lark stepped into the doorway. The horsemistress glared at her, and Lark glared back, chin up, spine straight, cheeks burning.

Her voice sounded small but steady in her ears as she said, "I've come for Tup."

Tup whinnied at the sound of her voice, and his hooves battered the wall, more wood shattering. Jinson shouted something. Lark took a step forward, and then Duke William appeared at the horsemistress's shoulder.

Lark froze where she was, even as Tup whinnied again.

William wore his usual black, with a vest embroidered in gold and violet. His boots and trousers were dusty, and streaks of sweat marked his smooth-shaven cheeks, but he held himself as still as ever, his eyes as black and flat as the stone of the Uplands. His lip curled. "Ah," he said. "The brat."

"Oh, aye," Lark snapped. "And you're the thief!"

Mistress Strong said, "Larkyn! How dare you!"

Duke William only laughed. "It's not theft. I've taken what is mine by right."

"We serve you," Lark said hotly. "You don't own us."

"Oh, no?" He pulled his quirt from underneath his arm, and stroked it with his fingers. "You think you can stand in the way of the Duke of Oc?"

"If I have to!"

Mistress Strong stepped forward and gripped her arm. "Silence," she hissed. "Show respect for your liege lord!"

Mistress Strong's iron fingers pinched the skin beneath Lark's arm, making her yelp. Tup gave a fierce neigh, and Jinson called weakly, "Mistress Strong—"

Duke William seized Lark's other arm, and the two of them lifted her between them as if she was a naughty child. Lark screamed, "Let me go! Leave me be!"

Tup screamed in response. Hinges screeched under his battering hooves, and a great crash shook the walls of the stables. Jinson croaked something, and then Tup came pounding around the corner, ears laid back, teeth bared. He wore a halter with the lead broken, four inches of leather dangling beneath his chin.

Mistress Strong dropped Lark's arm when she saw the charging colt. William, too, released her, cursing. He leapt into the aisle, brandishing his quirt in front of him. Tup skidded to a halt in the sawdust, rearing, forefeet clawing the air inches from William's head. He gave the full-throated cry of an infuriated stallion, a sound that shivered in Lark's bones.

"Tup!" she cried. "Here!" She stood poised in the doorway to the tack room. Warily, Tup let his forefeet drop. His eyes rolled at William, and he tried to dodge past him.

William struck at him with the quirt, catching him on the point of his shoulder. Tup's neck stretched, his white teeth snapping at William's full sleeve. As William jumped aside, Tup sidestepped in the other direction, coming as close to Lark as the wall would allow.

She tensed her thighs, bent her knees, and gave a great leap.

The hundreds of standing mounts she had practiced served her well in that moment. As Tup flinched away from another blow, Lark's left hand found his neck, and her right reached over his back. For half a breath, she balanced on her belly across his withers, and then she swung her right leg up and over, winding both hands into Tup's mane. Her legs clamped over his wings, and she bent low over his neck. "Go! Tup, go!"

Tup leaped forward.

William jumped aside barely in time to avoid being flattened by the colt's lunge. Lark felt just the brush of his quirt on her calf as she and Tup pounded past him, out of the stables, and on toward the meadow.

PHILIPPA took to the air with Sunny in the cool violet light of early evening. Hester followed on Golden Morning, and Philippa was glad of her company. Though Hester was only a first-level student, her maturity gave Philippa confidence. Theirs was a strange mission, and their path was anything but clear.

They had concluded that William and Irina could not have taken Black Seraph far, since they had to go on foot. Irina's Strong Lady made a poor monitor. She was known to be testy with young horses, and surely, Philippa thought, even Irina would not take such a chance with a colt. They already knew Tup had not shown up at the Palace stables. Where would it be safe for William to hide a stolen winged horse? Philippa remembered the new stables built at Fleckham House, separated from the main estate by the grove of beech trees. It was the only place any of them could think of. If Black Seraph wasn't there . . . Kalla's heels, Philippa thought, if the colt wasn't at Fleckham House, and if Larkyn had followed him to someplace unknown . . . they might never know what had happened to either of them.

She tried to tell herself, as the horses rose into the darkening sky and banked to the west, that even William would not truly harm a winged horse or a young rider, but nothing eased the tension in her belly and the pain stabbing the back of her neck. It was a short flight to Fleckham House, but a strained one.

They flew to the north of the estate, and came to ground in the park in the dim light of evening. Philippa was a little worried about Hester flying back in the dark, but a full moon would soon be rising. If the sky stayed clear, they would have enough light.

The horses trotted to a halt, and Philippa peered ahead at the great house, its windows gleaming blank and empty with the last of the light.

"It looks deserted," Hester said.

"Yes, it does, and a good thing," Philippa said grimly. "Where I think—I hope—Black Seraph might be is beyond that beech copse, there. Come now, quietly."

The horses folded their wings, and they rode down a slope of grass. There was silence around them except for the brief song of an evening bird, a faint rustle of wind-stirred leaves. They heard nothing else until they reached the edge of the grove.

When the sounds exploded through the quiet, Philippa jumped as if someone had struck her. A horse squealed, and hooves banged on wood. There were voices, and then a great crash. Philippa urged Sunny to a canter.

Sunny dodged through the trees. Branches caught at Philippa's hair and her coat, and tugged her cap from her head. They broke from the grove into a grassy verge above the small stables. A dappled gray mare ran nervously to and fro in a paddock, and William's tall brown gelding was tethered just outside. Shouts erupted through the twilight, and then Philippa heard Larkyn's voice, clear and determined, crying, "Go! Tup, go!"

Philippa urged Sunny forward just as the girl and the horse dashed from the stables and galloped toward the meadow beyond. Behind them an oc-hound raced, tail low, ears flattened. The moon had only begun its rise above the hills to the east. The vale and the wood above it lay in near-darkness.

Tup and Larkyn had not gone a dozen strides before William came out of the stables at a dead run. He yanked his gelding's rein free and leaped into the saddle. He began to use his whip before his horse had even rounded the stables. His path led right past Philippa.

"William!" she shouted as he galloped by. "Let them go! This is dangerous!"

Over his shoulder, William snarled, "I'm going to kill that brat!"

Philippa gave Sunny her head, and the mare plunged after William's gelding. Hester and Goldie thundered after, the Foundation filly's feet sinking into the spongy ground as she labored to keep pace with Sunny.

In the faint moonlight, Philippa could see that William was gaining ground on Larkyn, and pulling away from Sunny. Sunny had already had a long day, and William's gelding was known for speed. The brown horse surged up the slope on the far side of the meadow just as Black Seraph, with Larkyn bent close over his neck, reached the top of the hill.

But there was a wood there, thick with ash and oak and spring-blooming hazel. It wouldn't be possible to gallop through it. Larkyn would be trapped.

Philippa urged Sunny faster, and felt the mare's wings flex against her stirrup leathers. Of course, Sunny would not understand why, if speed were required, she couldn't take to the sky. "Just run, Sunny," Philippa cried to her. She hoped the ground of the meadow was even. At this pace, a rodent's burrow or a stray rock could be disastrous.

Sunny sped faster, fairly leaping up the slope toward the wood, leaving the heavier Golden Morning far behind.

Black Seraph reached the dark thicket of the wood, where the moonlight could not penetrate. He turned right, racing along the upper edge of the meadow.

William also reined his horse to the right, angling across the open space on a course to intercept them. He slashed his gelding with the quirt, and screamed something, but his high-pitched voice didn't carry enough for Philippa to hear what it was. His path and that of Larkyn and Black Seraph would converge in seconds, and though Sunny was in a flat run, they would never arrive in time. If the gelding crashed into Black Seraph at such a speed, anything could happen—a leg, a wing, a neck could break—and not only those of the horses. Larkyn looked as fragile as a butterfly, clinging to her colt's back.

"Kalla protect us!" Philippa cried into the wind.

A heartbeat later something metal flew from Larkyn's hand, something that glittered in the growing light of the moon. A second time her hand came up, and she cast another shining object into the air. It twirled away, out of the light, disappearing into darkness. Philippa didn't understand what Larkyn had done until she saw Black Seraph's wings open, stretch, begin to catch the air.

Wing clips. Larkyn had thrown off Black Seraph's wing clips.

Half a dozen strides, and William's gelding would run head-long into Black Seraph. William must be mad! He could destroy the winged colt, injure the girl, even hurt his own mount. Still, his quirt rose and fell as he drove his horse faster and faster.

Philippa urged Sunny on, knowing she couldn't reach them in time, not knowing what else to do but try.

Another stride, and another. And then Black Seraph, with Larkyn clamped to his withers like a small, curly-headed burr, rose into the air.

Philippa watched, open-mouthed, her heart in her throat. Seraph's wings beat strongly, once, twice, three times, as he launched himself up into the moonlight.

William screamed a futile protest. His gelding reached the spot where Seraph had been, overran it, William's quirt still cutting at his hindquarters.

Philippa straightened, and murmured to Sunny. The mare slowed her gait to an easy gallop, and then to a trot. Golden Morning caught them at the far edge of the meadow, and all of them, including William, came to a stop, horses and riders breathing hard, every head tipped up to the sky.

Black Seraph, with no tack and little experience, rose above the wood, his bondmate's legs tucked beneath his wings, her hands entwined in his mane. The moon had risen above the hills, full and yellow, and its light framed the little stallion as he banked to the east. He looked like a dark bird with long, slender wings, flying steadily away from them.

"Shall we go after them, Mistress Winter?" Hester gasped.

"We must," Philippa said, struggling for breath. "But we can't launch here. I don't know how Seraph did it."

"She has no saddle, no bridle, nothing! And Lark has never flown!"

William wrenched his mount around, his hands cruel on the bit. His gelding snorted in protest, and chewed on the bit with a jangle of metal. William snarled, "I've warned you for the last time, Philippa."

Philippa turned on him, her jaw so tight it ached. "Have a care, my lord," she said, stressing his title. "I will expose you, Duke or no Duke!"

She shifted her weight to the right, and lifted her rein with the lightest hand. Sunny spun on her haunches, not making a sound, as if to show William's poor gelding how it should be done. She trotted easily down through the meadow. Philippa glanced back to see that Hester and Golden Morning were following, and caught her breath at the sight of Bramble loping out of the woods and down the slope to join them.

A moment later, William charged past them at an angry gallop. He flung himself from the saddle the moment he reached the stables.

Jinson was there to meet him, reaching for the gelding's reins, barely missing becoming another victim of William's slashing quirt. The Duke strode past him into the stables. Philippa said, "They'll head back to the Academy. Seraph knows the return paddock there."

"I hope so." Hester sounded doubtful. "I don't know where else they could go."

"Let's hurry. We can launch from the park. We can help them down."

They gave the hapless Jinson a wide berth, keeping to the trot as they wound their way through the grove to the park. Philippa said, "If Golden Morning seems tired, let me go ahead."

"We'll be all right," Hester said stoutly. "What about Bramble?"

"We'll have to trust her to find her own way home."

They hurried, emerging from the grove moments later, in time to see another winged horse rise into the moonlit sky. It was a long, low launch, a slow banking turn to the west. Irina Strong, and Strong Lady.

"Kalla's teeth," Philippa muttered, as she and Hester took their positions to gallop down the park. "Where do you suppose she's going?"

THIRTY-FOUR

LARK'S heart drummed in her chest, and the night wind whipped tears from her eyes as Tup drove them up, up, beyond the trees, beyond the hilltop, far beyond the reach of Duke William's quirt. Tup's wingbeats sent waves of power through Lark's calves and thighs, through her hands, through her feet tucked hard around his barrel.

The moon shone so brightly Lark thought it might blind them both. Tup turned into the light, and then, leveling his flight, he turned south and west. Lark clutched his mane, and held on. She had no rein, not even a halter rope, nor would she have known where to guide him if she had. He flew strongly, without hesitation, as if he knew exactly where he was going.

She had to trust him. He, at least, had flown before. For her, it was all new, and confusing, even in the brilliant moonlight. The landscape looked utterly different from the air. The twisting lanes, the peaked roofs, the oddly perfect rectangles of cultivated fields, were alien and confusing. She hardly knew where she was.

And she was frightened. In the rush to escape from William and Mistress Strong, there had been no time to think about what she was doing. She had pulled off Tup's wingclips as the only thing she could think of to get him free. And the flood of power from his beautiful wings, the reach of his slender neck, the smoothness of his flight filled her with such joy that for long moments the glories of flying intoxicated her.

Only now, looking down on the landscape flowing so swiftly beneath her, did her courage falter. Where would they go? How could she be sure Tup could come safely to ground?

Tup flew toward the western hills, over villages and lanes, hedgerows painted silver by the light of the moon. Lark wondered how long it was safe for Tup to stay in the air. What if he grew tired, if carrying her was too much for him?

He appeared to be untroubled by her slight weight. When the hills rose up before them, he climbed higher without effort, his wings finding purchase on the cold air, his body growing hot beneath her, but his breathing strong and steady.

Lark knew, though, that having a rider changed Tup's balance, most especially upon landing. She racked her brain for everything she had learned in her classes, had heard the horsemistresses tell the other new flyers. Weight down. Heels in. Hands low, and back straight but not rigid. She knew she had to grip with her thighs and calves. Chin in—or chin up? Weight forward, or weight back—she couldn't remember. There was always a first landing, of course . . . but that was at the Academy, where the return paddock was kept smooth, every hole filled, the grass as soft and thick as the groundskeepers could make it. And those flyers were fresh, having taken short flights, taking care not to fatigue their mounts, having horsemistresses to watch over them.

As Tup flew on into the west, Lark tried to put worry from her mind. There was nothing to be done about it now. They must return to ground sometime, and she only hoped Tup had an idea where that would be.

As they flew on, the houses grew farther apart, the fields broader, the lanes longer and narrower. The moon appeared to flee before them, beginning its sink into the west as they pursued it. The air grew noticeably colder, and Lark's thighs and calves and fingers began to ache. She tried to release their tension, just a bit, and found that she was perfectly secure in her seat. Still, she kept a tight hold on Tup's mane, and kept her heels firmly against his ribs. To fall from this height would be the end of everything.

She felt, after a time, almost euphoric with exhaustion. She had not slept for two nights, and had eaten nothing at all yesterday. Tup, she hoped, had at least had grain, perhaps some hay. She began to shiver. She peered cautiously past Tup's shoulder at the ground, and saw a formation of road and lane and hedgerow that seemed vaguely familiar. She wrinkled her brow, trying to see it from a different angle, to imagine what it would look like if she were on the ground instead of high in the air.

Suddenly the pieces came together, a jigsaw of images and impressions resolving into a landscape she knew as well as she knew her own face. Tup had flown directly to the Uplands, his path as unerring as that of a homing bird. The faint glow of windows reflecting moonlight, a little to the south, was the town of Dickering Park. There, just to the north, lay the quiet streets and modest homes of Willakeep. And soon, directly below, Lark saw the turning of the lane that led to Deeping Farm. The kitchen garden, the house with its sloping roof, the barnyard, the whitewashed barn gleaming in the light of the sinking moon. Home.

But where could Tup land? There was no return paddock. There was only the field of bloodbeets, studded with knee-high spring starts. There were the rough furrows plowed for the broomstraw crop. And there was the packed dirt of the lane.

Tup, it seemed, intended to come to ground just as Winter Sunset had, on that winter afternoon that now seemed so long ago. Sunny had landed in the lane, cantered into the barnyard, with Mistress Winter sitting effortlessly straight in her saddle.

Tup slowed, banked, and soared over the barnyard. Lark took a deep breath, and held it. Tup circled Deeping Farm once, twice, and then his wings stilled, spreading wide, pinions fluttering in the wind. She sensed him choose his spot, saw his neck stretch, felt his hooves begin to reach.

That was when she saw the other horse.

She was unmistakable, even in the fading moonlight, her wings half again as wide as Tup's, her nose and neck thick with muscle. The perfect Foundation specimen.

Of course, she could not fly as fast as Tup, but Foundation horses were known for stamina. She was not a pretty flyer, but she was a powerful one. She came winging in from the east, perhaps ten minutes behind them, and she had the advantage of experience, though she had never, as far as Lark knew, been to Deeping Farm.

Irina Strong and Strong Lady would be here in moments, and would betray Tup to Duke William.

"Tup!" Lark shrieked. She bent far forward over his neck, and felt his wings ripple, adjusting for the shift of her weight. "No! No! Look!" She dared to put out a hand, to point to the east.

Tup's wings shuddered, and then began to beat again, though the lane was no more than four rods beneath them. Now she felt, with a certain despair, her bondmate's fatigue. Tup drove them up again, but slowly. Her muscles labored with his, her heart thudded with his effort. The heat of his body burned her calves as he climbed, and she feared he was too tired to go on. What would they do? Where could they go? "Oh, Tup!" she cried. "I'm so sorry!"

As if to reassure her, to tell her it was all right, his wings beat faster. He didn't ascend, though, but skimmed the hedgerows, turning north toward the river, where they had once wandered the meadow by the grove of cottonwoods.

Lark looked over her shoulder, and saw the outline of Strong Lady and her rider against the stars that twinkled weakly in the wake of the setting moon. She saw now that they could use Tup's fatigue, that it was best to fly low, to disappear against the shadowed hills and woods of the Uplands, to fly where Strong Lady could not follow.

"Good!" she called to Tup, as he banked above the river and turned higher into the hills. "That's good! Just a little farther, lovely brave boy!" She prayed to Kalla to help them. It seemed to her, for an instant, that the icon that hung against her breast flared with heat, that if she could spare a glance at it, it would be glowing in the dark.

Just ahead, a small mountain meadow stretched beneath a blackstone butte. "There!" Lark called, and Tup seemed to understand. He tilted in his flight, took aim at the meadow, and once again stilled the beat of his wings.

She felt his shoulders move as he reached with his forelegs and extended his neck. His hindquarters gathered as the meadow surged up toward them, shadowed and frightening. Lark felt his weight shift forward, and she knew, somehow, she must keep hers back. She felt the heat of his body as she squeezed with the last strength of her legs, and she rocked back, ever so slightly, on her seat.

But it was coming up so fast, that hard, unforgiving ground. She gasped, and braced herself.

Tup's wings flexed, abruptly, as if trying to slow his descent. Lark felt her left calf jar free, pushed by the movement of his wing, and her weight drifted to the right.

She could feel Tup try to adjust to the shift, felt him reach with his left shoulder, his foreleg stretched for that first running step.

But Lark's hands, perspiring now, lost their grip on the silken strands of his mane. Her left foot lost its purchase.

All that mattered was Tup, that he come safely down on all four feet, free to run, to spend the dangerous speed of his landing. He was so close now, seconds away, but his balance was off. He was trying to hold her on, tipping himself to the left as she slipped to the right.

Lark released her hold on his mane. She let her left leg lift above his withers and his back, and she rolled. It was a somersault, her feet above her head, wisps of his tail brushing her face as she fell. She tried to curl herself against the impact to come. She fell for perhaps one full second, and then the ground met her with a solid blow against her shoulder and hip and heel. The breath she had been holding whooshed from her lungs, and she lay on her back, staring in amazement up at the wheeling stars.

But she heard Tup's hoofbeats on the turf, the rhythm of his gallop, slowing to the canter, and then the trot, the sounds coming closer as he wheeled about and came back for her.

She lay in the grass, desperate for a breath. Tup found her, his muzzle against her hair, his breath blowing on her neck, his familiar, dear whimper asking if she would get up, if she would mount again.

At last her lungs filled, and she gasped for air, once, twice, three times. "Oh, Tup," she rasped, when she could. "Oh. Oh." Something hurt in her right leg, and in her side, something that she thought might begin to hurt far worse in the next few moments.

She tried to lift her arm, to stroke Tup's cheek, but it brought a stab of pain through her shoulder, through her ribs, down into her hip. Tup's eyes shone down on her, the moonlight reflected in them. He nudged her with his nose.

"Tup," she moaned. "I just—just let me lie here a bit."

They were down, and Tup was safe. She tried to tell herself that was all that mattered.

But she hurt so much. Her hip throbbed, and even shallow breaths filled her chest with pain. A bonfire had begun in her ankle, its flames shooting up her calf to her knee. She knew she couldn't stand on her own. If she couldn't stand, she couldn't walk. And if . . .

What if she could never ride again? Tup would be as lost as if she had let Duke William destroy him.

Her choices had evaporated, one by one. Dawn was coming, and it would find them here, stranded in an Uplands meadow, fugitives brought to ground, at the mercy of their pursuers.

THIRTY-FIVE

PHILIPPA knew, before they even reached the Academy's return paddock, that Larkyn had chosen a different path—or that Black Seraph had. There was no sign of either of them as she and Hester circled the grounds for their moonlit landing.

Impotent fury, at William, at Jinson, and most especially at Irina Strong, made Philippa's muscles twitch with nervous energy. As she and Hester crossed the courtyard to the Hall, their horses fed and blanketed for the night, she wished she had one of them before her at this moment, when her rage was honed to its finest point. By morning, by the time she could accost William at the Palace, or find where Irina had gone, fatigue and worry would have dulled the fire that burned in her now.

The door of the Hall opened as they approached, and Philippa saw with surprise that Margareth was waiting for them, still fully dressed.

"Margareth!" she said. "It must be three in the morning! You should be in bed."

"It's four," Margareth said crisply. "And how could I sleep, with one of our girls missing and her horse stolen?"

Philippa gave a resigned nod. "Yes. I fear there will be no sleep for any of us tonight."

Margareth closed the door and turned the bolts, then led the way to her office. "I had Matron leave some sandwiches," she said. "And tea, though it's cold by now."

"Thank you," Philippa said. "Both will be welcome."

Hester also thanked her, and added, "I'm ravenous!"

Philippa and Margareth smiled. It was good, Philippa thought, to feel a smile on her lips, even as weary and wan a smile as this one. She dreaded the tension of the morning to come.

When they were settled, and Hester had most of an entire

sandwich in her mouth, Margareth said, "Tell me." Philippa began at the beginning, leaving nothing out, ending with Irina Strong's flight from Fleckham House.

"Will Black Seraph be able to make a safe return?" Margareth asked quietly.

"With Kalla's aid," Philippa said. She, too, spoke with her mouth full.

Margareth quirked an eyebrow at the unaccustomed piety. "His launch was good?"

"It was perfect," Hester declared. She drank thirstily from a cup of cold tea. "But you know, Headmistress, Black hardly weighs anything. I doubt he even noticed she was there!"

"I wish it were that simple," Philippa said. Now that she had eaten, she began to feel as if she could hardly rise to her feet again, even to go to her bed. "There's balance, and of course the landing surface . . . who knows where they might come to ground?"

At that, Hester put down her teacup, and her eyes abruptly reddened. She, too, Philippa knew, must be exhausted. "Oh, poor Black!" Hester whispered. "She hardly had a chance, from the very beginning."

"Now, now, Hester," Margareth said soothingly. "We must not give up yet. Our Larkyn is strong and stubborn, and Black Seraph is a clever young stallion. They may yet return to us, whole and well."

"You must rest, Hester," Philippa told her. "Go to bed, and sleep. The Headmistress and I will decide what to do next."

Hester pressed the heels of her hands to her eyes, and when she dropped them, her eyes were clear again. "I couldn't sleep, Mistress Winter," she said frankly. "I would lie and worry."

Philippa opened her mouth to order her, and then closed it. Hester, tonight, had earned the right to make this choice for herself. Dawn was only two hours off. She rubbed her own eyes, and then, wearily, came to her feet.

"Sunny and Goldie need rest," she said. "It would not be right, or even safe, to fly them again so soon. But we have to search for these two, without alarming the rest of the students."

"Oh! I'm so stupid!" Hester blurted. "They will have gone home, of course! I should have known that."

"But this is home," Margareth said in surprise.

"Not for them," Hester answered. "Lark thinks of herself as an Uplander first."

"Then they've gone to Deeping Farm," Philippa said.

"And so has Mistress Strong." Hester's angular face set in lines too hard for her tender years. "I think we should ask Mamá for the carriage. It will be the fastest way, without flying."

Margareth nodded. "Thank you, Hester. In the morning, I'll send a message."

"Tonight, please, Headmistress. I'll go myself, if I may have a horse. We can be on our way before morning, and rest a bit in the carriage."

"We'll go together," Philippa said.

LARK drifted in and out of a daze, waking at times to see the moon sinking in the west, at others to find her eyes burned by starlight. And always, always, Tup was there, his velvety muzzle at her ear, on her cheek, the whimper in his throat more comforting than inquiring. She knew, no matter what came, he would not leave her, and she let her eyelids close, welcoming the respite from pain and anxiety that oblivion brought.

It seemed only a few minutes before the sky began to lighten, and she opened her eyes to a rainbow dawn. She squinted up into the light, hoping to reassure Tup, whose anxious breathing had played background to her nightmares.

But it was not Tup's delicate face she saw, but one of wrinkles and dark skin, of faded green eyes beneath a frizzy halo of gray hair.

It was Dorsey. The witchwoman of Clellum. And behind her, a woman Lark didn't recognize, young, slender, with a long blond braid falling over one shoulder.

Lark pressed her eyelids closed, believing she was laboring through a fresh nightmare. When she opened them again, the sight of the two women was made credible by the light rising behind the witchwoman's aureole of hair, by the rustling of Tup's wings, by the smell of new spring grass and rain-washed earth beneath her head. Morning light glittered on the blackstone butte rising above the meadow, and the heady air of an Uplands spring morning filled her lungs.

"Oh!" she breathed. "I live."

"Oh, aye, aye, Missy," the witchwoman cackled. "You live, right enough, thanks to this lovely fine horse of yours. Such a sight that was, the two of you sailing down from heaven on a path of stars!"

"Tup," Lark tried to say, though it was more of a moan.

"Aye, lovely fine fellow, brought you safe to this meadow, and I'll bring you safe to my house. Come now, Missy, get you up! Just a few minutes' walk. You can lean on old Dorsey!"

Lark would not have believed she could stand, so wildly did her head spin when she lifted it, but Dorsey's bony hands were remarkably strong, her arms as thin and hard as the poles that fenced the paddocks of the Academy of the Air. Lark fumbled to her feet, unable to suppress a cry of pain. At least, with Dorsey on her right, she could keep her right foot off the ground. The blond woman—girl, really—took her left side. They made an awkward threesome as they hobbled with agonizing slowness across the meadow, to circle the blackstone butte. Tup followed. He had folded his wings tightly to his ribs, and his nose bumped Lark's back with every step.

Dorsey smelled of herbs and sweat and old smoke, and muttered to herself as they labored across the grass and around the cliff. The blond girl was silent, but her hands were warm, and her shoulder steady against Lark's. Lark's head began to clear, bringing awareness of fierce pain through her right side.

"I've broken something," she said, her breath catching noisily in her throat.

"Oh, aye, aye," Dorsey said. "Likely more than one something. We'll get you to my house, and Dorsey will have a look."

"Did anyone follow us?"

"Nay," Dorsey answered brightly. "None that I could see."

Lark glanced to her left, but the blond girl kept her eyes on the ground beneath their feet, her mouth pressed closed. She hadn't spoken at all.

Lark took another jarring hop, and then gasped at the fresh torment in her side. "How far?" she grunted.

"Not far, Missy, not far," Dorsey said cheerfully. "Just around there, down the path."

Lark gritted her teeth. Sweat trickled under her hair and down the back of her neck, and Tup, sensing her misery, whimpered. She had no strength to reassure him, but she felt a wave of gratitude that he, at least, was unhurt.

And soon they would be out of this meadow, out of sight, safe for the moment.

WILLIAM raged at Jinson for an hour, stamping through his half-ruined stables, frightening the hapless mare in the paddock so that she galloped to the far end and tried to hide herself under an overhang of branches. "Why didn't you just put the little stallion in with her when he got here?" he stormed. "You imbecile! She's in season now! That was the whole idea!"

Jinson, white-lipped and trembling, started to say something, but William shouted at him, "Don't tell me he might have hurt himself! What difference does that make?"

"But, my lord," Jinson said shakily. "Horsemistress Strong said . . ."

Wordless with fury, William slashed the man with his quirt, one glancing blow across his shoulders. It was beneath his dignity to lose control that way, but frustration made him blind with anger. He had sacrificed so much. And Philippa—damn Philippa, now that she had touched him, she would guess. He just needed one foal, one more winged foal, now that the potion was stronger, now that Eduard Crisp was out of his way . . .

Jinson cowered away from him, and then, trembling, stood straight against the wall the little black had smashed. "My lord, the second mare is with foal. Perhaps that one will—"

"I want *this* one!" William roared. "His dam and his sire— they threw winged colts every time! *This* is the bloodline I want, that I've been aiming toward for years, and I'll be damned if I'll let it get away from me! You . . ." He raised the quirt again. Jinson paled, but stood his ground like someone meeting a fate he could not escape.

And then Slater was there, slinking around the corner in his greasy greatcoat, daring to put his hand on the Duke's arm, to offer him a dram of something in a silver cup. William spun on his heel, stalking away from the sight of Jinson, of the splintered gate and broken wall. He let Slater lead him into the tack room, and he sat on a bench with his legs out, his head back against the wall. Slater urged the cup on him, and he drank from it, drank it all.

A certain lassitude began to overtake his rage, and his mind, cooling, began to function again. Slater was right. There was no point in losing control. He would go to the Academy in the morning, and he would take what was his. There would be no Black Seraph, after all, if it had not been for him. He was perfectly within his rights to demand to have the colt returned to him. And if they resisted . . . if anyone resisted . . . they would think what that fat stable-girl had received was a blessing from their goddess of horses!

Just thinking of the horsemistresses, of ordering them to do his bidding, of forcing them to obey, made a cold fire burn in his belly.

"Slater," he said, lisping slightly. His tongue felt a little thick, but his desire, impotent and turned though it was, felt as keen as the edge of a knife. "Get me a girl."

THIRTY-SIX

PHILIPPA and Hester managed to doze on the long journey by road into the Uplands. Lady Beeth's carriage was cushioned and comfortable, and they each had an entire seat to themselves. Lady Beeth, as composed as if she had not been roused from her bed in the darkness before dawn, had ordered a hamper packed for them while the carriage horses were harnessed, and had herself carried two comforters from Hester's own bedroom. She had, as Hester had promised, understood the situation instantly, nodding over the story of Irina's perfidy, frowning over the theft of a winged horse from the Academy stables.

As the driver, yawning and unwashed, climbed up on the seat of the carriage, Lady Beeth put her head in one last time. She spoke with a bluntness Philippa appreciated. "Whatever you do, Horsemistress Winter," she said, "don't underestimate our new Duke, or that vile Slater who attends him. Tales have reached me."

Philippa blinked her dry eyes, not sure she understood. Lack of sleep fogged her brain. She longed to be on the road, to close her eyes for a time and be lulled by the sounds of hooves against cobblestones.

"Hester can explain," Lady Beeth said. "I have no wish to speak treason, but we have these young women to protect. They are Oc's hope."

Before Philippa could say anything else, Lady Beeth withdrew, and closed the door smartly. "Good luck," she said. "Hester, beloved, take care."

"I will, Mamá."

Philippa managed only to say, "Thank you," before the carriage, on well-oiled wheels, spun out of the courtyard and into the broad lane.

Philippa leaned back against the cushions, and contemplated

the girl across from her. "What did she mean, Hester?" she asked. "The tales?"

Hester's gaze was clear, despite her fatigue. "It's the Duke, Mistress Winter. Mamá makes it her business to know what's being murmured around Osham."

"And what does she know?"

"He has strange appetites," Hester said, with admirable bluntness. "And his man Slater procures for him."

"But . . ." Philippa tried to make her weary brain follow Hester's words. "But, Hester, it's nothing new for a man to want—"

"They say he can't perform anymore, not in the normal way," Hester said. She showed no embarrassment over the subject matter, and Philippa blessed Lady Beeth's pragmatism. "Slater brings him young girls, and he—he abuses them. They say one died, perhaps more."

"Ah. I see." Philippa remembered the feel of William's chest beneath her palms, that swelling that was so normal in herself, in Hester . . . and so shocking in a man. "And does your mamá know why he is this way?"

Hester yawned. "Slater buys potions," she said. "But the apothecaries are afraid to say what is in them. Afraid for their daughters, granddaughters . . . The families who know simply stay out of his way as much as possible. Mamá wanted Papá to take it before the Council, but he said . . ." Her mouth twisted, making her look years older. "He said they were only tales, and unless someone came forward, there was little he could do."

"He was right, I'm afraid." Philippa sighed, and closed her eyes. She would have to ponder it all later, once she knew Larkyn and Black Seraph were safe. The carriage bowled swiftly along the road, the smooth road that Frederick had always said was the best in Oc, perhaps in all the principality. Frederick—oh, if only Frederick were still here! Frederick would never have allowed anyone to interfere with one of the winged horses, or one of the student flyers . . . Frederick would have disowned William if he had known. He could have elevated Francis.

But the loss of Pamella had broken Frederick as surely as if someone had killed him. And now William, with his abnormally smooth chin and high voice, the suspicious swelling of his chest . . .

Philippa's eyes flew open. Hester had fallen asleep, her head tipped back on a cushion, her riding cap askew. The curtains were drawn, and the carriage was comfortably dim, though Philippa could see through the parchment shades that the sun had risen.

William. Potions. Apothecaries, and Slater. The secret stables, a mare in season, a stolen winged stallion.

Her mind, exhausted, suddenly saw right through the labyrinth to the truth at its heart.

William wanted to fly. He wanted to fly enough to try to change his body in order to bond with a winged horse, and he was trying to breed a foal for himself.

If he succeeded, the horsemistresses of Oc would lose all prestige and power.

And he would endanger the very resource that kept their tiny, ancient Duchy safe.

She forced her eyelids to close again, and she slowed her breathing, focusing on her need for sleep. She would need her strength, and all her wits. The battle of the South Tower had been nothing compared to the coming battle with William.

DORSEY'S house should more rightly be called a hut, Lark thought. It was no more than a single high-ceilinged room with an open fireplace, a privy to one side, and a sort of herb-hung workroom on the other. Dorsey helped Lark to her own bed, a noisome pallet piled with pillows stuffed with what felt like broomstraw. Tup whickered and stamped from the doorway of the workroom, protesting being separated from Lark. The blond girl pumped water into a bucket and took it to him. Lark heard him drinking from it, and she tried to lift her head, but Dorsey put a gentle hand on her chest.

"Nay, nay, Missy," she said. "Lie back. Let Dorsey have a look."

"But Tup—" Lark said hoarsely.

"Never mind," Dorsey said. "Girl will take care of your little horse."

"Hide him," Lark croaked.

"Oh, aye, aye, if you want. He can stay in my workroom. No one goes in there but me."

Lark wanted to ask if the silent girl knew anything at all about horses, but Dorsey began to probe her wounds, and the pain of that drove even Tup from her mind. Her world seemed filled with pain, chest and hip and leg. She hardly recognized her own voice as she cried out.

Dorsey muttered, "There, there, Missy, I know. Just let old Dorsey find out what's the matter. Aye, aye, there's a rib, all right. And a bruised hip. And . . ." Her fingers ran on down Lark's leg, to where the swollen ankle bulged against her boot. "Aye. Have to cut this boot."

Lark lay back, panting and perspiring, as Dorsey hurried to her workroom. When she came back, she held out a dented tin cup. "Now, here, drink you this. Give it a moment to ease you, and then old Dorsey will find out what yon boot is hiding."

Gratefully, without even asking what was in it, Lark drank the potion. Relief began to steal over her at once. The pain was still there, but she seemed to feel it at a remove, as if a thick curtain separated the hurt from her mind. She sighed, and her muscles relaxed. As Dorsey went to work on her riding boot with a small, sharp knife, she thought she heard Tup clop across the rough wooden floor. It seemed his lips touched her cheek. Her fingers stole up to caress him, but her hand fell limply to her side before she could ascertain if he was truly there or not.

When she woke, the sunlight slanting through the single window came from the west. She had slept the day away. With wakefulness came a return of pain, but she tried to ignore it, struggling to sit up against the scratchy pillows, to see where Tup might be.

In seconds, the old witchwoman was at her side, grinning crazily down at her as if having an injured girl in her house was a special delight.

"Oh, aye, aye, awake, are ye?" she exclaimed. "Good, good. A little broth, and another potion. You're coming right along."

"No . . ." Lark protested. "Wait—where is Tup?"

"Tup? Tup? Oh, aye, your little winged horse! Why, he's right there, right outside Dorsey's workroom. I left the door open so he could see you."

"He needs—he needs oats. A blanket. Hay . . ."

"Aye, don't worry. Girl will bring something back. She had to fetch her little one."

"She—who is she?"

"She's the one I told you about!" Dorsey exclaimed, with an air of triumph. "At Erdlin, and again in Osham. I told you!"

Lark frowned, trying to remember, but her mind was muzzy with pain and the remnants of the potion. The day of the old Duke's funeral seemed long, long ago.

Dorsey bustled about, bringing Lark a bowl of soup, propping her a little more upright and pressing a thick-handled spoon into her hand.

She drank the soup, and spooned up every bit of meat and vegetables lingering in the bowl. Again, Dorsey gave her the tin cup, and Lark drank it swiftly, then lifted the blanket to look at her right ankle. It was splinted now, and wrapped in a thick gray bandage. "How bad is it?" she asked.

Dorsey touched the bandage with careful fingers. "It's bad enough," she said. "Broken."

"I think I broke a rib, too."

"Oh, aye," the witchwoman said, nodding, her flurry of gray hair blooming around her head. "I bound it up, see?" She poked Lark's side, and Lark flinched.

"Will I . . ." Lark began, and then sank back, afraid to ask the question.

Dorsey grinned, spreading a spiderweb of wrinkles across her face. "Walk? Oh, aye. Just a broken ankle."

"No," Lark whispered. The potion had begun to work on her, and her eyelids grew heavy again. "No, Dorsey. I know I will walk. But will I ride? Will I—will I fly?"

Dorsey's claw of a hand came gently down on Lark's forehead, and passed over her eyelids, helping them to close. "Aye, Larkyn Hamley, aye," she said softly. "You have your little icon there. Feel how warm it is against your skin? Your goddess brought you to Dorsey. You'll ride again. Your goddess protects you, and that's no smallmagic. You'll be one of the great flyers of Oc."

Lark doubted this, but the sound of it, the idea of it, soothed her. She sighed, and drifted on the soft cloud of whatever herb it was Dorsey used in her potion. The last thing she saw before she slept was Tup, lipping at her forehead, sniffing in her scent. This time her fingers reached him before she fell into unconsciousness. She stroked his silken cheek, hardly even surprised that old Dorsey allowed him into her house.

* * *

PHILIPPA roused from a heavy, overheated sleep in mid-afternoon, jarred awake by the carriage jouncing. Hester still curled improbably upon the narrow bench opposite, her face buried in a pillow, her hair falling out of its knot and trailing across her brow. Philippa grimaced, and stretched to loosen the kink in her neck. Only the young, she thought, could sleep anywhere, anytime.

She lifted a corner of the curtain, and was startled by the abundance of color that greeted her. Crops of green and red and yellow overhung the road. Hedgerows bustled with life, birds flitting in and out of their branches, brown rabbits skittering into the safety of their roots, away from the beat of the carriage horses' hooves. The road had narrowed, and grown bumpy. They must be well into the Uplands. The footman saw the twitch of the curtain, and called out to the driver. A few moments later, the carriage stopped, and the footman opened the door, bowing to Philippa.

She touched her finger to her lips, and whispered, "Hester is still sleeping."

"Yes, Mistress," the footman said. "Driver wants me to tell you we've passed Dickering Park, but down that lane is a village, Willakeep. Perhaps you would like to refresh yourself?"

Philippa glanced up at the sky. The sun was halfway down from its zenith. "What about the horses?" she asked.

"They're due a rest," he said. "But we understood haste was important."

"You understand rightly," Philippa said. She climbed out of the carriage, closing the door softly behind her, and stood stretching her arms over her head. "I believe Deeping Farm is an hour's drive from here. Is that too long?"

The driver looked down from his seat. "Horses have had water. They'll be all right for an hour, if we can rest them there."

"Very well," Philippa said. She cast about for some cover to relieve herself, and found it, just off the road. "Just wait for me a moment, and then we'll press on. There's still food in the hamper if you need something."

"No, thank you, Mistress," the footman said. "Lady Beeth sent us well provisioned."

"Indeed," Philippa said, with a nod. "She would."

An hour later, Hester now awake and having polished off the last of Lady Beeth's sustenance, they pulled off the road and down the rutted lane to Deeping Farm. Philippa was out of the carriage the moment it stopped, and halfway up the walk to the house before Hester could climb out. She rapped on the kitchen door, absently noticing that the rue-tree was in full bloom, the barn freshly whitewashed, the kitchen garden beyond its black-stone fence tilled and planted.

Hester caught up with her, saying, "Is this Black's home? How perfectly marvelous!"

A young woman Philippa didn't recognize opened the kitchen door, and raised her eyebrows at the sight of them. "Zito's ears!" she exclaimed. "Here's two more!"

She stepped back, and held the door wide.

Philippa moved past her into the kitchen, and then stopped dead in her tracks.

At the old table, with a thick mug and a plate of crooks before her, sat Irina Strong.

"They didn't make it, Philippa," she said, with an air of grim satisfaction. "They're gone."

THIRTY-SEVEN

PHILIPPA stood in the center of the Hamley kitchen, her fists on her hips. "So it's true, Irina," she said in her most cutting tone. "You never meant for Larkyn to learn to fly."

Irina stood up, and said sullenly, "She showed no ability."

"No ability? She just flew her colt for the first time with no tack, no flight paddock, no monitor, and in the dark! No ability?"

"She got lucky," Irina said sullenly.

"She made her luck," Philippa said. "She meant to land here, I have no doubt, and you frightened her off."

"I didn't even see her."

"Kalla's teeth," Philippa said bitterly. "We entrusted her to you. I don't know how you can live with yourself."

"I serve the Duke—" Irina began, but Philippa cut off her words with a gesture, and turned her back.

She demanded of the girl, "Where's Master Hamley?"

"Oh," the girl said. "You mean Brye, I suppose? Or Nick?"

"Brye. The eldest."

"He's out looking for his sister and her horse," the girl said hastily. "Well, Nick is, too. Worried sick, they both are. Bid me watch out for this one, here, though I don't know what I'm to do if she decides to leave, because I can't exactly stop a horsemistress from flying, can I? I gave her tea, and some breakfast, but—"

"Where's her horse?"

The girl pointed through the kitchen window to the barn. "In a stall. Fed and watered by Nick, this morning, before they went off in the oxcart. I don't know what's to become of the milk cans, all ready in the coldcellar . . ."

Hester took a step forward. "What's your name, Miss?"

"I'm Peony, as what does the housework here now that Lark

has gone off." Peony waved a hand around the tidy kitchen. "I do the garden, and the milk and butter, and—"

"Thank you, Peony," Hester said with authority. "Perhaps you could make us a pot of tea, as well."

Philippa drew a deep breath, relieved at having someone else to deal with the housekeeper. She faced Irina again.

"Irina," she said. "Dishonesty runs in your family, I am told."

Irina sank back into her chair. "I followed my orders," she muttered.

"You were a *horsemistress*," Philippa gritted. "How could you risk that?"

Slowly, Irina lifted her gaze. Her eyes were dull. "I'm still a horsemistress," she said.

"Who will work with you now? Certainly no one at the Academy! When word of your disloyalty gets about, I have no doubt you'll be sent straight to the most remote spot in all the principality!"

Irina's cheeks reddened to the color of old bricks. "The Duke promised me—"

"William has his own problems," Philippa said bitterly. "And visited them on us. If this comes out, and is judged to be treason . . . You will lose your patron, Irina."

Irina paled at that, and caught her lip between her teeth. Philippa was about to say something further, but the sound of voices in the barnyard drew her and Hester to the window.

The relief she felt at seeing Brye Hamley, in his shirtsleeves, climbing down from the oxcart made her knees weak. He eyed the carriage waiting in the barnyard, and then strode toward the house while the younger brother led the ox away. Brye took off his broad-brimmed straw hat and ran his fingers through his thick shock of graying black hair. His brow was furrowed, and his jaw set.

This, Philippa thought, is Oc. Not an effete nobleman hiding his perversion behind embroidered vests, manipulating people, taking the law into his own hands, but an honest farmer, a hard-working man, a devoted brother. She turned to the door, and stood waiting for it to open, feeling as if a great weight were about to be lifted from her shoulders.

"So you're here at last," he said without ceremony. He indicated Irina with his chin. "This one's no help at all, except to tell us our sister's missing, and her horse with her."

"Master Hamley—you haven't found them?"

"No." He hooked a chair forward with his foot, sat down, and gestured for her to do the same. "I'll set out again tomorrow. I didn't know if I should let other people know or not, until I understand what's happened. This one wouldn't tell me, but you will." It was as much a command as any Philippa might have issued herself.

With a wry nod, she seated herself. "You're right to ask, Master Hamley," she said. "I'm not sure I can explain everything, but I'll do my best."

Peony came to the table with the pot of tea, and waved a tattered fetish at it. She stared at Philippa with wide eyes. Hester, with a sigh, took a chair opposite Irina.

"The new Duke," Philippa began, "apparently wishes to create his own bloodline of winged horses. By law this would be treason, but he is the Duke. Such a situation has never developed before, not in centuries." She glanced at Irina. "The important thing is to find Larkyn before Duke William does."

"What will he do?"

"I don't know," Philippa said. "She knows more than we do, at this moment, and he may wish to silence her. He's a ruthless man. And dangerous, in the way of the powerful. I don't know how far he might go."

LARK felt as if weights were attached to her eyelashes when she tried to lift them. She sighed, and blinked, and tried again. Her eyes opened gradually, and her pupils adjusted slowly to the light. She saw through the window that night had fallen again, the stars just beginning to show themselves in the black sky. She felt, all at once, ravenous.

Dorsey was at the crooked sink in the corner, humming to herself, rattling a spoon in a pan. Lark croaked, "Tup?"

Dorsey whirled, and grinned at her from across the room. "Oh, aye," she cackled. "Yon little winged horse is right there." She pointed to the workroom, and Lark lifted her head enough to peer past the hanging bundles of herbs and roots. She could just see Tup's hindquarters. His head was down, and he was cropping the sparse grass. Someone had wrapped him in a blanket, and tied it with twine.

Dorsey scuttled across the floor, and bent over Lark to press a palm to her forehead. "Nay, no fever, then, that's a good girl. Come now, we'll prop you up on these pillows and you'll drink something."

Lark drank thirstily from a cup of clear mountain water, holding it in her two hands. When she had drained it, she said, a little diffidently, "I'm awfully hungry, Dorsey."

Dorsey clapped her hands and cackled as if she had just won a great prize. "Aye, aye, now there's a good sign! Hungry!" She hurried back to the sink, and returned with a plate piled with sliced preserved bloodbeets, a wedge of yellow goat cheese, and a slice of dense brown bread. There were even two buttery crooks at the edge of the plate. "There, now, you eat your fill. Dorsey will build up the fire."

The food tasted better than anything Lark could remember. She tried to think when she had last eaten, but all she could figure was that it had been more than a day. Perhaps she had not eaten since the pastries in Osham.

When she had eaten, she began to think of the privy, but she was afraid to put weight on her leg. Dorsey, though, anticipated her. She supported Lark as she hobbled across the floor, and stayed with her until her necessaries were done, then helped her back to the bed. It all hurt surprisingly, and Lark was glad to lie down again.

"Dorsey," she said. She ran a hand through her muddled hair, and tried to think. "Does anyone know?"

"Nay, nay, old Dorsey keeps her own counsel, doesn't she? And Girl doesn't talk at all."

"I can't stay here," Lark protested weakly. "Tup needs exercise, and I need clothes. And a bath," she finished, looking down at herself. How was she to manage a bath, bound as she was, ribs and ankle?

Dorsey handed her another cup of the pain-relieving potion, patted her shoulder, and scuffled across the room to the tilting stone sink. "Now, now, you're home in the Uplands. We know how to take care of our own, don't we? We'll manage a bath tomorrow."

"But Tup," Lark said. "Who will take care of Tup? And what if someone sees him?" This thought made her try to wriggle upright, until pain laid her flat again.

Dorsey came back, a frayed towel in her hands. She twisted it as she looked down at Lark. "You don't want to be found, then," she said. "Girl didn't either."

"Who is she?" Lark said.

Dorsey shrugged. "I don't know. She can't tell me. But she had a horse, too, when she came here."

"Horse? What—" Lark's eyelids drooped again, pain receding, darkness overtaking her.

"Oh, aye," Dorsey murmured. "She knows how to take care of a horse. You sleep now, Larkyn Hamley, and don't worry. You'll feel better soon. The first day is always the worst."

PHILIPPA was surprised to find that the upper floor of the farmhouse boasted six bedrooms. Brye pushed open a door to one, and stood back to let her pass through.

"Nothing fancy," he said, "but comfortable."

He was right. The room was low-ceilinged and narrow, but the bed was soft, and a quilt that might have been a hundred years old lay ready at its foot. Peony bustled in after them with a stack of pillows, and came back a moment later with a ewer and a basin. Philippa went to stand beside the small window to watch the carriage pull away. She had not bothered to watch Irina and Strong Lady depart. There was no more they could do to harm Larkyn, she decided, so she made no move to stop her. She also didn't bother to ask Irina where she was going. It didn't seem to matter. She could hardly search for Larkyn and Black Seraph in the dark. She could go back to Fleckham House, or even to the Palace, but it would make no difference.

There was a hostelry in Willakeep, Nick had told them, small but adequate, where the carriage horses could rest and the Beeth servants could find rooms and meals. Hester assured Philippa that Lady Beeth had foreseen such a circumstance, and sent her servants with a letter of credit. Hester was to be put up in the room next to Philippa's. "It's Lark's," she said, coming to stand in the doorway. "Some of her things are still here."

"Aye," Brye Hamley said gruffly. "Always be a room for Lark at Deeping Farm."

"Of course," Hester said warmly. She smiled at him, startling Philippa again with her maturity. She was very like her esteemed mamá already. "You and your home are everything Black—I mean, Lark—told us, Master Hamley."

He inclined his head to her in a gesture of such simple grace that Philippa just stopped herself from pressing one hand to her heart. "Peony is setting out dinner," he said. "We'd best eat, and search again in the morning."

Philippa felt as if she had run through her last reserves of strength, and she doubted she could eat anything, but Hester seemed to have been revived by her lengthy nap in the carriage. She said eagerly, "Good. I'm starving!"

Brye Hamley nodded. "And so Lark always is, when she comes home." He turned, and led the way downstairs to the kitchen.

Darkness enfolded the farmhouse as they sat down in the mismatched, comfortable chairs. The brothers were all there, silent Edmar, handsome Nick, and the brooding Brye. Peony dished up a pottage of stewed hare, carrots and potatoes and bloodbeets, and put a fresh brown loaf on the table with a dish of sweet butter. Faces were dour, but appetites were strong. Even Philippa found the simple fare to be just what her body needed. Like the others, she ate everything in the pottery bowl, and used a thick slice of bread to sop up the juices. When she had finished, she felt as drowsy as a child, and was relieved at Brye's suggestion that they go early to bed and get an early start in the morning.

She and Hester trudged up the stairs. Philippa had just turned to her own room when Hester said softly, "I hope she's all right." She was standing in the doorway, looking into Larkyn's room. "It seems wrong to sleep in her bed, when she might be— anywhere."

"I know," Philippa said. "But she would want you to be comfortable. Brye will search for her in the morning, and you and I will be back with our horses by evening."

"I just keep thinking . . . if she fell, or if Seraph stumbled on his return . . ."

"Don't think about it anymore tonight, Hester. It doesn't help. We must expect the best." Philippa tried to speak with confidence, but her own anxiety put an edge in her voice.

Hester nodded, and Philippa could see she understood. "Good night, then," the girl said.

"Good night. Sleep well."

Hester closed the door, and Philippa turned toward her own room. She found Brye Hamley standing at the top of the stairs, his eyes stony.

"What will he do, Mistress Winter, if he finds her before we do?"

"It is the horse he wants," Philippa said wearily. "Your sister is simply in his way."

"But I understood—a winged horse, bonded, is useless without its bondmate."

"He would never fly again."

"Surely there are other horses. Why does the Duke want this one?"

"Master Hamley." Philippa felt as if she could barely keep her head up. She rubbed her temples, trying to think of a way to explain William. "I have known the Duke all his life. When he fixes his mind on something . . . nothing can distract him. He can be cruel, even to those closest to him. I knew his father better than I know him. Old Duke Frederick worried about his son's character."

"With good reason, it seems."

"Yes." Philippa took a step, and to her dismay, stumbled, and almost fell. Brye Hamley was there, one hand beneath her elbow, another supporting her back. He radiated such warmth and strength that she feared she might dissolve into the weakness of tears.

"Here," he said. "I'm keeping you from your bed. You're worn out."

"It's true," she said shakily. "I'm sorry."

"No need," he said gruffly. He helped her to her door, and showed her inside. "Rest well, Mistress Winter."

She managed to close the door, strip off most of her clothes, and fall into bed. She pulled the worn quilt up to her chin. It smelled of sunshine and fresh air, as if it had recently hung on a clothesline. The old farmhouse creaked gently around her. Doors opened and closed softly, and masculine steps sounded on the stairs as the brothers went to their own beds. Wind sang across the roof and ruffled the leaves of the rue-tree. From the barn, a goat bleated, but everything else was quiet.

Philippa turned on her side. Her back tingled where Brye Hamley's strong hand had touched her, and the pillow beneath her cheek was soft with age. Philippa, uncharacteristically, prayed to Kalla that Larkyn, too, would have a soft bed to sleep in this night. And that Black Seraph would be safe.

THIRTY-EIGHT

FOR two days, Lark drifted in and out of awareness. She woke to pain and thirst and hunger, and after Dorsey dealt with those things, she slept again. On the third day she woke to sunshine and the soft scents of a mountain spring streaming into the hut through the open front door. She was hungry and thirsty again, but her pain had receded to a dull throb instead of the piercing agony it had been. She lifted her head, and looked around her.

The blond girl was working at the sink, and a toddler with the same pale hair sat at her feet, playing with a wooden spoon. When Lark tried to sit up, the girl and the child both turned surprisingly dark eyes in her direction. The girl hurried across the room to help Lark to the privy. When that was accomplished, she urged her into one of two rickety chairs beside a small table. It felt good, Lark thought, to sit upright, though her head swam.

The girl brought a small basin and a clean, ragged cloth. Lark dipped the cloth in the water, and scrubbed at her face.

"I don't know your name," she said to the girl as she washed her neck and her hands. The girl shook her head, and shrugged. The toddler eyed Lark solemnly, as silent as his mother.

"Tup?" Lark asked, with a sudden pang of fear.

The girl pointed through the workroom. Past the bundles of hanging herbs, Lark saw Tup with his nose in a basket. "Is it oats?" Lark said. The girl nodded again. "Thank you." She nodded in response. Lark wrung out the cloth and stretched it across the basin.

When the silent girl came to take the basin, her eyes met Lark's briefly, then flickered away. Her eyes were dull, as if there was no hope in her.

She brought Lark a cup of strong tea. The toddler watched gravely as she drank it. Lark wondered if he didn't speak, either.

Dorsey scuttled in a moment later, coming in through the workroom with a handful of some sort of feathery plant. She bent over Lark, pressing her palms against her leg, probing at her bound ribs. Lark pressed her lips together against the pain this caused, but she made no sound. She wanted no more of the sleep-inducing potion. She wanted to stay awake.

She sensed something coming, felt its advent as surely as she felt the vigor of growth around her, the trees budding, the vines setting fruit, the grass at the foot of the butte thickening.

Dorsey brought her an old stick with a padded crosspiece, and Lark, leaning on the stick, hobbled out through the workroom into the sunshine. Tup was well supplied with a large bucket of clear water. The girl—Dorsey always called her simply Girl—had removed the blanket and folded it on the step. Tup trotted to Lark, whickering, and then dashed across the grass in clear invitation. His wings opened, ebony-bright in the sunshine.

"No, Tup!" Lark called. "No flying! I can't even ride, much less fly!"

He wheeled, and faced her, ears forward, head high. Had he been a dog, she thought, he would have smiled. She wondered what had become of Bramble. She hoped the oc-hound had found her way back to the Academy.

She held out her hand to Tup, and he trotted back to touch her palm with his muzzle, then raced away again, circling the grassy field. Lark bit her lip, wishing in vain for wingclips. Tup ran the length of the grass to the point of the butte. He bucked, and spread his wings, turning to see if she appreciated his display.

When he came back to her, she seized a handful of his mane and shook it. "No, Tup," she repeated. "No flying! It's not safe. Someone might see you!"

He blew, and stamped his feet, but he folded his wings. A moment later he dipped his head to the bucket of water, and then began to graze again.

Dorsey brought a stool from the workroom for Lark to sit on, and she accepted it gratefully. "He won't fly off, then?" Dorsey asked.

"I hope not," Lark said. "He needs exercise, but . . . I don't want him to be seen. Does anyone else know we're here?"

"Nay, nay," Dorsey said. She crouched on the sill, lifting her wrinkled face up to the balm of the sun. "Nay, only Girl and me.

Nearest house is in Clellum, and that's a half mile at least. Girl doesn't talk, as you see, and I don't unless I want to!" She cackled, and shook her head. "You ran away, then, did you? Decided the Academy wasn't for you?"

"Oh, no," Lark said. "No, I love it there, even though . . ."

Dorsey peered at her. "Even though . . . ?"

"Well. Some of the girls don't like me, because I'm an Uplander, and a farm girl."

"But you love it."

"I do. I want to fly, more than anything."

Dorsey tipped her head to one side in that birdlike fashion, her small eyes glittering. "Oh, aye? Why run off, then?"

"Someone tried to take Tup from me."

"Thought they couldn't do that. Bonded, and that."

"Aye. It's wrong. He would never fly again, but this—someone—doesn't care about that."

Dorsey pushed out her lips, creating a purse of wrinkles. "Someone?"

Lark tipped her head back against the wall. The sound of Tup crunching new grass comforted her, gave her an illusion of well-being despite the dull ache of her leg, the constricting tightness of her ribs. Softly, she said, "It's the new Duke. The one person who may hold power over even the Academy. And he'll be looking for us."

A soft gasp surprised them both. Dorsey turned her head to look up into the doorway, and Lark straightened, wincing at the twinge in her ribs.

The mute girl stood there, staring wide-eyed at Lark.

"Eh, Girl? What is it?" Dorsey asked.

The girl opened her mouth, and closed it, and then turned and fled, back through the workroom, out through the front door of the house. A moment later they saw her running awkwardly away through the field, burdened by the child in her arms.

PHILIPPA returned to Deeping Farm on the evening of the second day. She left Hester at the Academy, over her strong objections.

"It's too risky," Philippa told her, in Margareth's office. "I don't know what's going to happen, or where we might find Larkyn, and I don't want to worry about both of you."

"Goldie and I will be fine," Hester said. "You need us!"

"No, Hester," Margareth said. Her eyelids drooped, as if she had slept no more than Philippa and Hester in the past two days. "No, you must resume your studies. Behave as if nothing has happened. I know we can trust you in that."

"Girls are beginning to wonder, though," Hester said. "With Mistress Winter gone, and Mistress Strong, too."

"You must simply tell them you don't know," Philippa said.

"And the Master Breeder was here this afternoon," Margareth told them. "He made an excuse, but I think he was trying to find out if Black Seraph had returned to our stables."

"But William didn't come."

"No. Nor Irina."

"He will never let it lie," Philippa said bitterly. "It's not only the risk of our exposing him. It has become an issue of pride."

Hester began again. "Let me come back to the Uplands with you!"

The day was wearing on, and it was a relief to leave the argument to Margareth. Philippa and Sunny returned to the Uplands, arriving at Deeping Farm before dark.

She spent a second night in the comfortable bedroom of the old farmhouse, rising with the first streaks of light in the eastern sky to drink a cup of bracing tea and take flight once again.

She and Brye had pored over an ancient map he kept rolled up in a corner of an enormous oak desk. They divided up the countryside, trying to guess how far Black Seraph might have been able to fly, where the pair might have chosen to come to ground, how they might have hidden themselves. Brye headed south, down the twisting lanes he knew best. Philippa and Sunny turned north, to follow the Black River.

They flew low over the fields and hedgerows, gliding over the twists of the river. The air was alive with birds, and farmers stopped their work to stare upward at the rare sight of a winged horse in the Uplands. On a different day, Philippa would have savored every moment of such a flight. The air was pungent with growing things, even at altitude, and the mountains to the west sported grassy meadows punctuated by gleaming black cliffs. She saw roofs and haymows, stone fences and kitchen gardens. Cows and sheep and long-haired brown goats like little Molly grazed in the spring grass.

She stopped to rest Sunny, coming to ground in a fallow field after making a careful pass above it to look for holes or other obstacles. They both drank from the river, and Philippa ate the cheese and dried apples Peony had packed for her. She pulled Sunny's saddle off for a bit, letting her cool herself in the shade of some old cottonwoods whose branches drooped over the riverbank. Then, restless and worried, she took to the air again.

When she began to fear wearing Sunny out, she turned back to Deeping Farm. The sun had begun to slant from the west, and clouds piled above the mountaintops. Philippa gritted her teeth as she saw the storm building. Searching in a rainstorm would be misery, but there was no more she could do today.

She and Brye met in the barn, where Philippa was rubbing Sunny down with a towel. Their eyes met, but for a long moment neither of them spoke. They didn't need to ask.

After a time, Philippa laid the towel aside, and gave Sunny a final pat. "She'll be hiding somewhere, surely," she said. "Since we've seen no sign of . . ." She faltered. She couldn't bring herself to say it.

Brye finished her thought for her. "No sign of a fall." He stood well back from the stall, so as not to upset Sunny. "Aye. But even if they fell, we might not see them. This is the Uplands, and there are fells and copses enough to hide anything."

Philippa rested her cheek against Sunny's sleek neck. "I'm sorry, Brye," she whispered. "I was hard on Larkyn. I never understood how much Irina was holding her back. And I never dreamed any of this could happen."

"Come, now, Philippa," he said gruffly. "A bit of food, a rest, we'll both feel better. We'll start again tomorrow."

"Yes," she said, but she didn't move right away. Her eyes burned with unshed tears, and she needed a moment to control them. Philippa had not wept in years, and she had no intention of starting now. Especially not in the company of Brye Hamley.

"MY lord," Jinson said tentatively. "Perhaps you should just let it go? We can find another stallion . . . part of the regular breeding program . . ."

"Either she's dead or she's not," Irina said. "But if a winged horse were seen in the Uplands, you would know."

Her monotone inflamed William's already-thin temper. For two days he had raged, despite Slater's having procured the girl as requested. She had been unsatisfactory, trying to play coquette with him, acting like a common whore. He had a damnable time making her scream, and by the time he found some release, she was trying to seduce him again. As if, even if he could, he would have wanted to actually bed such a creature.

What he wanted was to kill her, had been tempted, but the outcry over the last one stayed his hand. At such a time, it wasn't wise to create more grist for the mill of the Council of Lords. Slater pointed that out, and though William had thrown a porcelain pitcher at him, narrowly missing his head, he knew Slater was right. Slater was remarkably clever, though no better-born than the girls he procured.

"Oh, she's not dead," William said in an icy tone. "Slater has discovered where she is. And we're in danger of that bitch Philippa finding her."

"Where is she?" Irina asked.

"It's a tiny place in the Uplands. I want you to go and get her."

"Back to the Uplands? What about Philippa?"

"What do you think, you stupid woman!" William shrilled, and then set his jaw to stop himself. It had gotten increasingly difficult to keep his voice in a deep register. His chest swelled against his vest, which was an irritation, but he hoped it might mean the next attempt at bonding would be successful. He crossed his arms, and glared at Irina. "You should never have left the Uplands until you knew where they were."

"Your Grace," she began, "there was no point, with Philippa there—"

"You're afraid of her."

"No. But I have to work with them, and she threatened me . . ."

"You work for me!" he said. "She can't threaten you!"

"But she said when the Council learns what you've . . ." She stopped, her mouth still open, her face paling as he jumped to his feet.

An idea formed in his mind, and he drew a slow breath, letting it crystallize. He took a step closer to her, leaning forward, taking pleasure in her slight shift away. He said, very softly, "Irina. There's no need for Philippa Winter to speak to the Council at all. No need for her to put you in jeopardy, or me."

She got slowly to her feet, and shuffled backward until she stood behind her chair. As if that would protect her! The fear on her face gratified him. He pulled his quirt out of his belt and ran it through his fingers.

"Go back to the Uplands," he said in his silkiest tone. "Deal with her."

"What do you mean, deal with her?"

"Don't be stupid," he said. He held up the quirt, and she flinched away from it. "If Philippa doesn't come back from the Uplands, none of the rest of it will matter, not even that farm brat."

"My lord . . ." Irina stared at him, her eyes round, the pupils beginning to swell. "My lord Duke—what are you asking me?"

He allowed his lips to curl, and he took a long step toward her, holding out the quirt. "Stop her," he said smoothly. "Flying is dangerous, isn't it? Accidents happen from time to time, tragic incidents." Even more quietly, enjoying Jinson's mesmerized stare, and the stupid woman's look of horror, he said, "Horse-mistresses die."

"Duke William," Irina said faintly. "I could never— deliberately—"

"You could never what?" he asked, still smiling. "You'll do as I tell you, Irina. You've gone too far to back out now. I am your only hope." He pressed the quirt into her hands. Her face was as white and stiff as a field of snow. She would do it. She had left herself no choice.

"Jinson." He turned to his Master Breeder, speaking almost casually. "Don't bring in another stallion. We'll wait for the little black to be returned. And this time, we'll bring the brat with him."

He tugged down his vest with both hands, and walked from the room. It was good to be in control, to have authority. It was worth any sacrifice. And surely, had his father understood, he would have approved.

THIRTY-NINE

THROUGH another day they searched, and then another. Nick resumed his rounds, asking questions everywhere he went, but his inquiries yielded nothing. In truth, he said sorrowfully, he doubted there could be a winged horse in the Uplands without everyone knowing of it.

On the fourth day Philippa, washing with water from the ewer in the bedroom at Deeping Farm, caught sight of herself in the old, shadowy glass above the bureau. She stopped, her hands dripping above the basin, and gazed at her gaunt face, her hollow eyes, her dry lips. She looked far older, she thought, than her thirty-seven years. The days of flying in circles, of little sleep, of bedeviling nightmares, had taken their toll.

She seized the towel from its hook and turned her back on the glass. There was nothing she could do about her appearance, and she shouldn't care. Still, she brushed her hair thoroughly before twisting it into the rider's knot, and she rubbed a little almond cream into her skin. She avoided the mirror as she pulled on her riding habit and boots.

Brye showed the strain of the past days as well. He seemed thinner, and he spoke less and less when they met at breakfast and at supper. Today he would take the oxcart to the west and north, to the mountain villages. Philippa, having exhausted the nearer neighborhoods, would fly ahead of him, starting at the top of the mountain and working her way down, scanning the meadows and valleys as best she could from the air.

"I've been there before," she told him, as they drank black tea and ate Peony's coddled eggs. "I can find Mossyrock again."

Brye rose from the table, and took his hat from its peg beside the kitchen door.

Philippa pulled on her own cap as she followed him out into

the barnyard. After days of balmy sunshine, a spring storm threatened above the mountains. She frowned up at the sky. "Let's hope the rain holds off."

Brye followed her gaze. "Can you fly in the rain?"

"As long as it's not too heavy. Lightning makes things a bit tricky. And wind."

He grunted acknowledgment.

Philippa found Sunny well fed and rested, eager to fly. She saddled her, and led her out toward the lane. Brye was there with the oxcart. Nick, with a borrowed pullcart, had already set out with his milk and butter. The Hamleys had set out a mounting block, but Philippa ignored it. She sprang to Sunny's back, and heard Brye murmur something. She avoided his eye, but she was gratified. Her standing mount restored a bit of her self-respect, welcome after her misadventure with the mirror.

She fitted her boots into her stirrups, and wheeled Sunny. They passed the waiting ox at a posting trot, and Philippa raised her hand to Brye. "Good luck," she called.

He touched his fingers to the brim of his hat, and climbed up onto the driving seat of the cart. Sunny cantered, then galloped, and moments later, bore Philippa up into the cool grayness of the morning, turning without being asked toward the northwest. She had caught their purpose, Philippa thought. She imagined that Sunny, too, turned her eye on every open field, every clearing, every inch of ground where a winged horse and its rider might have come to ground.

She put her gloved hand on Sunny's neck, and murmured, beneath the wind of their flight, "You're a grand girl, Winter Sunset. Let's find our missing chicks today, shall we?"

As if in answer, Sunny's wings beat more strongly, and she banked sharply toward the green hills.

The weather held through the morning and into the early afternoon. Philippa followed the pattern of the last few days, searching, returning to ground to rest and eat, then taking to the air to search again. They worked their way up into the hills in the direction of Mossyrock. They came upon the same meadow where they had landed months before, when Philippa came to investigate the saddle for sale in the country market. A misty rain began to fall just as Sunny touched down, slicking the grass and glistening on the blackstone butte that divided the meadow from the field beyond. Philippa buttoned her riding coat up to her neck, and led Sunny under a tree to keep as dry as possible.

The mare dropped her head to nibble at the grass just beyond the cover of the branches. Philippa let her graze while she sat on the ground, her back against the sticky trunk. She felt stiff with fatigue. Rain pattered through the leaves to spot the bare dirt around her boots.

She measured the dwindling light of the day, and had almost decided to turn back to Deeping Farm when Sunny threw up her head. Her ears pricked forward, and she whickered.

Philippa knew that whicker. She jumped to her feet, stiffness forgotten, and moved out into the drizzle to see what had attracted the mare's attention.

In the gray distance, a flyer circled above the butte, apparently making ready to land.

Philippa turned to Sunny, and mounted in one swift leap. Sunny whirled on her haunches, beginning her canter down the meadow before Philippa had settled properly into the saddle. Her wings flexed eagerly over Philippa's calves as she increased her pace. Before they reached the end, Philippa cried, "Sunny! Hup!" and they took to the air.

The other flyer was Irina.

Strong Lady's silhouette was unmistakable, the broad red-brown wings, the thick, short tail. Irina had always flown with a slight backward tilt to her spine, as if she was not quite sure where she was going.

In this case, despite her posture, Philippa had no doubt Irina knew her destination. She could lead her to Larkyn and Black Seraph.

Sunny's wings beat with steady strength, all fatigue vanished now that their purpose was clear. Philippa felt the same. She leaned forward, her hands and her feet alive with fresh energy. The rain intensified, and soon her face was wet, her eyelashes beaded with sparkling drops as Sunny circled the butte, following Lady.

Philippa saw that a small, plain house nestled on the other side, almost hidden by a jutting ledge of blackstone. A narrow shed protruded from one side, and smoke rose from a tin chimney pot in a narrow gray stream that blended with the mist and disappeared.

And in the lee of the shed, a small black horse stood out of the rain. A winged horse.

"Kalla's heels!" Philippa cursed. "How did I miss him?"

She knew, though, of course. If she had not come around the cliff from the south side, if Irina had not showed her the way, the house and shed would have shielded Black Seraph from her view. She might never have found him.

Strong Lady banked to the left in her descent, and Philippa and Sunny followed in the same circular pattern. They would come to ground just behind the other pair.

Rain ran from Sunny's mane and dripped from Philippa's cap, falling faster and harder every moment. Philippa peered ahead through the grayness. As Lady turned, preparing for her last circuit of the field, both horse and rider caught sight of Philippa and Sunny. Irina's body jerked, and Lady's wings fluttered. Sunny spread her own wings wide, beginning her glide. Philippa sensed Black Seraph's sudden attention as he caught sight of the two mares. She spared a glance to see that he had come out from beneath his shelter to stand with his head up, staring through the rain.

Philippa looked forward again, and caught her breath in shock.

Irina and Lady had broken off their descending pattern, and begun to climb, right into Sunny's path. Lady's wings beat laboriously, and Irina hunched over her neck. Lady's neck stretched forward, and she flew directly toward Sunny, gathering speed with every stroke of her powerful wings.

Below them, Black Seraph gave a full-throated neigh. Philippa felt Sunny hesitate, a question in the flicker of her ears. Her wings thrust them slightly upward. Seraph whinnied again, a long, clear sound.

Philippa gave Sunny her head, and Sunny drove hard with her wings, making a sharp ascent, averting a possible collision. The two pairs of flyers passed each other, Sunny above, Lady below. Irina was using her quirt on Lady's neck.

"Irina!" Philippa cried. "What are you doing?"

Black Seraph neighed again as Sunny wheeled in the mist at the far end of the field. Irina turned at the opposite end, Strong Lady making a ghostly figure against the blackstone of the butte. Philippa was about to give Sunny the signal to descend, when she realized, with a cold shock, that the near-collision had been no accident. Irina's maneuvers were deliberate. Strong Lady had the thick body and neck of a Foundation, and she weighed half again what Sunny did. Lady might survive a collision in the air, but Sunny wouldn't. And neither would Philippa.

But she must reach Black Seraph before Irina did. And find Larkyn! Irina had nothing left to lose. She might be capable of anything.

Again they passed each other, and again Sunny rose above Strong Lady's path. Philippa shouted at Irina, "Get away, you fool! Let me land!"

Irina only glared at her, and raised her quirt as if it were a sword.

The challenge was unmistakable. Sunny felt it, too, and her body vibrated with defiant energy. Philippa had felt that vibration only once before. Sunny had been right then, and she was right now. This was a battle, and one they dared not lose.

They flew one more arc above the field, and then the horses flew at each other, ears back, teeth bared, the battle engaged.

Someone, Philippa thought grimly, was going to die today.

LARK sat in Dorsey's single chair, her leg propped on a pile of firewood. Dorsey had been called to the village to attend an illness, leaving the girl and her child with Lark.

It had been a better day than the one before. She had taken no potion at all, and had eaten a bowl of pottage for lunch, along with more of the heavy brown bread and a slice of goatmilk cheese. She felt more lucid than at any time since her fall. The girl, silent as always, was working at the sink, but her little boy came to stand at Lark's knee, staring up at her.

She smiled at him. "Do you have a name?" she asked.

He only gazed at her, his mouth open. She knew he could speak, because she had heard him chattering at Dorsey earlier, though his prattle had made no sense. He was, she judged, not quite two. About as old, in truth, as Tup. She had no idea when children should begin to talk, or to know their names. Dorsey didn't seem to care, but it seemed wrong to Lark, somehow demeaning, that they should be simply Girl and the Child.

"Shall I name you?" Lark asked.

The girl looked up at her question, and left the sink to come toward them.

Lark glanced up at her. "I know you can't speak," she said. "But perhaps you can write? Tell me who you are, and what your child should be called?"

The girl's face brightened, just a bit. Lark thought it likely that Dorsey couldn't read. Many of the mountain people didn't.

Lark looked about her, wondering if any writing materials would be available in this place. The girl followed her glance, and then shaking her head, she knelt to pick a piece of charcoal from the cold hearth. She bent to begin writing something on the stones of the fireplace.

Lark could just see past her shoulder. B-r-a-n-d-o-n. "Brandon? Is his name Brandon?"

The girl nodded, with as much enthusiasm as Lark had seen from her. "He doesn't know his name, does he?" Lark murmured. "Of course not, if he never hears it. I'm so—"

At that moment, Tup whinnied loudly from outside the work-room.

Lark sat up, wincing at the pain in her right side, but alarm quickening her heart. Tup neighed again, a sound full of alarm. "Girl!" she exclaimed. "Go see if—no, help me up! Please, Girl, hurry!"

Another neigh shook the boards of the workroom. As if in answer, the rain intensified, pounding on the tin roof of the hut, spattering down the chimney to splash in the dead embers of last night's fire.

The girl cast one wide-eyed glance at the workroom, and then bent to put her shoulder beneath Lark's arm. Lark struggled to stand. Her right side took fire, but she didn't care. She hopped on her left foot. Her right leg felt as if it had hot coals inside its bandage. The little boy sat staring up at his mother and Lark, open-mouthed, and then, as they moved painfully into the workroom, he began to wail.

Lark would always remember, when she thought back on this day, the cacophony that seemed to attend every detail. The child screamed for his mother, the rain pummeled the hut. When she managed to make her way outside, her short curls were immediately soaked. And Tup, the moment he saw Lark emerge from the hut, pounded away across the field, head and tail high, calling fiercely to the flyers circling above.

Even through the thickening veil of rain, Lark knew who they were. Mistress Winter was a slender, straight figure in Winter Sunset's saddle. Irina Strong was thicker, and hunched somehow, her mare laboring through the rain. But what were they doing? Why did they fly at each other in that way, directly, as if they were . . .

"Kalla's teeth!" Lark cried. "They're fighting!"

And they were. Mistress Winter and Sunny dropped sharply toward the rainsoaked field, but Irina Strong flew into their path, coming precipitously close to them. They would surely have collided had Winter Sunset not darted swiftly to her left, her agile wings seeming almost to swim through the clouds of rain, lifting her out of the way.

In an abrupt, awkward turn, Strong Lady reversed, her effort obvious in the way she flew, her rider leaning into the turn, brandishing her quirt above her head.

"Tup! Come here!" Lark cried, but the rain drowned her voice. Tup stampeded beneath Winter Sunset, whirling as she did, racing headlong across the untilled ground. Lark screamed his name again, and again, but he was following his monitor, yearning to fly.

As Lark sank back against the girl's shoulder, weak with fear, Tup spread his wings and lifted from the ground to join Winter Sunset. Lark saw Mistress Winter glance down at him, and then forward to Irina and Strong Lady, who once again angled across her path. Mistress Winter looked the other way, just a quick glance, and when she saw Lark, it was as if a spark passed between them, an understanding.

"Yes, oh, yes," Lark moaned. "Get him away, please! Lead Tup away!"

Strong Lady's wings streamed rain as she drove at Winter Sunset again. Tup was behind Sunny, rising fast. If Sunny and Lady struck each other, Tup would never be able to evade the disaster. Lark clutched at the girl's supporting arms, her mouth open, raindrops weighting her eyelashes and dripping down her cheeks. The flyers drew closer, and closer still, until Lark thought her heart would stop. Then, with a deft movement, Mistress Winter and Sunny executed the tightest, swiftest Grand Reverse Lark could imagine was possible.

The Grand Reverse was the hardest of all maneuvers for the flying horses. It meant a complete reversal of direction, while at the same time changing the plane of flight, increasing or decreasing altitude. It was the perfect evasive action for a Noble to take under the attack of a Foundation, because the Noble was lighter, more agile than the Foundation.

And Tup, following Sunny, performed a perfect Grand Reverse. The dip of his wings and the angle of his small body were deft as a sparrow's. The two horses lifted, and turned to the right, out of the way of Irina and her horse.

And Strong Lady, trying to match them, tilted wildly to her left, her wings beating unevenly as she struggled to maintain her balance.

Irina Strong clutched at the wet saddle, at Lady's mane, but the angle was too sharp.

Lark's shout of warning died in her throat as she watched the horsemistress lose her seat, and slip backward over her horse's haunches. Irina Strong threw her arms out as if in surrender, and then fell.

The quirt flew from her fingers and tumbled through the rain after her, end over end.

A shudder of horror shook Lark's body. All sound faded from her ears as she watched Mistress Strong fall to the ground, strike the wet soil, and lie utterly, perfectly still.

The next moments passed in a sort of leaden shock for Lark. She stood trembling, leaning on the girl's arm, gazing numbly at the motionless form of what had been a woman. She was barely aware that Sunny led Tup neatly to the end of the field, made a cautious descent, and came to ground. Strong Lady, reins flying loosely behind her, circled the field, over and over, as if she didn't know what to do. She called to her bondmate, and called again. Her wings flapped more and more heavily as she began to tire, until at last she, too, made an awkward, stumbling landing, galloping up to Irina's body, circling it as if she could persuade her to rise.

Mistress Winter came toward the hut at a brisk canter, Tup following. When they were half a dozen rods away, Philippa leaped from her saddle to stride toward Lark.

"Larkyn! I am so relieved to see you alive, I can hardly . . ."

And then Mistress Winter broke off, staring at the nameless girl.

Lark was aware, all at once, of how the girl trembled. Her face had gone pale, and her lips worked as she struggled to speak. Lark looked back at Mistress Winter, mystified.

"By Kalla's heels!" Philippa exclaimed. "Pamella Fleckham!"

FORTY

THE next hours flowed by in a blur of confused feelings for Philippa. Paramount, of course, was that Larkyn and Black Seraph were safe. Though Larkyn had been badly injured, it seemed someone had cared for her hurts. Black Seraph was his usual self, spirited, independent, but unharmed. The pointless death of Irina Strong oppressed her, another weight on the scales measuring William's offenses.

And the discovery of Pamella, Frederick's lost daughter, hiding in the cramped hut of a witchwoman, staggered her with its implications.

For some time, she was too busy even to ask questions. She was shocked to see Pamella, whom she remembered as a willful, spoiled girl, acting as nurse to Larkyn, and then come out into the rainsoaked field to help carry Irina Strong into the shelter of the workroom. Sunny and Black Seraph and the bereft Strong Lady, her head hanging, crowded together beneath the eaves, out of the wet. They laid Irina on the floor of the workroom. Pamella went into the hut for a moment, and returned with a ragged blanket, which Philippa unfolded, and stretched over Irina's broken body. Pamella ran out into the field one more time, coming back with Irina's quirt, holding it out mutely to Philippa.

Philippa took it in her own hands, and almost gasped at the sensation. It was William's, she saw now, black braided leather with the silver ducal insignia affixed to the handle. It burned her palms with a kind of cold fire. Her hands trembled slightly as she laid it across Irina's breast, even as she chided herself for being credulous.

In the middle of this operation, the witchwoman herself appeared. She was a wrinkled old peasant named Dorsey, who dropped an absurd curtsy and peered up at Philippa with unrepentant glee.

Philippa was on her knees beside Irina. She pulled the blanket over her bruised face, lingering a moment when it was done, thinking how high a price Irina had paid for her ambition. When she stood up, she glared at the old woman, seizing the opportunity to vent her anger and grief. "You have had a winged horse and his rider here for a week," she snapped. "And yet you made no report?"

"Oh, nay, nay, Mistress," the crone said. Her hair hung in greasy strands about her head. "Oh, nay," she said again, "because Larkyn was afraid! Just like Girl, here, not wanting anyone to know. Old Dorsey minds her own business! Uplanders stick together, oh, aye, aye!"

"This . . ." Philippa used her whole arm to point directly at Pamella. "This girl is no Uplander. She's a Duke's daughter, the Lady Pamella! Why did you not tell anyone?"

The crone seemed unabashed by Philippa's scolding. She grinned, showing yellowed, sharp teeth. "Haven't heard a word from her!" she cackled, as if she had won a great argument. She led them into her hut, her boots shuffling across the rough floor. "Don't know her name, don't care," she said over her shoulder. "She lives here with me, does her share of work, and makes no bother of conversation!"

Philippa glanced at Pamella, who stood near a slanting stone sink, a toddler balanced on one hip, her eyes cast down to her feet. She rounded on the old woman again.

"You don't seem to realize the trouble you're in," she began, but Larkyn interrupted.

"Mistress Winter," she said, a little shakily, but with that familiar lift of her chin. "Please don't scold Dorsey. She would have sent a message—at least to Brye—but I was afraid that he—that the Duke—"

Philippa noticed how Pamella avoided her eyes, and she realized that she had not spoken a word. "Lady Pamella," she said, trying to moderate her tone. "No one expected to see you alive again."

Pamella's lips parted, and her throat worked, but no sound came. The child, a little boy, was as blond as all the Fleckhams, and the eyes fixed on Philippa were midnight dark.

"She doesn't talk, Mistress Winter," Larkyn said quietly. "She can write, though. Her baby's name is Brandon."

Dorsey whirled to gaze with toothy delight at Larkyn. "Brandon, is it? Now isn't that a wonder! More than a year she's been with me, and I never knew that! And Pamella, Pamella—now there's a pretty name!" She spun about in a flourish of grimy wool skirts, and went to build up the fire. "Now, now, do all of you make yourselves comfortable. I'm sorry, Mistress, that I have only the one chair, what Larkyn needs. There's yon stool, though, if you like."

Philippa said coldly, "No, thank you. I will stand, for the moment." She looked around at the single, dingy room, the narrow cot, the long workroom hung with bundles of things she supposed were herbs and so forth. "The Lady Pamella has not been living here, surely?"

Dorsey straightened, and faced her. "Oh, aye," she said. "She had no place to go, and swelling with child, she was."

Pamella's eyes swam with tears, and she hugged the little boy closer. Philippa laid down her hat and gloves, and went to stand beside her. "Pamella," she said. "Is this child yours? Why did you not come home?"

"Oh, she won't tell you," Dorsey said. She was pumping water to fill a teakettle. She turned with the kettle in her hand. "Haven't heard her speak a word, ever."

But Pamella's lips parted, and Philippa could see her tongue struggling to form words. Dorsey drew breath, but Philippa put up a hand. "Be quiet," she commanded.

The fire crackled in the hearth, and the teakettle began to steam. The little boy squirmed, and Pamella set him down. She made what appeared to be a supreme effort, the veins in her slender throat standing out above the collar of her worn tabard. Her voice was little more than a whisper when it came, and Philippa leaned closer to hear.

"Father," Pamella managed, and then she dropped her head into her hands, and sobbed silently.

Philippa pushed the stool forward, and pressed the weeping girl onto it. She glanced back at the wide-eyed Larkyn, who had one arm around the little boy, and Dorsey, who had poured boiling water in the teapot and laid it on the battered table, and was waving a fetish over it. Dorsey said, as if all that had happened were no more than trivialities, "Well, then, the tea's ready. Let's have a cup, and think what to do!"

PHILIPPA gave up, after a time, trying to understand exactly what had happened to Pamella, and how she came to be living in a witchwoman's hut in Clellum. The girl's struggles to speak were painful to watch, and no real information came from them. Philippa ended by patting her shoulder, and assuring her that it would all come right in the end, though she didn't know if that were true.

She learned from Larkyn that Black Seraph had been allowed to spend his nights in the workroom, and that Dorsey and Pamella had found feed for him, and wrapped him in blankets against the chilly mountain nights. Larkyn had slept in the only bed, with the other women and the child sleeping on the floor.

Philippa, before leaving, offered a stiff apology to the witchwoman. "I was grieved over the loss of a flyer," she told her. "I was rude to you, and I'm sorry for that."

Dorsey nodded. "Oh, aye, aye, old Dorsey understands all about that. You'll come back for Lark, then? With a cart? She won't be riding for a time yet."

"Her brother will come for her. And for her horse. It's best for Black Seraph to stay here, I think, just one more day."

"Oh, aye, aye, that will do. And Girl?"

"I beg your pardon?"

The witchwoman pointed to Pamella. "You'll take Girl back where she belongs?"

Pamella's eyes brimmed as she waited for Philippa's answer. Philippa tried to look away, but the events of the last days had laid her heart bare. She took a deep breath. "Pamella. You and I never got along, really, but that was long ago. I don't understand what's happened to you."

Pamella tried again to speak, spasms of effort making her lips twist. All she could manage was, "William," before she gave up.

Philippa stiffened. "William?" Pamella nodded, and looked at her feet. Philippa sighed. This was a burden she wished she did not have to take on, but there was no one else to do it. "Do you want to come with me, Pamella?"

Pamella's throat worked. It took her a full minute to scrape out, "Palace," while shaking her head.

"Not the Palace. Your mother's city house, then?"

Again, Pamella shook her head. More tears fell, and her mouth twisted with grief.

Behind Philippa, Larkyn spoke. "She can come to us, Mistress Winter."

Philippa turned. "The Academy? Larkyn, I don't think—"

"I meant Deeping Farm. Brye will take her in. Brandon will be happy there, with Peony, and Nick, and Edmar."

Philippa only nodded, and pulled her riding cap from her belt. It was, at least, a practical solution. And until Pamella could explain herself, it probably was best.

As Philippa pulled on her riding coat and walked out to Sunny, waiting beneath the eaves, she thought of poor Frederick, grieving for his lost daughter. If Pamella had turned up in time . . . Frederick might still be in his rightful place, and William would not have gained the power to hurt them all. She paused, looking back at the firelit group in the hut. Could William have brought this about, somehow?

Philippa forced herself to turn away, to walk past Irina's blanketed form. It had been years since she had watched a horse-mistress die, and it had grown no easier. The grief in her breast hardened into anger.

Someday, somehow, William would answer for this.

As she mounted, and turned Sunny away from the witch-woman's hut, she imagined Margareth's wise voice counseling patience. Oh, yes, she told herself, as Sunny began her canter through the damp evening light. Oh, yes, I'll be patient. But I won't forget.

FORTY-ONE

"I suppose we'll have to postpone your testing, Larkyn," Mistress Winter said.

Lark, leaning on the cane Edmar had cut for her, put down her currycomb, and hobbled to the gate of Tup's stall. "No, Mistress Winter, please," she said. "I'll be back at the Academy after Estian, and I'll be able to fly! I promise I will!"

Mistress Winter shook her head. "It seems too soon, after such an injury." As Lark came through the gate, she added, with a little purse of her lips, "Although, crude though she is, the witch-woman took good care of you."

Lark let the remark about Dorsey pass. They had been at Deeping Farm two days, making arrangements for the transfer of Irina Strong's body to her family, and settling Pamella and little Brandon with the Hamleys. Mistress Winter's eyes had not brightened once in that time, and Lark knew she grieved for the loss of a horsemistress, even a troublesome one. Strong Lady was already beginning to show signs of distress at the loss of her bondmate, and Lark knew that weighed on Mistress Winter, too.

Mistress Winter watched Pamella with an odd expression, as if not quite believing her own eyes. Pamella had still said nothing, but she had already found work to do around the farmhouse, helping Peony in the kitchen, carting laundry out to hang on the clotheslines, even bringing in lettuce and searching out early tomatoes in the kitchen garden. This, too, Mistress Winter observed with a furrow in her brow, and Lark could only think that seeing a Duke's daughter doing farm work was outside her experience. Brandon followed his mother about, clutching a wooden toy carved for him by Edmar. Edmar, of course, was almost as silent as Pamella herself, but Brandon had taken to leaning against his knee as he carved, babbling and laughing. Edmar nodded to the little boy as if it all made perfect sense.

None of this seemed unnatural to Lark. Everyone she had ever known worked hard from morning till night, even at the Academy. She supposed Hester could have had a different life, if she had wanted. Perhaps, when she arrived with her mamá this afternoon, to carry away Irina Strong's body in her carriage, she could ask her.

"Mistress Winter," she said, hobbling alongside her instructor, trying to hide the pain it caused her. "I want to stay with my class. With Hester, and Anabel."

Mistress Winter started to say something, but the sounds of hoofbeats from the lane distracted her. Lark followed her gaze. A chill spread through her belly. Automatically, she took a step back toward the barn, as if to stand between Tup and her enemy.

Duke William approached the barnyard at a posting trot, his black coat flying out behind him. His brown gelding was lathered and blowing, and stood trembling as William dismounted and tossed the reins over the post. William tugged down his vest with his hands, and smoothed the tails of his coat.

Beside Lark, Philippa Winter stood stiff and straight. "William," she said in an icy tone. "I wish you would not abuse your horse."

"Mind your own business, Philippa," he snarled at her. "Where's Irina?"

Lark turned her eyes up to Mistress Winter, wondering what she would say.

A ripple seemed to pass over Philippa Winter's face, and something hard gleamed from her eyes. She lifted her arm to point to the slanting door beneath the farmhouse, and she spoke with a knife-edge to her voice. "Irina is there. In the coldcellar. Awaiting her burial."

William's eyelids flickered, once, and his features froze. Philippa and William stared at each other, narrow-eyed, neither moving, barely breathing.

"What happened?" William finally asked, his lips stiff.

"She attacked me," Philippa said. Lark thought she could feel the cold fire of her fury in her own body, and she wondered that Duke William did not step back, away from it. "I hold you responsible, William."

"You killed her, then," was his answer.

Philippa's indrawn breath was loud in the silence. "I defended myself."

He leaned forward, his eyes glittering beneath half-lowered lids. "We will see what the Council has to say about that."

"The Council?" Philippa took a step forward, and now the Duke did step back. "The Council, William? I hardly think you want to take this before the Council. You abducted a winged horse!"

"I did not."

"Your people did. They took him to Fleckham House—and we saw you there!"

"Who will believe you, Philippa? You're guilty of a horse-mistress's death."

"What did you expect her to do, William? Kill me, and Winter Sunset? Bring you the little black, and let him go mad without his bondmate?"

William shrugged. "It was a mistake, to take the horse and not the rider. Jinson should have known."

Lark opened her lips to protest, but Mistress Winter shot her a swift, repressive glance, and she closed her mouth again. The Duke and the horsemistress glared at each other, and the only sound was that of Strong Lady, pulling against her tether, nickering, stamping her feet.

"Irina's horse will have to be destroyed," Mistress Winter said. "And that, too, is on your shoulders."

William sighed, as if it were all a game he had grown tired of. "She had my quirt," he said lightly, as if they were speaking of someone who had merely stepped out of the room. "I want it back."

"By all means," Philippa said. "Help yourself."

William's jaw muscles flexed, and another silence stretched before he turned his black eyes on Lark. "So, brat," he said. "You simply wouldn't listen to reason, would you?"

Lark felt as if her tongue were as paralyzed as Pamella's. Because she had no answer, she lifted her chin, and tried her best to stare into the Duke's eyes as bravely as Philippa had.

His lip curled. "Very well," he said. "Your family will pay. Take a good look at all of this, brat, because it is forfeit." He made a gesture that included the barn, the fields, the kitchen garden, the farmhouse. "You and your bumpkin brothers will have to find other . . ."

His voice trailed off, and his eyes, looking past Lark to the farmhouse, widened.

Lark, turning awkwardly on her cane, followed his gaze.

In the upper-story window, looking out of Lark's own bedroom, was Pamella. Her white-blond hair was unmistakable, despite the gleam of sun on the glass. She held something in her arms, sheets or towels, which dropped to the floor as she beheld her older brother.

In a low, tense voice, Mistress Winter said, "Larkyn. Hurry. Keep Pamella indoors."

William stared at her, and then at Larkyn. "What has she told you?" he said, his voice cracking at the end of the question.

"Larkyn. Go!"

Lark went. She hobbled across the yard and passed beneath the rue-tree, coming into the kitchen and closing the door firmly behind her. She peered out past the foliage to see Mistress Winter with her hands on her hips, and Duke William turning toward the coldcellar. His man, Slater, made a belated appearance on a dusty piebald horse, with the Master Breeder just behind him on a tired bay. By the time they dismounted and reached the Duke, William had gone into the coldcellar and come back with his quirt under his arm. He was already replacing his hat and drawing on his gloves.

Lark heard a step behind her, and turned to see Pamella, with Brandon at her knee, clutching the banister and trying to choke out something.

"Sit down," Lark urged, coming to her, helping her to sit on the stair. "Breathe, Pamella. Here, Brandon, come with me."

The little boy toddled toward her, a wooden lamb Edmar had carved for him clutched tightly in his hands. Lark swept the child up in her arms, and then stood before Pamella, blocking her view of the yard. "What is it, Pamella? Mistress Winter tells us he's your brother. Why does he frighten you so?"

"Take . . . take . . ." Pamella's mouth worked, her lips stopped on the next word, pressing together, trembling with effort.

Lark tried to guess. She pressed her own lips together. P, m, b—B, of course. "Brandon," she breathed. "He threatened to take Brandon."

Pamella, ashen and shaking, nodded, over and over. Lark hugged the little boy tighter.

"Never mind," she said fiercely. "Never you mind! Yon Duke can try all he wants, but we Uplanders don't give away children!"

Despite her brave words, she was shocked when she heard the sounds of three horses clipping away up the lane. She whirled, and found Mistress Winter standing alone in the open kitchen doorway, her still, narrow face framed by the branches of the rue-tree.

"Is he gone?" Lark blurted, hardly daring to hope.

Mistress Winter nodded. She said bitterly, "He knew where she was all along. When she was pregnant, he took her to Clellum and left her there. Worse, he let his father die believing his daughter already dead."

Pamella burst into silent, painful sobs. Brandon, seeing her, began to wail, too, and Lark set him down to run to his mother. Slowly, she straightened, and crossed the kitchen to stand before Mistress Winter.

"He threatened to take Brandon from her," she said quietly.

"So I surmised."

"And our farm?" Lark asked. "Will we lose Deeping Farm?"

Philippa Winter's lips twisted, and she shook her head. "No, Larkyn. He won't dare, not with Pamella here. He's afraid of what Pamella can tell the Council of Lords."

"But she doesn't speak!"

"William doesn't know that. And I chose not to tell him."

LADY Beeth and Hester arrived together in the carriage to transport Irina Strong for her burial. Hester and Lark went out to the barn to see to Tup and Sunny and help the carriage driver water and rub down the draught horses. Strong Lady was growing more and more distraught, and none of them dared go near her flashing hooves. Lark managed to fill her water bucket, and then for a time, she and Hester merely stood and stared at the poor mare, their hearts aching.

Philippa and Lady Beeth vanished into the farmhouse, and spent an hour closeted with Brye. When they emerged, grim-faced, the girls went in to join them at the table.

Peony, wide-eyed and silent, for once, in the presence of the lady of a Council Lord, served them all with cups of strong tea and laid out a fresh platter of crooks. Pamella stayed near the hearth, with Brandon asleep on her lap, his fingers wrapped around the wooden lamb.

"Mamá," Hester said bluntly, before even tasting the crooks. "Papá will settle this, won't he? You'll see to it."

Lark watched the mother and daughter, marveling at their likeness. It was not only that they resembled each other, but their forthrightness, their directness, were the same. She remembered round little Lord Beeth, with his doubtful manner, and she felt a momentary stab of sympathy for him. He was overmatched in his household. Lark had no doubt that Lady Beeth had a firm voice in the Council of Lords, though it wasn't her own.

Lady Beeth straightened her girdled tabard, and then sat back in the old, comfortable chair. "There will be little he can do," she said slowly. "The Dukes own the winged horses, but their management is a matter of tradition, rather than of law. Except, of course, for the bloodlines. Duke Frederick's great-great-grandfather Francis was a man of foresight, and he codified the bloodlines so that violating them would be treason."

"Then Duke William . . ." Lark began, and then fell silent. It was confusing to her that William had stolen Tup from the Academy stables, set Irina Strong chasing after them, threatened his own sister, and yet might escape unscathed.

Hester, however, nodded as though she understood perfectly. "And so," she said. "As long as the Lady Pamella cannot stand in the Council to accuse him, and as long as we have no proof that he's been crossbreeding the winged horses, we are at an impasse."

"But we *do* have proof!" Lark burst out. "I saw and heard him myself!"

Hester put out her long arm and covered Lark's hand with hers. "We know, Black," she said. "But the Council won't hear a commoner."

"You mean an Uplander," Brye said with a sour edge to his voice.

"No, Master Hamley," Lady Beeth said crisply. "Hester is right. The Council takes testimony only from peers or their direct representatives."

"What will we do, then?" Lark cried. She thought of Tup, of William's whip cracking against his silky skin, of the feel of that whip against her own body.

Mistress Winter set down her mug of tea with a decisive click of pottery on wood. "We will carry on, Larkyn, as if you merely had an accident. You will return to the Academy after Estian, and we will put it about you are healing, and your colt, of course, stays with you."

"And His Grace," Lady Beeth said in a wry tone, "will keep his distance from Lady Pamella. One hopes he will lie awake at night, wondering when she will turn on him."

Involuntarily, Lark glanced at the fireplace where Pamella sat with her arms protectively circling her son. Pamella laid her cheek against Brandon's pale hair, and closed her eyes. Lark asked, "Will Pamella—I mean, will the Lady Pamella—return to Osham, then?"

At this, Pamella lifted her head, and shook it sharply, her eyes pleading with Lark and with Mistress Winter.

Mistress Winter said, "No. I think not, Larkyn. Your brother has agreed with your suggestion that she stay here, at Deeping Farm."

Lark watched Pamella's eyelids close with relief. "But . . ." Lark began. "But—when her mother—won't her family want her back?"

Mistress Winter said, "Come now, Larkyn. You're old enough to understand. She's been shamed."

"Her son has no name," Hester said bluntly. "He will be shunned in the White City. And in the Palace."

"Oh." Lark bit her lip, trying to take this in.

Lady Beeth said quietly, "I will pay a call on Duchess Sophia. I doubt she will disagree with her daughter's decision." Her lips pursed, and she glanced sidelong at her daughter, who nodded. "Yes. She hardly dares add further scandal to the Fleckham name."

Such a cool assessment still mystified Lark, but Hester, apparently satisfied, started in on the crooks. Lady Beeth, too, nibbled at one, making Peony blush with pride. Mistress Winter turned her level gaze to Lark.

"You're worried about Black Seraph."

"Aye," Lark said. "If Duke William wants him . . . will he try again?"

"We will be on guard, Larkyn," Mistress Winter said. Her lips thinned, and a look passed between her and Brye. "You must concentrate on getting well, and rejoining your class. And we will be on guard."

FORTY-TWO

THE Estian holiday passed in a blaze of sunshine and birdsong, it seemed, for everyone except Philippa. The death of Irina haunted her. She saw Irina's fall in her nightmares, the outflung arms, the distant, silent impact, the crushed body. Even waking, the memory darkened the bright summer days, and she went about her duties with a heavy heart. There was no word from Duke William, and Margareth and Lady Beeth and Philippa decided that the fear of exposure was too great for him to make good his threat to report Philippa to the Council. Lady Beeth assured them her husband understood the truth of the matter. If a Council session were called, the Academy would have a champion. It seemed best to all of them, though, to keep William's incursion into the bloodlines a matter of confidence, at least for the moment. Irina's betrayal of her colleagues would not help the Academy's reputation, and dragging out the arguments before the Council would not bring her back.

Nor would it bring back Strong Lady. The death of the winged horse affected Philippa at least as much as the death of her rider. She had summoned the indolent Amberly Cloud from Dickering Park to assist her, and they had put the Foundation mare down as quickly and kindly as possible. Brye Hamley and his brothers had buried her next to the little mare they called Char. They could only guess that Char had been Pamella's mare. The saddle in the Mossyrock market had been hers, sold to pay the midwife when Brandon was born. They still did not know how it had all come about.

But now, Estian was over. Philippa tried, as she watched the girls return to the Academy, to put away her dark mood and look forward to Ribbon Day. The students could think of nothing else. They were as twittery as nesting birds as they dashed between the Dormitory and the Hall and the stables. Even the winged horses were restive, whinnying, turning in their stalls, flexing their wings. The very buildings seemed to vibrate with anticipation.

And at last, just when she had almost given her up, Larkyn Black returned.

Philippa was smoothing her hair into its rider's knot when she heard the familiar creak of the oxcart. She returned to the window, drawn by a little, girlish spurt of hope.

She forced a laugh over her disappointment at seeing that it was not Brye Hamley, but Nick who drove the cart up to the steps of the Dormitory and leaped down to help his sister from the seat. Black Seraph whinnied across the courtyard to Sunny, and Larkyn was swept up, laughing, by Hester and Anabel. Even Grace and Beryl came to greet her, though not so effusively. Larkyn hugged her brother, and waved farewell to him before she parted from her classmates to lead Black Seraph across the courtyard. She was hardly limping at all.

Philippa finished dressing, and hurried downstairs and out to the stables. She stepped inside just as Larkyn turned Seraph into his stall. The brown goat bleated with joy, and nuzzled the little stallion's chest. Bramble, the oc-hound, was already there, and now stood with her forepaws on the gate, watching Larkyn fill Seraph's water and grain buckets and check his wingclips. Larkyn stroked the dog's head, murmuring to her.

Philippa started down the aisle toward Larkyn, but she stopped when she saw Petra Sweet approaching from the other direction. The older girl stood with her arms folded, staring over the gate at Larkyn and Black Seraph. Philippa stepped aside, into an empty stall, where the girls couldn't see her. She put her back to a wall, and listened.

"I can't say I'm glad to see you, Goat-girl." Petra's forced accent carried easily down the aisle. "We all hoped you and the Crybaby had gone back where you belonged."

"Aye," Larkyn said. "And so we have."

"I meant the Uplands," Petra retorted. "That dirt farm you come from."

"And did you spend Estian at the shoe factory, Petra?" Larkyn asked brightly. "Hammering hobnails, or whatever it is you do there?"

Philippa clapped a hand over her mouth to stop her snort of laughter.

"Don't be vulgar," Petra said.

"Then don't be an ass," Larkyn snapped. Philippa heard the stall gate open and close, and the rustle of boots in the sawdust of the aisle.

Petra sneered, "You simply *must* learn not to speak to your betters that way!"

"I promise you, Sweet," Lark said tightly, "that when I am in the presence of one of my betters, I won't!"

There was a hiss of indrawn breath, and then Petra said, "I don't know why you bother, Black. You'll never fly your Airs. You're hopeless."

Black Seraph, as if he understood this insult, kicked the wall of his stall, and gave a loud complaining cry.

"Oh, by Kalla's teeth!" Petra snapped. "Is your little mongrel horse *ever* going to outgrow that habit?"

"What did you call him?" Larkyn's voice dropped low, to a pitch Philippa had never heard before. Only Petra Sweet, her temper now in full spate, could have missed the danger in it.

"You heard me," she said.

Larkyn said, her voice almost inaudible, "Take it back."

"Take what back? You mean, calling your Crybaby a mongrel? But that's what he is, isn't he!"

"I'm warning you, Petra," Larkyn breathed.

"Warning me? Who do you think you are, Black? And what do you think he is?"

Petra still didn't understand. Philippa did. An explosion was coming. She opened the gate of her hiding place, and stepped out into the aisle.

Petra said, "You've caused nothing but trouble from the moment you arrived, Goat-girl! You should have let the little mongrel die at birth rather than—"

Philippa broke into a run at that. Too late. She heard the smack of a small fist connecting with something hard, and a yell of shock from Petra. By the time Philippa reached them, Petra Sweet lay flat on her back in the sawdust. Her eye was already blackening, and tears of outrage streamed down her cheeks. Larkyn stood over her, both fists clenched, her small body rigid with fury. "Take. It. Back," she repeated. "Now. Or I'll—"

"Larkyn! Never mind," Philippa called belatedly. "I'll deal with her. Go to dinner."

The girl spun about, and Philippa almost fell back on her heels. Her eyes were violet with anger, and her cheeks blazed. Bramble stood at her side, her tail rigid.

Philippa put out a calming hand, hardly knowing whether to scold or laugh.

"She said . . ." Larkyn began. Her voice shook with fury. "She called Tup—"

"Yes, Larkyn, I heard. But you can't solve things with your fists, you know."

Larkyn looked down at her hands, and slowly, slowly, opened them.

"Now. Go to the Hall. We'll discuss an appropriate discipline later."

It seemed for a long moment the child might refuse.

"It won't be harsh, Larkyn. I think you were provoked."

Larkyn nodded. She drew a deep, trembling breath, and wheeled about to march out of the stables, jaw set, small boots spurting puffs of sawdust. Bramble trotted at her heels, and Black Seraph and Molly both cried after her.

Philippa waited until she was well out into the courtyard, and then offered Petra a hand. "Get up, Sweet," she said evenly.

Petra clambered to her feet, one hand covering her bruised eye, the other pointing after Larkyn. "Mistress Winter!" she said shrilly. "I demand something be done about that *bumpkin*!"

Philippa's lips twitched. "I believe you stepped over the line, Petra."

"She *hit* me!"

"You insulted her bondmate."

"But—but . . ." Petra sputtered her way to silence.

"Come," Philippa said. "Let's go to the kitchen. Matron will get you some ice for your bruise, and you can explain to her how you ran into a door."

And I, she thought bemusedly, can try to explain Larkyn's latest escapade to Margareth.

RIBBON Day arrived with a rush of early autumn color, rust and gold and scarlet. The third-level girls approached it somberly, already feeling the mantle of adulthood settle over their shoulders. The second-level girls swaggered, experienced now, sure of their success. And the first-level girls, Hester and Anabel and their classmates, fluttered and fidgeted, anxious and hopeful and edgy. Their mounts, too, grew nervous, sensing the mood. Even the oc-hounds were snappish and restive.

When the day dawned at last, Lark's stomach clenched so tightly that she could eat nothing at breakfast. She sipped a little tea, and then put that down, too, afraid it would come right back up. Hester leaned close to her.

"Black," she whispered. "You should eat something. It's going to be a long, long day."

"I know," Lark told her. "But I can't. I'm just so—"

Anabel crumbled a piece of toast between her fingers. "I can't eat, either," she mourned. "I'm terrified."

"You'll be fine," Hester said firmly. "You're ready, and so is Take a Chance."

Lark dropped her eyes, twisting her fingers in her lap. Hester was too honest to offer her such assurance. She and Tup weren't ready, and everyone knew it.

Drills had been agony for both of them. Mistress Dancer insisted they use a flying saddle, a bridle, a chest strap, all the equipment the other flyers carried. As long as she wasn't riding him, Tup could launch and land without faltering or stumbling, but the moment Lark sat in the saddle, all balance and grace fell away. They flew, but not beautifully. They wallowed through Reverses, wobbled in Points, spoiled the Graces. Mistress Dancer refused to let Lark show her what she could do bareback.

"My dear," she had said quietly, when no one else was around. "I know you're struggling. My preference would be that you stay back, train with the next class. But the worst would be another— that is, a fall."

Everyone, it seemed, knew of the mishap in the Uplands. The other girls and instructors looked at Lark with a sort of bemused wonderment. A hundred times she hid in the stall with Tup and Molly, burying her face in Tup's mane and remembering the freedom and exhilaration of that moment when they rose from the meadow behind Fleckham House into the cool night air, the moon on their faces, the wind like a hand lifting them up. And they had flown so far, without any trouble at all, and without the hindrance of a flying saddle. Everything had been perfect—well, until the end.

Lark understood now how to come to ground, how to sit, how to shift her weight, how to be part of Tup's movement as his hooves reached forward and down. But she couldn't *feel* it through the saddle!

For Ribbon Day, she formulated a plan, and she persuaded Rosellen to help her.

Rosellen muttered dire warnings throughout, even as she supplied the leather and the awl, the buckles and thongs. "Best think hard about this, Lark," she said. "Them horsemistresses catch on, they'll hold you back for sure. Maybe better just to muddle through."

"No, Rosellen. That's not good enough. I need to do this my way."

Rosellen shook her head, and grumbled on about punishments and penalties, but she lent her hands just the same, holding and stretching and beveling and fitting, until the project was complete.

And now, the day was here.

Because the Council Lords and their ladies were eager to see who would become Oc's newest horsemistresses, the third-level students performed their Airs first, when the sun was at its highest and the horses could be shown to best effect. The winged horses gleamed with brushing, the membranes of their wings were rubbed till they shone, and each bit of tack glowed with saddle soap. Every buckle and snap glittered with polish, every mane and tail sported black and silver ribbons. The girls, who would be women by the end of the day, walked with self-conscious pride as they approached the flight paddock. Their riding coats and divided skirts were immaculate, their boots spotless, their peaked caps tilted just so above their perfect riding knots.

The aristocracy of the White City sat in rows of chairs in the courtyard. They wore elaborately girdled tabards and jeweled caps, ropes of pearls from the coast, soft high-heeled shoes. A few of their children sat with them, hushed and stiff in rich clothes too old for them. Lark and Hester and Anabel leaned on the fence of the flight paddock, shoulder to shoulder, gazing hungrily at Elizabeth and Ardith and the others. Their horses were six years old now, mature, well schooled. Lark hardly breathed as the flight began its canter down the paddock. They lifted into the bright sky, haloed by fluffs of white cloud. Philippa Winter led the way, the ideal figure of a horsemistress at the height of her abilities.

Lark thought there could be no more beautiful sight than Horsemistress Winter and Winter Sunset banking, dipping, soaring above the flight. Lark knew, now, what the signals were she made with her quirt. The flight performed a Half Reverse, a Grand Reverse, hovered at Quarters. The Lords of the Council and their ladies patted their hands together, which was silly. The flyers above couldn't possibly hear them.

When the flight formed for Arrows and the flyers made their sharp descent, flashing down toward the courtyard and up again into the hot sunlight, the ladies in the chairs gasped. Hester said, "Thank Kalla we don't have to do that!"

"Nor the Grand Reverse," Anabel whispered. "At least, not this year."

Lark, who had managed for a moment not to think about her own upcoming ordeal, said nothing. The third-level flyers spun above them in the first and then the second of the Graces, lovely balletic patterns designed to impress. Lark tilted her head back to watch.

As she straightened, she caught sight of Duke William's tall, slender figure on the steps of the Hall. His pale hair caught the sunlight. His eyes, like blackstone pebbles, met hers, and even across the courtyard, she could see how his thin lips curled.

Lark pressed herself closer to the fence, and averted her eyes.

William had caught her in the aisle of the stables, just as she went to braid the ribbons into Tup's tail. He held out that magicked quirt and dared her with his cold gaze. Only Hester coming along had stopped him. If he had touched her . . . she feared she might have lost what little nerve she had left. It was, she thought, exactly what he intended.

The afternoon seemed endless to the first-level girls awaiting their turn. After the third level finished their triumphant display, they dismounted and presented themselves to the Headmistress and the Duke for the formal recognition of their achievement. The ribbons for which the day was named were pinned to their tabards, and they accepted the Duke's congratulations with stiff nods, then the accolades of the Council Lords. An hour passed in this fashion before the second-level flyers took to the air.

The gallery in the courtyard began to shrink even before the second-level girls had finished their demonstration. As the sun sank in the western sky, carriages were brought round from behind the stables, and the ladies were driven away, one by one. As the second-level girls received their ribbons from the Headmistress, the gallery was reduced by half. Even some of the Lords began to depart after that ceremony was finished. Petra Sweet, smirking with pride, was the last to receive her ribbon. Lord and Lady Beeth remained to watch their daughter fly, and a few of the Council Lords also stayed. The Lady Constance, William's colorless little wife, had been whisked away.

Anabel said, "Look! The Duke is still here."

"I see him," Hester said. "Right behind Mamá and Papá. It's odd. Usually he leaves the moment the third-levels have finished their Airs."

Lark's stomach turned over. She knew it was because of her, and because of Tup. He had stayed to watch them. And if they failed . . . He would claim Tup for his own purposes. Mistress Winter and Mistress Morgan would fight him, but the Council Lords would have seen for themselves, and they would have no chance.

By the time Mistress Dancer summoned the first-level flyers to the stables to prepare, the disc of the harvest moon, broad and yellow, already showed above the eastern horizon. Lark glanced at it over her shoulder as she slipped into the stables. She touched the icon beneath her tabard, and whispered a prayer to Kalla to hurry the sun down, to slow the moon's rise, to provide a little darkness.

When the first-level flyers emerged from the stables, torches had been lighted in their sconces around the courtyard. The Lords of the Council sat in their flickering glow. The flight paddock, by contrast, seemed gloomy, but when the girls and their horses moved away from the torchlight, their eyes adjusted quickly. Horsemistress Dancer cantered down the flight paddock, leading the way. Hester came directly behind the horsemistress, and then Lillian, Beatrice, Beryl, Isobel, and Grace. Next to last came Anabel and Take a Chance, increasing the pace to a hand gallop.

And last, lest their wobbling affect the rest of the flight, came Lark and Tup.

She knew, the moment she felt the shiver of power that radiated from his great chest muscles through her calves and thighs, that she had made the right choice. The wind streamed above and below his wings, and her hands felt his confidence as he banked and ascended after the others. They aligned themselves in the circle for the first of the Graces, and Lark felt as if nothing, nothing at all, could stop them.

PHILIPPA, with Sunny already brushed and blanketed, stood on the top step of the Hall. She had not changed her riding skirt, and in the cooling air she could still smell Sunny on her clothes, and on the gloves tucked into her waistband. She breathed in the scent, reminded as she always was of the nerves and excitement of her own Ribbon Days. William still leaned against one of the pillars, two steps below her. He cast her a single cool glance, and then turned back to watch the first-level flight assemble in the paddock.

Philippa tried not to think about him, nor about the welling anxiety that had nagged at her all day. She stood with her arms folded and her back straight. She tried to expect good things for Larkyn and Black Seraph, but in truth, she had scarce confidence of their success.

She had watched their drill the day before, and she could see that Larkyn simply had no seat in the saddle. She had flown better when she made her escape from Fleckham House than she had, even once, since her return to the Academy. And if she failed now . . . in the presence of these Lords of the Council, in the presence of the Master Breeder and Margareth . . . if she failed, William would win after all.

The torches dazzled her eyes, haloing the winged horses in a golden fog as they cantered, then galloped, their wings spreading, catching the air, beginning to beat. They rose above the grove, one after the other, flying into the fading light of evening. Mistress Dancer led them in a slow pattern above the courtyard. Heads tipped up, and there were appreciative murmurs as the horses circled in the first of the three required Graces, legs curled, wings steady, girls erect. One after another they came, faces blurred by the torchlight. When the flight had arrayed itself around the Academy grounds, Kathryn Dancer twirled her quirt, and they executed the first of their Airs, a Half Reverse that opened their formation like the petals of a flower.

Philippa found she was holding her breath. She peered through the dazzle of light, and she sensed William, below her, doing the same. She willed Larkyn and Black Seraph to perfection, and she knew William did the opposite, searching for any sign of weakness, unsteadiness, anything he could use.

But there was nothing. Each of the flyers performed the Half Reverse, and then held a nearly perfect pattern at Quarters, following their flight leader. Black Seraph looked, to Philippa's hopeful eyes, as steady as Hester's Golden Morning. Nor could she find any fault with his rider. Through the haze of torchlight, Larkyn appeared to sit as straight as any other flyer, settled deeply into her seat, her heels down, her head up.

The second Grace was a loop, each of the flyers turning outward on a precise count of wingbeats, turning back to face each other at Quarters. Surely Black Seraph's loop was the smoothest of all, Philippa thought, his slender wings moving effortlessly, his small body at the perfect angle, his rider leaning into the turn with just the right shift of weight! How could this be? It was as if the two of them, overnight, had found the answer they needed, the balance of strength and position and speed.

It was enough, Philippa thought wryly, to make one believe in smallmagics.

Kathryn led her flight in a short demonstration of Points, appropriate for the first level, and then came the last of their Graces.

It was an elliptical pattern, the flyers soaring low, then ascending in a great curve. Kathryn led, with Hester and Golden Morning close behind, and then the others. As Goldie set her wings and glided above the heads of the watchers, a patter of applause broke out at the dramatic sight of the palomino Foundation with her hooves shining in the torchlight and the rising light of the moon. The other flyers matched her, soaring down as if they would land on the cobblestones, angling sharply up. The applause grew. Philippa had never seen such a fine performance from a first-level class. She hugged herself with delight.

The last pair to perform the Grace were Larkyn and Black Seraph.

Seraph was small, even for an Ocmarin, but he had flair. His tail arched, and his mane fluttered prettily over his rider's hands. His ears, small and finely cut, turned eagerly forward. His neck stretched, showing the great muscles of his chest. And Larkyn!

Larkyn sat Black Seraph as if she had grown there, her heels snug against his ribs, her slight body barely moving as Seraph glided downward. They reached the nadir of the pattern, seeming almost to float above the glowing circle of the torchlight. Philippa heard the little intake of breath from the watchers, and then Seraph beat his wings again, once, twice, three times, the membranes rippling like silk. He lifted easily into the twilight as if the ascent cost him nothing. In half a dozen heartbeats the two rejoined their flight, Seraph tilting, banking, finding perfect synchrony with the others.

The moon was fully up now, bathing the return paddock in golden light. The flight circled, and began to settle, one by one, each coming to ground more nimbly than the one before, until all of them were trotting smoothly toward the stables.

It was done. And it was nearly perfect. Kathryn Dancer would be walking on clouds for weeks to come.

Philippa felt as if a knot in her breast had been suddenly untied. She turned abruptly on her heel, to march along the top step, away from William. She did it deliberately, resisting the urge to say something triumphant to him. Only as she crossed the cobblestones toward the stables did she cast one swift glance back. The Duke was stalking away, his man Slater scuttling after him. One or two of the Lords still in the courtyard started toward him, but then stopped. When William reached his carriage, he lifted his head, and glared across the courtyard at Philippa.

She inclined her head to him. He turned his back without responding, leaped up into the carriage, and moments later was gone.

Philippa felt a great smile spread across her face as she hurried to the stables to congratulate Kathryn and her flyers.

FORTY-THREE

LARK leapt down from Tup's back. The grass beneath her boots felt like clouds, and her heart swelled with such joy she wanted to dance. Instead, she disciplined her feet, and led Tup toward the stables at a moderate pace, avoiding the circle of torchlight, staying well behind the rest of her flight. He pranced beside her, his head tossing with pride, folded wings rustling as if he would do it all over again.

Rosellen met them in the doorway, her gappy grin so wide it seemed her cheeks must ache. "Hurry, Lark! Get him into the stall before someone sees . . ."

"Larkyn!" Lark and Rosellen froze at the sound of Mistress Winter's voice. They stared at each other, wide-eyed, and then turned slowly to see the horsemistress striding in from the courtyard. A rare smile curved Mistress Winter's lips. "Well done, Larkyn!"

Tup danced impatiently, and whimpered, but Lark knew she couldn't simply walk away from Philippa Winter. Hastily, she released Tup's rein to Rosellen, and faced the horsemistress.

"Thank you, Mistress Winter," she said.

"I see I was mistaken to be worried about you," Mistress Winter said. "Your Reverses were smooth, and your Graces were remarkable. Such improvement! How did you manage it?"

Lark took a step forward, hoping to block the view of Tup and Rosellen walking away down the aisle. "Well, I—that is, we—"

But she was too late. The horsemistress stared past her, watching Tup and Rosellen walk down the aisle. "What—Rosellen! Stop!"

Rosellen stopped. Tup stopped beside her, his ears flicking.

Mistress Winter passed Lark in two decisive strides, and reached Tup in another two. She ran her hand up over his hindquarters to his bare spine, where the flying saddle should have been—should still be. She touched the slender leather band Rosellen and Lark had worked so hard on. She put her fingers into the shallow loop at the top, and tapped the thin metal buckle that allowed it to be adjusted for length. A breast strap, no more than two fingers wide, ran from one shoulder, around Tup's chest, and buckled in to the band at the other shoulder. Mistress Winter traced all of this with her fingers. She slipped her whole hand into the loop, and tugged. It held, of course. It had held for Lark all through her flight. Tup twisted his neck to look at her, and whickered a question at Lark.

Lark drew a deep breath as she came to him. Rosellen backed away a few steps.

Philippa Winter's smile had vanished, leaving her narrow lips set in a grim line. "This is how you did it," she said. "You flew bareback."

Lark's cheeks burned, but she lifted her chin, and met the horsemistress's steely gaze as steadily as she could. "Not exactly," she said, in a voice that shook only a little. "I used the breast strap, as you see."

"You were expressly forbidden to fly without a saddle ever again."

"Aye," Lark said. "But the Duke wants Tup, and if I failed, he would take him."

"You could have repeated the first level."

Lark, without intending to, snorted. The sound, even to her own ears, was very like the sound Mistress Winter so often made.

And Philippa Winter recognized it. Her lips twitched, and she put a hand to her mouth. Lark breathed easier, knowing the horsemistress had covered a laugh. Mistress Winter coughed a little, and then lowered her hand. "You are right, Larkyn," she said. "I admit it. Holding you back would have exposed you more to . . . to interference."

Rosellen said, "Excuse me, Mistress. Them Lords are going to be eager to leave. Lark should go get her ribbon."

"Yes," Mistress Winter said. "Indeed she should. Rosellen, take Seraph to his stall, would you? You can untack him for Lark." She glanced to her right, where the other girls were beginning to emerge from their horses' stalls, and she took a step to block Tup from their view. "And perhaps, Rosellen, you could hurry."

"Aye, Mistress." Rosellen took Tup's lead, and the two of them trotted down the aisle.

A heartbeat later, Hester and Anabel came bounding up to Lark, faces shining. "You were brilliant, Black!" Hester said.

Anabel cried, "We did it! We won our ribbons!" Isobel and Grace and the others dashed past, glowing. Mistress Dancer came after, a little slower, but a wide smile lighting her face. She touched Lark's shoulder as she passed. "Well done, Larkyn. Very well done!"

When they had gone, Lark faced Mistress Winter, awaiting her judgment.

"I hardly know what to say to you, Larkyn."

"Yes, Mistress."

"There's no denying you performed well. And so did Black Seraph."

"Oh, wasn't he marvelous?" Lark burst out. "I hardly had to do a thing!"

The smile began to return to Mistress Winter's face, first brightening her eyes, then softening her lips. "My dear . . . you can't go on this way."

"It's different for us, Mistress Winter. For Tup and me."

"Well." Mistress Winter turned her face toward the courtyard, and faint torchlight glimmered on her cheekbones, on her long, slender nose. Lark thought she looked, just for that moment, like the girl she must once have been, young and vulnerable. "Well, Larkyn, that may be. And you have certainly earned your ribbon. But we will talk about this later."

"Oh, thank you!" Lark cried. She spun about to run to the courtyard, but Mistress Winter caught her back.

Lark looked up at her, biting her lip with renewed anxiety.

Mistress Winter laughed, and shook her head. She pointed to the back of Lark's skirt.

"You're covered in horsehair, Larkyn," she said. "Quick, brush it off. And then go! They'll be waiting."

Please visit www.tobybishop.net
or e-mail the author at DuchyofOc@aol.com.